ALSO BY DAVID GRAND

Louse

The Disappearing Body

MOUNT TERMINUS

MOUNT TERMINUS

DAVID GRAND

FARRAR, STRAUS AND GIROUX   NEW YORK

Farrar, Straus and Giroux
18 West 18th Street, New York 10011

Printed in the United States of America
First edition, 2014

Library of Congress Cataloging-in-Publication Data
Grand, David, 1968–
Mount Terminus : a novel / David Grand.
    pages   cm
    ISBN 978-0-374-28088-8 (hardback)
    1. Motion picture industry—California—Los Angeles—Fiction.
    2. Hollywood (Los Angeles, Calif.)—Fiction.   I. Title.

PS3557.R247 M68 2014
813'.54—dc23
                                                2013033025

Designed by Jonathan D. Lippincott

Farrar, Straus and Giroux books may be purchased for educational, business, or
promotional use. For information on bulk purchases, please contact the
Macmillan Corporate and Premium Sales Department at 1-800-221-7945,
extension 5442, or write to specialmarkets@macmillan.com.

www.fsgbooks.com
www.twitter.com/fsgbooks • www.facebook.com/fsgbooks

1 2 3 4 5 6 7 8 9 10

For my mother

And in loving memory of my grandmother,
Bessie Buschel (1914–2013)

CONTENTS

DARKNESS

No one knew where the spring on Mount Terminus originated. They could only conjecture from the warmth of its waters that the aquifer lay deep underground, near the hearth of the Earth. Jacob sounded out for Bloom the hiss and groan he would hear when the vapors rose and expanded into the pipes of their new home. He spoke of flowering gardens and bulky vegetable patches, the scents of citrus groves and the perfume of trees canopied in mentholated leaves, of a narrow promontory pointing like a finger over an ancient seabed to a distant shore, and he said to his son, Please, my dear, tell me you want to see it.

Bloom wanted to say, No, I don't want to see it. I want to go home.

But he said, instead, Yes, of course, Father, I want to see it all.

For this kindness, Jacob thanked his son, and thanked him again; he bent over and squeezed Bloom tight, pressed his cheek against the stiff collar of his shirt, and, for several moments too long, held him there.

Father and son dwelled in the comfort of prolonged silences thereafter. They listened to the clatter of rails beat the rhythm of their progress across the prairies. On the Sabbath, Jacob covered his head and adorned his shoulders in a prayer shawl. He kindled the light, blessed the wine, the bread. The young Bloom tried to invent an image of the place his father had described, but his thoughts returned to the familiar surface of Woodhaven's lake mirroring the rise of its valley and its sky, and he recalled memories of his mother standing in profile before a succession of windows.

In the expanse of the Chihuahuan Desert, he awoke from a

dream in which he saw just such an ephemeral image, and he called out to his mother, at which time Jacob gently reminded him she was no longer with them. While passing the painted archways of the Sonoran Desert, Bloom wondered aloud how it was possible she could have died so young, and the elder Rosenbloom, who appeared at a loss to answer Bloom, drew for his son an illustration of a heart in its anatomical intricacy, and pointed to its various chambers to better show him how the muscle in his mother's chest had ceased to function.

Jacob asked the boy if he now comprehended the cause, and Bloom said he did, but, in truth, he didn't, and even if he had, neither his father's scientific reason nor the warm touch of his hand would come to fill the desert air with moisture. It wouldn't soften the stark light of its sun. It wouldn't curtail the boy's expectations of seeing his mother's silhouette materialize in the shadows of their berth.

The train thundered through tunnels and canyon passes, whispered along the outer edges of mountains. When they turned southwest from Mojave into the sierra, they joined the path of a river Bloom mistook for a stream. The thin, lazy current delivered them from the foothills of the San Gabriel Mountains onto the great basin. Here the air of their compartment warmed with the scent of orange blossoms and the stench of industry. Opposite the river, foundry stacks disgorged black smoke, wisps of which swept northward on a pulsating breeze, over the flat tops of brick buildings whose uneven lines foregrounded the range. The mountains, the city, their combined measure, the immensity of their weight, the boy felt in his chest, and more so than before, he wanted to retrace the rail lines east so that so he might once again feel the balance of Woodhaven's valley, watch the August rains thrash its lake, meander the damp trails of its hills, but they had come this far and Bloom knew his father wouldn't be persuaded to turn back. For reasons the boy couldn't understand, Jacob was determined to reside here, as if he had been commanded to do so by God. *Go forth. Go forth to the desolate end of the world.*

There, said his father when the train began to slow, there, ahead, is our new beginning.

A golden dome cast an amber glow onto a sprawling platform where a multitude of hat brims shone with the intensity of small suns. They shadowed the rough-hewn faces of men; they shadowed the softer, rounder features of women. At the center of the throng, in the most luminous point of the dome's light, were three figures, tall and broad, all approximately the same height and build, standing shoulder to shoulder, dressed identically, wearing in the heat of the afternoon black mackintoshes and black bowler hats, black gloves, black boots, the collective garments so dark they appeared to absorb all the light within their sphere. Bloom was moved to remark what a strange sight the dark triumvirate was, but the boy's attention had been arrested by the void they formed in the crowd. Before he could turn to make his father aware of the phenomenon, and turn back, the figures had vanished.

What was it? Jacob asked.

Nothing, said Bloom, nothing at all.

The elder Rosenbloom hired a porter to cart their trunks through the station's rotunda to the exit, where, at the curb, they hired an open carriage. They moved through unpaved streets whose grit caught in their teeth and coated the front of their mourning clothes in granite residue. As they proceeded through the city's crosscurrents of streets and avenues, Bloom watched his father's grave profile flash in and out of darkened storefront windows, and when the density of the city center opened onto a series of empty squares whose fountains were dry, whose lawns were balding, Jacob said it would be some hours yet before they reached Mount Terminus.

In their new life, he told his son, they would live apart from the world at large. Apart from the assembly of men. Outside the reach of their influence. Beyond the boundaries of trivial concerns.

On the outskirts of town, they rode past small adobe homes shadowed by the lattices of oil derricks. Children scrambled around barrels and beds of tar, kicked up scythes of dust which drifted over the road and settled onto the browned backs of a chain gang hauling sledgehammers and casks of water. The hunched figures formed a slow procession behind a sheriff whose denim jacket and pant legs were embroidered with lightning bolts. Soon Bloom and his father passed no one at all. The coachman, a blue-eyed mestizo with pitted skin and a thick, crooked nose, tried to make conversation with Jacob, but the driver spoke little English and neither Bloom nor his father spoke any Spanish. The driver occasionally pointed to faraway places off the empty road, to the burned husk of a hacienda through the gates of a dead ranchero, and tried to explain an incident involving his cousin and his uncle and a woman who stepped between them, but the story was lost to the grind of the carriage's wheels and the driver's rapid flights into Spanish. No matter, he said with a shake of the head when the elder Rosenbloom apologized for not understanding. No matter.

They turned onto the mountain just as the glare of the sun had fallen to meet their eyes; they rode into the canyon's shadows and switched back and forth over its trail's rutted curves; the higher they scaled the grade, the more the vistas widened, the wider the ancient seabed expanded in diagonal rows of trees. They directed Bloom's sight to the distant shore, to the north, where the folding range was mantled in bramble, olive and drab, for as far as he could see.

For as far as he could see, there was emptiness. No homes. No people. No vestiges of civilization past or present. When they reached a series of escalating plateaus stepping up to the mountain's peak, they stopped at a blackened gate, beyond which was land so bright with color, in these barren wastes it seemed implausible it should exist. The father contrived a smile for the boy and told the driver to drive on; with a jolt, the horse kicked past the perimeter, up a long gravel path bisecting two garden mazes whose hedgerows were overgrown with tendrils of bougainvillea. The tall windbreak framed the front of the villa, its fading yellow walls, its thatched roof layered in terra-cotta. Overshadowing the roof's ridges rose a tower, at its vertex a columned portico warmed by saffron light.

Upon noticing the day's wane, Jacob told the driver to stop. He paid the man his fee and asked him to leave the trunks at the villa's front door. Jacob then took hold of Bloom's hand, and together, father and son walked along the edge of the garden maze to an empty field. Blond grass swept at the boy's knees and the father's shins all the way to the leveled acreage of the grove, where they were met by a sickly odor, of fruit moldering in heaps at the cephalopod roots of trees. Their sleeves covering their noses, they continued on to a long stand of eucalyptus, at which a hill descended to a large empty plot of land aswirl in dust; and here they turned onto the eroded earth at their property's end, to the promontory pointing to the sea, less like a finger than the bow of a ship. The headland jutted out over a deep ravine, at whose precipice Jacob stood and stared into the bruised light of the setting sun, and with his eyes filled with its gloaming he seemed to be contemplating the oncoming darkness. For the time it took the spectrum of colors to submerge into the ocean's depths, he said nothing; and when all that was left was some violet sediment on the horizon, the father touched his son's cheek with his finger and said how very sorry he was for the fate that had befallen them. He wished he could revisit their past and amend it. For Bloom's sake, he wished he were a different man.

Bloom looked to his father to better understand what had altered his mood; in the dim light, Jacob's dark Semitic features were difficult to read, but the boy could see the elder Rosenbloom's eyes were no longer cast toward the horizon; rather, they were fixed on a turn along the mountain road beyond the gorge; and when Bloom followed his father's gaze he saw three silhouettes of men astride three horses.

What is it? asked the boy. What do you see?

Nothing, said his father. An illusion. A trick of the light. But the elder Rosenbloom's voice sounded uncertain. He turned his head to Mount Terminus's peak, and Bloom turned with him. Like a fog arriving from the sea, stars had already begun to cluster through the moonless sky, and upon seeing this, Jacob made Bloom promise that when he became a man and fell in love, he would protect his love better than Jacob had protected his.

✺

The Rosenblooms were conceived somewhere on the other side of the world. In a country whose name they didn't know. To mothers and fathers who were most likely dead. Those who told them about their origin could say with any certainty only that they had been carried by many caretakers to a port on the shore of the Adriatic Sea, where they were placed on a ship and into the arms of an old rabbi and his wife, who bundled Bloom's father together with his mother and her twin sister in a bread basket. Each child, so far as the rabbi and his wife knew, had yet to be named. From the story of Joseph, the rabbi called the boy Jacob; the sisters, the rabbi's wife called Rachel and Leah, and they passed down to each of them their family name. When the ship landed, the elderly couple claimed them as their grandchildren. To the gatekeeper, the old man swore on the scrolls of the Torah cradled in his arms that they had been borne by his two daughters, both of whom, he said, had died in childbirth. Because they were too old and poor to parent the children themselves, the rabbi and his wife carried Jacob, Rachel, and Leah to the Hebrew Orphan Asylum on the lower east end of the city, where they lived for many years.

The three infants had grown so accustomed to sleeping with one another over the course of their long journey, the two girls and the boy wouldn't be separated at night without a great disturbance up-setting the nursery. Their new guardians allowed them to sleep to-gether in the same crib until they were two, then moved them to the same bed until they were five, at which time they required them to reside in separate wings, but the children met every day between les-sons to play in the courtyard, and without fail, they sat side by side when they dined. So Jacob wouldn't be lonely at night, the girls cut pieces from the ribbons holding back the thick curls of their hair, and they pinned the shiny material to the lapel of his jacket, and each night before curfew they placed into his pockets notes in-scribed with wishes he was meant to read before the dormitory lights were extinguished. The girls longed for things all children long for: sweets and toys and pets. They desired, too, things only orphans desire: a mother and a father, a room in which to sit alone, for silence lasting days and nights with no end. Jacob never made such wishes, as he had only one, of such great importance that he never dared write it down or articulate it.

His only wish was to remain with Rachel and Leah.

To never be apart from them.

To be reunited with them in his bed.

Anyone who had eyes could see in what ways the twins would blossom into great beauties. At the age of nine, they already comported themselves with the poise of young women, and on their own initiative they endeavored to refine their characters so they might better resemble the figures living in the novels they read at night under the glow of streetlamps hanging outside their dormitory windows. Leah taught herself to sing and play the spinet; Rachel taught herself how to draw and paint; their eyes, in turn, retained a hopeful glimmer, and projected an intellect neither sharp nor oppressive.

On Saturday afternoons, they walked with their sister orphans to the long meadow in the park, where, instead of running wild with the others, they presented themselves for public view at the edge of the promenade. There they watched the men and women of privilege stroll by, evaluated their faces as they passed, read into them what goodness they believed they were capable of. On one such Saturday, the identical sisters, dressed in their identical dresses, attracted the attention of an unaccompanied woman who, on her approach, saw them point her out of the crowd, then watched them lift a dandelion to their lips, and blow away the downy tuft in her direction.

What, the woman asked, had they wished for?

The girls said they had wished she would stop and talk with them.

Why? asked the woman.

And they told her why.

And what more would you wish for if I handed you all the dandelions in the world?

And they listed all the wishes they had written in the notes they had slipped into Jacob's pockets. The following day, they were invited to visit the woman's home. And off they went, and never returned. Without so much as a final note to wish Jacob well, they were gone, and would remain estranged from him for almost a dozen years.

To dull the loneliness Jacob felt in Rachel and Leah's absence, he immersed himself in his studies, and he discovered one day in the Asylum's library the writings of the Cambridge scryer, John Dee. He grew increasingly fascinated by Dee's pursuit to devise a numeric code in which one could see the pure verities that underlay the visible world. He dreamed of a universe in which it was possible to prove there was a mystical unity in all creation, and marveled over the thought of an obsidian mirror that the old scholar acquired from a soldier who claimed Aztec priests had found within it the angels of God.

For two years, Jacob spent his free time absorbed by the principals of optics he'd discovered in Dee's writings, in the drawings of Goethe, the treatises of Newton, and when his enthusiasm for this field was brought to the attention of one of the orphanage's trustees, he was introduced to a man named Jonah Liebeskind, an inventor and craftsman, who made his living shaping lenses for cameras and naval telescopes. Mr. Liebeskind was a fastidious bachelor who saw the smallest imperfections in all things. In objects. In architecture. In the manners of men. In the appearance of women. His intention, he would one day explain to Jacob, was not to be unkind by pointing out the deficits in people and the objects they created, he simply could not tolerate mediocrity.

He said to Jacob the afternoon they met that if he was willing to work hard and do everything in his power to live up to his standards, if he was willing to pledge to him his diligence, and promise he would attempt to rise above his circumstances, he would make Jacob his apprentice.

To this, Jacob agreed.

In return, he was given a room of his own in Mr. Liebeskind's splendid home, a key to the garden, a pair of coveralls to be worn in the machine shop, a new suit to be worn on days they made their deliveries, an additional suit, even more refined, to be worn to shul on the high holidays, to the theater, where they would spend each Sabbath eve, to the museum, where they would spend each Sabbath day studying art, and always to dinner.

Mr. Liebeskind was fond of saying, We will not be unseemly Jews. We will not look or speak like men spawned from the gutter. *We* will rise above. He settled for nothing less. Sartorial perfection. Clean hands. Buffed nails. Hair groomed. Shoes shined. Posture erect. Words pronounced without guttural inflection. Manners. Always manners. Always serving the aesthetics of grace. Jacob adopted Mr. Liebeskind's regimen. A small sacrifice to make for a room of his own and for the opportunity to handle such beautiful tools. In a night and a day, the upright Mr. Liebeskind transformed him from an unkempt boy into a pristine little man, and in ten years' time, all the while playing his role accordingly, Jacob absorbed everything Mr. Liebeskind imparted to him. He learned from him all there was to know about the properties of glass and shaping lenses, the mechanisms of photographic equipment, the physical nature of light, the internal workings of reflecting telescopes. His mentor had an impeccable eye for painting and believed there was no reason why he and Jacob, with a forthright application of ingenuity, couldn't, one day, craft lenses and mechanisms that would make it possible for the photographers to whom they sold their equipment to be as great as Hals and Van Dyck. Tiepolo. Poussin. Guardi. He dreamed of traveling abroad like a proper gentleman, to meet with other opticians, to research their methods of shaping lenses, but they were always too consumed with work to take time for a holiday.

With Mr. Liebeskind's permission, Jacob dissected the early projection and viewing devices his mentor had acquired over his lifetime; the components of his magic lanterns, the spinning carousel of his zoetropes, the synchronized disks of his phenakistoscope, the mandalas of his Wheel of Life; and with the little money he earned from Mr. Liebeskind, he bought materials with which he re-created, from designs he'd seen illustrated in the journal *Phantasmagoria*, an electrotachyscope and a phasmatrope. In this same journal, he read one night before bedtime an article about Thomas Edison's search for a method by which he might deliver clear and consistent images on his Kinetoscope. Jacob visited the patent office to study the blueprints of Edison's motion picture viewer, and saw in the drawings that the flaw wasn't, as Edison claimed, with the width and length and tensile strength of the celluloid, or, for that matter, with the placement of perforations along the film's edge, but rather with the rate at which each framed image moved past the device's aperture. The instant Jacob looked at it, he saw the wondrous flaw, and in the instant that followed, its remedy occurred to him as if it were handed down from heaven by the angels of God the Aztec priests witnessed in Dee's obsidian stone.

He spent the next year constituting Edison's Kinetoscope, re-engineering its system of feeds and loops, sprockets and pulleys, and when it was completed, he added to it a singular item, deceptively simple: a timing mechanism—not unlike what one might find inside a common pocket watch—that would make it possible to deliver however many frames of film per second one desired to the viewing piece of any motion picture device. In keeping with his character, the evening after he observed the successful operation of Jacob's invention, Jonah Liebeskind—as if he had recognized at that moment that he was on the cusp of declining into the middling state of mediocrity he so abhorred—died peacefully in his sleep, leaving not the slightest indication on his face that he'd struggled to stay alive.

To Jacob, who had proved himself over the years a devoted acolyte, Mr. Liebeskind willed his splendid home, his machine shop, his tools, his collection of optical devices, and the type of small fortune a fastidious bachelor accumulates after so many years of hard work without holidays. And once again, Jacob found himself alone, without friends or companions, better off only in riches.

With a small portion of the money left to him by his mentor, Jacob bought a suit more refined than the suit he wore to shul on the high holidays, and, dressed in this new ensemble, he traveled to West Orange to see Edison, who, after studying the patent for Jacob's timing mechanism, had agreed to sit for a demonstration. When presenting his invention to the great man, Jacob said, See, sir, see how simple and elegant. And he showed how simply and elegantly his invention rotated the device's shutter as it intermittently halted and reengaged the scrolling film, how it left just the right length of slack for the sprockets of Edison's Kinetoscope to move the frames of celluloid past the aperture, to create for the eye fluid imagery. And at this sight, Edison remarked, Now, why hadn't I thought of that?

Jacob sold Edison the rights to use what he would come to call the Rosenbloom Drive for a modest royalty, and he reserved the privilege of being the sole manufacturer and distributor of the mechanism. Jacob's modest riches wouldn't yet accrue into a fortune, but they would soon thereafter, when, several years later, a former associate of Mr. Edison's, a Mr. W.K.L. Dickson, who had been impressed by the young Rosenbloom's ingenuity, sought Jacob out in his deceased mentor's machine shop, and presented to him a new challenge: to build a mechanical system that would allow a projection device to cast a life-size image of a continuous action of prolonged duration. At present, because of the fussy internal configuration and limited capacity of Edison's Kinetoscope, only the shortest of moving pictures could be observed—of the most minuscule physical gestures, of the most meager displays of human nature—and they could only be seen by stooping over a box and squinting into a hole. Mr. Dickson placed in Jacob's hands a design for an apparatus he called a Phantoscope, and Jacob, again, after a short period of study, saw—as if God had breathed the solution into his mind—what Mr. Dickson and his colleagues could not. He set forth his terms—a greater royalty than the one he asked of Edison and the right to be the sole manufacturer of whatever moving parts he invented—and Mr. Dickson agreed.

In a few months' time, Jacob built for him a mechanism more complex, but equally as elegant as the one he had built for Edison: a labyrinth of rolling roundabouts and reversals, metallic passages, clips and levers, all of which fed and guided a length of film on a wayward journey from one magazine up top to another below, with each frame of film stopping intermittently in front of the projector's condenser lens and light source. This device he named the Rosenbloom Loop, which included in its design the Rosenbloom Drive. When Mr. Dickson saw in what an ingenious manner Jacob had made it possible to roll over as many feet of film that could be scrolled into the two magazines, and that the images they produced were larger than life, Dickson, who was not nearly as arrogant or prideful a man as Edison, said, Now, I would have *never* thought of that.

At which time, Jacob's modest riches began to transform into lasting wealth.

In Jonah Liebeskind's former machine shop, Jacob manufactured his mechanisms, and continued to attend to Mr. Liebeskind's longstanding clients. And as the old man's regimen had served him well thus far, he continued it on his own. He dressed in coveralls when working in the machine shop; when making deliveries, he dressed in his delivery suit; for dinner he dressed in his finest attire. On Friday nights after Sabbath prayers, he sat for a theater performance, sometimes two; on Saturdays he perused the wings of the museum. For many years he kept to these routines, and in doing so began to inhabit the character of his deceased mentor. More and more he resembled the fastidious bachelor whose work left him no time for holidays. And then, one Sabbath afternoon, a dozen years after he had watched Rachel and Leah slip away through the narrow opening of the Asylum's doors, an event he had long ago stopped hoping for befell him. On a bench in the museum, a sketch pad on her lap, a nub of charcoal in her hand, Rachel sat, drawing, re-creating in her own style Tiepolo's *The Rest on the Flight into Egypt*. There she was, the same little girl, now grown into the woman she had once pretended to be.

Jacob watched for a long while, well aware as he observed her in what ways he had become a man she wouldn't recognize, so precise and regimented, tailored and mannered, manicured, as upright as a soldier. For so long now, the boy she was familiar with had long since vacated his body. Even if he wanted to, he knew he wouldn't be able to summon him back. He rounded the stone bench on which she sat and continued to stare at her. He regarded with wonderment the movement of her hand and the shape of her lines, the curve of her wrist, and as soon as he formed her name on his lips, tears welled in his eyes. He thought for a moment that he should walk on and hide his face, but she sensed his presence and turned to see him crying in the silent manner he sometimes cried as a child, and upon seeing him this way, she recognized him.

Jacob? she said. Is it you? Is it really you?

That she knew his face without a moment's hesitation left him unable to speak.

My dear, dear, Jacob, she said. It's Rachel.

Yes, I know, he said. Of course, I know. How could I not?

And now, her eyes, too, filled with tears. They fell from the soft bulb of her chin and ran rivulets through the pitch, down the arm of the virgin mother, over the lines forming the newborn's head. He sat beside her and took her hand, and for a long time they remained there, silent, expressing their awe with searching looks, looking at each other with immense curiosity, imagining in their recollection of each other how they must have appeared in the intervening years. After a long while, she expressed her regret for not having said good-bye to him the day they departed the orphanage. She said how often she'd thought of Jacob, described in what ways she continued to feel his absence as if he were a phantom limb. She told him she had returned to the Asylum after she and Leah had settled into their new lives. She had hoped to find him there, but he had already moved on, and, she thought, perhaps he was angry with her for having been so selfish and unfeeling, angry enough to have irreversibly broken the bond they shared. That she sat beside him now, Jacob told her, was all that mattered. And they continued to study each other until she no longer saw the boy she once knew and began to apprehend what he had become. Touching the corners of his eyes with her charcoaled fingers, she said, Look at you. So young, yet so old. She could intuit how alone he had been. She could see in the lines that had begun to prematurely form on his face at what an unnatural rate he had grown into a man, and she promised him in that instant, We will never be apart again.

Every Saturday, they met at the bench set before Tiepolo's painting, and every Saturday, Jacob asked why Leah hadn't come to see him, and every Saturday, Rachel made excuses for her sister, until she could make no more. Leah, she confessed, hadn't visited him not because she didn't have the desire to see him, but because she was unaware she and Jacob had been reunited. Rachel, in short, had no way of telling her, as it had been some years since she had been estranged from her sister. This Jacob couldn't begin to comprehend. It was incomprehensible to Rachel as well, but it was the truth. Jacob asked how such a thing was possible. And Rachel described the ways in which their adopted mother, Alexandra Reuben, had deliberately and maliciously undermined Rachel and Leah's devotion to each other. From the moment they moved into their new home, Alexandra favored Rachel; she appealed to her better self; enticed her with gifts and rewards, with love and affection. When Rachel conducted herself well in company or performed well at school, when she met her potential, her mother praised her and held her up as exemplary. Leah, on the other hand, could do nothing to satisfy her. No matter how much effort Leah put into her music, her appearance, the manners with which she conducted herself, Alexandra voiced displeasure. Disheartening displeasure. No matter how well her sister played or sang at her recitals, Alexandra escorted her through the reception hall with her arm entwined in hers and in the most anodyne tones made apologies to her friends for her daughter's inferiority. If Leah expressed an opinion in company about a book she had enjoyed or about a fashion she found appealing, Alexandra twisted her words and revised her sentiments to make them sound foolish and uninformed. Once their adopted mother had successfully undermined Leah's confidence, she began to appeal to her baser instincts; she imparted to her dark secrets and gossip about the men and women who visited their home; and when she did so, she expressed, on the one hand, her disgust with the improprieties perpetrated by members of their closed circle, while, on the other hand, she whispered her tacit approval. About a young woman traveling unescorted by a man of standing, or about a mistress engaged in an affair with a married man, she might say: They should feel the blackest shame choke at them in the darkest hour of the night. Of course, she would say in the same breath, One must consider, how does a young woman not unlike yourself, Leah, rise above her lowly position?

It wasn't enough for Alexandra to merely encourage Leah to commit her own acts of transgression, she went so far as to manufacture them for her, by whispering, in the strictest confidence to her fellow matrons, lies about her own daughter's exploits with strange men. Rachel and Leah dismissed their mother's cruel and unscrupulous behavior as that of an unhappy woman too long alone and uncared for. They tried to take pity on her, but as time passed, as the sisters' obscurity fell into relief and became more and more a distant memory, Leah's resolve to deflect her mother's fictions weakened, and she began to believe in and embody the character Alexandra invented for her. Taboo began to fascinate her. She began to imagine, to speak of ways in which she could challenge the limits of propriety, and soon thereafter she started to embrace her mother's vision of her. While Rachel studied or painted, Leah dressed provocatively for evenings out with young men; she returned late in the evening. When this didn't provoke the desired reaction, she extended her stay out until the early morning. When Alexandra continued to show her indifference, Leah didn't return for days at a time; and then, not long after she turned sixteen, she fulfilled her mother's expectations of her, and didn't return at all. Rachel lost her sister to the city streets. Her own image of herself, the sound and smell of herself, her own flesh, disappeared into the shadows; the most intimate and integral part of her had become estranged. And this absence weighed upon her, she told Jacob, expressing itself in darker and darker visions of the world.

Jacob promised Rachel he would find Leah, and when he did, he would set things right and care for them both. Rachel's shame, however, was too great to immediately agree to this course of action. She feared facing Leah again. She was unaware of it at the time, but was now convinced she had played a part in alienating her sister from the small, precious world they had entered together. She could have spoken her mind, but chose not to. She could have defied Alexandra, but didn't. She could have fought more obstinately against her self-interest, but she didn't want to lose her favored position in her mother's heart, or, for that matter, put at risk the comforts of her mother's home. It was evident to her now in hindsight, the many ways she had betrayed her sister. She had spent a great deal of time trying to imagine the life Leah had been leading, and she wasn't convinced she wanted to become acquainted with its details. If I were Leah, she said to Jacob, I would be unforgiving, perhaps even vengeful.

Despite Rachel's reservations, Jacob felt obligated to discover what had become of Leah. He had the means to look after her, and, if she were willing, he intended to extend his hand. On the bench in the museum, he and Rachel had fallen in love. He wanted to marry her, and she wanted to marry him, and Jacob, who for so many years had missed both sisters equally, couldn't imagine a wedding without Leah. Wouldn't she feel greater shame, he asked Rachel, if they didn't search for her, to tell her of their plans, to have her present on the day they were joined? If they didn't make the effort to search her out, wouldn't it then be impossible to reconcile with her? To this, Rachel reluctantly agreed. Jacob hired an investigator, who instructed them some weeks later to visit the Freed Music Hall and take in an evening performance. On a Friday night, they sat together at the foot of the orchestra, and from there watched descend from the rafters on the seat of a swing whose ropes were twined in vines, Leah, singing the role of the ingénue, Eloise, a sylph whose songs were composed with melodies sweet and light, with lyrics laden with double meanings that left the gruffest men in the audience rapt with celestial and indelicate thoughts of streams and meadows, and Eloise, as she had been billed: dressed in white linen, her red lips spread in a girlish smile, golden locks curled over the nape of her neck, her bust bulging forth against the constraint of a corset, her pink fingers pulling up a silken slip to her naked thigh.

The reunion that evening was more pleasant than Jacob and Rachel anticipated. It appeared all of Rachel's fears were unfounded. Leah warmly embraced her. She shed tears over the time lost between them, but over a meal in a nearby tavern, she insisted she had no regrets. She assured them she was content. In fact, she couldn't have been more enthusiastic when speaking of the life she had chosen for herself. She had traveled to many cities, performed before a great number of audiences. Foolish men regularly sent expensive gifts to her dressing room, and Samuel Freed, for whom the hall was named, paid her a salary that afforded her a fine suite in a hotel not very far from the park's promenade, where she and Rachel had stood so many times as young girls. She had missed Rachel, she said, but she couldn't bear to complicate the fragile world Rachel occupied with Alexandra, so she decided when she left home to spare Rachel any trouble she might cause her. She was confident they would be together again, when the time was right.

Upon hearing of Leah's success and happiness, Jacob could see in Rachel's face how greatly relieved she was. She embraced her sister again and told her of their plans, and when Leah heard the news, the two sisters embraced a third time, and Leah said how wonderful and appropriate it was that she and Jacob should once again fall into each other's company by happenstance. Like Rachel, she expressed her profound regrets for having abandoned Jacob in the manner they did, and told him how often she had thought of her beloved companion over the years. Let us all forgive one another, shall we? she said. Let's say we'll let the past lie in ruins. In the months leading up to the wedding, Leah was consistently in good spirits and full of good cheer, whether she sat with Rachel in Jacob's home for dinner or was out with Rachel, making preparations for the reception. She graciously arranged with Samuel Freed to hire musicians from the hall and introduced Rachel to the florist who arranged the flowers in its lobby. Leah went so far as to sit beside Alexandra in grudging silence on the day the young couple stood under the chuppah to exchange their vows. All, it seemed, was reconstituted. All, it seemed, was how it should have been.

The newlyweds spent their wedding night in a hotel in the city and the following day rode a steamer upriver into the countryside, where they stayed at an inn on the edge of a lake. For several weeks they honeymooned, and it was there, on a walk up a hill overlooking the lake, they discovered the Woodhaven home in which they would live. Leah helped Rachel pack the items she would take with her from Alexandra's home, and sent stagehands to assist Jacob in dismantling Mr. Liebeskind's machine shop, to relocate it upriver. On the day the boxes were unloaded, Jacob was called away to the city on business. He would be gone for only three days, but he wanted Rachel to join him. He didn't want to be away from her for a moment, but she insisted she remain behind to unpack. Jacob traveled by train from Woodhaven and was ferried across the river to the naval yard, where he spent the afternoon installing a research telescope in the captain's quarters of the U.S.S. *Maine*. The following day, he did the same, and that night he returned to Mr. Liebeskind's home to find Rachel had changed her mind. She had decided to join him after all. They dined out together, then went to bed, and because they had nowhere to be, they stayed wrapped in each other's limbs for the better part of the following day and night. The next morning when they awoke, Rachel packed their bags and on they went to the train. All this time, at the station, inside the carriage on their journey home, they held each other close, and when they reached the threshold of their new house, Jacob playfully lifted up his new bride in his arms and carried her inside, only to find standing there Rachel, who looked at Leah in Jacob's arms.

There was her sister, dressed in her clothes, her hair mussed, her face flushed. All Rachel could say was that she didn't understand. To which, Leah said, Look at me. Look at me and tell me you don't know my reasons. Jacob set Leah down and, as the two sisters stood before each other in a frozen moment in time, he looked from Leah to Rachel and back again to Leah, and for the life of him, he couldn't tell them apart. All he could do was look away as Rachel listened to her sister unburden herself of the great unhappiness and hardship she had endured since she was driven out of Alexandra's home. There was no great success. She had no suite by the park. She was, more or less, kept by Samuel Freed in a small room inside the music hall, where he took from her whatever he wanted, whenever he wanted. For years, this had been their arrangement. For years, she had been his favored girl. This was the sacrifice she had made to escape the cruel woman who raised them. Now do you understand? she asked Rachel. Do you not understand why I want you to endure the lasting discomfort of this moment? Rachel was too hurt and dumbfounded to speak. Leah removed a slim paper tube from her pocket, marked Jacob's cheek with a streak of red lipstick, and made her exit. When Rachel found her voice, all she could say to Jacob was, How could you not know it wasn't me? How could you not know it was her? Jacob had no answer and, as he rubbed away the stain on his face, he was left to wonder if, perhaps, he had known. But how could he? . . . Yet how could he not?

For many months, Jacob and Rachel lived as if they were in mourning. Rachel covered all the mirrors in black cloth so she wouldn't be reminded of Leah. She ordered Jacob to the springs near their home, where she insisted he be ritually cleansed in the presence of a rabbi. She fasted and prayed, and, in the company of the rabbi's wife, she, too, visited the springs to immerse her body and cleanse her spirit in the living waters. Only after these rituals and further months of reflection was she prepared to once again accept her husband. Not long after she had managed to achieve some semblance of inner harmony, however, Rachel received from Leah a birth announcement and a photograph of Simon Abraham Reuben, a child whose face resembled Jacob's, and all she had worked to forget was now undone. She fell into a dark state of melancholy, refused to eat or get out of bed. For weeks she barely uttered a word. One morning Jacob awoke, in the room to which his wife had long since banished him, to find Rachel wasn't in the house. He searched for her everywhere, and eventually discovered at the train station that she had departed for the city early that morning. Jacob, instinctively knowing where to go, went directly to the music hall, where he learned from a stage-hand that Rachel had been there and moved on. The stagehand had sent her to Samuel Freed's residence, and there, too, Jacob went, and when he arrived, he walked into the entryway, where, to his hor-ror, he saw Samuel Freed sitting at the bottom of a stairwell, weeping over an unmoving Leah, whose dead body was still thick from preg-nancy. Samuel Freed looked at Jacob and described to him in what raving manner Rachel had barged in. She ran upstairs, lifted Leah's child out of its crib, and, claiming the boy was rightfully hers, started walking out with it. Leah chased after her. When she reached for the baby, Rachel stepped out of the way and Leah tumbled down the stairs. She has the child, Samuel told Jacob. You'll find her, and the boy, and you'll bring him back to me. Do this, and I'll show you mercy. Don't do it, and I swear to you, Rosenbloom, I will see you and your wife destroyed.

All Jacob could think to do was return home to Woodhaven and wait. When three days passed, he began to think the worst. The evening of the third night, however, a carriage pulled into the drive, and out of it Rachel emerged with the bundled infant. His wife's de-meanor wasn't her own. She glowed with the pride of a new mother, made faces at the babe in her arms, acted as if she, herself, had given birth to it. Jacob went outside and asked the driver to wait a mo-ment. Without disturbing Rachel's fragile state of mind, he escorted her inside and laid her and his son down to rest. When he returned to the cabbie he asked if he would take a message to the telegraph office. He scribbled a note addressed to Mr. Freed, telling him if he wanted the boy he would have to come and collect him. And back inside he went and sat with his wife and Simon until morning. Mr. Freed arrived with his men and a nurse at dawn, and while Rachel slept, Jacob pulled Simon from her arms, walked him outside, and handed him to the woman.

When you next see him, said Freed, he will be a man. He will know who you are. He will know what you've done. He will know what she has done. And he will come to claim what's his. Until then, you and she will not go near him. Is that understood?

Jacob understood.

Until then, your wife will not be safe from me.

Jacob understood.

Freed motioned his arm at the men who had traveled with him to Jacob and Rachel's home. You'll be visited by these men from time to time, and when they come to you, you will give them whatever they ask for. Anything.

Yes, said Jacob. Anything.

If you become disagreeable, said Freed, you see the nurse? I will send her to the police. She will tell them, in no uncertain terms, that your lovely wife is a murderess. Say you understand.

I understand, said Jacob.

I have never been an ideal man for any woman, Rosenbloom. I might not have always treated Leah as I should have, but, whatever my faults, whatever passed between us, I adored that woman more than you can possibly imagine. I was prepared to give her whatever her heart desired.

I am sorry for you, said Jacob. I'm sorry for it all.

Well, Freed said, I am glad we have an understanding.

When Rachel awoke, Jacob told her what he had done. More important, he told her what she had done. Leah is dead, he said. A statement Rachel refused to believe. Leah is dead, he said. Again and again he said it, for him to hear as much as for her. He must have said it to her a hundred times, and not even then would she believe him. He could hardly believe it himself. Not until she read in the paper that Leah Reuben, who played Eloise at the Freed Music Hall, had died under suspicious circumstances, did Rachel accept Leah was gone, at which point she fell into an inconsolable bereavement.

✲✦

The triumvirate sometimes appeared in the distance. In dark gaps on the road. In shadows across the canyons. As phantasms standing atop vistas high up on the trails. They were there. And then they were gone. Never present long enough for Bloom to see their forms clarified. When the days began to shorten, the young Rosenbloom longed to feel the harvest chill break the summer heat. He yearned to feel the mornings' moisture soak into his shoes, to smell the redolence of decaying wood, to see beds of moss thicken over hardened earth. But the autumnal heat intensified instead of diminished, and the more the moisture evaporated from the soil and radiated in waves across the basin, the more he pined for Woodhaven. Soon, desert gales arrived to further petrify the brush blanketing the vistas, and not long after, somewhere on the uninhabited range, plumes of amber smoke breasted the sky; the air filled with a sulfurous stink, and down snowed stinging flakes of ash. It would be many months after the winds arrived and the fires had exhausted themselves before they would feel the relief of winter rains. Torrential bursts washed away precipices and turned Mount Terminus's canyons into muddy rivers. When spring arrived, and then summer, Bloom wouldn't have been able to differentiate one season from the other were it not for the fact that as the Earth's vernal orbit concluded, the spindling limbs of the eucalyptus trees appeared too tired to hold up the clusters of their leathery leaves. It would be many years before he would grow accustomed to the bright skies circumscribing the passage of time; to the eruption of wildfires and flash floods, the violent quakes of the Earth; but he would never feel at ease with the effect their new surroundings had on his father. Jacob's spirit had discernibly dusted over, not unlike the preponderance of terrain about their new home. Only on the rarest occasions, when, perhaps, a stellar phenomenon presented itself in the sky, or if, by chance, the elder Rosenbloom was stirred by a passage of poetry or philosophy, did Bloom perceive the enthusiasm Jacob once enjoyed when discussing a small scientific truth or a metaphysical curiosity. He had never been a demonstrative man, but neither had his eyes ever appeared as dull and inert as they did now. Jacob regularly muddled away the diurnal hours inside the labyrinths of the front gardens, where, shortly after their arrival, he cut back the heliotrope blooms and the clinging appendages of the bougainvillea, edged hedgerows, planted beds of geraniums, crowns of thorn. When he had tidied the gardens' extremities, he began sculpting topiary from shrubs long unattended. With a stubborn devotion, he pruned from verdant protozoa, legs and torsos, arms and heads, and when, over the period of their first year on Mount Terminus, he had refined their curves and given shape to their faces, their hair, their hips, the figures transformed into women; into the same woman; in variegated poses, they stood mirroring one another in their respective corners and corridors, each figure expressing in her own distinct manner a profound disenchantment. Through the tall hedges Jacob cut ovals slightly wider in dimension than the faces, so each set of leafy eyes looked off in the direction of the villa, onto the mountain's range, out to the haze blanketing the sea, to the canyon's crags, to the promontory on which Bloom and his father continued to meet at day's end. The elder Rosenbloom constantly and fastidiously trimmed back his anthropomorphic shrubs, and, as he did so, he talked with them lovingly and intimately, in conspiratorial whispers about a past he would keep secret from his son for some years to come.

➤✦

Left to his own devices, the innocent Bloom walked the trails to Mount Terminus's peak, where, facing the eastward expanse of the valley, he read and sketched and carried on lengthy conversations with himself. In the evenings, while the elder Rosenbloom sat in his study, reading ledgers and writing correspondence to an associate he'd charged with the responsibility of attending to the business he had abandoned, Bloom went from room to room, lighting sconces, illuminating the villa's coffered ceilings, the colorful mosaics of its floor tile, the spiderwebs of fissures expanding through its walls. Their furnishings had been shipped from Woodhaven and set in place by his father throughout the villa's corresponding chambers. Bloom took comfort living among the many familiar items. The piano in the parlor. The armchair in which the elder Rosenbloom reclined in the later evening with a bottle of schnapps, with his fellow lens grinder Baruch Spinoza, with his beloved scryer, John Dee. Their dining room table and brocade chairs, the Georgian sideboard, the floral-rimmed china. Upstairs in a library even more spacious than the one in Woodhaven, his father's collection of books and optical devices—his Indonesian shadow puppets, his magic lanterns and zoetropes, the synchronized disks of a phenakistoscope, the mandalas of a Wheel of Life—filled cupboards and shelves climbing to the heights of a telescopic ceiling. The elder Rosenbloom's drafting table, at which he once sketched his optical designs, was present; present, too, were the leather sofas on which Bloom's growing body left its impressions. In a room overlooking a courtyard bordered by two cottages were Bloom's bed and night tables, a rolltop desk, Turkish rugs with opalescent borders, a wingback chair and a threadbare footstool erupting with fluff. Most comforting of all to him was the gallery in which Aphrodite reclined in relief above the mantelshelf of the fireplace. In this room, at the level of the goddess's eyes, his father had hung the Woodhaven landscapes Bloom's mother had painted, and under them arranged a chaise longue and two wooden chairs with clawed arms and clawed feet. One chair was slightly smaller than the other, and etched in Hebrew into the backside of the smaller one was the name of the boy's mother, and into the larger one, the name of his father. Whenever Bloom asked about the sadness he had observed in his mother's face in the days before her death, Jacob said to him, There is no need for you to dwell in darkness, my dear Bloom. When he asked about the fog consuming his mother's paintings, he said the same. My dear Bloom, there is no need for you to dwell in darkness. It was this room Bloom often visited in the middle of the night when he had difficulty sleeping. He wrapped himself in his mother's shawl and looked at her heavy brushwork, at Woodhaven as perceived through her studio window, its view of the lake, the placid cobalt water reflecting the slopes of the valley, the summits of its fern green hills bridged by gray mists. On the glare of the window's glass shimmered a ghostly portrait of his mother's profile, the elegant slope of her brow, her bold, aquiline nose, one of her otherworldly eyes whose gaze appeared to simultaneously stare onto the landscape below, and at him, her observer. While listening to the hum and groan of vapors expanding through the pipes behind the walls, while looking at the iridescent image of his mother, and breathing in what remained of her dying scent, Bloom was able to recall the days he spent in her company, copying images from her collection of lithographs. She would set before him the paintings of Tiepolo, *The Prophet Isaiah*, *Rachel Hiding the Idols*, *Jacob's Dream*; Rembrandt's *Joseph Tells His Dream to Jacob*; Gelder's *Judah and Joseph*, and she would say, One day the sun and the moon will bow to you, my dear Bloom. Like his mother, she would tell him, he possessed a steady hand and enjoyed a strange talent for seeing shapes within shapes. Like her, she said, he needed only to look at an object once before he could retain all its aspects in his mind. On several occasions, Bloom overheard her say to his father, In his eyes, I can see the face of God; in the lines he draws, I can hear His voice; when I watch his hand move, I can sense His presence. To these assertions, Jacob said to her, Please, my love, please don't. Please settle your mind. And he would take her by the hand and escort her to bed, or sit her before the fire in the parlor, where, wrapped in paisley, she stared into the blaze with a daemonic gaze. This memory of her still and quiet eyes filled with flames, and this memory alone, delivered Bloom into unshakable slumbers.

>‹

On the sixth day of Yamim Noraim, in the month of Tishri, on the third day before the sun descended onto Yom Kippur, one year and two months after their arrival, Bloom, now a boy of ten, gathered at Jacob's request a collection of trimmings pruned from the garden topiary and bound them in twine. When he completed this task, he helped his father unearth two fledgling juniper trees. That morning Bloom gathered candles and lanterns, filled several jugs of water, packed loaves of bread and jam, dried fruit, salted meat, a sack of oats, a bunch of carrots. He rolled up blankets and pillows into a tarp, and retrieved from the library a miniature book titled *Death, Forlorn*, which he tucked into the pocket of his father's jacket. When Jacob finished harnessing their mare to the buckboard, Bloom loaded the cargo he'd collected throughout the day. In the kitchen that evening, they ate a heavy stew, and when they were through, they set out into the darkest hour, the only lights the lanterns hanging from hooks on either side of their seats, a sliver of moon, the gauzy haze of the firmament. At sunrise, when the great valley brightened, Bloom noticed far behind them a dark fleck on the horizon; as they rode northeast in the direction of Mojave, he watched it trail after them, but just as every time he felt the presence of the men he had seen at the station, he wasn't certain they were, in fact, there.

At the pace of a funeral march, they traveled the valley's entire expanse, and when they reached the range beyond Mount Terminus, they entered a canyon pass. It deposited them onto a desolate plain, onto a hard, grooved road that delivered them to a region of cultivated earth abutting the desert's edge. For two days Jacob had gone without sleep or food, and each time Bloom insisted he stop and take some nourishment and close his eyes, his father refused. He would only break for an hour every now and again to rest the mare, during which time he looked through a spyglass in the direction from which they had ridden. Bloom asked him what he saw, and his father said, Men on horseback. Riding this way. Bloom asked who they were, and his father said, They are men. On horseback. Nothing more.

They soon met the embankment of a river and turned in the direction of the current. For several hours they followed it to the shores of a lake taking on the shape of the rift valley in which the river's water had settled, and when they arrived there, father and son made camp. Bloom gathered brush to build a fire while Jacob arranged, before the lapping water of the shore, the candles and the lanterns, the trimmings and the trees. When the boy returned, Jacob told him to stand beside him, and after a few moments of silence, the elder Rosenbloom lit the yahrzeit candle with a match and slipped it under the fogged glass of a lantern, and recited, *God full of mercy who dwells on high, grant perfect rest on the wings of your divine presence among the holy and the pure who shine in the brightness of the heavens to the soul of who has gone to her eternal rest as all her family pray for the elevation of her soul. Her resting place shall be in the Garden of Eden. The master of mercy will care for her under the protection of His wings for all time and bind her soul in the bond of everlasting life. God is her inheritance and she will rest in peace.* When the elder Rosenbloom finished the kaddish, Bloom watched his father untie the bundles of trimmings, and with the clippings piled on either side of his feet, he bent down and picked one up, rose, and cast it onto the water. He bent, he rose, davening, and with each offering, said, Forgive me. Please, my love, please forgive me. Forgive me, please forgive me. Forgive me, he said, please, my love, forgive me.

And when he had begged for his wife's forgiveness more times than Bloom could bear to hear, when the trimmings seemed to cover the vast surface of the lake, the sun started its descent behind the range. His father gathered some rocks, and with the brush Bloom had collected, he started a fire to keep Bloom warm and told him to eat the bread and meat, to drink some water. He told him he would be watching over him through the night and throughout the following day.

But where are you going? asked Bloom.

His father told him he would see soon enough. Don't wander off, he said. And don't follow me. He handed Bloom his spyglass, then lifted the juniper saplings in his arms, and through the eyepiece of the small telescope, Bloom watched him climb.

The elder Rosenbloom climbed high up the escarpment above the lake, and there, under the gnarled limbs of mature trees of the same variety he carried, Bloom could see him dig into the rocky earth with his spade. He watched him submerge the trees into their holes, cover over their roots, and sprinkle them with water, at which time Bloom could see no more, as his father's figure and his trees were soon shrouded in darkness. For the entirety of the night his father didn't return, for the entirety of the night the blue flame of the yahrzeit candle burned, and when the sun rose in the morning, Bloom discovered him sitting between the fledgling trees, and he discovered, too, high up the escarpment on the opposite side of the lake, three dark figures standing tall under the shade of a boulder. For the entirety of the following morning, Bloom sat between them and his father without moving. For the entirety of that afternoon, the men stood under cover of the overhang, watching Jacob. For the entirety of the afternoon, Jacob sat under buzzards perched in heraldic poses.

The birds, unmoving and silent, clutched at pale blue berries with their talons, Jacob's only cover the shadows cast from their outstretched wings. In the desert heat, Bloom watched his father fast and pray, and stare beyond the grand deposit of lake water, up the mouth of the river, whose bounty Bloom could see evidenced through his scope by the meandering lines cut through the plains, in the oblong curves etched into the earth from its overflow, in the argent veins of irrigation canals running to plots growing high and green. He imagined his father fortifying his weakening body with images of ice melt flowing from the mountains beyond, with thoughts of the rushing cascade falling through the gorge of a volcanic crater. How else could he sustain himself if not by envisioning the way in which the waters fell down steep cliffs into the maw of jagged rock? He must have seen it streaming through canyons in his mind, rounding its tortuous route through the scrub and bramble, pooling into the graben over which he sat. Over the water, onto the expanse of the panorama, Jacob stared for the entirety of the day. Not until the arc of the sun once again kissed the summit of the distant range did he lift his weary body and begin his descent down the trail he'd yesterday negotiated upward.

When the elder Rosenbloom returned to the campsite, he asked Bloom if he wouldn't mind packing up. Bloom did as his father requested. He rolled up his bedding into his tarp, and collected and stored the lanterns. Jacob, meanwhile, watered and fed the mare, and drank some water and ate some food himself, and when Bloom had finished his task, Jacob climbed into his seat and took hold of the reins; and when Bloom joined him, he said, Father?

Yes, my dear?

Did you see them?

Did I see who?

The men. Up there, he said, pointing, sitting opposite you.

Yes, I saw them.

Who are they?

They are men.

What sort of men?

Men whose interests happen to coincide with ours for the time being. Nothing more.

Bloom looked up to where the three dark figures had been biding their time, and he asked his father what those interests were. Jacob said they were none of Bloom's concern. It is not for you to worry about, he said. The worry is mine, and mine alone. They are only men, he repeated for Bloom. They will do us no harm. This I promise you.

✣

Some weeks later over breakfast, Jacob said to Bloom, You are lonely, my dear.

To this Bloom said, No, father. We, together, are all that I need.

The following day, the elder Rosenbloom traveled to Mission Santa Theresa de Avila, and hired from its refectory two sisters to be their cook and maid. Before they arrived, Jacob told his son he was never to say a cross word to their new cook. For a young woman of twenty-three, she had been through an ordeal a boy wouldn't understand, and he expected Bloom to treat her with the kindness of a pure heart even when he didn't feel like being kind.

The young woman Jacob referred to was Meralda, the elder sister, the larger and heartier of the two, the one more worn around the eyes. She possessed plump ankles and wrists, and had fingers like overstuffed sausages, which, in the first days she took up residence on the estate, she used to knead the boy's cheeks as she kneaded the dough she flattened into tortillas and shaped into loaves of bread.

She would then stop and hold him firmly in her grip for a few moments, at which point a doleful expression overcame the corners of
her mouth; her eyes moistened, and in that instant, Bloom found
his nose buried in the smell of flour powdered about the heft of her
breast. Any motherless child would have been fortunate to be
embraced so tenderly. However, Bloom concluded, from the way
Meralda would release him to gaze out through the kitchen's open
shutters onto the sky, that her affection was meant for some boy
other than him. To the sound of wood burning in the stove, to its
crack and hiss, he watched her disappear into memory, and he, whose
boyish frame prompted this reverie, became invisible to her.

Bloom was better disposed toward spending his time in the dim
presence of Roya, who had been born into a chrysalis of silence almost four years to the day before he entered the world. Deaf and
mute, she wandered with a somnambulist's gait from room to room
without acknowledging Bloom was there observing her. Unlike
Meralda, whose fleshy features readily displayed her most internal
thoughts and feelings, Roya's youthful lineaments were more delicate and narrow and remained fixed in beatific remove. They hardly
ever changed, and if they did, the changes were so subtle, Bloom
could never be certain if what he saw wasn't an invention of his
imagination. Each morning after breakfast, he trailed after her to
watch her sweep aimlessly at surfaces with the bright green plumage of her feather duster. And when she had tucked away the corners of their beds, and had pressed and hung the elder Rosenbloom's
shirts, she broke from her chores and sat in the courtyard with her
feet submerged in the reflecting pool. Bloom would sit beside her,
and together they would stare down at the ripples of water moving
through the reflection of a crescent-shaped building terraced onto
the shelf of a short, crescent-shaped mesa. Sometime, long ago, his
father had told him, this dwelling had burned from within, and was
now derelict and forbidden. For this reason, its shutters had been
nailed tight, and its door fixed with a sturdy lock, its only dwellers
brown lizards warting its stucco walls.

It was at the edge of the reflecting pool, some months after the sisters' arrival, that Roya presented to Bloom an object that would connect him to a part of his past about which he wouldn't have otherwise known. From a pocket in her skirt, she removed a folded piece of paper whose seams were thin and worn, then pulled at the corners one by one to reveal an ink drawing crafted with heavy lines Bloom recognized to be his mother's. It was a portrait of his father standing in the shadows of Mount Terminus's gate, looking very much as he appeared at present: drawn and longing and mournful. Bloom stared at the image for a time, trying to divine from the dark warrens composing his father's expression how this was possible.

Where did you find this? he asked Roya.

In the same manner with which she had presented the drawing to him, she folded it into a square and placed it back in her pocket. He expected this would be the extent to which she would answer a question she couldn't hear, but after she had dried her feet with the hem of her skirt and had pinched her toes into her shoes, she tugged on the collar of Bloom's shirt and began walking toward the house. He trailed behind her through the arcing shadows of the courtyard's loggia and followed her inside, up the stairs, along the landing. They passed Jacob's bedroom, and Bloom's, then entered the gallery, where Roya approached one of Rachel's paintings; one at whose vanishing point was a church on a hilltop, nearly all of it lost in a heavy mist, all for a muted yellow glow emanating from a window in its spire. She pulled away from the wall the bottom of its frame, retrieved the piece of paper from her pocket, and slipped it into a worn crevice between the canvas and the wooden slat. And then, as if nothing unusual at all had transpired, Roya went about her duties as if Bloom wasn't there.

Over dinner that evening, when Bloom set his mother's drawing down at the head of the table, his father, who wore the same expression as the one in the picture, nodded at the image—as if to say he already knew of its existence and knew where Bloom had found it. He then folded it over along its worn seams and slipped it into the inner pocket of his dinner jacket.

For a long time Jacob stared into steam rising up from a tureen of broth fogging the lusters of the dining room's chandelier, and, after this period of contemplation, he turned to his son and said with a thin smile all he was going to say. He said, It was a very long time ago.

Bloom wanted to know if the time in the past spent on Mount Terminus with his mother was a time like now, one filled with sorrow. But his father, anticipating a question, said, I will tell you more when you've become a man. The boy wasn't aware of what his face revealed, but whatever he had shown of his interior, of his hunger to know more about his mother and his father, Jacob said: I promise, my dear, you will know everything you need to know when you have grown.

Bloom didn't object. He knew his father's resolve well. He knew it was a futile endeavor to extract from him what he wanted with childish emotion, so he said, Yes, Father, when I have grown.

✣

Bloom began to imagine, when he reclined in the library, or walked the dusty trails, or sat with her likenesses in the gardens, his mother observing him from across the room, or from somewhere ahead in the distance, or while sitting at the opposite end of a bench. And when he sat with Roya at the edge of the reflecting pool, he would wonder aloud about what might have occurred in his mother and father's life to have made them travel to the end of the world. Why, he asked more than once, would they willingly choose desolation? Bloom discovered on his nightstand, the morning after he had posed this question to Roya, a wooden cross with acorns engraved on the front and on the back a primitive figure of a whale. As soon as he dressed, he carried it to the garden, where he found his father standing on a ladder, narrowing the shape of his mother's face where it had grown plump in the cheeks.

Have we become Christians? he asked as he lifted the cross.

His father stepped down and took it from him, examined it, and then handed it back, saying, No, my dear, we have not become Christians.

Then why did you leave this beside my bed?

To which Jacob said as he climbed back onto the ladder, I'll have a talk with Meralda.

Bloom suspected it wouldn't have been Meralda who had left the cross. Indeed, he was certain it would have been Roya. But because he wanted to protect her from any discomfort she might feel in his father's presence, and because he hoped his silent companion would one day introduce him to something else belonging to his mother, he didn't want to say as much. So he said nothing. And having said nothing, he began to believe in the causality between his omission and the great number of objects that appeared beside his bed. The morning after he found the cross, he discovered next to his pillow a Latin Bible, its pages oxidized brown and illustrated with images intended for the eyes of a child. Soon, artifacts fashioned in the same style as the cross began to appear; such things as clay pots and dolls carved from oak, a leather pouch filled with charms, talismans shaped from polished bone.

Each morning these objects appeared, and each evening after Bloom had fallen asleep, they were taken from his possession. He tried to remain awake into the early hours of the morning, after his father had quietly drunk himself into unconsciousness, when he could sneak out of his room and follow Roya to wherever it was she retrieved these items. Every night he went in search of her, it was as if she didn't exist.

Everywhere he looked, in the many rooms and halls, in the maids' quarters, in the outbuildings, she was never present. And so he would return to his bed and wait for her to arrive, but as if he had been put under a spell, his anticipation weakened; his eyes grew heavy, his small body fell into a deep pit of darkness, and when he awoke to the sun filling his room, there appeared a new curio. In several notes he left on his bedside table, he wrote, *Where do you go at night to find these?* But there was never a reply, only more and more objects left in exchange for his inquiries. He soon found colorful pictures printed from woodblocks, meticulous etchings whose compilation over time shaped for the boy a tragic tale.

The story began under dusty blue skies, where a tribe of Indians gathered at the mouth of the spring that now filled the estate's cisterns and irrigated its land. There were no eucalyptus or orange trees, no avocado or olive trees, no rosebushes or manicured gardens, only a wilderness of oaks, into which Indian children climbed and shook from their limbs acorns into waiting baskets below. Under a bright canopy of stars, under a full moon, in the crepuscular glow of distant wildfire, the women ground acorn into meal. Before sunrise, the men departed for the sea, and returned to the fires in the afternoon, wearing lines of fish hung over their shoulders. All the tableaus from this time resembled an Eden, vignettes of a people free from adversity, until one day Franciscan priests led a serpentine trail of soldiers, armored and helmeted, strapped with muskets and swords and rapiers, to the heights of the mountain. They forced the tribe in its entirety to lie prostrate before the crosses mounted to their saddles, to witness them fell the oaks and cap the spring. When the trees had all fallen and the spring had ceased to flow, the eyes of the captive men and women collectively darkened. Their faces contorted, as if afflicted with palsy. The priests marched away the women and children to a glowing cross by the sea. Behind remained their men, who the soldiers felled as easily as they had felled the oaks. And in place of the spring water that had streamed down the mountainside ran the men's blood. In the aftermath of the atrocity, the priests returned the women to the mountain, to make them handle at the point of swords the gruesome corpses of their husbands and brothers, fathers and sons, cousins and uncles. One after the next, they were appointed to drag their men into a ravine in which buzzards and coyotes tore away at their remains. The land afterward was cleared by oxen, the fallen trees stripped of their bark and cut for lumber that would be used in the construction of the villa, in which the women would live as servants, on whose property their daughters terraced the mountain for orange and lemon groves, where they could see to the east from the peak of Mount Terminus their sons raising swine in the valley below.

><

When this vision of Mount Terminus's past reached its conclusion, Bloom's nightstand in the morning was bare. Without the expectation he felt before he fell asleep and the excitement he experienced when he awoke, the ghostly visions of his mother, which had subsided in the intervening months, returned, and in her company he now could see in the lacunae of the estate's grounds, could hear in the clattering leaves of the groves, in the upsurge of the running spring, the phantoms of Mount Terminus's aborigines. Absent forethought, unaware of his intent, he began to draw scenes of the vivid chimera his imagination imposed on the estate. Not unlike the progression of events he had observed in the prints, he drew into the gardens and the groves life-affirming idylls. He set his mother in the company of children hanging from limbs of trees. She sat with women who ground acorn into meal. She presided over a feast held under a moon-lit sky. And as he had witnessed his father do when he set out to perfect his topiary, the boy tended to these Arcadian hymns to his mother with the same fastidious and loving care. Bloom refined each line of each composition until the ink he pressed onto paper with a fountain pen resembled the heavy strokes of his mother's brush; and only when he was satisfied that they reflected in their totality what he had envisaged, in the instance the phantasmagorias were born, did he present the drawings to his father, who, upon receiving the very first one, and upon receiving many more thereafter, appeared elevated in spirit.

With each presentation of his handiwork, Bloom could see color flush his father's face. He took great pleasure watching him handle the paper's edges before studying the complexities, looking on the fig-ments of his imagination as if he might discover within the details of the drawings' configurations a hidden map to free him from his present condition. Jacob sent the drawings to town with Meralda, to have them framed, and when they returned, he hung them in the parlor, on the cracked wall facing the chair in which he reclined at night to drink and smoke. Orderly rows formed, and by flickering gaslight, he stared at them, meditated over them, at times spoke to them under his breath.

Having witnessed the revival of his father's spirit, Bloom grew determined to further animate it. He was convinced if he continued to provide him more and more of what he saw in the stillness of his days, the elder Rosenbloom would begin to live in the world. Bloom, therefore, withdrew from the activities that provided him solace. He withdrew from his books. He withdrew from taking his daily sojourns to Mount Terminus's peak. Instead, in the estate's quietest corners, sometimes with Roya, sometimes without, he dutifully day-dreamed and drew what he saw in the shadows. He didn't quite understand why, but the more absorbed his father became by his drawings, Bloom was visited again and again by the image of the serpentine trail formed by the missionaries and their soldiers. Again and again, he envisioned the events that followed their arrival, and as hard as he tried to resist the impulse to draw his mother into the violent, ghastly scenes they perpetrated, he couldn't stop himself. Not unlike the prints his silent companion had left for him at his bedside, his narrative devolved. His once sunny idylls darkened into subterranean spectacle. He thought to hide these images from his father, but, perhaps to better understand the reason he couldn't re-lease them from his mind, when his father asked one morning over breakfast if he had more drawings to share with him, Bloom handed them over, and when he did, he watched his father's face change. His expression grew disturbed, and in an injured voice, he said, No, no, my dear, these won't do. No, we mustn't allow this to happen to you. Not to you, too.

He didn't send these drawings to the framer. Rather, he quietly hid them away. They disappeared to some secret place. Out of sight. When Bloom asked where they had gone, his father shook his head and said, It was wrong of me to encourage you. Jacob didn't admon-ish the boy. He didn't punish him. On the contrary, his tone was kind and contrite. But it was admonishment enough for Bloom to see, in the wake of this expression of regret, his father's features re-turn to their fragile, disconsolate shape. It was punishment enough to see his fascination wane, to watch it turn limpid and resigned. Once again the idle glaze to which Bloom had grown accustomed frosted his father's eyes, and once again the inconsolable man es-caped into his garden labyrinths, into the dark shadows of a past Bloom couldn't see, and within the passages of the narrow warrens,

Jacob paced. Around plantings and trimmings, he mindlessly wandered, migrated from one figure to the next. From the tower's pavilion Bloom observed his father pace a tortuous route through the desert gales. On he paced when the fire season delivered flames to Mount Terminus's nearby canyons. He paced until, one day, he did not.

And on that day, Bloom watched him ride down the mountain dressed in a suit, cleaned and pressed. And for some weeks after this first trip down the switchback, he frequently repeated the journey, sometimes staying away for several nights at a time. When Bloom would ask where he had gone and what he had been doing, his father said he had been tending to a business matter he could no longer avoid.

⤞⤝

Out of pity, Bloom wondered, or perhaps because this was her preferred method of entertaining herself—through mysteries and intrigues—he began to receive from Roya unusual notes, which she left in the most peculiar places. The first he felt inside the toe of his left shoe when he was dressing one morning. As if written by a child with an unsteady hand, it read, *I have a secret.* The following day he discovered in the toe of his right shoe another note that read, *In the library is a book on whose cover is a blue pyramid.* For several hours Bloom browsed the library's lower shelves and for several hours more from the rungs of a ladder he browsed the library's upper shelves, and only after having glanced at nearly every book cover in their large collection did he locate on the highest shelf in the library's farthest corner the cover he was looking for. There on a thin volume titled *Too Loud a Solitude* was a blue pyramid, at the center of which was inset a figure of a pharaoh, sitting upright in a sarcophagus. The pharaoh's eyes were open and his mouth was agape, and behind the cover when he turned it over he found a bookmark on which was written in Roya's penmanship: *The house has a secret.* As it served no purpose to implore a woman who couldn't hear and didn't speak to reveal what she uncovered during her furtive movements through their corridors and rooms, Bloom trusted Roya would soon enough deliver a new clue to draw the mystery she had set in motion to a point of comprehension. Bloom's patience was rewarded one afternoon, when, at lunch, Roya served him a sandwich and a glass of lemonade. Rolled inside the cloth napkin accompanying his meal were three sheets of parchment. On each was a miniature drawing whose lines were straight and whose corners were square and whose images were three skeletal representations of each level of their home. These illustrations, however, delineated neither the rooms with which Bloom was familiar nor the passageways leading to these rooms, but rather an elaborate system of connecting stairwells and corridors that, so far as he knew, had never been built. To Roya, who was standing across from where he sat in the dining room, Bloom silently mouthed: Did you draw these? She turned and walked around the long table at whose center he sat, and when she arrived at his side she pointed to a corner of the parchment where he could see, obscured by the tint of the paper's border, a signature: *Manuel Salazar*. So she could see his lips, he looked up at her and asked, Who is Manuel Salazar? As she had done on the day she handed him his mother's drawing of his father, she reached into the pocket of her skirt and removed a clipping from a page of a book. It read: *The parallax of time helps us to the true positions of a conception.* Then, from her opposite pocket, she removed another clipping on which was printed: *As the parallax of space helps us to that of a star.* To this, Bloom shook his head. She looked at him with the same indifference with which she looked at everything. She replaced the slips of paper in her pocket, along with the illustrations she had presented to the boy with his meal, and pointed with the same hand to his sandwich and then to the lemonade, indicating to him that he should eat. So he ate, and while he ate, she stood over him and watched him eat, and when Bloom had taken his last bite, he looked up again to Roya's face to see, this time, a chink of light in the darkness of her eyes. For an instant, he could see a violet-tinged nimbus flare on the circumferences of her pupils, and he knew when she turned and walked away

from him and rounded the head of the table, he was meant to follow her.

They entered the kitchen through a swinging door and walked
past halved heads of cabbage arranged on a woodblock, and on they
went to the service entrance at the base of the tower, where from a
leather pouch nailed to the cellar door Roya removed two flashlights,
one for him and one for her, and together they descended below
ground. Shining his light onto the pleats of her skirt, Bloom followed
her through the archways separating food stores from wine racks, old
furniture from hot water tanks, empty space from empty space, and
in one of the vacant vaults, in which the dry afternoon heat was
trapped and felt most oppressive, in which the hiss and groan of
the plumbing sounded most monstrous, Roya stopped and stood
before a brick pillar wider than any of the other supports that bol-
stered the load of the villa. She paused for a moment to look at Bloom.
She stood very still with the light shining up the middle of her blouse
and onto her chin; then, for the first time Bloom had ever seen it happen, Roya smiled. She smiled not a radiant smile, or a smile that
signified hope or delight. She smiled as she would if she were asleep
and dreaming of something colorful and airy. And with this listless
expression from which glistened a thin sliver of her teeth, she reached
out her free hand, pressed it against the bricks, and, with only the
slightest force of her weight leaning onto the pillar's exterior, its face
gave way and swung inward to reveal at its crack the hinges of a door.
When the door had opened fully, there before Bloom was a dark
shaft.

Roya stepped back now and stretched out her free hand. Twice
she pressed at the air with her palm. Then a third time. At which
point the boy stepped inside and pointed his flashlight upward. The
dim bulb cast a cone of orange incandescence onto the rungs of a
wooden ladder that so far as Bloom could see climbed into a thicker
darkness. He turned to look back at Roya, but she was no longer
there. Into the darkness of the cellar, she had silently withdrawn.
Into the darkness, she had noiselessly stepped away as only she could.
The boy thought for a moment he hadn't the courage to climb the

ladder to see what secret was at its top. But as soon as he placed his flashlight in his trouser pocket, whatever trepidation he felt was overtaken by curiosity, and in no time at all he had scaled high enough so that when he looked down to see what progress he had made, darkness filled the space below him. At the ladder's end, he arrived at a door, behind which he anticipated finding a corridor like one of those he had seen in the diagrams presented to him by Roya in the dining room, one that would take him on a Thesean journey through internal passageways, but when he lifted the door's lever and pushed it away from him, instead of encountering what he saw imprinted on the parchment, he was met by a soft expulsion of stale air and the sight of an enclosed room whose ceiling slanted with the pitch of the roof.

There were no windows here, yet, strangely, the space filled with a dull gray glow that misted out into the chamber and clung to him as would a fine silt. He stepped into the pall, and with each footfall forward, the floorboards creaked with vague, cacophonous sounds, not unlike those a chick might hear from the interior of its shell at the moment of its birth. On the wall adjacent to the door was painted in fresco the face of Cyclops, whose eye was a convex piece of glass rimmed with gold. Out of it, a beam of light illuminated an oval mirror hung at an angle on the opposite wall, and, on this day, the mirror projected onto a round table a granular image—awash in grays—of Roya, who was now sitting on the chaise longue in the gallery. She faced the frieze above the fireplace, staring through it to him with a knowing grin. For quite some time Bloom marveled at Roya's unmoving image and then gravitated to the wall opposite the entrance, where encased behind beveled glass were shelves on which he found all the objects his silent companion had brought to his bedside. And a great deal more. Stacks of unused parchment. Baskets filled with nibs and quills. Tins of pigment. Etched wood-blocks bundled in twine. In a brass chamber pot, a collection of hairpins, each rusted tooth crowned by a bouquet of black roses. Above the shelves was a long cabinet anchored to the wall, behind whose doors he discovered a leather-bound diary written in Spanish and signed on the opening page by the same hand that had drawn the hidden labyrinths. Although he didn't read a word of Spanish, there were a great number of drawings in these pages to hold the boy's interest, sketches of the pastoral and gruesome scenes with which he was already familiar, and then more detailed drawings of grand villas that might have been, variations on rooms and gardens and statuary, on towers and their arcaded pavilions. And finally appeared the plans for the villa that would be. That was.

Before the table holding Roya's still image, he sat in an armchair positioned so whoever occupied its seat saw the gallery projected upright. And there, in his silent companion's company, he sorted through the remaining pages, in which landscape and architecture no longer existed as Manuel Salazar's sole preoccupations. In these pages lived evidence of a burgeoning obsession with a woman who appeared at first as a shadow on the periphery of the estate's construction, and who, slowly, after many months, inched closer and closer to the foreground, until she occupied it completely. From thereafter, the scale of the unfinished buildings and the unfinished grounds diminished, receded, to vanishing points, until they disappeared altogether and were replaced by the woman, alone. As if floodlit on an empty stage. Bloom had yet to reach the age at which he could appreciate what moved a man of free will to devote himself to what he beheld in a single subject, but he was nevertheless captivated, image after image, by the only facet of this woman's countenance that was at all telling. Whereas her face was a vision of cold, hard balance and structure, whereas her eyes were perfect orbs that reflected neither light nor warmth, whereas her neck was slim and fixed, poised with the rigidity of an idealized human form, her left hand, whether it was at rest on her hip or holding a charm to the outline of her breast, held its fingers splayed, with a single digit dimpling a soft curve of flesh, a detail that, had it not been there, would have moved the boy to wonder if a woman such as the one drawn by Manuel Salazar could have ever been conceived in a world other than that of a man's dream. More engrossing still were the pages he discovered at the end of this volume, in which he saw drawings as exacting as he would ever see. Only to these, his attention focused not on this grand lady's face or the way she positioned her hands on her body, but to her garments, which were not the style of dress one would presume a woman would wear into the untidiness of desecrated ground. Rather, she was dressed in gowns and robes so rich with ornamentation that—if stretched flat and hung on cloistered walls—they could have been medieval tapestry. In their stitching, however, were no obvious symbols from which to divine any religious design. Instead, woven into the fabric were visions of unrequited love and architectural despair, of ruined Eastern cities, topographies of shattered teeth, decaying civilizations, home to no one but one man and one woman, who, from great distances, stood apart, the woman never seeing the man, the man always gazing from atop the rubble of fallen minarets, through cracks in ruptured walls, across dry beds of garden oases, his arms entwined in vines of tropical trees, in ivy clinging to crumbled walls, the man looking at the woman, his expression, like his father's, entrenched with lines formed from ceaseless longing, from never-ending despair.

❧

The attraction of Manuel Salazar's secret chamber drew Bloom back to face the eye of Cyclops many times in the months that followed. He often lay awake at night preoccupied with the dark cavity hidden inside the villa's walls, and he imagined there the face of a man resembling his father's, and he imagined reflected on the projection table the unblemished visage he had come to memorize from Salazar's diary, and he wondered, Had she sat as still for Salazar as Roya sat for him? Did she know he was there observing her? Could she feel his need to be nearby? On one such night he weighed these thoughts, Bloom's father appeared to him in what he thought at first was a dream. A barely visible outline of a man, a shock of white hair glimmering like the twilight's gloaming, rose up over him, and said, Come, my dear, we have a journey to take.

Bloom reached out to touch his father, and when he was convinced that what he saw and heard was real, he protested, But, Father, the sun hasn't risen.

It will soon enough.

I want to sleep.

Later, Jacob said, you'll sleep.

Bloom, as he neared the end of his twelfth year, had grown to the height of a man, still thin and lanky, but sizable enough that his father grunted when he pulled his weight upright. Jacob wet his hands in the washbasin on the dressing table, and with more attention than Bloom was accustomed to receiving from him, the elder Rosenbloom crept his fingers through his hair and pulled back the tight coils that stubbornly clung to the corners of his eyes when his forehead moistened in the heat.

There now, he said. Dress yourself and meet me downstairs.

Outside, Jacob sat atop the buckboard, holding the reins of the mare, which appeared to Bloom hypnotized by the lightening colors stratifying the sky. When he climbed on board and took his seat, his father placed an attaché case on his lap, and just as Jacob was about to turn away from him, he looked onto his son's face not unlike the way the horse had become transfixed by the aurora. The grooves between his brow squeezed shut, and appearing as if he wanted to elaborate on the purpose of their trip, or on something else altogether, Jacob shook his head to cast away whatever was on his mind, and turning his focus to the mare's ass, he snapped the leather straps, sending them on their way. They rode over the gravel drive dividing the gardens in which Jacob spent his days, and because it was rare he and Bloom ever ventured beyond Mount Terminus's gates, because Bloom felt a deepening connection to the estate's creator, he was drawn back to the villa's grandeur. He watched it fade into the distance, and as he did so, he noticed, standing in silhouette between two pillars of the tower's arcaded pavilion, the diminutive figure of Roya. He watched her stand there before a crimson sky for as long as he could see her and looked away only when his father said in a conciliatory voice, There, there, we are not going very far.

They switched back and forth down the mountain road without

talking, and cantered past citrus groves rooted to ruts of desiccated earth. Extending into the distance as far as they could see, baubles of fruit weighted down muscular limbs. Dust devils formed in the wake of their tracks and spun into Aeolian wisps of smoke whose tendrils dispersed upward into vapor trails, on which a condor lofted and circled about. When some hours later they reached the bluff overlooking the ocean's expanse, they descended a slope to the coastal trail, not far from whose head stood alone at the edge of the beach a blinding structure, tall and long and molten white. Illuminated by the morning sun, it appeared to Bloom a mirage, as liquid and form-less as the sea. As they neared it, the building's shape solidified into what looked like a steamship three tiers high, along each of whose decks ambled figures neutered of their gender by white gowns and wide-brimmed hats. Beyond this building was a smaller vessel, where a horseshoe hung on a brace over a pair of barn doors. It was to this structure the father steered the mare, and here the man and his son disembarked, and left the horse and buckboard with a liv-eryman. Jacob handed the attendant a coin and said they would only be a moment. He then took the attaché case from Bloom and pressed his hand to his back to set him in motion. They walked to-gether onto white planks filling the gap between the two buildings, where, before they reached its end, Jacob halted. He turned to his son and looked into his eyes with the same probing uncertainty with which he had searched his face earlier that morning. As if he were apologizing in advance for doing something he knew to be of questionable judgment, he said, You needn't say a word. You must come with me, but if you don't feel moved to, you needn't utter a sound. It was impossible for Bloom to comprehend the meaning of his father's caution, the reason for his contrition, but when they reached the end of the boardwalk and turned the corner, it became clear. Spread out before him on a deck overlooking a significant re-gion of the beach, the same gowned figures he had witnessed am-bling along the landings reclined in rows of white chaises arranged like the groves they had just ridden through, and standing in con-trast to everyone and everything about them at the far end, were the

three dark figures who came and went, to and from Mount Terminus, dressed in black long coats and bowler hats.

The three men whose faces Bloom had never seen. There they
were, forming a dark constellation around one of the lounge chairs.
Bloom's father placed a hand on his shoulder and said again: You
needn't utter a sound. They walked in and out of shadows cast by
white umbrellas, past gaunt faces lathered in zinc. Bloom noticed
hands clutching handkerchiefs spotted with blood; he avoided the
stare of milky eyes thick with jaundice. At regular intervals, the
sickliest of the patients appeared to suffer simultaneous fits. Bodies
convulsed in on themselves, rasping coughs from lungs too damaged to expel whatever invading substance occupied them. The sad
noises once trumpeted into the ocean breeze acted like a contagion,
setting off a percussive echo of croaks and caws into the crash of
waves. I needn't say a word, thought Bloom when he and his father
halted before the humorless faces of the grim triumvirate, whose
motives remained concealed in the cloudy rheum of their eyes. Lank
hair fell from under the brims of their hats, dampening insipid brows;
sweat gathered on the thick bulbs of their noses and occasionally
dripped onto the toes of their boots. Their mouths were thin, their
jaws locked, and each possessed a unique taxonomy of pink, worm-
like scars fossilized on their jaws, around the orbits of their eyes, on
the knuckles of their brawny hands. They held a perimeter around
an invalid, passing an unlit cigar under his nose. Unlike the other
infirm, this man didn't wear the wide-brimmed hat or the cake of
zinc on his face. Nor did he wear the white gown. Instead, he reclined
in a cream silk robe tied off with a purple sash. While his thick arms
and chest were matted with wiry hair, the crown of his head was
bald and browned, and what hair remained above the ear and around
the pate was white and cropped close to the scalp. His face belonged to that of a caricature. Wide nostrils. Fat lips. Heavy jowls.
Hooded eyes. It belonged to a man who had inflicted, who had been
afflicted by, pain.

At the first sight of Bloom, the steely eyes of the reclining brute
softened and became those of a moody, quizzical child. His cigar

fell limp between his thick fingers as he said in a voice deep and graveled and full of bent foreign syllables, Remarkable. Absolutely remarkable. Without breaking his open gaze, he told Bloom to come closer, to sit with him. The young Rosenbloom looked at his father, who nodded his assurance. And with that, Bloom left his father's side and sat at the man's hip.

Your papa has said who I am?

Bloom shook his head.

No, of course he hasn't. The old man set his cigar in his lap and rested a coarse palm on Bloom's cheek. You're a fortunate young man to have such a sensible papa. With his brow raised, he drew his chin to his chest. He has done good today. For you, young man, he has done good. He searched Bloom's eyes again, this time as if he were hunting for evidence of something intimate they shared. He now withdrew his hand from Bloom's cheek and turned his attention to Jacob. The air. The sound of the salted sea. These men of God here, they say it will do miracles for me. But they say in the same breath, I don't help myself because I don't believe. What do you say, Mr. Rosenbloom? Do I suffer from a lack of faith? Bloom's father stepped forward without replying and presented the attaché to the sickly man, who lifted it into the waiting hands of the nearest member of the triumvirate. He then reached into a pocket stitched onto his robe and removed a silver pendant, half of a coin embossed with a full moon, bright and shiny on one side, dark with tarnish on the other. Give me your hand, *malchik*. It is for this I've asked your father to bring you here today. Bloom lifted his hand and in it the man placed his gift. One day soon, he said as he looked at Bloom's father, as if he were speaking to him as much as to his son, you will know its other half. He then smiled as he closed Bloom's fist. This world of ours, young Rosenbloom, it is a world of wondrous surprises, is it not? Bloom nodded in agreement. One never knows what astonishments await us. Isn't that so, Papa? The old man lifted his heavy lids and once again directed his eyes at the elder Rosenbloom. Jacob didn't answer the man. He instead tugged on Bloom's collar, and when the young man looked up he saw his father's chin motioning him away. At that moment, he could see in the hollows of his father's eyes the malignant influence these dark figures held over his will. For the first time, he could see in the tightening folds of his father's face how terrified he was of these men. As they walked off in the direction from which they had come, rather than upset Jacob's pride by asking where these brutes derived their power, or what the significance of the pendant was, Bloom took hold of his hand and said, When we return home, shall we climb to the top of the tower and look at the sea?

>‹

Neither Bloom nor his father mentioned in the following days and weeks anything about their journey to the sea or the identity of the man who had set his hand on the younger Rosenbloom's cheek. Bloom asked no questions about what the attaché case contained or what might have been the meaning of the pendant. He was deeply curious, of course, and at times was tempted to breach the darkness his father had forbidden him to enter all his life, but Bloom sensed the questions he was keeping to himself would be answered soon enough. He intuited from the softening of his father's manner, from the warmth he heard in the tone of his voice, from the concern he expressed for Bloom's well-being, his forbearance would not persist.

Bloom, now approaching the age of manhood, had become familiar enough with his father's character to know that whatever the nature of the transaction he had witnessed on the beach, it was most certainly one marking a significant change in his association with this man. Something of consequence had transpired. Something momentous enough, his father was compelled to break from the comfort of his routines to ready Bloom for what was to come. Jacob ceased spending the entirety of his days tending to the grounds and communing with the animist spirits of his topiary; instead, he approached the courtyard each morning from a vanishing point at the end of a path dividing the dark grove of avocado trees from the bright lattices of the rose garden. His arrivals coincided with Roya's departures: as she entered the shadows of the loggia and disappeared behind the villa's walls, he walked between the twin cottages forming the yard's border, bowed his head through a pergola wearing a toupee of bougainvillea, and announced his presence with a grim smile.

In the same manner Bloom sat with his mute companion, he sat with his father, who drew their attention to the crescent-shaped building terraced onto the shelf of the short, crescent-shaped mesa. One afternoon while looking at this structure, Jacob described a place on the sluggish Belus River where in the middle of the first century a ship belonging to soda traders spread out along the Phoenician shore to prepare a meal of fish stew. He told his son they had no stones to support their cooking pots, so they placed lumps of soda from the ship under them, and when these became hot and fused with the sand on the beach, streams of an unknown, translucent liquid flowed. This, he said, was the origin of glass. This, he said, has given our eyes their greatest purpose. His father patted the air with his long fingers, indicating to Bloom that he should remain still, and off he went up the stone steps with a skeleton key dangling from a string tied to his wrist. When he reached the landing, Bloom watched him follow the curve of the building until he rounded its side. A gust of desert wind rustled the grove, through which he could hear the unmistakable cry of a long-unopened door. The sharp noise of the stiff hinges scattered the lizards on the building's surface; they scurried and refixed themselves into a new configuration, until a few moments later, with as little ease as it had opened, the door shut, and a new pattern was formed. Around the corner his father walked, pressing to the chest of his coveralls a wooden case nearly as tall and wide as he. When he had descended the stairs and reached Bloom, he said, Today we will give your eyes greater purpose. Climb the tower after lunch and this will be waiting for you. He turned to go, and then turned back. Looking at his dusty boots, he said, You must prepare yourself, my dear.

What for?

Jacob tapped the case with his knuckle. With this, you will see.

>⋵

Assembled inside the tower's pavilion was a reflecting telescope whose optical tube was crafted from ash and trimmed with cast iron. It was mounted to a decorative globe resting atop a pedestal whose thin base was held secure by metal supports. All was affixed to a dais that snugly fit onto the shoulders of a tripod. The lacquer applied to preserve the wood had darkened and in places was altogether stripped bare; aquamarine streaks of oxidation had begun to accrete over the iron's surface; and whatever words had been etched into the brass plaque set onto the dais's foundation had long since been rubbed away into a flat sheen. Old as the telescope might have been, when Bloom set the orbit of his eye against the viewing piece, the mirrors magnified into his mind a wide field of vision, full of clear images, their colors crisp and containing no aberrations, all of it so impressive and bright, when he saw what was in its sights, it summoned within the young man the thrill of being present at the focal point. But when this initial excitement wore off, and he was left to contemplate the substance of what he saw, he wanted some explanation for what was out there. His father had trained the tube's aperture onto the section of winding road that snaked up to the estate's gates, and there, occupying the annular frame, was a team of hulking men swinging picks, driving them in unison into the ground. Following them, a line of laborers turned over earth with shovels, and beyond them, a line pulled rakes; next rolled carts piled high with tarmac, and what was beyond that, Bloom wouldn't see until some time later, when the men who spread the pitch onto the raked earth edged out from behind a turn on the road. It would then be some more time before he saw the stacks of the steamrollers belch black smoke as they paved the tarred macadam into a smooth surface. And there the parade came to its end, all for the three dark figures he had encountered on the beach. They casually strolled up the grade, each biting down on a smoldering cigar; the tails of their long coats, the brims of their hats, catching the steam rising up from the cooling pavement.

When they sat down to dinner that evening, Bloom's mind remained fixed on the images he observed that afternoon through the eyepiece of the telescope. Seeing as it was his father who revealed to him the brigade of laborers advancing up the mountain, he assumed he would explain the circumstances of their arrival. But the elder Rosenbloom deliberately avoided the subject, and, instead, spoke for the entirety of their meal about the many ways the visible world had excited his boyhood imagination. He spoke of the philosophers and men of science whose intent was to prove there was a mystical unity in all creation. He spoke of the ways in which he saw the world as ecstatically alive, to what extent he believed light to be the exuberance of God's great goodness and truth, how mirrors and prisms divine the means to reflect that truth. He spoke of Shakespeare's Prospero and Marlowe's Faust, of a disciple of John Dee's who descended into an erupting Vesuvius to study its smoking vents, of a mad fantasist who spent his life's work disproving the Tower of Babel could have ever reached the moon. For as long as men of imagination appreciate the wonders of the mind, he insisted, they will draw inspiration from such men; throughout the ages, their spirits will continue to manifest themselves in characters we can only now dream of.

That, my dear Bloom, was the type of man I wanted to become, Jacob said. One whose ideas and inventions had the power to shape visions.

Here his father paused. And here Bloom looked up from his meal, and he could see a wet film had formed over his father's eyes. But you can see in my face every day what I've become.

No, said Bloom.

Yes, insisted his father. He pushed back his chair and stood up. Come, there's something I want to share with you in the drawing room. Something, I believe, you need to see.

☀

If we lived one hundred years ago, his father said as he led Bloom to the parlor after dinner, if this were a great ballroom or cathedral, and held in it several hundred spectators, I might introduce what I am about to show you by declaring, That which is about to happen before your eyes is not frivolous spectacle. It is made for the man who thinks, for the philosopher who likes to lose his way. This is a spectacle that man can use to instruct himself in the bizarre effects of the imagination. When it combines vigor and derangement. If I were the great Etienne-Gaspard, who began all his phantasmagorias this way, I would spread open my arms in some grand gesture and you would see floating into the center of the room an apparition, or a phantom, or the head of Medusa, or, perhaps, have rising up out of Daedalus's labyrinth the waxen wings of Icarus moving toward the radiance of the sun. And, I daresay, Jacob said with a hush, you would be dazzled.

The elder Rosenbloom ushered his son toward a table in the center of the room and said, Open it. There on the table rested a wooden box not unlike the one his father had retrieved earlier that day from the crescent-shaped dwelling. The young Rosenbloom did as he was told: he unlatched an iron clasp and pushed open the lid, underneath which he found, immersed in fitted compartments, two copper objects with thick veins of patina running through their wear. The shape of the first resembled an oil lamp; the other was a cylindrical lens at whose base was a slot into which one could slide a silver dollar. Within the tube, Bloom saw when he pulled it out, was a configuration of mirrors; in its orbit was fixed a clouded lens. Careful now, said his father as he removed the lamp, it's very old. Jacob took the tube from Bloom's hands, delicately fitted the two parts together, and set them on the table. From a separate compartment, he pulled out a box within the box, and when he opened it, he asked Bloom to extinguish the drawing room's flames. As soon as Bloom had done this, and they were ensconced in darkness, his father struck a match and lit the lamp, and he instructed the young Rosenbloom to sit facing the empty wall. Bloom sat down in the armchair his father slept in most evenings and heard the first of the slides slip through the slot. When it was illuminated by the lamplight, he saw an image of his mother standing before a window in which he could see, reflecting back, her profile. She painted these, said his father. With a very fine brush and a magnifier, she reduced herself into miniature. Always with a shadow image standing somewhere nearby, watching, observing. Do you see, my dear? It's important that you see.

Bloom, who hadn't initially seen the shadow, now saw it quite clearly and said as much to his father. Yes, Father, I see.

The elder Rosenbloom changed the slide to a likeness of his wife standing before a mirror in which her reflection stared past her to the ghostly double, this one's lines better defined, bold enough that he could see expressed, in the creases of its eyes, scorn and contempt for the image reflecting from the mirror. And this one?

Yes, Father, this one is clear.

And then, said his father, she disposed of the windows and mirrors altogether, and, well, you can see here—again he switched the slide—and here—and again switched—and here, how the shade becomes more and more lifelike, and begins to resemble your mother in every way. You see, my dear, what she saw?

Yes, Father, I see what she saw.

Yes, said his father.

But why? asked Bloom. Why did she depict herself this way?

Bloom heard the tink of glass, and then the sound repeated, and then again, and he knew from that sound, and from the pauses between them, as much as his father wanted to continue with this, he had reached an impasse.

Tomorrow, Father, said the young Rosenbloom. There is always tomorrow.

Yes, his father agreed. Tomorrow.

➤✦

The following evening, and for several more evenings afterward, Bloom's father produced a new optical device, and with each new device, Bloom witnessed the furtherance of his mother's peculiar preoccupation. Animated on spinning disks and carousels and drums, his mother ran away from herself through long corridors, hid from herself in dark closets, knelt before herself to beg for forgiveness.

Do you see? was his father's refrain.

To which Bloom said, Yes, Father, I see.

Do you see how she suffered?

Yes, Father, I see. But I still don't understand the cause of her suffering.

No, said Jacob. How could you?

And as these viewings went on night after night, Bloom said on more than one occasion, Please, Father, you needn't subject yourself to these if it causes you pain.

Yes, said his father, I do.

⁂

At home, in Woodhaven, his father told Bloom on one of these nights, Mother was so possessed by these visions she could no longer be left to her solitude. Both her doctor and our rabbi thought she should be committed to an asylum, but I couldn't do that to her. I decided for both our sakes to take her away. I put the foundry in the hands of my associate, Mr. Geller, who you may or may not remember . . . I packed a few trunks and we boarded a train with no destination in mind. We traveled aimlessly for several months, wandered deeper and deeper into the heartland, and along the way, if your mother chose to be stubborn or defiant, if her condition made her listless or confused, I didn't care—I would carry her in my arms if need be, and force her to stand on her feet, to open her eyes, to look upon the wondrous beauty we encountered along the route of our journey, and the more distance we gained from home, the more westward we moved, the more I agitated your mother to be active, the more she began to resemble the woman I had fallen in love with. By happenstance, we met a man in town who told us of this place, this estate, and one day we visited it. Mother was immediately drawn to the gardens and the groves, to the view at the edge of the promontory; on the summit of the mountain, in the quiet of the parlors, she felt at peace with her thoughts and at ease with me, so the day following, I bought it, I bought it all, the entire mountain and a great deal of the land extending to the sea, so no soul could intrude on Mother's happiness. And not very long after we arrived, some several months had passed, perhaps, no more, Mother started painting again, and took pleasure in her work. In landscapes, and only landscapes. Absent from them were any human figures at all. I, of course, encouraged this. And to show her how much so, we periodically ventured out into the valley in search of new terrain. To inspire her eye. And when she tired of the valley's barrenness, we journeyed beyond it. One day, while roaming trails we weren't familiar with, we arrived at the river I have taken you to, and then at the lake, and when we reached that enormous body of water, and looked upon its calm surface, Mother saw in her reflection something of herself she hadn't observed in a very long time. Whatever it was she saw, she felt moved to wade into that water, fully clothed, to the knees at first, then to the waist, and the neck, until she was immersed, her yellow skirt floating around the top of her head, she looked like a daisy, full of warmth and light. In that instance, on the shore of those waters we stand before on the Day of Atonement, your mother transformed. She was reborn. As if some agent of God had revived her spirit.

And in the days that followed, as a gesture of love, I suppose, or perhaps as a way to preserve the place where I witnessed this miracle, I was compelled to seek out the men who owned the water rights to the lake, and, to protect that place of sacred beauty, to preserve the landmark that filled me with hope, I bought them as well. I hired a local family to manage the irrigation of the farms in the region, to manage the lands and the wildlife, and for the few years Mother and I lived on the estate, we frequently traveled there, often enough, for certain . . . But then we were happy. More happy than we had ever been. And with our happiness constant for an extended passage of time—as people are prone to do—we both began to forget our troubles. We forgot what condition of mind Mother was in when we first arrived on Mount Terminus. She and I, both, took for granted the miracle we had experienced in the rift valley, at the lakeshore, and I, thinking Mother's change was irreversible, started to feel restless. She had become pregnant with you, my dear, and as I saw her growing larger and larger, I selfishly longed for Woodhaven, to return to the business, to my workshop, to the foundry, to do something more industrious than caring for my wife, and I began to wonder, what precisely was keeping us from going home? Mother, after all, had been well for so long, I didn't think it wrong or unfair, I certainly didn't think it a risky proposition to return. And, of course, when I did make the proposal, Mother convinced me I had sacrificed enough of my time for her. She said it was important I return to my work. She said herself she felt the pull of Woodhaven, that she dreamed of raising you in our old home. And while I was convinced these words were spoken from her heart, I did see something in her eyes during that conversation, something I chose to ignore. It was little more than a flicker of light, what amounted to no more than a few frames in one of her projections, a miniature moment cautioning me she was still as fragile as she had ever been. In that exchange—had I only been more alert—I would have seen how easily she could reverse course. Instead, who knows what my mind did? Disregarded the possibility? Interpreted it as a vestigial fear from a period in our marriage I believed to be long since past? And so, we packed away what we had accumulated here over the years, and returned to the East, where, in reverse course, she experienced a decline in such small gradations I wasn't even aware it was taking place. Not until it was too late. Not until she had disappeared from me again did I understand to what extent she was irretrievably lost.

You must remember, Jacob said after a long silence, how faraway her eyes could be. And Bloom recalled how she stared into the fires at night.

You do remember, don't you?

Yes, Father. I do.

Yes?

Yes. Like you. In the gardens.

Yes, said the elder Rosenbloom with a contemplative pause. Like me in the gardens.

><

The morning after his father confessed to Bloom what had been weighing on his conscience these many years, the elder Rosenbloom walked into the courtyard carrying a crowbar, and proceeded up the steps to the crescent dwelling. Bloom watched from his bedroom window as his father wedged the bar's bucked teeth behind the shutters and pressed his body into the work of dislodging them. A creak sounded, followed by a loud crack. Jacob maneuvered his way around the edges, one window after the next, the creak and crack building into a steady rhythm, and before the sun had reached its apex in the sky, a pile of discarded wood gathered on the landing. Meralda went and returned with a mop and pail, and when she had finished her part, the elder Rosenbloom stood at his son's door and said, There is more to say, and soon enough, I will say it all, but for the time being, my dear, come along. Bloom followed his father out of his room and down the stairs, into the yard and up the stone steps to the top of the mesa, and there Bloom saw through the windows, a room, far from derelict, certainly never burned from within, but, rather, a spacious opening, bright and clean and white. I've cleared everything away and arranged it in the library, said his father, then he pointed to a large wooden cabinet with a scope rising out of the top, All for that.

What is it? asked Bloom.

It was for that, he said, I sacrificed your mother's calm.

They walked around the corner and entered the dwelling, and once there his father led him to the back of the cabinet. He pulled away its covering to reveal inside a complex system of spools and feeds, clips and mechanisms throughout which snaked a gray film. This one, Bloom's father said as he touched his finger to a network of cogs, is the Rosenbloom Drive. Without which, neither this device nor any motion picture projector can function properly. From this, he said, we want for nothing. As he turned the reels with his finger, he said, It's little more than a timepiece, really, a mechanism that makes it possible for your eye to perceive a crisp and fluid movement of light and shadow, leaving the mind free from distraction to interpret the images as it would the life passing before you. His father reached into a compartment, pulled out a battery the size of an ingot, and replaced it with another of the same. He then handed Bloom a nickel and said he should go ahead and give it a try. Bloom walked around and slipped the coin into the slot at the front of the box, and as soon as it clunked into a metal bin, the viewer's mechanisms sounded a whir and a continuous clicking, and up through the eyepiece, he witnessed a flickering of light. Do you hear it? asked his father. The clicks?

Yes, said Bloom.

That, he told him, is the sound of the Rosenbloom Drive at work. Bloom listened to it for a moment, and imagined his father listening to the original clicks of the very first machine, and he then placed his hands on the sturdy wooden box to feel its vibration. Go on, said his father, tell me what's inside. Bloom bent over and rested his eyes against the mask of the peephole and felt himself aroused at the sight of a woman balancing on her right foot atop the capital of a Corinthian column. Her left foot she rested flatly against the inner thigh of her extended leg. Her arms she encircled over a Corinthian mound of ivy-twined hair. Very slowly, as if her fingers were rays of light, she broke the halo over her head and reached into the darkness behind her. With an extraordinary display of flexibility, she shifted her hips forward and extended her arms and curled back into the shape of a dewdrop, at which point her hands enfolded her ankle and the column began to rotate. It revolved once and then twice, and at the beginning of the third revolution, a translucent shroud billowed from out of the darkness above and collapsed over her body. When the column finished its rotation, a light flashed and the woman disappeared, leaving only the shroud limply hanging over the capital's leaves.

A woman, said Bloom. Spinning and disappearing.

Yes, said his father with an amused grin, I know it well.

And with that, Jacob reached into his pocket and pulled out the skeleton key he had used for the padlock the other day. The room, he said, is yours. Your mother practiced her art here, and so should you. And then from his other pocket, he removed *Death, Forlorn,* the miniature book he carried with him everywhere, and he said, If you would, I would like you to illustrate this for me.

➤≺

A young couple, newly wed, travels to the sea. At the end of a mountain pass, they arrive at a parcel of land surrounded by a fortress wall. They ride the entire length of the circular road around it, and as far as they can see, the wall appears to be perfectly enclosed, without entrance or exit. When they descend to the bottom of the mountain, they stop for a meal at an inn where they meet a cloaked figure sitting at the bar. The stranger, they learn, lives behind the enclosed walls. He is about to explain how it is he accesses his home, when the waitress walks by and drops a tray of dishes. The kindhearted husband leaves the table for a moment to offer his help, and when he returns from the kitchen, his wife and the strange man have disappeared. The husband searches the woods and the storefronts of the town, and when he's reached the apothecary at the end of the road, he notices in the front window a terrarium of mandrakes, and at the sight of them, his panic turns to despair. He enters the shop and takes from a shelf a bottle of arsenic, which he gulps down until there is no more. His body begins to wither, but before he has fallen to the floor, he is transported to a bed of nettles lying in the shadows of the enclosure at the top of the mountain, where, before him, a section of stones dematerializes to create a dark opening through which he can enter. The stranger he met at the inn is waiting for him when he has completed his passage. I am Death, he announces, and he asks why he has come to him without being called. The husband says to Death that he's come in search of his wife, and Death says that his wife is beyond hope. He leads the husband into a cathedral whose cupola is lit by candlelight. Each candle, he explains, is a life, and when its flame is extinguished, the life is lost. Death confesses to the husband that he has grown weary. He is tired of being feared and wishes that the inevitable consequences of his actions weren't absolute. He, therefore, offers the man a chance to save his wife. Let us see, he says, if you can alter the boundaries of fate. He makes appear three candles and says to him that if he can keep one of these three candles lit, his wife will be returned to him unharmed. Death first sends the man to save the lover of the Caliph of Baghdad from being buried alive by the Caliph's gardener. He fails, and a candle is extinguished. Death sends him to save the lover of the Chinese emperor from the emperor's archer, and at this task, too, the man fails, and a candle is extinguished. Death sends the man to save the fiancée of a Venetian tyrant, and here too, he fails, and the third candle is extinguished. Because he desires to see the young man succeed, Death offers him a final chance. He tells him that if before noon he can find a life that has yet to meet its fate, he will return his wife in exchange. Death returns the husband to the apothecary just as he is about to swallow the arsenic, and at that moment the clock strikes eleven. He returns to the inn, where he recalls having seen in the window of the second floor a feeble old woman. The old woman, happy for the company, invites him in to sit by the fire. He asks her if she would be willing to give up what remains of her life so that he can live his with his wife. To this, she says, Not one day, not one hour, not one breath. When the old woman is finished speaking, out of the fire pops an ember. The ember falls at the ruffle of a curtain and sets it ablaze. The fire laps at the walls and licks at the ceiling and spreads across the room. The home, it turns out, is the home of the waitress, who, from the street below, is now screaming for her child. As the fire continues to consume the room, the man finds the baby, sitting up in its bassinet near the edge of the flames. Death now appears and reaches out for the child. He says that if he places the babe in his arms, his wife will be returned to him. But the man has already decided what sacrifice he is willing to make for his beloved. He hurries to the window and drops the child into the arms of its mother, then walks into the inferno, from which Death sweeps him up in his arms, and says, This is meant to be. Moments later, the newly wed wife appears on the main road. She searches for her husband as her husband did for her, and once again the story begins.

✦

After his father had placed the frail pages of Death's allegory in his hand, Bloom began to spend his mornings in the studio. Every day after breakfast, he sat at a drawing table set before a pane of glass framing the courtyard, the walls of the villa, the cottages, the reflecting pool. And with each successive morning after breakfast he felt a keener and keener appetency to better understand the deeper meaning of his mother's visions. While weighing in his mind the story handed to him by his father, he wondered if the fate of his sanity was in some way tethered to his mother's. He wrote of what transpired between him and his father and left his summaries for Roya to find, and when the sheets of paper disappeared, he wrote such questions as *Was it a natural deterioration she experienced? Or was there a precipitating cause? Am I destined to confuse the visions I see in my mind for what I perceived in my perceptions of world?* But she never answered him. She did, however, sit beside him in his studio as he worked, sometimes for many hours. These were worrying thoughts, he told her on several occasions, ones from which he didn't know how to dissociate himself. If he were, perhaps, a more typical young man, one who didn't empathize with his father's sensitivities, one who hadn't been conditioned to tolerate his secrets and his silence, he might have pressed Jacob to explain his mother's condition in more detail, but he couldn't in good conscience—not for the time being, at any rate—ask him to confide in him any more than he had already. He had observed the great strength it took for his father to reveal what little he had. He had heard the hesitation in his voice, witnessed the way his nerves had been shaken. To ask more of him now, Bloom said to Roya, would be cruel, would it not? And so Bloom decided to wait, to exercise, as he had done for so long, patience.

✦

Before long the sound of picks and shovels reached the top of the mountain, and not long afterward they heard, through the open windows and all about the grounds, the call and response of song keeping rhythm with the thwack and scrape of the men's toil.

It's a lo-o-o-ng John!
A lo-o-ng John!
He's a lo-o-o-ng gone!
A l-o-o-ng gone!
Like a turkey through the corn!
A turkey through the corn!
Through the lo-o-o-ng corn!
The l-o-o-ng corn!
. . . Well, my John say-ed!
My John say-ed!
In the ten chap ten!
Ten chap ten!
If a man die!
A man die!
He will live again!
He will live again!

And from their camps each night just before the noise waned, Bloom heard:

Wait and let me tell you what your brother will do:
Fo' your face, have a love for you.
'Hind your back, scandalize your name.
Jest the same you have to bear the blame.
O Lord, trouble so hard. O Lord, trouble so hard.
Don't nobody know my troubles but God.
Yes, indeed, my troubles so hard.

When it was finished, the road ended well before Mount Terminus's gate; it turned inward onto the long plateau downhill from the stand of eucalyptus. Early the next morning, not a full day after the completion of the work, Bloom heard, for the first time, the fiery combustion of motorcars. When the sound of the engines quieted, he looked out of his bedroom window to see, at the end of the cobbled path, his father, standing on a boulder under the long, spindling limbs at the edge of the estate. Bloom dressed and walked down into the courtyard and on through the pergola to the path's end, and when he arrived, his father handed him a pair of binoculars. Bloom watched through the lenses the dozen or so men who had convened at the center of the clearing. Three carried scrolls of blueprints, three carried theodolites, the others held mallets and stakes and cones of twine.

But that's our land, Bloom said to his father.

No, said his father. Not since the day we traveled to the sea.

For all these years, said Bloom, this is what they wanted?

This, said his father, and a great deal more.

And what have you given them?

Everything they've asked for.

I don't understand.

I know, my dear. But you will soon enough.

The men carrying the tools gathered around a young man, tall and slim, dressed in a white suit whose cut was sharp in the shoulders and along the lapel. His hair had been tussled from the wind, and falling over his eyes was a rakish curl. He had a natural ease about him when he spoke, yet he held himself upright in such a way he appeared superior to those around him. He formed the men into groups and sent them on their way to different areas of the plateau, and when these men had set about their tasks, the young man turned his head to where Bloom and his father stood, and with a cold, hard gaze acknowledged he knew he was being observed. He made no attempt to wave or nod; he only tucked his hands into his trouser pockets and glared at them. And with his face now unobstructed by the others, Bloom was overcome by the uncanny feeling that he knew this young man. He was somehow familiar to him. Strangely so. He eased the binoculars away from his face and looked at his father, who said, They will be coming for a share of our water next.

And we will give it to them?

Yes, said Jacob.

The man below continued to look up to Bloom and his father, and Bloom could see when he raised the binoculars again, a dark emotion had entered the young man's eyes. He began to tilt in their direction, and an instant later he was walking toward them. I want you to leave me now, said the elder Rosenbloom. I'd like to have a few words alone with this man.

Do you know him?

Please, my dear, be on your way.

Bloom did as he was told. He stepped back and walked the way he had come, and when he reached the courtyard, he climbed up to the studio landing, where he looked down to the stand of eucalyptus and saw through the binoculars the man emerge from the steep hike up the hill. The elder Rosenbloom extended his hand, but the young man didn't take it. His father said a few words now, to which came no response. The elder Rosenbloom tried once more, but the young man stood his ground, and this time when his father failed to elicit a reaction, he made a polite gesture and walked away in the direction of his gardens. The young man watched the elder Rosenbloom walk off, and then, with his fists clenched at his sides, he followed.

This disturbing behavior concerned Bloom, so he, too, followed. He ran down the steps, into the villa, through the kitchen, and leaped up the stairwell of the tower, taking steps two by two, to the pavilion landing. Once there, he saw Jacob's head wending through the maze of hedgerows, and saw his pursuer wasn't very far behind. When they reached the corner of the garden for which his father was bound, the young man in the white suit looked up to see the topiary, and at the sight of it, he allowed his eyes to wander from the elder Rosenbloom to the leafy figure. He circled around it once, and then again, this time shaking his head. Bloom watched him through the eyepiece of the telescope now, and could see an expression of disbelief in the openness of his mouth and eyes. He now said something. What, Bloom, of course, couldn't hear, but he believed he saw form on his lips No or How. And then You as he pointed a finger at the elder Rosenbloom. And another No or How. The sensation Bloom felt earlier returned. There was something familiar about this young man's face, something familial, perhaps. And now his father's pursuer circled the topiary one last time, and when he said his last words, he spat at Jacob's feet and threw up a hand in disgust. When he reached the drive, Bloom could clearly see the shadows of his arms casting rude gestures onto the gravel below.

><

Over dinner that evening, Bloom asked his father why the man from the plateau had been so angry with him. He wanted to know if they had met each other before today. The elder Rosenbloom would only say, I would like for you to go out and make his acquaintance. The questions you have for me, pose them to him. And then we will talk. On the subject of the angry young man, he would say no more.

><

As the elder Rosenbloom said would happen, the same group of engineers and surveyors they had watched shape the lots below walked onto the estate some days later and began marking the land for a pipeline. Bloom, who, in Roya's constant company, had begun to sketch his illustrations of *Death, Forlorn* in the meticulous style of drawing he discovered in Manuel Salazar's sketchbook, watched from the studio as they staked a route from the spring's outlet. Through the courtyard. Between the cottages. Along the path. Down the hill. Soon afterward arrived a team of Chinese ditchdiggers whose long braided hair swung like pendulums as they lifted and set aside the walkway's paving stones. Under lines of twine the surveyors had strung to demarcate the water's route, they broke into the hard earth with pickaxes and dug a trench, into which they laid the pipe. When they had coupled all the conduits, they joined one end to a cistern, and continued their labors on the plateau. The day the water began to surge downhill, Bloom noticed the young man walking along the line of eucalyptus with a camera case strapped across his chest and a tripod slung over his shoulder. He stopped occasionally to admire the villa, then pressed on up toward the trailhead beyond the rose garden. From where Bloom sat, this figure, dressed as he was in his elegant white suit, and carrying himself with the determination of a man dividing a throng on a city street, appeared misplaced. He moved his body with little regard for the desiccated earth that scuffed at his shoes and kicked up eddies of desert silt onto the cuffs of his pants. He obviously didn't know or care about what fits of volatile temper this place was capable of, nor did he sense what Bloom saw from this distance, how small and insignificant his presence was on this giant rise of sediment and rock. He walked uphill with his shoulders square and his free hand thrust into his pocket, surveying the land with a keen eye, as if he were the behemoth and Mount Terminus merely a small mound of dirt, which he could flatten with the bottom of his shoe should he choose to. The intensity of spirit, this display of self-importance, disconcerted Bloom; yet, when the young man rounded the turn onto the trail, he was compelled to make himself known. He wanted to face him, to confirm what he suspected: that he and this man were somehow related. He placed aside his work and set out into the courtyard, onto the path, up onto the initial grade, and where it leveled out at a vista overlooking the plateau, Bloom came upon him standing before the camera mounted to the tripod. When the young man heard Bloom's approach, he turned, and when he saw him, he stopped what he was doing and stared, not with the same angry glare with which he confronted the elder Rosenbloom; rather, he appeared entranced. Bloom walked on and saw before him what he had seen through the binoculars and then again through the lens of his telescope: their commonality was manifest. Here stood a man, eight or ten years older than he, strikingly similar to himself. Their faces shared the same handsome lines around the jaw and the chin. Both bore bold noses, neither too long nor too wide. Their hairline rounded high on the forehead and they each had the same Tatar curve to their eyes. Their dark complexions, the coarse texture of their hair, were identical. The hands were long and narrow to suit their tall and slender frames. Even the eyebrows contrived the same herringbone weave.

Remarkable, said the young man.

Yes, said Bloom, nodding in agreement. The young man nodded along with Bloom and then said, with the same certainty and self-possession Bloom had witnessed from the window of the studio, You're Jacob's son.

Yes. Joseph.

But you are called Bloom.

That's what my father calls me.

The young man now moved away from the camera and took a step downhill. Do you know who I am?

Bloom, too, took an additional step forward. No, I don't think so.

Simon? . . . Simon Reuben? He inflected the pronunciation of his name in such a way that there was an expectation Bloom should have recognized it; but he didn't, and could only say in response that he was pleased to meet him.

You don't recognize the name?

No, I'm afraid I don't.

No one in the entirety of your life has ever so much as whispered my name?

No, said Bloom, never. He took another step toward the man to see if this even closer proximity would somehow enable him to re-call a hidden memory. What, he asked from this short distance, should I know about you?

Why, said Simon with an edge of indignation in his voice, you *should* know *everything* about me. At the very least, you should know my name. You should have been carrying it around with you all your life. It should be filling your mind with mystery and wonder, as yours does mine.

Bloom could only shake his head. About the past, my father says very little. Almost nothing at all.

That shouldn't surprise me, said Simon, but I find it disheartening all the same.

I don't understand.

No, Simon said angrily, how could you?

And then arrived a pause.

The two young men, who were identical in almost every way except for their age, looked each other over for a prolonged moment in which Simon appeared, from the movement of his eyes, engaged in an internal deliberation. When he concluded this inner discourse, he regained his equanimity and said, I'm sorry, but I must be on my way. Simon Reuben lifted the tripod with the camera attached and continued charging the trail upward.

I wish you would take just a few minutes to explain.

No, said Simon from over his shoulder, it's for your father to explain. Ask him. Ask him what became of Leah. Ask him who Leah was to your mother. Ask him how I am related to you.

Upon hearing this, Bloom set after him. Then we *are* related?

Ask your father.

Please try to understand, said Bloom as he ran to catch up, I will, but I assure you, nothing will come of it.

For years, Simon said, speaking to Bloom as if his concerns belonged to a world beyond the one on which they walked, I've been chasing the sun. Do you know what kind of displeasure it brings me to chase the sun from season to season?

I'm sorry?

Like Moses and the tribes of Israel must have felt wandering the desert. You see there, he said, pointing with the toes of the tripod in the direction of the plateau. That is my Promised Land, and today I refuse to allow God or anyone else to keep me from it. He took three long strides and then, talking more to himself than to Bloom, said, When I return, it is here that I'll stay. No more running. When the construction is complete, I'll return, and when I do, you and I will become better acquainted. Until then, I must continue on. Simon quickened his pace.

Please, Bloom pleaded. He's sent me to you for the answer. I don't have the patience to wait.

As abruptly as he had reengaged his movement up the mountain,

Simon Reuben stopped, and with a plume of dust drifting beyond him, he turned back and grabbed hold of Bloom's left hand. *Look*, he said as he held out his same hand, it couldn't be more plain. On Bloom's palm, just below his thumb, was a brown birthmark resembling a thorn growing from a stalk. On Simon's palm, in precisely the same location, was the identical blemish.

There, he said. Take that back to him and see what he says.

Bloom looked up at the familiar face and asked in a voice upset from the unexpected turn, You are my *brother*?

Go home and talk with our father.

He turned again and continued his charge up the mountain. Bloom didn't follow this time. He looked at his hand and then looked at Simon's. He watched it clench into a fist, which he used to drive himself ahead to the appointment he was keeping with himself at the top of the trail.

><

It was almost too much for Bloom to apprehend. He had a brother? An elder brother? How was it possible he had a brother? Headstrong and ambitious. Self-absorbed and easy to anger. A man who knew something of the world. Had he not been so astounded by this revelation, he might have stopped to wonder about his father's motives for having concealed his existence from him, but Bloom, for the time being, could only feel the preternatural thrill of the event. For the moment, he was filled with a joy he had never known before. He had a brother! An elder brother! Alive. Vibrant. Determined. Nothing else mattered to him. His only desire was to know Simon better, to stand with him when he did whatever it was he was going to do under Mount Terminus's unyielding light.

Father! he called out when he reached the front gardens.

Father! he called again into the mazes of hedgerows.

I've seen him! I've talked with him! I've done as you've asked! Father?

Up here, Bloom heard from above. He pitched his head back

and saw the elder Rosenbloom's profile edge out over the rail of the tower's arcade. I am here, my dear.

I'll come to you! And on Bloom continued in his enlivened state to the tower stairs. When he had climbed to the pavilion's landing, he discovered his father standing before the telescope, its small aperture pointing to the slope Bloom had just descended. Jacob's eyes wouldn't turn to his son; they gazed out in the same direction as the hollowed tube. He looked off into the distance as if he were still imagining the dramatic turn on the mountainside. Bloom was accustomed to his father's reserved silences, but this reticence to engage him he had never before encountered. His remove unnerved Bloom, and he couldn't help but wonder if by doing what his father had asked, he had somehow betrayed him; if by allowing himself to experience the quiver of exultation he felt in his joy, had he in some way breached the elder Rosenbloom's trust?

Father?

With his eyes still unable to look onto his son, Jacob said in a plaintive voice, The two of you, you're nearly one and the same.

Yes, said Bloom in a tone now matching his father's.

Yes, Jacob repeated, nearly one and the same. He nodded as a philosopher might when formulating a complicated course of logic. After a long silence, he turned, not to Bloom, but in the direction of the sea, and said, I've envisioned this day many times, you know. And each time I've lived this moment in my mind, I've never been able to move beyond this point in the conversation. You and I have often stood together in these temporal events of mine, very much as we are right now, and they've all concluded with the same result. Always we end as participants in a stillborn scene, one in which I'm unable to form the words of the story I must tell you. And here I am, paralyzed by the same hesitation, the same reluctance to say what I must say.

Please, Father, said Bloom. I must know. It's time I knew.

Jacob looked into his son's eyes for a few moments, almost as if he were bidding him farewell, then said, Come along.

>‹

In the drawing room that afternoon, the elder Rosenbloom placed in his son's hands a photograph and said, Tell me what you see. Bloom took the silver plate from him and saw on it a lustrous image of his young mother standing on either side of his father. Two mothers, each holding one of his father's arms. Is it an illusion? asked Bloom.

No, it isn't an illusion. On my left arm is your mother, Rachel. And on my right is her sister, Leah.

One was indistinguishable from the other. They were identical in every way. With no trace of a physical inconsistency. Pointing to Leah's image, Jacob said, *This* is Simon's mother. And Bloom now understood his father's hesitation in the tower. He now comprehended his unease, as he could hear a disquieting voice emerge within his mind, one calling into question everything he once thought he knew about the man who had fathered him. It was as if a mask had been lifted, revealing to him a face with which he wasn't at all familiar.

Jacob reached for the pouch of tobacco on the table beside his chair and with trembling hands packed the bowl of his pipe. With your mother's sister, he said, with Leah, I had a son. And before there could be any recriminations, Jacob began at the beginning. He told Bloom of the obscure origin of his, his mother's, and his aunt's birth, of their epic journey to and across the sea. He told him of the old Rabbi Rosenbloom and his wife, the life he, Rachel, and Leah shared at the orphanage. He described the day he learned they were lost to him, the years he apprenticed with Jonah Liebeskind, the circumstances in which he and Rachel found each other again. He told Bloom about his mother and his aunt's estrangement, how, together, he and Rachel searched out Leah. He recounted their happy reunion, the happy wedding, how content they felt upon their move to Woodhaven. He told Bloom the tale of Leah's deception, detailed the extent to which her betrayal destroyed his mother's spirit, described how devastated Rachel was when she received the announcement of Simon's birth, set out the order of events that led to Leah's death, to his mother's descent into madness, revealed to Bloom the identity of the man he had met at the sanitarium on the beach, explained to him how Simon had come to be in Samuel Freed's care.

They moved from the drawing room to the dining room, and Jacob continued to speak through dinner, during which time he chronicled for Bloom the history of Samuel Freed's extortion.

Some days after Leah died, Jacob told him, Sam Freed arranged for his men to meet him at his bank. On that day, Jacob provided them a large sum of money, more than enough, he thought, to provide for Simon's care for an entire lifetime. He thought, perhaps, that would be the extent of it. The following year, however, and every year afterward on the anniversary of Leah's death, Freed demanded more, and, having no recourse, Jacob provided him larger and larger amounts of money. With this money, he learned, Sam Freed was purchasing a great many burlesque and vaudeville houses throughout the city, and from all accounts Freed's fortunes rose. The theaters flourished and Freed prospered greatly, particularly after he had gathered his theatrical talent, hired photographers, and put them to work in an open-air studio on the riverfront.

There they made dozens of short pictures. Novelty acts mostly. Dancing bears. Sword swallowers. Circus freaks. Sideshow featurettes, he called them. Freed purchased Kinetoscopes from the Edison Manufacturing Company, which he lined up in the lobbies of his theaters, and in his new machines he presented his productions. He was so impressed by the return on his investment, he started converting his theaters into motion picture palaces. He realized if he could make his pictures last the duration of a theatrical performance, he could run them through the day and late into the night, and collect a continuous source of revenue at a fraction of the expense of putting on live acts.

When Edison Studios learned Sam Freed had gone into the picture business, they started after him for unfair use of their equipment. Freed simply did what every other production company did:

he sent his crew off to traverse country byways and make pictures out of the reach of Edison's lawyers. Soon enough, it became apparent to him, he could further cut his costs if he had a fixed base of operation. He wanted to eliminate the fees his itinerants were laying out to local townships—the bribes paid to politicians, the location payments made to property owners, the rates for lodging and food. He realized his overhead would be significantly lower if they consolidated everyone in one place and remained stationary on a single plot of land. It just so happened, at the time he began to dream of a permanent place in the sun, he sent his men to collect his annual alms from me, but on the day they arrived at the bank, they discovered I wasn't there. Mother had already passed away, and seeing as Freed no longer had any leverage over us, I no longer had cause to continue paying him.

When they saw Jacob wasn't at the bank, the elder Rosenbloom explained, Freed's men went to the house in Woodhaven, where they saw Bloom and his father board a carriage bound for the train station. They followed them there, and, after making a few inquiries, learned where they were going. Freed sent a telegram to one of his production teams, and they sent the three men who had been observing them. They reported back about what was on Mount Terminus— open land drenched in light, coastal desert kept alive by an eternal spring—and not long after that, they learned about Jacob's holdings at the lake up near Mojave. Several times they approached Jacob in town and tried to influence him to sign over a portion of the Mount Terminus property and the water rights to the lake. They threatened to implicate him in Leah's death in place of Rachel. But Jacob refused to give in to their pressure. They eventually offered him money for both the land and access to the water, and he refused them still, as he couldn't imagine parting with either property for the sentimental reasons that precipitated him to purchase them in the first place.

But as I watched you grow older and more self-aware, said the elder Rosenbloom, the more I was reminded of the loneliness I knew as a child, and the more I recalled the longing I felt to be rejoined with your mother and her sister, the need I felt to be reconnected to the only true family I had ever known. And the more I was reminded of the routines in which I had cycled through alone for such a long period of time, the more insurmountable the regret I felt for having concealed from you that you had a brother, the more I regretted and reproached myself for having abandoned Simon to my blackmailer. I no longer could pretend I had done something noble by sacrificing my child for your mother's welfare. I could no longer ignore the truth. Without a struggle, without voicing any opposition, I'd deposited an innocent child, my own flesh and blood, into the hands of an unscrupulous thug whose only motive for wanting the boy was to harm me, and your mother, for the roles we played in Leah's death. I could no longer ignore the fact that I owed Simon more than I could possibly provide him. There was no material recompense adequate enough. And so, in the end, I agreed to provide *him*, not Freed, the land and the water rights to bring the two of you together and help him realize his dreams.

Which are what? asked Bloom.

Pictures, said Jacob. He makes pictures. And down there, he will be able to do as he pleases. With you. If that's what you wish.

But why sacrifice the lake?

Because he has plans for it. But, more important, because he knows what it means to me.

※

When the elder Rosenbloom had finished his confession, he fell quiet for a long while, presumably waiting for Bloom's response. Bloom could see in his father's face that he needed him to express some assurance that he'd one day find it within himself to accept the complicated history of their family and forgive him. But, as Jacob rightly anticipated when imagining this moment all these years, Bloom found himself caught in a schism taking shape in his mind. On the one hand, he was filled with compassion and pity for his father. He had seen in what ways the great abyss at the core of his story had taken its toll on him. For this reason Bloom was compelled to find words to comfort him. But he couldn't. What, after all, did one say to the figure of such a tragedy? How did one console a Hamlet or a Lear or an Othello? Even if he could find the right words, he wondered if he'd share them. He couldn't help but ask himself if the preservation of his memories, of the way Bloom perceived him and his mother, was reason enough to conceal from him the fact that Simon existed, that Bloom wasn't alone in the world. Certainly he would have been capable of forgiving his mother's frailties, of comprehending the circumstances surrounding the choice his father was forced to make. But now he couldn't help but think selfishly, of what had been lost to him in the passage of time. For the entirety of his life, he had a brother, and knew nothing of him, not even his name. And when he reflected on this, Bloom wasn't convinced there was a sensible explanation sufficient to provide this episode a heartening conclusion. He had never before felt distrustful of his father. He had never before thought it was possible he would give him cause to feel this way. But he had. He had deceived him. Intentionally designed an illusion in which he had been dwelling for the entirety of his life.

There were a great number of thoughts and emotions Bloom wanted to express, none of which squared with the relationship he had had with Jacob. No words he possessed could properly articulate his disappointment, his confusion, his anger. All he could think to do, therefore, was contain his true sentiments and say what he would have said on some other occasion preceding this one, one with which he was more familiar. In a controlled manner, with as much hope in his voice as he could summon, Bloom said, We'll find our way past this.

Will we? said Jacob circumspectly.

Yes, said Bloom. We will. I'm certain of it.

Unable to say anything more than this, Bloom backed away from his father. At the door, he turned and climbed the stairs to his bedroom, inside which he stared out the window into the night sky and in it he saw the nightmare of miniatures his mother had painted for his father's devices, his mother running from Leah's shadow, on her knees before her, begging for forgiveness, and he recalled more clearly the emptiness in her eyes when he was a young child. He could see now, they were the eyes of a woman whose heart had been irreparably harmed, whose spirit had been crushed by her own hand. So devastated, he thought, not even the abiding love of a child, Bloom's love, could repair it.

✸

For almost a year, the top of Mount Terminus filled with industry. In Simon's absence, concrete poured into foundations, lumber arrived by the cartload, plumbers and electricians, carpenters and masons overtook the camps, and while they remained in residence, geometric skeletons cast higher and longer shadows onto the mountain. Technicians erected poles along the edge of the road and connected them with high-tension wire spun out from man-sized spools. After some time, the glow of electrified light illuminated the night sky a bright hue of orange, so that from Bloom's bedroom window it appeared as if the sun were always about to rise over the ridge.

Ever since the night Jacob had recounted the circumstances that led him to abandon Simon, Jacob, perhaps out of respect for Bloom's need to absorb what he had learned, perhaps because he sensed in what way Bloom's estimation of him had been lowered, perhaps so as not to burden his son any further, removed himself to seclusion and returned to his routines. He returned to his gardens, where, to dull the noise of the construction, he stuffed tufts of cotton into his ears, and when he could no longer stand even the muted drumbeat of labor echoing from the plateau, he locked himself away for the remainder of the day in the gallery, where, as a form of penance, Bloom speculated, he stared into his mother's Woodhaven landscapes to recall his wife gazing vacantly at the countryside without seeing its beauty or feeling the possibility of its sanctuary, seeing, rather, visions of her sister. In the gallery, the elder Rosebloom drank. From Manuel Salazar's chamber Bloom watched him drink until he could drink no more, and as the construction beat on, as its noise continued to disturb his father's communion with the two women he'd loved since before he could remember being alive, as the sounds of the pneumatic drills bored deeper into his interior, he visited the gallery earlier and earlier, oftentimes falling unconscious well before the sun dipped below the horizon.

Bloom witnessed his father surrender. In the furrows of his brow, in the gauntness of his cheeks, in the dark depressions under his eyes. He could clearly see drain from the elder Rosenbloom's body what remained of its vitality. It was as if the telling of his story had released him from his obligation to his son. It was the withholding of this information, it occurred to Bloom, that motivated Jacob to keep on living, and now that it had been released, the largest artery of his spirit had been depleted, the reason for his being, exhausted, and to watch him fade, without a glimmer of resistance, unsettled Bloom. He didn't know what to do. He had grown accustomed to the oblivion in which his father had dwelled for so long, an oblivion that now seemed to him mild compared with this one. He couldn't fathom the rate of such an unnatural decline. In less than six months, his father appeared to have aged ten years. His life no longer nurtured the gardens in which he dwelled; rather, it leeched into them, drained into the soil holding firm the roots of the hedgerows. He grew so feeble, Bloom was afraid to leave him alone at night. He feared he would set himself on fire with his pipe's burning cherry of tobacco, that he would, perhaps, take a drunken tumble down the stairs, or worse, stumble upon the courage to exact his own destruction.

When the elder Rosenbloom entered the gallery in the late afternoons, the younger Rosenbloom climbed to the heights of Salazar's chamber, where, sitting across from Cyclops and before the dim reflection of the projection table, he kept a watchful eye. He watched and labored on the illustrations of *Death, Forlorn*, hoping he could prove his devotion through the dedication of his work, his exacting lines. He thought, surely this would show him he was still loved and needed by Bloom, that his presence continued to fortify him. Perhaps then he would return to him, if not in full measure, as some small fraction of a man. And so the younger Rosenbloom worked through the nights with Salazar's journal by his side, learning from his hand how to draw strong, flowing lines and embed detail into his compositions in such a way his father would feel as awestruck as Bloom felt the first time he set his eyes upon Salazar's pages.

During the day, he now refused to leave his father's side. He took Roya by the hand and led her to the gardens, where amid the hammering of the construction, he sat with her in case he could no longer fight his fatigue. And it was here, when Bloom's face had begun to resemble what it would look like when he became a man, Roya reached out and pressed into his hand a note that read, in her childlike script, *I will watch over him.* She then reached out and took the younger Rosenbloom by the neck and placed his head on her thighs, at which point she opened a second note and placed it in front of his eyes. It read: *Now sleep.* Roya's palm pressed itself against Bloom's ear, and the world grew silent, and Bloom slept. And every day afterward he slept with his nose buried in the pungent scent of Roya's lap.

><

On the sixth morning of Yamim Noraim, just as the autumnal winds began to blow, the team of craftsmen put the finishing touches on their work. By the afternoon, when the gales began to howl their fiercest, the last of them departed, leaving behind an arrangement of unremarkable architecture. Out of the materials that had traveled such a great distance to the top of Mount Terminus, they formed a cul de sac at the plateau's far end. At its center, some form of French chateau with an odd configuration of asymmetrical towers and spires. On either side of this huddled a colorful collection of smaller-scale construction, an incongruent assortment of Samoan huts, Tudor cottages, a Rhine castle, odd little shacks with domes and minarets, all built up with plaster, lath, and paper. Where the long stretch of property abutted the mountainside, they had built two sizable warehouses whose roofs were lined with skylights. Across the road from these structures were a dozen wooden stages with latticed roofs. It all amounted to a small settlement. Seventeen buildings in all. Impressive to the eye only insofar as it was something of a monstrosity, a pastiche conceived in a mind holding little regard for balance or symmetry.

When the last of the tools had sounded, and the last of the workmen had departed, the elder Rosenbloom left his garden and joined Bloom at the overlook. For the first time since the start of the construction, Jacob looked down onto the land he had provided his estranged son, and upon seeing what had been built, he said with a brave smile, I hope you will try to find your place there. Bloom could see his father's eyes dampen in this instance, and he thought for a moment he was going to reach out and pull him into his chest the way he did when Bloom was small, but just as a tear had welled with enough volume to fall onto his cheek, his father turned and walked away. He meandered through the avocado grove, brushing his long fingers over a burr forming on the trunk of a male tree whose flowers had wilted, and every few paces thereafter, he bent down under the limbs of a female and lifted from the ground her blackened, withered fruit. And when his thin arms bulged with misshapen avocados, he returned to his garden's labyrinth, where he would stare into the leafy eyes of his topiary for the last time.

✦

Jacob didn't return to the house at the wane of day. As he did every year on this sixth day of Yamim Noraim, he collected the trimmings he had cut from his topiary and bundled them in twine; he unearthed the juniper saplings he had planted the year before, gathered his candles and his lanterns, the jug of water and sack of oats, and carried his cargo to the stables. On this third twilight before the Day of Atonement, however, he remained in the gardens after the sun set, and continued to stay there into the night. He refused Meralda's over-tures to come in for the dinner that would fortify him for his fast, and he refused her again later when she begged him to take shelter from the winds. Bloom watched over Jacob from the tower's pavil-ion until a dry electrical storm cracked the black glass of the sky. He descended the tower stairs and walked out into the flashing light, to where Jacob knelt at the feet of the sculpted shrub staring out over the promontory. Please, Father, he said, the storm. He took his father by the hand and tugged at the weight of his arm. The elder Rosen-bloom wouldn't lift his head to look at his son, but with his eyes turned away, he rose to his feet and allowed himself to be led away. Bloom sat him down in the drawing room and poured him a drink, which he placed into his father's hand. He then ran upstairs to the gallery and retrieved his pipe and pouch of tobacco. When he re-turned to the parlor, he emptied the bowl the way he had observed his father do it so many times before, with three gentle taps to the side of the silver tray. He dipped his fingers into the pouch and pinched enough of the moist leaves to fill the pipe; he struck a match and puffed at the lip—three small kisses—then sucked in his cheeks in the same manner his father did when he breathed the smoke into his body. When the burning smoke hit the back of his throat, he wanted to cough it out, but he suppressed the urge—no more than a hiccup sounded from him—and he blew out a steady stream, did it again, this time allowing the smoke to enter into him without so much as a sniffle.

This performance of Bloom's amused his father. With the most melancholy of eyes and the most joyful of smiles, he said, You have been watching me, I see.

Yes, said Bloom as he placed the pipe into his father's palm.

Joseph Rosenbloom, said his father, look at you. You've become a man.

Yes, Father.

Yes, my dear. Yes, indeed.

Bloom removed his father's shoes and tucked a blanket around his legs. A loud clap of thunder rattled the windows, and when it quieted, Bloom knelt beside the elder Rosenbloom and said, Father, I worry about you.

His father tried to hold Bloom's gaze, but he couldn't. He tried to find the courage to say what Bloom needed to hear, but he could only say with his son's face so near to his, My dear Joseph. My gift from God. And the elder Rosenbloom could say no more.

Please, said Bloom, don't leave until morning. If you leave in the morning, I will go with you, as always.

Jacob smiled at his son and drank down his brandy, and with his sunken eyes, he looked up at Bloom, and Bloom without saying another word stood up, took the tumbler from his father's hand, and poured him another drink, thinking if he could get him drunk enough, he would fall asleep in his chair and be safe until the storm passed. And then it occurred to him how he might do just this. Don't move, said Bloom. I have a gift for you. And Bloom ran off again, this time to the library, where he retrieved the magic lantern and the box of slides on which he had been laboring. He unpacked the magic lantern and set it up on the table behind his father's chair. He then lit the lantern's lamp and extinguished the lights of the drawing room. You recall, said Bloom, you asked me some time ago to illustrate *Death, Forlorn*?

I do, yes.

I'd like to share it with you now, if I may.

Please do.

Bloom opened the wooden box and removed the first slide, that of the couple standing under a wedding chuppah, gazing into each other's eyes. He slipped it into the slot before the flame and removed the lens cap to reveal his mother and his father.

Look how beautiful you've made us. Jacob turned his face to the light, and there Bloom saw the pride in his eyes. I have never seen such lines, he said. Never. He blinked, and blinked again, then returned his gaze to the image, and on Bloom went through the entire box, and when he was through and had brightened the lights, his father wept openly in front of him for the first time since his mother died.

※

That night the desert winds mixed with storm clouds from the sea. They gathered over the great basin and pressed their combined forces onto Mount Terminus. Bloom sat beside his father, filled his glass several more times, and together, in silence, they listened to the intemperate mood of the world. A hard driving rain began to lash at the villa, and when it did, the lines that had etched themselves onto his father's brow and around the corners of his eyes appeared to soften, and Bloom was able to see in him an image of the much younger, more vibrant man they had just observed in his slides, an image in which his father's features were still fine, in which he wore a suit and tie, his hair slicked back, his fingernails buffed, his shoes shined. His father soon dozed off, and when he did, a calm came over Bloom, and in that calm, he felt weary. He dimmed the lights of the parlor to a blue glow and, for the first time in a long time, he retired to his bed, where he counted the passing seconds between the lightning flashes that brightened his room and the thunderclaps that followed them. And as the storm began to subside, he drifted off to sleep.

※

The sun had long since risen when Bloom was startled awake by an explosion of shattering glass. A paroxysm of wind had blown one of his bedroom windows around the axis of its hinges to crash against the wall. The young man dressed and put on his shoes. He walked over the glimmering shards to discover the latch had snapped. The rain had ceased and the skies had cleared. The fiery desert heat, it appeared, had overpowered the moisture from the sea. Bloom looked out over the courtyard and down the path of paving stones under which their water now flowed, and there he saw an odd sight. He saw their mare attempting to shake off a long rope lassoed to its neck. With the rope dragging under her, the mare galloped up the path and through the pergola and came to a halt at the reflecting pool. She

looked up at Bloom and for a long time stared at him with obsidian eyes, then as quickly as she approached, she turned and galloped
off in the direction from which she came. When Bloom saw her
turn toward the front of the estate, he ran down the landing, calling
out to his father. He ran downstairs and into the parlor, where he
had left him. Jacob's blanket had been pushed aside, the tumbler
from which he drank, with which Bloom had plied him with drink,
the pipe, were just where the young Rosenbloom had left them, but
no father. Meralda called out from the kitchen, asking what had
happened, but Bloom ignored her and ran out onto the drive and into
the maze of the garden, calling out at every turn, Father! and when
he reached the plots in the garden where the elder Rosenbloom had
appointed his topiary, Bloom discovered, with a deepening sense of
dread, that each figure his father had spent perfecting all these years,
each and every figure he had communed with in his irreparable state
of grief, had been irreparably damaged. Their limbs torn from their
torsos. Their torsos torn at the waist. Their heads severed at the neck.
When he exited the maze of the first garden, he entered the maze
of the second and found the same devastation. Father! he called out.
And when he exited this garden, he noticed the mare standing on
the promontory. She no longer was trying to shake herself free from
her rope. She just stood there, her long neck tipping into the ravine.
Bloom approached the mare with some caution, and when he had
reached her, he saw the outer edge of the headland had fallen away.
He advanced toward the precipice and looked down, and there he
saw some twenty yards into the chasm a deposit of mud mixed with
brush and rock, and rising up out of this, a shoulder and an outstretched arm, both of which remained perfectly still. As soon as he
comprehended what he was looking at and what had happened,
Bloom averted his eyes, and when he did, he noticed, standing beside a motorcar at a turn on the road, the three men in dark long
coats holding against their chests their bowler hats.

He should have wanted to scream out at them, to curse them,
shame them, chase them down, but he couldn't, he simply couldn't,
and not because he was afraid, rather, because contrary to what he

was supposed to have felt at this moment in which his worst fear had been made real, he was overtaken by a profound feeling of release. He could feel the intensity of his father's torment lift. He could sense it being swept out to sea by the desert winds. Vaporized by the heat. It was wrong, it was all wrong, but Bloom, who was, indeed, doing his best to struggle against this deviant emotion, couldn't help himself.

The euphoria outweighed him.

PART II

LIFE

Meralda wept. And wept. And wept. She sat vigil at the promontory's edge for a day and a half until the sheriff arrived with two deputies and a mule. They dragged the elder Rosenbloom out of the ravine and set his broken body on the dining room table. There she continued to weep at his side until the gravediggers, along with the rabbi and three members of the *chevra kadisha*—tailors all—entered through Mount Terminus's blackened gate. Roya led the men carrying picks and shovels to the burial site. The rabbi, who was forbidden by religious law to sit in the same dwelling as the dead, consoled Meralda in the courtyard. The tailors, meanwhile, performed the *tahara*. They lifted Jacob into a metal basin and lit candles all around. They covered the remains with a shroud and disposed of the dirty clothes, all the time careful not to breach the space over his body where the soul was believed to make its departure. They carried in pails of water and washed him clean; they wrapped him in a tallith and cocooned him in knotted linen, recited at the end *Tahara he Tahara he Tahara he.* He is pure. He is pure. He is pure. *Jacob, orphaned child, we ask forgiveness from you if we did not treat you respectfully, but we did as is our custom. May you be a messenger for all of Israel. Go in peace, rest in peace, and arise in your turn at the end of days.* Bloom, all this time, sat with Roya in the rose garden, watching the two bearded gravediggers labor into the earth. The young Rosenbloom couldn't fathom the idea of burying his father's remains inside the garden labyrinths among his dismembered creatures. He chose instead to walk about the estate until he was drawn to the right burial place. For the day and a half he waited for the sheriff to arrive, for that one day more he waited for the rabbi and his cohort, he walked and went without sleep, until he heard in his delirium through the rushes of wind the faintest whisper of his name, so faint, he disregarded it as a figment and began to move on. But he then heard it again, again as if his name had been spoken by the currents of air, and this time he turned around, and found nothing, only roses, clustered and swaying, red upon yellow upon white upon red, roses set against strata of veined rock and blue sky. The garden radiated outward in concentric circles at the center of which rose up Cupid and Psyche fixed in marble embrace. The desert wind again swept over Mount Terminus, but this time Joseph didn't hear his name; rather, this time, a short burst of sunlight reflected into his eyes. He now wandered into the garden, to the source of the light, followed one of the gravel paths that joined the circles at each quarter turn, and when he reached the innermost ring—the one whose circumference enclosed the naked angel holding in his arms his love sleeping the Sleep of Death— he stepped onto a bed of red petals disseminated from their buds, and walked onto nests of thorny stalks uprooted in the storm, and there at Psyche's lifeless feet, he decided, was where he would bury his lifeless father. Here, on the last day of Yamim Noraim, on the morning before the sun would set onto Yom Kippur, on the day he and his father would have atoned at the lakeshore, they all gathered. Here, the rabbi sent his father on his way with a few prayers and a few kind words about a man he didn't know. And beginning with Bloom, they each emptied a fistful of dry earth over the linen shroud, and left the gravediggers to their chore.

>‹‹

As the small processional wound its way out of the rose garden on the day of Jacob's funeral, Roya handed Bloom a note. *It is time for you to lead the way.* Every day for seven weeks, Roya followed him to the headland overlooking the ravine that had swallowed Jacob Rosenbloom, and every day for seven weeks, Bloom recited the mourner's prayer he had heard his father recite for his mother; and every day for seven weeks, Roya followed him back to the villa, to his bedroom, where she sat with him and fed him his meals. At night, she remained at his bedside. She reclined in an armchair set under a shrouded mirror, and watched him sleep, and if he stirred, she moved to the edge of his mattress to stroke his hair until he settled back to rest. And if he became restless from a disturbing dream, she pursed her lips and blew on his neck until his body was once again still.

One night when Bloom felt this pleasant sensation, he extended his arm until his hand had reached the source of the breeze, and felt in his grasp a soft fabric, beneath which his fingers discovered the weight and warmth of some tender and unfamiliar thing. He was neither awake nor asleep when he opened his eyes, but when he saw his hand had become acquainted with the rise of Roya's chest, he grew more alert in all the ways one expects a young man to do so. His silent companion sat at the edge of the bed, and he could make out, in the glow of gaslight, her eyes shut and her hand hidden under the pleats of her skirt. She occasionally drew in a sharp breath through her nose and arched her back, not pulling away from Joseph, as he expected she would, but, rather, the more the bed shuddered with the small motions of her concealed hand, the harder she pressed herself into his palm. Bloom thought he saw her mouth frown a rictus of disapproval at his unconscious act, but he soon became aware of the spirited pulse in her chest. The bed continued to tremble and the more vibrant the movement, the more shallow Roya's breaths. The motion and the excitement he saw flare on her nose, in the shape of her lips, he could sense, was building to something; to precisely what, he didn't know, but in that instance she appeared as if she were going to speak. For the first time, he believed he would hear Roya's voice bellow an animalistic howl or screech. It was for this, with great anticipation, he waited, wondered with some excitement as to what the sound would be. But when the moment arrived, other than the respiration from her lungs and the rhythmic creak of the chair, Roya produced no sound at all. Instead, a silent tremor radiated over her entire musculature. Her body contracted in on itself. Her lips quivered. The tendons in her neck attenuated. Her free hand clenched into a fist. And then, an aftershock, and then one more, each new tremor diminished in strength from the one preceding it. And then, a deep inhalation, expressed in one last audible breath. And then, calm. And then, silence. Her eyes now opened, awakening the darkness with their light, and when her sight adjusted to the dim luster of the burning gas lamps, and she saw Bloom had borne witness to her pleasure, she reacted with the same composure she reacted to the most joyful and most tragic of events. With placid temper, she reached for his wrist and gently pulled his hand away so the tips of his fingers relaxed and skimmed over the nub of her breast. And with this, she did what she did with any other nocturnal disturbance: she stroked away the hair from the young Rosenbloom's eyes and brushed her fingers over his cheek, to say, in her way, he had done nothing for which he needed to be forgiven. And neither had she.

><

Bloom awoke the following morning uncertain if what he had experienced in the night was real or if it was a dream. When he roused, he felt his nightshirt and his sheets wet and sticky; and when he removed his covering and his garment to inspect further, he discovered pearly beads nesting in his pubis. He dipped the tips of his fingers into the sticky liquid and observed as he pulled his hand away how it clung to his skin and expanded into glimmering strands. He would have spent the better part of the day wondering if this was some symptom of a disease or the product of some infection, but Roya, who was asleep in the armchair beside Bloom's bed, awoke, and saw how bewildered and concerned the naked Rosenbloom was, and without hesitation, she rose and sat by Bloom's side, where she unbuttoned her blouse and exposed the breast Bloom had dreamed of touching in the night. She took hold of his hand and placed it on the soft mound of flesh. Bloom rose to greet the hand now reaching out for him, and with Roya's eyes glancing down to her breast, she stroked the young Rosenbloom up and down, until he felt as if his body might levitate, at which point out shot a small butterfly of this same substance he had earlier discovered. It flapped its wings to the height of his nose, only to land unceremoniously in the depression of his navel. And with that, Roya brushed her hands together, buttoned her blouse, and for the first time in seven weeks left Bloom to his solitude, so that he might fully appreciate his new discovery.

※

When he had washed and dressed, Bloom felt himself enlivened. The weight of his grief no longer pressed against his chest and hung on his shoulders as it had only moments before his silent companion performed her compassionate act. He had no purpose to speak of, but at the very least he would greet the day and make himself part of it. He found a biscuit and a cup of coffee waiting for him in the kitchen and took both up the stairs of the tower. The higher he rose, the more he believed he heard the rustle of wings, a great many wings. Or, he wondered, was it the autumnal winds beginning to blow again? The closer he neared the pavilion's landing, the more distinct the restless flutter sounded. Staccato yips and plaited song soon met his ear. They were sounds not of this place, not screeches of the condor or the vulture; rather, they were the cries of some other, more exotic world whose soil was rich and whose plants and trees were verdant and wet and overgrown, and with these noises growing louder and more complex with each step upward, he experienced a psychic sundering. It was only after he had reached the last of the stairs and saw overhead four wrought-iron cages hanging from hooks and chains that he was once again grounded. Above him, enclosed in their respective aviaries, were yellow canaries and green parakeets, albino cockatiels and lovebirds wearing black masks and red beaks. They frantically hopped up and down the limbs of iron trees; some sat perched, nuzzling one another, burying their bills into fluff. Bloom marveled at the vibrant colors, at the boundless energy, and, for the time being, felt one with them. He visited each cage and fed the birds small morsels of his biscuit and tried to see if there was a way to tell the members of one species apart from each other. The variations were so minute, it would take him some time to recognize them individually, but he would try, and when he succeeded, he would name them all. As the birds squawked and sang and reacted to one another's calls, Bloom rested his coffee on the rail and noticed that, during this time he had been bedridden, Meralda had hired a gardener to remove his father's dismembered topiary from the front gardens. The living statues of his mother were gone. The only reminders of them, the holes in the hedgerows through which they looked out onto their vistas. The sight of her absence pained Bloom, but as his eyes explored the new landscape further, this brief ache dissipated. Not only could he see how beautiful these empty gardens were, but also he was comforted in knowing that with the mazes bared, there would no longer be the continual reminder of what had been lost. In time he'd have the opportunity to forget and begin anew. For the moment, however, he could still see his father refining the edges of his mother's face with his shears, and in this, too, he took solace.

><

Bloom would learn upon his descent from the tower that morning that the aviary was a gift from two men presently sitting in the courtyard drinking coffee. One was named Saul Geller, his father's lifelong business associate. He possessed a round face and a pair of frowning eyes Bloom vaguely recalled from his boyhood in Woodhaven. The other man was Mr. Geller's cousin, Gerald Stern, a local attorney who kept an office in the Pico House Hotel downtown. Mr. Stern was a perfectly bald middle-aged man with a freckled head and nose. Unlike his relation, he stood as tall and thin as Bloom, and was fitted into a bespoke suit whose fine cloth and stitching shimmered in the sunlight. Mr. Geller told Bloom he had traveled the entire breadth of the country to spend only one day on Mount Terminus. He had come to deliver Bloom the aviary bought for him by his daughters, to pay his respects to Jacob, and then there was the matter of witnessing Mr. Stern's execution of Jacob's will.

Geller wished he had more time, but for reasons he didn't specify, he was needed at home and at the foundry. As it was, he feared his world would be turned upside down when he landed in Woodhaven. When the mild-mannered Mr. Geller had established this much, he told Bloom a story, the very same story he said he'd told Jacob the day they met.

When they were much younger men, Bloom's father had placed an advertisement in the newspaper, calling for a man of considerable ambition who had some understanding of optics and mechanical engineering to represent his interests in the marketplace. An army of candidates called on Jacob at his home in Woodhaven, any one of whom would have suited his needs to one extent or another, but it wasn't until he sat down with Mr. Geller, and listened to the events of his life, did Bloom's father feel the sort of kinship he thought necessary for such an intimate association. The sad tale Geller told Jacob that day was about how a family of Russian criminals who, with the help of a government minister, stole his father's livelihood. With a perverse pleasure, these men drove Geller's father into their debt for money he never borrowed and for services he never requested. They used these invented arrears against him to take his property: his storefront, his home, his carts and horses. Over and over again, the bailiffs arrived with ministerial papers and took what was his. This succession of seizures, which elapsed over a period of years, exhausted his father's nerves so completely he fell into a paralytic malaise. One day, when the elder Geller appeared to be returning to some semblance of the man he used to be, he dressed in his finest clothes, kissed and hugged his wife and children, and said he was going for a stroll to clear his head. He walked out of their rented rooms and proceeded to the bank of the river. With no fear, without hesitation, with a smile, said one witness, he stuffed his pockets full of stones and waded out into the frozen current until he was submerged. In the end, Geller told Bloom, he, his two younger sisters, and his mother possessed nothing but a small trunk in which they kept a bolt of linen and three pieces of silver: one fork, a serving spoon, and a Kaddish cup, which they used to mourn his father's passing. When his mother suffered the indignity of asking the authorities for the smallest pittance of charity to see them through their troubles, the very same men who had taken everything from them, and who they believed could take no more, took away the country they had known for as many generations as their familial memory could recall. They placed them in one of their father's former carts, drove them to the border, and forced them into exile on foot.

At this juncture, Bloom acknowledged what a maddening tale of injustice Mr. Geller's was. That, said Geller, is precisely what your father said to me. In return, Jacob described to Mr. Geller the unfortunate events of his own life and the predicament he found himself in with Sam Freed. Their shared experience, said Geller, created a deep bond of trust and loyalty between the two men. Jacob, who had recently secured terms with Dickson, entrusted Mr. Geller with the prototype of the Rosenbloom Loop, and for his new employer and friend, Geller signed contracts with Siegfried Lubin and Ruff & Gammon; and with the biggest manufacturers of motion picture projectors endorsing Jacob's device, its reputation grew; and as news of the Rosenbloom Loop spread, Geller received requests for Jacob's invention from projector manufacturers around the world. In less than a year, the demand was overwhelming, so great, the small workshop Jacob had established in his Woodhaven home proved inadequate. Mr. Geller, therefore, searched out a proper facility, and discovered, on a tract of land not far from the Rosenbloom residence, an abandoned candle factory. Jacob bought the title, and he and Mr. Geller transformed the old brick building into a manufacturing plant, hired metallurgists and engineers, who, under Jacob's direction at first, and Mr. Geller's to follow, duplicated the individual parts of the device, and then arranged an assembly line. There, Geller said, I have made my living. For every year since the foundry opened, he had managed it, grown its business, and for every year Jacob and Bloom had lived on Mount Terminus, he and his sisters, his mother, his daughters, and his wife had looked after Jacob's interests, his accounts, his investments. It is because of your father's genius and generosity, said Geller, I have my beautiful family, have built homes for my mother and my sisters, have more than I ever dreamed of having. To your father, said Mr. Geller, I owe my life. To you, he told Bloom, I owe the same. And so, he said, I make this promise to you, Joseph. You have my loyalty and devotion. For as long as I live, I am yours to rely on.

Bloom, who was deeply touched and uplifted by these words, thanked Mr. Geller for the kind sentiment, and then Mr. Stern, who had been listening quietly, reached for an attaché case resting at his feet, and removed from it some papers. Your father's will, he said to Bloom. The fastidious man dug a pair of spectacles from his pocket, clipped them to his freckled nose, and began to list his father's last wishes. Bloom was informed by Mr. Stern that morning, Mr. Geller would retain full autonomy over the foundry's operation for as long as he was willing and able, and from this day forward would own a forty percent share of the company. The remaining sixty percent would be held by Bloom. In addition to operating the foundry and its day-to-day business, Geller would manage and hold in trust Bloom's substantial holdings until he turned twenty years of age, at which time he hoped Geller would continue to dispense his invaluable advice. Bloom now held an interest in things and places holding no interest to him at all. He owned a certain percentage of a small oil field twenty miles to the south of the estate; five hundred miles to the north, a logging company; in the far reaches of the valley, a dairy farm and a cattle ranch; somewhere in the tropics, in a country he had never heard of, he held majority ownership of a sugarcane plantation; not very far from Mount Terminus sat an observatory whose rotunda was endowed in his father's name, housed inside which was a telescope dedicated to studying the reversing polarities of sunspots, and, to which, he would, as his father had done, make a handsome donation annually. With the exception of the plateau on which Simon had built his studio, all the land on Mount Terminus, from top to bottom, was now his, as was the house and adjoining property in Woodhaven. Finally, he now possessed a considerable amount of gold bullion secured in a bank vault back east, and a sizable collection of precious gems stored in a bank downtown. To Simon, Mr. Stern told him, his father had added to his already substantial holdings the parcels of land Jacob held throughout the valley and the basin, what amounted to tens of thousands of acres, all of which he determined Simon should develop or sell as he saw fit to realize his future plans. You and your brother, and the generations that follow you, Stern said in conclusion, should want for nothing.

When Stern had finished the formalities of his recitation, Bloom wondered if there were any personal sentiments expressed in the will. The will, Stern told him, had been amended not long before Jacob died. As is the case with us all, he said, I'm sure he believed he had more time. Upon hearing this, Mr. Geller told Bloom his brother had been contacted about his inheritance and Mr. Stern had already made arrangements with Simon's attorney to transfer the property. Mr. Geller then asked his cousin if he wouldn't mind giving him a moment alone with Bloom. Stern excused himself and wandered out of the courtyard in the direction of the grove, and when he had disappeared from sight, Mr. Geller said to Bloom in a hushed voice, My cousin, Stern, he can be somewhat cold and humorless, but he is a good man, and I believe you need a good man nearby to serve your capital and show you how to maintain it when you come of age. I'm simply too far away and too preoccupied with the business of the foundry to be of any use to you here. Gerald, therefore, will be looking after your holdings and advising you about the decisions he makes on your behalf. Geller assured Bloom that Stern would hold his interests above all others and take his side in all circumstances. He would see to his investments as if they were his own, and to Bloom, to his wellbeing. Please, Joseph, he said, tell me I have your blessing. Humor an *alte kaker* who grows weary with the burdens he carries.

Yes, Bloom said, yes, of course, you have my blessing. If that's what you think best, then I think it best, too.

Geller said what a fine young man Bloom had become, and he removed a business card from a pocket in his jacket and gently placed it in Bloom's hand. Here is Stern's card. If you need anything at all, call on him. He knows your business as well as I do. If you have concerns about anything at all, if you need help of any kind, Gerald is the man to go to. He'll be doing a good deal of traveling for you, but when he's here, he'll look in on you without fail. Please, make good use of him.

And with that said, Mr. Geller vigorously shook Bloom's hand. Your father might not have put it down on paper, he said in parting, but you and I both know what his last wish was for you. More than anything, he wanted to see you and your brother united and made whole. I very much hope this is what comes to pass. Should this dream of his go unfulfilled for any reason, be assured, you always have me, and my family, to turn to.

Thank you, Mr. Geller.

I mean it, said Geller. Every word of it. Mr. Geller now took Bloom by the arm and walked him in the same direction Mr. Stern had gone. Together they meandered through the grove of trees until they reached the head of the drive, where Stern was waiting in his sedan. Bloom wished Mr. Geller safe travels and thanked him for having come all this way, and he asked him to thank his daughters for their wonderful gift. The birds, said Bloom, have lifted my spirits, as has your visit.

Mr. Geller was pleased to hear it.

I will be seeing you, said Mr. Stern from behind the wheel. I'm available to you anytime.

Goodbye, Joseph, Geller called as they drove off. And good luck!

✣

That afternoon, Bloom did as he had done before so many times in the past. Filled with the warmth and kindness he felt from Saul Geller's visit, he returned to the courtyard and sat with Roya on the wall of the reflecting pool, sank his feet into its water. He reclined in the library for some time and read *The Fall of the House of Usher*.

During the whole of a dull, dark, and soundless day in the autumn of the year, when the clouds hung oppressively low in the heavens, I had been passing alone, on horseback, through

a singularly dreary tract of country; and at length found myself, as the shades of the evening drew on, within view of the
melancholy House of Usher.

He took the book with him for a walk up the trail to Mount Terminus's peak and remained there to read it three times over. Three
times, he saw the mighty walls rush asunder. He returned in time
for dinner, and when he walked into the dining room with his book
in hand, he was pleased to find the walls freshened with a coat of
whitewash. The table and the rugs, the sideboards and the drapery
had all been substituted for furniture and material of a similarly
baroque shape and pattern, yet dissimilar enough that the room
appeared to Bloom sufficiently altered. Meralda placed a plate of
enchiladas before him, bent over him, and pressed her cheek to his.
I'm so happy to see you at your place again, she said. As she swung
through the kitchen door, Bloom turned his attention to where his
father would have been seated, and he was reminded of his shattered body lying atop the table, and with that image in mind, the
buoyant mood he had fostered that morning and throughout the
day was undone. He stared at the bands of color that had begun
to streak the sky outside the window, and in this storm of particles,
he felt nothing of its beauty, only the oncoming death of the day.
Through the duration of the twilight, he waited for the fall of night,
and sat with an emptiness within him, which wouldn't be filled with
food. When Meralda returned and saw he hadn't eaten, and was
entranced by the sight of the empty chair, she sat beside him and
said, Tomorrow, let's try the parlor, shall we? To this, Bloom nodded
his consent. The aches, she acknowledged, they rise and fall with a
mind all their own. In time, she said. In time.

✸

Each morning now, he returned to the tower to commune with
the birds given to him by Mr. Geller's daughters, hoping he might
recapture the exultation he'd experienced upon discovering them.

He named the male cockatiel Elijah and taught him to say the meaning of his name.

My God is Yahweh, he repeated over and over until the bird squawked back, My God is Yahweh, My God is Yahweh.

To Bloom's greeting, Hello, my dear Elijah, he taught Elijah to respond: Hello, my dear Bloom. Where have you been?

I've been here and there, Bloom would say.

To which Elijah responded, My God is Yahweh.

When Bloom asked Elijah, Do you want to be free?

Elijah responded, Open the door and we shall see.

No, Bloom would say. I need you here with me.

To which Elijah would say, My God is Yahweh.

Such amusements held Bloom's interest for only so long before he found himself revisiting again and again the House of Usher. It began to inhabit him so thoroughly, when he wandered in and around the estate there grew in his mind a strange fancy. About him emerged an atmosphere, which had no affinity with the air of heaven. Around the villa's exterior, within the walls of its rooms, hung a pestilent and mystic vapor, dull, sluggish, leaden-hued. He sat at the opening of the gate for hours at a time and in pencil and ink laid over the façade minute fungi . . . hanging in a fine tangled webwork from the eaves. Throughout the stucco walls, he inlaid a zigzag of fissures. He turned the roof's clay tiles an ebon black, the white gravel of the drive, of the gardens, a dusty gray. He withered leaves, flowers, and fruit. He blew into the sky clouds of ash, lit the cadaverous landscape with feeble gleams of encrimsoned light, laid waste to livestock throughout the depression of the valley, turned the sea into an inky stain, scattered from the top of the tower into the wind the exotic feathers of his birds.

In time, said Meralda each evening, in time.

✦

Weeks passed in this gloom, until one morning, while under the archways of the pavilion, the combustion and grind of a car shifting gears turned his attention outward. The birds noticed it before he did. The noise quieted their song and movement, and their silence disrupted his contemplation. On the final switchback at the top of the mountain, a white roadster motored into view, and in only a few minutes' time, it entered the gates. When it had traveled the length of the drive and had come to a stop, it took Bloom a moment to apprehend who was there. For the better part of a year, he had been reminded of his brother each time the strike of a hammer resounded from the construction site. He knew he would return before long, but the circumstances of the past months had pushed the thought of him a vast distance away. That Simon now sat in the sunlight below, staring off through a pair of goggles in the direction of the promontory, took Bloom aback. He thought to call out to him, but his brother had yet to disengage the motor and likely wouldn't hear him, so he started down the stairs. When he reached the bottom, he walked out the service entrance to discover the car absent its driver, its engine no longer idling, his brother's goggles hanging from the rearview mirror. He looked in the direction to which Simon had focused his attention when he arrived, and there Bloom saw his white suit reflecting the sun's morning light onto the tall grass of the field. Bloom trailed after him, on toward the estate's end, where the yellow meadow met brush and rock, and as he neared the headland, he recalled most vividly the first time he and his father stood together at the bluff's edge to watch the twilight reflect off the surface of the sea, and for the first time in many years, he recalled the vow he had taken. Like a hypnotic melody he couldn't detach himself from, he heard the words over and over again within his mind; and in a quiet voice, in the voice of the child who once fit snugly under his father's arm, he repeated it in the form of a prayer. *Blessed art thou, O Lord Our God, Ruler of the Universe, when I am a man and I fall in love, I will protect my love better than he protected his. Blessed art thou, O Lord Our God . . .* When Bloom reached his brother at the edge of the bluff, the prayer turned into a whisper and was ended upon hearing Simon say, in a tone that held little recognition of Bloom's presence beside him, How strange it is to know I'll never have a complete picture of him. Not even a trace of his death remains.

As his elder brother continued to hang his head, Bloom stepped forward and inched his brow over the promontory's border. It was true. The mound of earth in which his father had been buried was no more. The mud, the rock, the bramble had in the months since the accident been reclaimed by the mountain; it had hardened in the heat, crumbled, and, with the aid of gravity's invisible hand, spread over the scree at the base of the ravine.

Tell me, Joseph. Do you think a man can fully assemble himself without having knowledge of his father?

I don't know, said Bloom.

No, said Simon, nor do I.

Simon said after a thoughtful pause, I've lived out so much of my life on a stage. I've acted so many roles, appeared as figments dreamed up in the minds of others, I'm not convinced I'd recognize the original inhabitant of my body if it introduced itself to me on the street one day; it's often the case I open a door to an unfamiliar room filled with unfamiliar faces, and find I haven't a clue who will arrive on the other side of the threshold.

Actors, said Simon. Hydras all.

He now stepped back and took in the sight of Bloom, and Bloom stepped back and took in the sight of Simon, and each, unaccustomed to seeing himself reflected so precisely on the surface of another, looked off in opposite directions.

Perhaps it was Bloom's new habit of dampening the light of the day into the darkest of shades, but when they turned back to each other a moment later, Simon appeared to him a duller version of himself. Paler in the cheek, more gray in complexion, more skeletal in stature. His eyes, too, appeared a dimmer version of what Bloom recalled. No longer were they burning with the same intensity he had encountered on the trail that day of their first meeting. He asked Bloom if he'd mind showing him where their father had been buried. To this, Bloom said, Not at all.

The brothers turned their backs on the ravine and wended a

path through the grove. They circled into the center of the rose garden, where, at the foot of the grave, they stood in silence until Simon
reached into the neck of his shirt and pulled out a silver chain;
attached to it was the other half of the pendant Bloom had received
the day he and his father traveled to the sanitarium by the sea.

As long as I can remember, Simon said, this has been such a
weight around my neck. It's a wonder I can hold my head upright.
He gripped the pendant in his fist and, with his jaw braced tight, he
yanked the chain hard enough to break one of the fastenings. Bloom
eyed the shimmering links that had fallen over his brother's knuckles. When Simon saw Bloom observing his closed hand, he said, I
understand you have one just like it.

I do, said Bloom, but I know nothing about it.

Simon pointed to the grave. Didn't he say?

No.

No, said Simon, why would he? There was a note of scorn in
Simon's voice, sharp enough it troubled Bloom. His brother seemed
to have heard it as well, because when he spoke next, he was more
measured. He didn't tell you because the gift of the pendant, it was
a morbid gesture. To have told you would have been perverse.

I don't understand.

I was told the story when I was a child. Sam, the man who placed
the other half of this in your hand the day you visited him on the
beach, he related it to me. Mother told him. Simon opened his fist to
reveal the charm. It was a gift from our father. This coin was his only
true possession when he arrived at the orphanage. It had been sewn
into his swaddling, presumably by his parents. As a loving gesture to
your mother and mine, he went to the orphanage's tool shop to divide
it in two and presented it to them on their eighth birthday. Simon's
eyes studied the object in his hand for a moment as if he hadn't looked
at it for a long time. Sam, he removed this half of the coin from my
mother's neck the day she died, and he clasped it here around mine the
night he retrieved me from your home in Woodhaven.

Simon glanced over at Bloom. You know the night?

Yes.

He told you, then.

Yes. He told me everything.

Well, what he didn't tell you was the half of the pendant Sam placed in your hand the day you visited him at the sanitarium was the half my mother pulled from your mother's neck as my mother fell to her death.

No, said Bloom, no he didn't.

No, said Simon with a thin smile. A thoughtful man wouldn't burden a child with such an ugly account. A calm now came over his face and for a few moments he lost himself to his thoughts. When he returned, he breathed out a tremor of laughter that made Bloom wonder if he was taking some pleasure at his expense. But his brother then shook his head and said, as if dumbfounded by an idea he couldn't fully grasp, Sam, on the other hand . . .

What about him?

He was the type of man who was mostly unaware he was an affront to all things decent. Simon laughed. A different sort of man altogether. One who took great pleasure in delivering the cruelest aspects of the world with an avuncular smile. As I'm sure he did when he handed the other half of this to you.

Why are you speaking of him in the past?

Simon turned to observe Bloom. His eyes narrowed as if he were trying to puzzle out a riddle. He now gripped the pendant between thumb and forefinger and rubbed at its surface. He walked around their father's grave to the base of the statue and ran his finger over the contours of Psyche's arm. Observing the languid features of her face, he said over his shoulder, I truly was hoping to know him. I hoped in time I would come to forgive him. To better understand him . . . He's always been present in my life, you know. Sam never allowed me to forget. He always reminded me there was a father, my father, a Jacob Rosenbloom, who played a part in my mother's ruin, a Jacob Rosenbloom who owed me more than he could ever repay me. I would have preferred the knowledge of his existence to fade, but Sam wouldn't allow it. Simon turned back to Bloom and said with some seriousness, I would have preferred to live as you have.

Quietly. In peace. Without a thought about what I was owed, in what ways I had been wronged. He set the pendant and its chain into Psyche's lifeless hand. But you had him, and I, I had Sam. The petty. The unprincipled. The very hungry Sam. Simon laughed again at the thought of his protector and benefactor one last time, and then meandered off through the garden's rings. Bloom thought to walk after him, but he could sense, from his brother's shift in tone and the way he turned away from him, this was his exit.

Instead of trailing after him, Bloom walked to the pendant and picked it up, and noticed all along the coin's curve, on its face, wear so thorough from touch the edge had been thinned to a point, and the moon on both sides had been nearly rubbed away. With the pendant in hand, he followed the path his brother had taken, hoping now to catch up to him, to invite him inside, so they might talk, so Bloom might better comprehend the source of his sorrow, but before he reached the rose garden's outermost circle, the roadster's engine combusted, and Bloom heard the whine and grind of its motor descending the mountain, and with each step he took along the path to the courtyard, the noise grew less and less audible.

❧

That night Bloom dreamed every surface of the villa had become a mirror, and reflecting from every mirror was his image. Everywhere he turned, he was there, yet it was some manifestation of himself he hardly recognized. Every countenance was disturbed, every feature that composed his form, a distortion. When he shut his eyes to escape his image, the interior of his lids opened a door to another room replete with mirrors. He climbed the mirrored stairs of the tower and set his eye onto the night sky; but even there, the combined light from the stars formed in the firmament a projection of his face. He reached out to it and found himself stepping off the pavilion's rail. Down he went, and as he plummeted, the villa broke apart and fell with him. It shattered into mirrored shards refracting crimson points of light, all of which gathered into a core sounding a heavy beat, a throbbing pulse, followed by a terrible moan. When he awoke from this heavy slumber, he recoiled from fright at the sight of his brother hovering over him.

There, there, said Simon. All is well with the world. He removed a handkerchief from his trouser pocket and pressed it to Bloom's brow, then placed the soft piece of linen in his hand.

What time is it?

It's after ten.

Bloom looked at the dark velvet curtains drawn across his bedroom windows and saw a piping of white light brightening the borders. Yes, said Bloom as he dabbed at his temples, it's late.

I've been waiting for some time, said Simon. He took Bloom by the arm and helped sit him up.

What for?

To apologize for having been so unpleasant and abrupt yesterday. It's been a trying week.

How so?

It seems we are both now fatherless. Me, twice over.

Mr. Freed is dead?

Simon nodded. It was a long time coming.

I'm sorry, said Bloom.

You shouldn't be. I know he was a great source of grief for you.

Nevertheless . . .

To the world at large, said Simon, Sam could be a nasty piece of work. A tyrant on his best days. To me, however, he was decent and kind. Out of the love he felt for my mother, he treated me like a son. Did for me as he said he would. Fulfilled his promises. Gave me all I have. And having done as much, I prefer to let others talk of his flaws. Simon smiled at Bloom, reached out to his head, and shook his curls. Wash up, do what you do, and meet me downstairs in the drawing room. And off went Simon out the door.

Then he returned and asked, Breakfast?

Yes, said Bloom, rubbing the sleep from his eyes, please. I'll be along in a minute.

Simon nodded, and off he went again.

>‹<

Because Meralda couldn't bring herself to remove them to the library, where they belonged, on the parlor table sat the magic lantern and the box of slides Bloom had illustrated for his father. Standing upright next to these items today was a film projector not like any Bloom recognized from his father's collection. With his head still clearing from his long sleep, he studied its components. Simon, meanwhile, walked the length of the parlor wall, shutting the curtains to the view of the canyon. When the room had been sufficiently darkened, he sat at the piano, lifted the lid, and with impressive dexterity, ran his fingers over the keys. This will do nicely, he said. Do you play?

No. I have no talent for it.

For me, there's no better way I can think of to spend my time.

Bloom was pleased to hear Simon sounding so affable. The somber mood on display at the edge of the promontory, in the heart of the rose garden, had all but disappeared.

I can't begin to tell you how many hours I spent as a child in Sam's theaters when they were dark. It was my greatest pleasure to sit alone at the piano in the orchestra pit, living between the notes, anticipating the next bar, modifying my internal tempo to the changing time signatures. Simon played a run up and down the board then settled onto a pleasant melody. Over the music he said, with his nose directing Bloom to the projector, It's an automatic. See the mechanism? The knob? There on the back?

Yes, I see it.

Turn it to the right and take a seat.

Bloom did as he was told. He turned the knob on the back of the projector then walked to the sofa through a mist of silvery dust.

I think you'll enjoy this, said Simon.

Over the clicks of the Rosenbloom Loop turning on its axis within the projector, Simon now produced an amusing rag, which modulated its rhythm to suit the movement of images Bloom saw on the wall before him. As he nibbled on eggs and toast, he watched a magnificent picture in which a vessel shaped like an exotic fish propelled itself from Earth's surface and traveled through a region of space rich with sparkling showgirls. The spacecraft collided point first with the monocled eye of the moon, where it sank into a meringue crust. Graybeard scientists, bespectacled and hunched over, disembarked and wandered subterranean passageways. They encountered Hottentot moon dwellers wearing grass skirts and bones through their noses, and with a vitality that defied belief, the aged travelers gave chase. When they caught the tribal moon people, they thwacked them over the head with their canes, turning them into spectacular puffs of smoke.

Bloom was so entertained by this, his mood so elevated, it felt to him as if yesterday's bleak encounter with Simon happened long ago. And without inhibition, he turned to his brother and asked, May we? Again?

Simon obliged. He rose from his seat, and acting the role of the obsequious servant, he bowed and then went on to feed the film into the reel out of which it had spooled. He cranked it back to its start, and again he performed the same syncopated rag he had played moments before, and Bloom, again, sat leaning forward over his knees, marveling at the fantastical spectacle flickering on the wall. Never before had he thought it possible for such enjoyment to be taken from a visual experience, short of watching the nighttime glow of a distant wildfire.

That morning, Simon showed him half a dozen more pictures made by the same motion picture director, the last of which he introduced as a metaphor for the life of the actor: a movie about a man who fell into a film projector and was made malleable. His head expanded and shrank in size and was replaced by a variety of animal visage. And this movie, like the first, Bloom asked to watch again. But in response to this request, Simon consulted his watch and said, As soon as we return.

Return from where?

I've arranged a short voyage of our own.

Simon took Joseph by the arm and started walking him to the

front door. Bloom told him he really wasn't prepared to voyage anywhere today.

I understand, said Simon. But I assure you: you won't leave the
grounds, not for a moment.

Then from where exactly will we be returning?

When they stepped out of the house and onto the drive, he said
to Bloom, Right there.

><-

Right there, Bloom found an inflated hot-air balloon whose silken
bubble rose almost as tall as the villa's tower. It was weighed down
by sandbags and moored in place by three stakes driven into the
ground, and attached to the basket's undercarriage was a hook connected to a thick rope wound around a winch bolted to the bed of a
truck. Simon removed a pair of azure coveralls from the passenger
seat of the cab and slipped them on, and, acting as if it were the most
ordinary activity to embark on an aeronautical adventure in the
middle of the day, at the start of the rainy season, he said to Bloom,
Shall we? Given the effort his brother had made to begin anew,
Bloom couldn't think of a courteous way to refuse him. He followed
Simon up a ladder into the carriage, and when they were inside and
secure, Bloom's brother waved his hand. A man of considerable height
and heft, who possessed a rather prolific nose, appeared with an ax in
hand from behind the cab of the truck, and with three swift swings,
he cut them free. Simon cast off several sandbags, then pulled on a
string dangling from a lit stove rigged below the balloon's opening.
An azure flame the same color as Simon's outfit spiked into the cavity
of the bubble. They rose at a moderate rate. They rose over the tops
of the eucalyptus, over the tower's pavilion, inside which Bloom could
see his colorful birds fluttering about in their cages. The brothers
steadily ascended to a point in the sky from which they could see in
one direction the horizon line grow more distant from the edge of the
ocean; in the opposite direction, the humpbacked mountain range;
and beyond it, the depression of the valley. And because it was a

rare winter day, in that it was extraordinarily calm, no matter how high they rose, the balloon remained remarkably still. They drifted in no direction. Against all intuition, they hovered over the same point on the Earth from which they had taken off, and at this altitude Simon pointed to the plateau and said, It doesn't look like much from up here, does it?

No, said Bloom as he looked down onto the miniature village his brother had built, it doesn't.

Tell me. Did Jacob explain to you what we'll be doing down there?

Yes.

Then you know all you have known is going to change.

In what ways?

In the most significant ways. I should think in the most remarkable ways. The balloon swayed a little. Tugged against the tether tied to the bottom of the carriage. People, said his brother. A jungle of them, all variety of apes and monkeys and lower order of primates will soon populate the land down there. A whole colony of baboons and chimpanzees, orangutans and marmosets, will be swinging from those trees. Men and women filled with desire and passion and purpose.

I've known so few women. And even fewer men.

You'll soon be acquainted with more than your fair share of both orders. Simon bent down and removed from a case by his feet a motion picture camera, and he mounted it onto one of the metal rods securing the sandbags. Here, look in here and tell me if what you see is in focus. Simon reached out and guided Bloom's hand to the camera's lens. Bloom switched places with Simon, set his cheek and brow against the viewfinder and adjusted the lens slightly to make the image of the plateau crisp, and when he offered the eyepiece to Simon, his brother leaned forward and said, Well done. He now described to him what he wanted next. He said he should allow the camera to run for a short while, to then turn it slowly, first to the right in the direction of the valley, and then to the left in the direction of the sea, and while he continued to roll the film, to push left all the way to him, where he should set him off-center within the frame. Nice and easy turns, said Simon.

Bloom did as Simon asked. He rested his eye on the viewfinder and started to turn the camera's crank. He wound the reel of film around the magazine as he remained focused on the stretch of the plateau; he slowly turned the lens to the right, and after a few breaths in and out, he proceeded to the left. And now all the way to me, said Simon. Farther to the left Bloom turned the camera to face Simon, and with his brother fixed right of center frame, he swung his arm around in a sweeping gesture, then stepped away to reveal the great expanse of the basin, its shore, the infinite ocean, all of it shone down upon by the coastal desert sun. And in that instant, every detail of the world Bloom had come to know so intimately was magically captured and contained in a way he had never captured it before.

What do you think? asked Simon as Bloom continued to feel in his hands, against his cheek, the sensation of the camera's moving parts working in unison.

It's wonderful, said Bloom. Behind the camera, I feel as if . . . He couldn't quite find the right words to describe what he felt. It feels like . . . he tried once more.

Disappearing?

Yes, said Bloom. Like disappearing.

→←

They remained aloft for the better part of an hour, and after the driver had cranked them back to Earth, Simon accepted Bloom's invitation to lunch in the dining room. In her excitement at seeing the young Rosenbloom's brother sitting in Jacob's place at the head of the table, and perhaps because she was eager to please the first proper guest she'd had the opportunity to serve since having taken her position on Mount Terminus, Meralda swung into the room at regular intervals, with, it seemed, every morsel of food she had available to her in the kitchen. She presented to the young men shredded chicken in mole, a stack of steaming tortillas fresh from the oven, guacamole, rice and beans, salsa with sliced orange, an assortment of olives picked, cured, and pitted by her own hands, a pitcher of lemonade, and for dessert, a glazed custard flan. With each entrance she made into the dining room, her complexion appeared to Bloom as if it were lit from within, and he was nearly certain he could see evidence of tears having been wiped from her eyes. This display of emotion didn't escape Simon's notice, and at one point during the meal, he reached out for Meralda's thick hand and asked, Have we upset you?

Oh, no, she said, dabbing the corners of her eyes with the cuff of her sleeve.

But you're crying.

Yes, but they are good tears, Mr. Reuben, I promise you.

Simon continued to hold her hand and looked at the full features of her face in search of a further explanation.

Just look at him, she said, her focus turning to Bloom. Look how your company brightens his eyes.

Is that my doing? asked Simon, who was now studying Bloom's face as intently as Meralda.

Meralda removed her hand from Simon's and touched it to his cheek. Bless you, she said with a tearful smile. Bless you. And off she went through the swinging door, and both young men could hear from within the kitchen Meralda sound a soft snuffle.

➤<

They lingered over lunch for some hours, during which time Simon was more than happy to do most of the talking. Bloom, after all, wasn't disposed toward, nor practiced in, the art of conversation. He was, however, the finest of listeners and the most astute of observers, and, as such, the perfect audience for his loquacious brother, who appeared to be performing for Bloom an extended monologue, one containing within it the broad strokes of his past. As a result of his brother's generosity of spirit and the gift he possessed to reveal himself in abbreviated fashion, Bloom came to know more about Simon over the course of this one afternoon than he had ever known about the man with whom he had shared his life up to this point. As Bloom had anticipated from having witnessed him walk the trails of Mount Terminus on the day they met, he was, indeed, a man of the world, but an even wider world than Bloom had imagined. Having come of age in the theater, he knew the idiosyncrasies of stage people. Having grown up at the side of Sam Freed, he knew the hypocrisy and corruption of men who conducted business and civic affairs. He knew the dirty habits of lowly thugs, the weaknesses of gangsters, the nonsense of rowdies and fancy men, the dreams of small-minded civil servants, the petty vanity of lofty politicians, the ill-mannered spirits of the moneyed, old and new. His education extended beyond the chain of Freed's theaters and his production company. At Freed's insistence, he had been sent to good schools, and at Freed's insistence, he was made to work while he studied. In the theater, he acted away his childhood, and when he came of age he produced and directed. He photographed motion pictures, negotiated business deals. As part of Freed's effort to shape him into a man of industry, as a means to groom him and better him, Simon attended a fine college, where, at the age of nineteen, he took an early degree in law and philosophy. At Freed's insistence, to finish him off properly, he was sent abroad; he traveled widely, and from spending time in the world's great museums, he learned about art and fashion. In salons and opera halls, he learned literature and music. From observing the workshop of the Lumière brothers, from having worked in the studio of Georges Méliès, he learned something of the craft of making motion pictures. When he returned from his travels abroad, he continued on with travels at home. He set out on dusty roads to manage one of Freed's itinerant crews.

There was, it seemed to Bloom, so little his brother hadn't done or seen or knew, and although, in Bloom's estimation, Simon had already lived several lifetimes, he could sense his ambitions were boundless, and for reasons he didn't entirely understand, Bloom was unsettled in his stomach at the mere thought of their enormity. And so when it came time for him to recall for Simon the events of his life that had preceded their meeting, he demurred. He told Simon he knew everything important that had ever happened to him, and that this latest development—Simon's arrival on Mount Terminus—was surely his most exciting affair to date.

No, said Simon, I know for a fact there is more.

What more?

I'm afraid, he said as he glanced at his watch, that is a question you'll need to reflect on until tomorrow. With an apologetic grin, Simon told Bloom he needed to keep an appointment in town, but he assured him he would return the following day. Bloom walked him outside. The driver had, in the time they had eaten their lunch and Simon had outlined the defining moments of his past, deflated the balloon and stored it on the truck. Until tomorrow! said Simon as they drove off. Until tomorrow!

>‹

Simon returned the following morning, and every morning afterward for the next several weeks, and each morning he and Bloom met, their day began as the day before, with a new picture or two to view, adventures and farces, parlor intrigues, tales of romantic love and longing, some exciting, some ridiculous, some sublime and full of wonder. Simon's long reach strode the length of the piano's keys in search of rhythms and melodies to capture the spirit of the images moving before them. Over lunch in the dining room, Bloom's brother often invited him to speak about how he passed his time on the estate, how it was he could bear the long silences and the isolation, but Bloom, who still didn't know how to articulate the ways in which he took pleasure losing himself to the still waters of the reflecting pool, to the soft cushions of the library sofas, to the gardens and the trails, to the tower's pavilion and aviary, to the temporal expanse of his studio atop the mesa, encouraged his brother to ignore the simplicity of his life, and instead to tell him more about the strange and beautiful people he had met in the exotic places he had visited, about the colorful and dangerous characters who populated his past. Day after day, Bloom listened to his brother speak at length, and as his brother's presence, and the places he described, grew in dimension, Bloom continued to search for some commonality he and Simon shared beyond their physical resemblance, for some deeper root that anchored them together, a familial trait, a mannerism, a movement, some similar characteristic he had observed in their father, but the more he listened and the more his brother performed his rehearsed speeches, the more Bloom marveled at the fact that, while born from the same man's seed, from two women whose outward appearances were indecipherably identical, there couldn't be anyone in the world more unlike him or Jacob than Simon. From top to bottom, from his theatrical expressions to his calculated style of elocution, he was a man, it seemed, entirely of his own making, and Bloom was left to wonder if beyond the information his stories imparted, if belying the bounty of language he enjoyed the feel of in his mouth, Simon had yet to show Bloom his authentic self, the unadorned spirit that lived within him. Or was it possible that his existence was composed of, as he claimed on the day of their reunion, the disparate roles he played in life and on the stage? Perhaps he *was* merely a composite of invented personae. Or, Bloom wondered, was there more to him buried beneath the fragments, somewhere under the amalgam constituted by his own will? Or was it in that act of self-invention, in the absence of a mother and a father, that Simon and Jacob were alike? They, at the very least, retained *this* similarity.

Bloom imagined if he'd had the opportunity to stand Simon and Jacob back to back, to bind them together, they would have formed a countervailing force in whose reversed polarity could be manifested the one attribute he was now convinced Jacob did pass on to Simon, and, for that matter, to Bloom: the invisible quality of being unknowable.

For days, Simon filled the void created by Bloom's reserve with amusing backstage dramas, of vaudeville routines gone wrong, of performances so good and so bad they resulted in small riots, until one day it occurred to Simon in the middle of a perfectly entertaining anecdote about a mezzo soprano who had accidentally fallen through a magician's trapdoor that he should stop speaking altogether. Listen to me, he said to Bloom. Just listen to me. How I go on and on. You must forgive me, he said, and quieted, and after a minute or two of a perfectly restful stillness, he asked, and then insisted, that Bloom take charge of the day, which left Bloom feeling quite uncertain as to how to proceed. He eventually stood up, took Simon by the elbow, and led him to the sanctuary of the library, where he showed him the shelves on which he kept his favorite books, his Homer and Bulfinch, Pliny the Elder, the Brothers Grimm, his Poe, Hawthorne and Dickinson, Byron and Keats, Wordsworth, Cervantes, Chekhov, Melville, Flaubert, Dickens . . . and after summoning the courage to speak of their father, he directed Simon's attention to Jacob's optical devices, the blueprints of his inventions, the patents he filed when he was a younger man, the artifacts he inherited from Jonah Liebeskind. And when he saw in Simon's open expression that he was receptive to learning something more about their father, he told Simon about Jacob's apprenticeship with the master optician; described how the fastidious man lived at the altar of greatness and progress, and how he died at the moment he had outlived his relevance. He told Simon about their father's brief meeting with Thomas Edison, about Edison's humorous retort upon seeing the Rosenbloom Drive function for the first time. And when Simon laughed at the idea that his young father had outwitted the great man of the modern world, Bloom escorted him through the villa's many rooms and up the tower stairs, where he introduced him to Elijah and ran him through his routine, all the way through to Open the door and we shall see . . . No, I need you here with me. They gazed through the telescope's lens, over the basin to the sea, and Simon pivoted the eye to align with a clear path running through the groves, and said, In three weeks from tomorrow, they will all arrive at the same time, a convoy of trucks along the port road. If you look for us, he said, pointing over the scope's hollow tube, you will see. And Bloom said in three weeks from tomorrow, he would seek them out.

When they returned indoors, Bloom, feeling that much more at ease with his brother, returned Simon up the stairs to his mother's gallery, where he sat him down on the chaise longue and explained to him what his mother's paintings meant to him, how as a child he cast his eyes onto their horizons in search of sleep and the few memories he could recall of his mother sitting before the fires, and he explained what the landscapes represented to their father; and as their father had done for Bloom, he sat Simon down in the drawing room and displayed through the eye of the magic lantern, on the mandala of the Wheel of Life, on all the various devices he had introduced to Simon in the library, the miniature images Bloom's mother had so carefully and masterfully crafted, the numerous ways in which she had been haunted by the ghosts of Simon's mother; he allowed Simon to see the heavy burden, the madness, she carried within her until her heart, quite literally, broke. Do you see? Bloom asked as their father had once asked Bloom. Do you see how she suffered?

Yes, said Simon. Yes, I see.

On a late-afternoon walk to the top of Mount Terminus, Bloom recounted for Simon the year he was absent, the year during which the noise from the construction site resounded over the grounds of the estate, and he told him how their father suffered his shame as vigorously and unyieldingly as Bloom's mother had suffered her lament. He lent his brother the flimsy copy of *Death, Forlorn*, which Bloom now carried with him in the inner pocket of his jacket, and when Simon had read it, Bloom escorted him to his studio, and there showed him the panels of finished drawings he had made for Jacob, showed him the multitude of sketches on which they were based, showed him the pages of Manuel Salazar's journal from which their style was born, and he then returned his brother to the parlor, where Bloom proceeded to show him how, inspired by his mother's miniatures and the lines of Salazar, he reduced the panels to fit onto the glass slides of the magic lantern. And upon seeing the last of these images projected onto the wall, Simon turned to Bloom and said, with his eyes squinting into the lamplight, I hadn't realized.

Realized what?

That you're a luftmensch. A true one, at that.

A what?

A dreamer. Always with his head in the clouds. The *true luftmenschen* is what Sam and I called the dreamers who could pull the clouds from the sky and bring them down to Earth for us lesser people to behold. You, brother, are a true luftmensch . . . And now I understand. Now I understand why it was that Jacob insisted I make a place for you. For the exchange of the land, for the rights to the water, he insisted I make a place for you at the studio. Now I understand why.

But I don't know the first thing about making pictures.

No, said Simon. You know everything. Everything you need to know. It is all here, he said with a hush as he pointed the glowing embers of a cigarette toward the lantern and then to the wall. You were born for this. And do you want to know how I know this to be true?

How?

Because, at this very moment, I envy you.

You? Envy me? That's . . . unlikely.

No. Your eye, your lines, Joseph, they are enviable.

Bloom shook his head at his brother.

Trust me, said Simon as he shook his head back at Bloom, the envy I feel is the envy all middling artists will feel when they look at your work.

Bloom continued to shake his head at this. You overestimate me.

If anyone's to be disappointed, said Simon, I'm afraid it's going to be you. The majority of pictures we make are rough and crass. There are a few true artists in my stable, but, if you can bring pictures such as these to life, you're going to make all of them look artless by comparison. You must believe me, Joseph: if you weren't my brother, if our father hadn't put these conditions on me, I would have sought you out all on my own. Understand? It's rare I find such a gift. With a talent like yours, you can do anything you like in this business. Anything.

Bloom took a moment to consider this. He saw no mendacity in his brother's face, not in his eyes, in the shape of his mouth. When he had convinced himself that what his brother had said to him was genuine, Bloom said with some lingering skepticism in his voice, Anything?

Anything. Anything at all.

><

Before I left, said Simon the next day, I wanted you to see this. When you're ready, when we've put some experience behind you, this is the man I want you to work with. This man, Gottlieb, is, I think, the man for you. As he did every morning for the past several weeks, Simon fed a reel into the projector and took his place at the piano, and as he began to play, Bloom watched a picture that matched the quality of the very first pictures Simon had run for him, and, maybe, even surpassed them. It was a living dream, artful and serene, yet funny and human. It relied on techniques he had thus far not seen in any of the other pictures Simon had shown him. This man, Gottlieb, transcended the cinematic rules of storytelling set down by—so far as Bloom knew—no one in particular. In a seemingly arbitrary manner, Gottlieb's perspectives cut away from scenes to the natural world—to trees, to bodies of water, to open sky, a character's fidgeting hands, a finger working out a wrinkle in a dress, to symbolic objects placed in the most unlikely places. He shifted camera angles to alter the frame of reference in such a subtle and seamless manner he enabled the viewer to see within, to reflect on, to reflect with, the subject before him. He made it possible for his audience to feel the echoes of what had already passed, to foreshadow—to anticipate—what was to come. With these invisible manipulations, with an illusionist's sleight of hand, he inspired within his observer the type of spiritual dissociation Bloom had experienced only from reading the Romantic poets on his favorite shelf. In this last picture he watched with his brother during this period on Mount Terminus—Gottlieb's *The Magnetic Eye*—Myron Bishop, a bitter curmudgeon, awakened one morning possessed by an eye charged with an unusual

magnetism, one whose force worked in vexing opposition to Bishop's
truest desires. The people and objects he despised most, the magnetic
eye attracted; the people and objects he most wanted to attract, it
repelled. *The cruelest of jokes*, read the intertitle upon the revelation
of the eye's logic. To illuminate Bishop's repulsion, Gottlieb introduced first the figure of a cantankerous old hag whom Bishop had
seen in the distance and tried to avoid by crossing the street. Gottlieb cut away to Bishop's fantasy about what cruel act he wanted to
perpetrate on her, but the magnetic eye had other designs. When
Bishop drew near to her, a Kewpie doll flew out a shop door and
into Bishop's hand, and, in its wake, the ugly old wretch lifted off
the ground and followed. When her nose was only inches from his,
and she saw what he held in his hand, she plucked the gift from
Bishop's fingers as she would a flower, observed the mawkish sentiment expressed on the Kewpie's porcelain face, and then looked
to Bishop with tearful eyes. The act of kindness softened her so,
she smothered Bishop with unwanted kisses. Everywhere he went
from thereon, Bishop found himself embracing the most wretched
creatures—the infirm and impoverished, the town drunkard, an
amputee, a forlorn dwarf, a widowed malcontent more malcontent
than Bishop himself. Meanwhile, each time he tried to draw near the
magnificent woman he adored, a bespectacled beauty whose white
hair Gottlieb lit as if to appear on fire, the magnetic eye repelled her,
in one instance by removing her spectacles from her face and cata-
pulting them through the air into the hands of a handsome young
gentleman, more well-to-do and free spirited than Bishop could ever
dream of being. Gottlieb used proximity to the love interest to show
Bishop's spirit defeated. The camera, assuming Bishop's point of view,
pulled back farther and farther from the young woman, leaving him
to observe her from a great distance away, and only from there was
he able to see with what kindness and grace she embraced all the
people he found so repulsive. From this distance, he came to understand it was this woman's selfless qualities with which he longed
to be acquainted, and from this distance, he began to model her
example. Those he once felt most in opposition to, he now grabbed

hold of freely. He expressed his affection for them, offered them his undivided attention. His face, once fallen and disturbed, transformed. With each act of kindness, it grew more attractive, appeared healthier, more sound, more alive, and soon he found that the poor wretches he now embraced with a full, compassionate heart were unable to enter his sphere. The magnetic eye wouldn't allow it, as their company was now desired. *The cruelest of jokes*, the intertitle read again. Bishop stood alone, isolated and untouched, and as such, the world about him—brought to life by a sequence of Gottlieb cutaways—began to look glorious in all its aspects, at which point the polarity of the magnetism was neutralized by the unlikeliest hero. A mosquito flew into Bishop's magnetic eye and pressed its proboscis into the dark center of its pupil.

For the moment, Bishop was blinded—the screen faded to black, over the lens a shudder blinked to simulate Bishop's frenetic lid—and when the camera lens moved from soft to sharp focus, he saw the glowing hair of the bespectacled woman, there she was, examining the eye that had caused him his troubles. With the corner of a kerchief, she wiped from his cheek a bloody tear left by the mosquito, then extended him a hand, lifted him to his feet, and off Bishop walked down the street with her until the camera's iris closed around them.

><

Bloom thought it marvelous, and before his brother could solicit his opinion, he said so.

As Simon stood before the projector and wound back the reel, he told Bloom that when he was ready, when Bloom had acquired the skills to be useful to Gottlieb, when he had matured a little more, Simon would do everything in his power to arrange for him to work as his assistant.

For this Bloom thanked his brother.

Simon removed Gottlieb's reel and replaced it with another. When he had fed the leader into the machine and switched on the projector, he walked to Bloom's side, took a seat on the sofa beside him, and together the brothers watched the picture Bloom had filmed on their aeronautical adventure over Mount Terminus. There, said Simon, the first of many pictures you'll be responsible for. Bloom watched with the thrill of seeing his memory of that day re-created and projected onto the wall. He watched as the scope turned and constructed the panorama of the valley and the range, the basin and the sea. This print is for you, said Simon when the film had run through and all that remained on the wall was a square of light shining forth from the burning filament of the unobstructed bulb. Bloom watched his brother rewind the short reel and close up the metal canister in which it was housed. You must keep it safe, in a warm, dry place.

I will.

Be sure that you do, he said when he stepped forward and placed the container in Bloom's hands, which felt warm to the touch. Before letting go, Simon added with a serious note, I mean it. It will be a memorial soon enough.

How so?

What I told you a few weeks ago, about the changes that are to come?

Yes.

I wasn't only speaking about the immediate changes on the studio lot. Simon waved his hand through the light. It cast a wave of a shadow across the wall. The fact of the matter is it won't be long before the land all around us is changed forever. All of what you see today from the peak of Mount Terminus, you won't recognize in the years to come.

I don't understand.

Simon stood up and began walking about the room. Before I explain how and why, understand this: I won't be deterred from my plans. They're already set in motion. But, he said as he pulled back the curtains to let in the light, I thought, perhaps if I prepared you for what's to come, the impact wouldn't be as unsettling as it might have been otherwise. He walked to the case in which he carried his daily allotment of film canisters, reached into it, and pulled out a map. He returned to his seat beside Bloom, unpacked the map's sections, and, with his eyes focused on the terrain, pointed to symbols and lines drawn over the topography of the region. Here, he said with his finger resting in the middle of Pacheta Lake's outline, at the center of the source of his mother and father's brief happiness together. I know you're familiar with this place.

Yes, said Bloom.

Yes, said Simon. He pulled his chin to the knot of his tie, and said, Here. You see the line marked here? Simon ran his finger over a line of red ink running southwest from the lake to the northern edge of the valley to a red triangle near the canyon pass. I've made a deal with the county's water authority to divert the lake water. Here, where the pass is, we're going to build a dam for a reservoir. Simon's finger now followed a tangential line west from the red triangle at the far reaches of the valley up along the ridge of the mountains leading to the basin on the opposite side of Mount Terminus. That water, it will flow through an outlet into the valley here, and through another outlet here, into the basin. Here, where for some years now, I've been buying up the property not owned by our father. Simon traced the red line until it stopped in the middle of the vast stretch of land leading to the sea. What I didn't inherit from Jacob, what Jacob didn't own, what I haven't yet been able to acquire, I'm now in the process of purchasing.

What for?

To make the land habitable. To build on it. To expand the city center outward by road and rail. All the way to the sea.

Simon handed the map to Bloom so that he might study it more thoroughly, to take in the full extent of his brother's vision, but Bloom couldn't begin to imagine the outcome, nor could he fathom how in the world Simon would achieve it. The engineering. The machinery. The laborers. It seemed to him an endeavor on the order of a Chinese emperor, an Egyptian pharaoh, a Mayan god. He tried to recall the city center's congested landscape, its architecture and industry, its tramways and public squares, and he tried to imagine it all superimposed onto the surface of the map, crowding the lens of his telescope, but the best he could do was to see a phantom image, a mirage on the edge of the desert shimmering in the heat and the wind.

When Bloom didn't respond, Simon said, The moment I looked out over the vistas of Mount Terminus, I saw what the land to the west should be. I saw how to make it habitable. How to populate an entire region of the Earth no one until now had ever thought to populate before. And I knew I was the one meant to shape it. I've spent enough time in the company of true artists to know, in my heart, Joseph, I'm not one of you. I'm a producer. That is the truth of it. As a businessman, understand? I, like you, have the potential to leave behind something great, something monumental. And what you see here? he said with his hand returning to the outline of Pacheta Lake, I know in my gut, will be the most important thing I ever do. The running of the studio, it's been my trade, a vocation like any other, for which I'll be admired for a while, and then forgotten, but *this*, *this*, Joseph, will leave a permanent mark on the land that will live long after you and I have both turned to dust. Surely, you can understand?

Bloom nodded, if only to indicate he followed his brother's reasoning, and recognized his conviction. He was able to comprehend Simon's plans, but he wasn't certain he understood the ambition that motivated him. Bloom had put little thought into what he would leave behind. He wasn't certain he cared what he left behind. Nor was he certain that he appreciated his brother's vision, as it stood in opposition to what he valued and cherished. He didn't wish to set himself apart from his brother, so he didn't express these thoughts out loud, but Simon was perceptive enough to see what weighed on Bloom's mind.

Simon lifted his hand and playfully tapped Bloom's forehead with the tip of his finger. We obviously have a great deal more to learn about each other, he said. I have come to see one thing quite clearly, however.

What's that?

How deeply attached you are to this place. I'm not blind. Simon repacked the map and placed it in his case. And when he had closed the clasps, he stood and said, No need to worry. We'll ease you into it. Before you find yourself in the thick of it, the least I can do is prepare you to become better acquainted with the terrain of what's to come.

Before Bloom could ask how exactly Simon proposed to do this, Simon asked the question himself. Yes, he said, but how, exactly? Simon stared off through the window whose view crossed the canyon. He stood quietly, intently twisting one of the curls on his head, occasionally glancing back at Bloom with what appeared to be a solution, and each time he appeared to have plotted a course of action, he made a theatrical turn, puckered his lips, and shook his head dismissively. After two and then three comic dismissals, he made his final turn and said, with a gleam in his eye, And there you have it!

There you have what?

The very thing, of course! My man Gus, he'll call on you tomorrow. He'll explain everything then.

Uncertain what arrangement he was agreeing to now, but trusting his brother well enough, and unable to help but feel appreciation for Simon's effort to lighten the blow of this news, Bloom said, All right. Yes, why not.

That's the spirit!

Bloom followed Simon out to his roadster, where his brother removed from the passenger's seat the case that held the fine-looking camera they had used on their aeronautical journey. Simon handed Bloom the container, and said, You'll be needing this. He then observed Bloom standing there with it in his arms, and, with brotherly affection, added, It suits you.

Does it?

It does. Simon nodded. He placed a hand on Bloom's shoulder. In all seriousness, he said. Do exactly as Gus says and we'll put you to work when I return.

Simon cranked the engine at the front of the automobile, and

when its interior sounded its combustion, he took to the seat behind
the wheel and said over the ruckus, Remember: three weeks! Twenty-
one days from today! Watch for us on the port road! Three weeks!
he called from the driver's seat. Until then! Simon turned the roadster
around now and sped off down the drive onto the winding road.
When the noise from his brother was no longer audible, Bloom set
the case his brother had handed him in the foyer and climbed to the
top of the tower, where he set his eye onto the viewfinder of his telescope and surveyed the land all around him, watched the ocean
breezes waft dust up from the fields and the roads and settle over the
canopy of the groves, and he tried once again to see into the future,
but, for the life of him, he couldn't fathom it.

>‹

From behind his veil of sleep the following morning, Bloom heard
a voice rich in timbre repeating his name. Joseph, it called. Joseph . . .
It's time to wake up, kid. When Bloom opened his eyes, he saw first
the inlay of his bedroom's coffered ceiling, and when he turned his
head he was given a start, as standing beside him in silhouette was
a man in a black mackintosh and bowler hat. Don't be startled. It's
only me, Gus.

Gus? said Bloom, recalling the name of Simon's man.

Yes. Gus.

Why are you dressed like that?

Gus looked himself over and looked back to Bloom with his
heavy brows pinching the bridge of his prodigious nose, and asked
as a child might, How else would I be dressed?

The enormous figure bent down and folded over the blanket
covering Bloom's body. He lifted it off, and he walked around the
bed, and when he set it in the lap of the armchair Roya had slept in
during his period of convalescence after his father's death, Bloom
couldn't help but notice the great pack of shoulder muscles shifting
under the material of the coat. The young lady is waiting, said Gus.

What young lady?

Your character study. Simon told me to tell you: You're to study the life within.

I'm to do what?

He wants to see what you can do with a living, breathing human being. She's waiting for you in your studio.

Bloom sat up and searched for Gus's eyes under the brim of his hat.

He said if you were to look at me the way you're looking at me now, I was to say this . . . He pulled from his jacket pocket a piece of notepaper, and after he wiped his extravagant nostrils with the back of his hand, he read: You're to become acquainted with her form and draw out what lives within. And then Simon said, if you still looked disorientated, like you look right now, I was to say, Let's go. On your feet. But only more like this: Let's go! On your feet! Only I don't think I'm going to have to do that now, am I?

No, Gus. That won't be necessary.

I'm glad for that. In spite of my appearance, I'm not the sort who enjoys making emphatic exclamations.

No, said Bloom for the sake of agreement, of course not.

Gus reached out to Bloom with his big paw and mussed his hair. You're a smart kid, he said, then told him he'd be waiting for him out on the landing.

After Bloom had washed and dressed, Gus escorted him into the courtyard and up to the dwelling atop the mesa. When they reached the door at the side of the building, Gus said, Remember. The inner life, not the outer beauty, is your concern. Simon says if you don't capture the inner life, he'll know. Like that, he said with a snap of his meaty fingers. He now opened the door and gave Bloom a little pat on the behind, which pushed him through the threshold. He then shut him in.

Sitting on a stool in the light shafting through the studio sky-lights, Bloom found a naked woman with a long braid of auburn hair hung on her shoulder. She sat nicely postured with her back to him, her skin appearing as if it had been treated with a golden-pink gouache. Bloom was reminded of the occasions he had seen this mix of soft color and texture from the tower's pavilion moments before the sun set, when a marine haze, whose moisture appeared more flowery than airy, hung on the horizon, and he further recalled how on such rare evenings when the sun slowly ebbed below the distant line of the sea to form in a few instants celestial bouquets of violet blue and saffron orange, all his worldly concerns ebbed into the arresting vision ahead, and vanished.

Hello, Bloom thought to say.

He said I shouldn't speak, said the woman. The sound of her voice was soothing and mild and Bloom tried to imagine from its tenor what her face might look like.

He told her she didn't need to speak to him if that was what she wanted.

She said it was, and then she said nothing more.

Forming a wide girth around his subject, Bloom gingerly placed the soles of his shoes on the planks of the floor, all the time observing along the way the cellolike curves of her back, the elongated tendons of her neck, the delicate bow of her left arm. When he reached the point in the studio where he could see her face and her chest in profile, he found she looked more like a girl than a woman. Although her cheeks were smooth, he could see pushing up through the taught skin a few white blemishes. Her jawline had yet to fully fill out, and to add to her youthful appearance, she had a petite nose and a full mouth, out of which poked at her lower lip a crooked bicuspid.

With each step, Bloom took none of the details composing her body and face for granted, as, other than in books and paintings and sculptures in and around the house, he had never seen a woman fully bared before him. He delighted in the way her small nose sloped at the same angle as her breasts, how the shape of her chin resembled the knobs of her knees, that the color of her lips was a shade darker than that of the broad rings of flesh circling her breasts. Her mouth was the same color as the crenellated flesh between her legs, which she opened for him with a coquette's good humor.

As if in search of sprites and nymphs, he studied with great fascination the sparkling triangle of auburn hair under the small bulge of her stomach. He followed beads of perspiration up from her navel to the notch at the base of her throat, where he paused before gazing for the first time into the powder-blue hydrangeas that were her eyes. It wasn't until he reached this most fragile and intimate of places that he discovered what he was meant to be looking for, and with this discovery of the young woman's inner beauty, the internal pressure one would expect the young Rosenbloom to feel at the sight of such lovely flowers began to mount.

Having no illusions that his subject would miss the ascent of his mood, Bloom retreated a few steps to an armchair sitting beside the camera and tripod Gus had presumably set out. He sat down, and here, in this position, he pressed his hands into his lap, and waited. With a hapless grin, his face aglow, he focused his attention on the young woman's feet. But here, too, he saw in the rise of her instep, in the delicacy of the tendons, a configuration of lines that reminded him of the curve of her hips and the shape of her face, and he returned in his mind to what beauty projected from her eyes. Wherever his thoughts turned now—to the shafts of light, to his birds in the tower, to the limbs of trees hung with fruit—he returned to what lived behind this woman's eyes. When a good amount of time had passed, the young woman—as if she couldn't bear witness to his mortification a moment longer, or perhaps because she had simply grown impatient with the stillness of the room—rolled her eyes to the skylight above, stepped down from the stool, and padded over the wooden planks. There she knelt down between Bloom's knees, placed a finger to her lips, and nodded her head as if they were in agreement. The young Rosenbloom's instinct was to protest, to protect the young woman's integrity, to save her from herself, but with her mouth only inches from the zipper of his pants, with her weighty breasts pressing upon his inner thighs, with the musty aromas rising from under her arms and between her legs, with the expectation he might experience the same levity and release he had felt with Roya, his senses were too overwhelmed to do anything other than nod back his consent, and before he knew it, in a few swift motions, his subject, with whom he had shared less than a dozen words, had undone the fly of his trousers and had taken him into her mouth.

This lush sensation was so unusual to him, he tried to push her away, but she acted possessed—or was at least very intent to do her good work—and not only did she manage to hold Bloom there, but she also overpowered him, outmaneuvered him. She thrust her head forward faster and faster until the young Rosenbloom gave in to her and arched his back, allowed himself to present to his full length, at which point, only then, she slowed, at which point, he, with one hand gripping her long braid and the other hand gripping her ear, gushed, and, to his great pleasure, felt the unique sensation of her nibbling away at him with her fang as she drank down every last drop of the very same substance that had landed in his navel so unceremoniously months before.

>‹

Now that the coil within Bloom had been unraveled, he was able to concentrate on what had been asked of him. The young woman daintily touched a finger to the corners of her mouth and returned to the stool, her braid coming undone, her lips spread in a mischievous grin, her eyes glowing as if electrified. Bloom wrapped around her shoulders his mother's paisley shawl and he gathered the tripod and the motion picture camera whose lens he set back a small distance from her shoulder. Look away from me, he said to her. Look over your other shoulder, he commanded, and when I say so, slowly turn to me with your eyes shut. When your chin touches this shoulder, slowly open them, and look at me the way you're looking at me right now.

He focused the lens on the back of her head and began turning the camera's crank.

And begin, he said.

And she began.

>‹

In the days he waited for his brother's return, the young Rosenbloom's education in inner beauty continued in this way. Every morning, Gus appeared beside his bed to announce the arrival of a new subject, and with each new arrival, Bloom now walked to the studio on his own, eager to see what type of woman awaited him; as every one Gus brought to the estate varied in size and shape and had such different features and temperaments, Bloom's ideas of physical and psychic beauty were constantly changing, and he began to understand the nature of his brother's exercise. He became, in this brief time, a great admirer of women, of all women, whether they were classically beautiful in balance and symmetry, or enormously imbalanced, with urn-sized breasts that hung to oversized waists. All forms, he found, appealed to him. Ever since his first experience in the studio, he particularly appreciated women with imperfect teeth. He found himself particularly aroused by one woman whose front two were substantially gapped. Because of the duality he observed in the face of another woman on another day, he thought women with high cheekbones and high foreheads were much more becoming if included in the composition of their faces was a small overbite. In profile, he was left with the impression that the woman was awkward and shy, but when he walked around her and looked at her directly, she appeared appealingly predatory. Gus introduced him to women who had peculiarly exaggerated physiognomies. A woman with a thin face and an aquiline nose. A woman with a large mouth full of oversized teeth. A woman with a narrow torso and wide hips. A woman with rolls and folds of flesh that lapped over her God-given curves. And he discovered, when he rolled the film over in the camera, he was more intrigued by the faces of these women, especially the shapeliest of the lot. The women with strong thighs and muscular rumps, those with hefty bellies and breasts, with broad shoulders and thick wrists. These women, unlike the women undistinguished in their shapeliness, didn't retreat to invisible and mysterious places in their minds. They didn't deflect the cold gaze of the lens. Rather, as one would reflect outward onto the night sky, they appeared to be searching for meaning in its darkness. In a few frames of film, Bloom discovered, a shapely woman, uninhibited, could reveal in an instant the full essence of her character, and to this he was drawn in, so closely, he was compelled to turn away.

✳

The women departed with Gus each morning at precisely eleven o'clock, and he would return just before two with a man who possessed an unusual talent. The object here, Gus said, is to capture the character behind the thrill of the event. He arrived first with a one-eyed Negro cowboy dressed in spurs and chaps. A scar like the tail of a rattlesnake curved down his cheek, ending near the opening of his ear. Like Gus, he wore a bowler hat, only his had two bullet holes on each side and had tucked into the band of its brim a mottled peacock feather. At his waist was a holster holding two six-shooters and in his right hand he held a rifle with a pewter finish. The sight of the man, who stood as tall and wide and as taciturn as Gus, frightened Bloom, until the cowboy walked into the grove and plucked from their respective trees an orange, then a lemon, an avocado, a plum. He handed them to Bloom and together they walked to the open field, some distance from the headland, and there the man pointed to the sky. Throw them all up, one after the next, real fast like, as high as you can, he said. Bloom looked to Gus and Gus said, Do as he says. Bloom readied himself and then, starting with the largest of the fruit, he threw them up in quick succession as hard as he could. Avocado. Orange. Lemon. Plum. As the avocado rose to its apex, the one-eyed cowboy drew each of his pistols and shot each piece of fruit out of the sky, the plum just as it started its descent. He then turned to Bloom and smiled, showing him where he'd lost his two front teeth. My wife smacked 'em right out o' my head. He laughed when he saw Bloom innocently gazing through the gap into the back of his mouth. Bloom spent the afternoon filming the cowboy's face in the afternoon light. Straight on. In profile. Close up, to take in the detail of his scar. He rolled film to capture the way he walked with his hands at rest on his pistol grips. From a distance he filmed him plucking fruit from trees. From up close he filmed his dark hand reaching up to grasp hold of a lemon. Lying on his back, he focused on the point in the sky where he could best capture the exploding fruit. At his side, he filmed the cowboy drawing his gun. From the front, from the back, from every angle he could think of to re-create that one moment in time, Bloom rolled and rolled the film in the magazine, until there was no more film to be rolled. And off went the one-eyed Negro cowboy sharpshooter with two missing teeth as the sun began to dip below the horizon.

In the days to come, Gus drove up to the top of Mount Terminus a Chinese dwarf who spun miniature plates at the end of bamboo poles, a dozen of them, simultaneously; a mustached, one-armed Greek who juggled five baseballs at a time with his one good arm, his shoulder, and a foot; a strongman who wrestled a wild pig; a team of Russian acrobats who formed atop a single bicycle a reverse pyramid; a lazy-eyed magician who failed to make Gus disappear; a six-foot-tall contortionist who squeezed into a small box from which he couldn't remove himself; and then there were several dipsomaniacs Gus plied with drink so Bloom could film them stumble about through the maze of the knotted gardens until they could stumble no more.

><

Except to say that Sam Freed had given him a chance at a new life after he'd fallen on hard times, Gus Levy shared little about his past. Yet Bloom felt at ease in his company. He trusted him. Inherently. Even if he was dressed as one of the henchmen from his childhood nightmares, he didn't resemble his father's tormentors. There was warmth and an innate kindness belying Gus's exterior. Even Mr. Stern, who had stopped by several times to advise Bloom on his holdings, took a liking to Gus. Despite his monumental presence, Gus, a man of his father's generation, more often than not struck Bloom as a small boy wearing an oversized suit. When he didn't know he was being observed, Bloom caught him on several occasions burying the tip of his proboscis in a rosebud to take in not a manly snort, but more a feminine whiff. Not long after he arrived, he carried with him—inside the internal pocket of his long coat—a pair of pruning shears, which he used for several purposes. Once, sometimes twice a week, while Bloom filmed his subjects, he would ask Meralda for a vase or a bowl and would clip flowers or fruit, and present them to her at sunset. On the days he wasn't arranging flowers in a vase or fruit in a bowl, he trimmed back branches in the grove, so they produced healthier fruit, he told Bloom. To occupy his time further, he lumbered up to the top of the tower, where he did as his young charge did: observed the world about them through the eye of the telescope. Communed with the birds. He even went so far as to take with him a bucket of water and a brush to clean the cages. What Bloom liked about him best of all, however, was the respect he showed the guests he delivered to the estate. No matter what variety of woman he met at the door of the studio, after Bloom had finished with her, Gus bowed his head, handed a yellow rose to her, and offered his arm for the walk back to the motorcar. To the one-eyed cowboy, to the one-armed Greek, to the dipsomaniacs who could hardly stand upright, Bloom was introduced as if they were respectable gentlemen. To the most unusual of the lot, he treated their differences with the nonchalance of a man who had experienced the world enough to know when to shrug his bulky shoulders at its most intriguing peculiarities.

>+<

One night after Gus had twice been to town and back, Roya appeared before Bloom in the parlor and touched his shoulder. He followed her out the front door and down the drive. When they reached the gate, she handed Bloom a flashlight and pointed to the right, along the stone wall. Bloom turned on the light and there he saw Gus's black sedan, and in it, Gus, snoozing upright with a shotgun's double barrel resting against his chest. Bloom approached and woke him. And said, Won't you come inside, Gus? There are more than enough rooms. Or, if you like, you can sleep in one of the cottages.

I can't, said Gus. Simon wouldn't like it.

Why not?

I'm supposed to be looking out.

What for?

He grimaced. It's nothing you need to concern yourself with.

You're hugging a shotgun, Gus.

The big man looked down at the two barrels in his arms, raised his thick brows as if to say, So I am, then said, Walk around and take a seat.

Bloom did as he was told, and when he was settled next to Gus, Gus said, Simon's told you of his plans? For the reservoir and the aqueduct?

Yes.

Well, the farmers up there near the lake haven't been in a particularly obliging mood. They sort of have it out for him at the moment. And seeing as it was Mr. Rosenbloom, the departed, who turned the lake's stewardship over to Simon, I'm afraid they're not too pleased with you, by association, see.

No, said Bloom, I don't see.

Look, said Gus, it's like this. You've got the farmers out at the edge of the desert there who aren't too pleased because they say the people down south are going to suck the water right out of their fields, and then you've got the citrus farmers over here on the other side of the mountains, he said, pointing out to the basin, who've yet to sell to Simon—they're not too pleased with the amount of money Simon's offered them for their groves. They feel like they're getting squeezed. They consider the way your brother does business something of an injustice. But the thing is, the courts have said it's Simon's right, and it's the water authority's right, to divert the water from the farms in the north, and put the squeeze on the farmers in the south, and it's the courts, in the end, that say what's what. So, said Gus, it's no surprise tempers are up, and, it's been my experience, when tempers run hot, right minds don't prevail. It doesn't matter whether or not you're part of Simon's venture, see? When people think their livelihood is threatened, anyone will do. Until now there have been whispers about some unpleasant business, nothing more than whispers; nevertheless, Simon wants me here to sit out the nights. As a precaution.

Despite the unsettling news, the sight of Gus, enormous and armed, made Bloom feel secure. Nothing, he thought, could penetrate this large barrier of a man, this amiable Golem. Nothing.

The lengths he goes to, Gus remarked after a long silence. It dizzies the mind. After another pause, he added, I know he wasn't Sam's natural-born child, but there are times when I wonder if he didn't inherit a little of his soul. Gus shifted his eyes to Bloom, and Bloom returned Gus's gaze, hoping Simon's man would continue on. Sam, Gus said after he and Bloom stared at each other for a little while, he had something of the dybbuk about him. And now I can see it in Simon. Same as Sam. Follow?

Bloom shook his head.

Gus went on at some length to explain how Sam Freed started off—not unlike Gus himself—as a dirty immigrant kid working the saloons back east along the city's Bowery. By all accounts, Sam was a decent, levelheaded boy until he took a job at P. T. Barnum's dime museum on Broadway, where, day after day, he spent his time attending to Barnum's cabinets of curiosities. While looking after them, Gus explained, something inside him changed. Gus was convinced a malevolent spirit, a dybbuk, came to attach itself to him. Got him fixated on the freaks and geeks. He fell in love with them, along with the variety acts, the animal shows, the acrobats, ventriloquists, melodramas, the panoramas, the living statuary. While working for Barnum, Gus told Bloom, Sam left behind his family, stopped attending shul, and took up running a numbers and booking racket, to make enough money to rent a small theater. When he secured a lease, he filled the small venue with lewd acts and minstrel shows, worked the same crowds everyone else did, the rowdies and the riffraff, the fancy men, the poor hardworking, hard-drinking bastards who needed to step out on their families at night. The small theater filled up every night—and while Sam might not have conducted himself in the most upright fashion, while he wasn't the most pleasant of human beings to pass the time with, the man knew his business. And he knew people. He could see right into them, what they wanted, what they needed—and with the profits he made from that small theater, he was in a position to rent a bigger theater, and after some time, Sam had enough dough to buy his own place. For a long time, he continued to work the East Side and the Bowery Boys, and one night he saw something that changed him. One night he saw one of his patrons assault a young, innocent girl in the most unspeakable manner, right there, in one of the balcony seats of his theater, and that night the dybbuk loosened its hold on him, and, like he'd just woken up from a nightmare, he had a vision of something altogether new. He started to imagine the money he could make by putting on a clean front and going broader, widening the appeal of his acts, making it so women and children didn't feel scared when walking out for a night of entertainment. They had their own troubles, their own concerns to forget, Sam had said to Gus when the idea struck him, and he took it upon himself to open a place uptown, right on the edge of privilege, at the doorstep of the upright native borns, and he got rid of the drink in the theaters, cleaned up the acts, brought in real, trained talent and mixed it up with the song of the street, clad the working girls in respectable garments, brought in a Henry Higgins to teach them some manners, and after a while found himself growing respectable, *a bridge builder*, some reporter said of him. And, Gus suspected, he would have continued bettering himself, but, he said after taking a pause, it wasn't too long after he'd thrown off the malevolent spirit, there was that business with your mother and Leah. Leah, she was the only woman Sam ever really loved. He loved her more than himself. And, well, that changed Sam, reacquainted him with his former scruples, and he began to see in what ways his business would benefit from pressing Jacob, by taking from him what he believed he needed. And, like I said, he knew his business, and it turned out his business benefited. He could always see what was next, Sam, always found the means to push what was new into the world, and for the worse, I think, he bred his ambition into Simon, poisoned him with the dybbuk's aspirations. And now Simon sees this place as his territory to conquer. To make of it what Sam made in the East, only bigger, a great deal bigger. His own empire, said Gus. With his enemies at the gate and all the rest that accompanies a big head. But you rest easy, kid. The big man patted the shotgun with his hand. I ain't gonna let nothing happen. And Bloom believed him. The big man gazed into the distance and looked off in the direction of Mount Terminus's peak for a long while. When he turned back to Bloom, he said, I could take you out there sometime if you like.

Where's that, Gus?

To the lake. On the High Holidays. To pray and fast. Maybe the three of us can go, all together.

I'd like that.

If you ask me, Simon could stand to find some solace. He could use a day of rest and peace, to reflect, be written into the Book of Life. If you can believe it, Gus said in the same manner he sniffed at the flowers in the gardens, I've been looking after your brother since he's in diapers. Long enough to know exactly what kind of fronts he puts on. Simon's not like Sam. He's got all the makings of a good man. But there's always some obstacle in his way, always some new affair twisting away at what lives in his heart. He doesn't know how to slow down long enough to enjoy what he's got. He *thinks* he's like Sam, thinks he's gotta make himself bigger than he is, that he's gotta be larger than life generally allows, but . . . Gus humphed through his cavernous nostrils and let out a sigh that sounded like a small laugh, I'm getting too slow and old to keep up with the size of him. You, Joseph, you can teach him a thing or two about what it is to be a man. A human being. He unconsciously patted the barrels of his gun, and when he did, his stomach rumbled through the sedan's interior.

You're hungry, Gus.

Gus looked to his wide midsection with some amazement at the sound it produced. I'm hardly at risk of fading away.

Never mind that. I'll send Meralda out with some food.

You shouldn't trouble yourself.

It's no trouble at all. Bloom opened the car door and returned to the gate, where he met Roya, and the two of them walked back up the drive, and when he found Meralda, he told her where Gus was and what he was doing. She would gather together a picnic for him, she said, and carry it out when it was ready.

><

Every night after this night, Bloom noticed Meralda left the kitchen earlier than she normally would after dinner. When she didn't return, he went out to check on her, and found her sitting in Gus's company. A short duration of time the first week, longer the second week, and by the time the three weeks had lapsed, she sat with him well after Bloom had fallen asleep in his bed.

><

On the twenty-first day of his brother's absence, Bloom stood in the company of his birds, his telescope pointed down the long stretch of road leading to the sea. He waited. And waited. And waited. And while he waited he searched for unique markings on each of his lovebirds, drew those with the most recognizable features into a book, and recorded their names. Three females he named Scheherazade, Desdemona, and Beatrice. Three males he named Bergerac, Roderick, and Candide. Did the ship skirt the coast of Tierra del Fuego? he asked Desdemona. Did it navigate the arctic waters around Cape Horn? he asked Candide. He returned to the telescope every few minutes to search the line that separated land from sea at the end of the port road, and a little before noon, a plume of dust no bigger than a granule of sand appeared at the edge of the basin, and at just half past noon he could see charging ahead of the burgeoning cloud the lead truck of the approaching convoy. As that truck grew larger in dimension within the telescope's frame, the tower's pavilion was overtaken by the same silence Bloom heard the day Simon arrived on Mount Terminus in his roadster. The calls and song sounding from the aviary silenced. The frenetic motion stilled. And a moment later, he heard echoing through the canyon pass below, a beehive of engines. He looked again into the viewfinder of his telescope to see what progress the trucks had made, and when he saw they remained some distance away from the start of the mountain road, he turned the aperture down onto the farthest turn visible to him, and there caught speeding in and out of frame three trucks whose beds were loaded with men. He turned to the next visible bend in the road and a few moments later they again moved in and out of his field of vision. And when they reached the final curve before the turnoff to the plateau, two of the trucks pulled over on either side of the pavement and one parked lengthwise across it. The beds of the trucks now emptied and Bloom could see step out into the sun no less than two dozen men, many of them dressed in overalls, every last one of them holding the barrels of a shotgun across his chest, some wore rifles slung across their backs, others holstered pistols on their waists. They congregated in small groups. Lit cigarettes. Smoked. Paced. Didn't talk. These weren't the faces of the conquistadors he knew so well from Salazar's prints, but like them they wore an expression resembling a religious conviction. The squint eye and pursed lip of piety and righteous intent. There was something about the clarity of their bearing that began to fill Bloom with dread. It was the alignment of faith and duty—the absolute presence of a visible motive—that distressed him.

He turned to Elijah and said, Some horrible thing is about to happen. To which Elijah responded, Open the door and we shall see. Bloom returned to the scope and watched on. The mob continued to pace without words shared between them, and then, some ten minutes later, the collective of birds again grew silent. Bloom searched the visible turns of the switchback and eventually saw a black sedan slowly making its way up the grade. Upon hearing the approaching vehicle, the rabble bunched together at the center of the road in a disorderly fashion, and when the sedan arrived, they surrounded it in such a way Bloom couldn't see the face behind the windshield. He prayed it wasn't Stern. Or Gus. Not even Gus was a match for this army of men. A man whose face was cast in shadow by the brim of a cowboy hat, presumably their leader, exchanged a few words with the driver, then a few words more, and in the next instant, this same man pulled open the car door and, the next thing Bloom knew, the driver—as if he had been swallowed by a mythic beast—disappeared into the scrum of bodies. Bloom watched the butts of shotguns and fists rise into the air, and then silent blows fell, one after the next. They silently pounded, and pounded, and, no doubt, they would have continued their assault had they not heard the rumble of trucks echo through the pass. Like Bloom's birds, their frenzy calmed. They abandoned the body on the roadside, left it there, facedown, unmoving. And again, they waited in silence, this time, their guns raised, their hands shaking from the aftermath of the violence, with thoughts of the impending violence. Those farmers who were still smoking flicked what remained of their cigarettes to the pavement and stood fixed when the lead truck rolled up before them and came to a stop.

Bloom trained his telescope on the cab, and he was able to see through the glare of the glass, Gus behind the wheel, and beside him on the passenger seat, Simon, his eyes looking cold and hard at the sight of the men, at the body laid out on the road's shoulder. Bloom's brother casually extended his arm out the window, at which point the young Rosenbloom noticed Simon's lips curl up one side of his face; a smirk transformed into a grin as he swung his arm down and smacked the side of the door several times. Hard enough, Bloom could hear the thud from this distance. The truck began to rock in such a way it looked as if it were to lurch forward, and then up along its sides, a number of armed men appeared, each and every one of them pointing a shotgun in the direction of those men aiming shotguns at them.

Simon allowed the tension to build for a few moments longer, allowed the men on the road to size one another up, before he stepped out onto the macadam in his gleaming white suit and tie, and when he did, Bloom watched his brother step up to the mob. He stared down as many of them in the eyes as he could. He then waited. The same man who pulled the driver from his car now stepped forward, and Simon, without a moment's hesitation, matched his step. For a long time they said nothing to each other so far as Bloom could see.

He could then see Simon's lips move. Nothing else. Only his lips. His face, otherwise, was stone. He showed no fear. No concern for the menacing figures before him. He pointed to the man on the side of the road and then made a brief speech. Another heavy silence passed. And then the farmer had his say, during which time Simon didn't so much as blink. He held his ground. And when the farmer had said his piece, he paused for a moment. Observed Simon's determined indifference, then gestured with the brim of his hat to a man standing behind him. The man he had appointed for the job strolled over to the truck blocking the road, climbed into the cab, and cleared the way. Simon didn't move. He stood in clear view of the farmer—in defiance of him—for what felt to Bloom like a very long time. He then turned his back on the mob and rejoined Gus in the truck. Two men lifted the beaten man from the roadside and sat him upright next to Simon, then remained on the road with their guns drawn until the convoy continued on its journey, and when it had, the farmers departed. They returned to their vehicles, started their engines, and motored away in the reverse order in which they had arrived. Bloom didn't move. He could hardly breathe. He stood frozen until the road was clear, and when it was, when Simon's men had continued their journey to the plateau on foot, he went to Elijah's cage and said, Thank God.

My God is Yahweh, squawked Elijah. My God is Yahweh.

To which Bloom said, Amen.

><

When he regained his composure, the young Rosenbloom descended the staircase of the tower and made his way to the stand of eucalyptus. He thought he should go down and greet Simon, but, after having witnessed what his brother had done on the road, he was reluctant to do so. There was something about Simon's doggedness he found unsettling and he grew wary of being in his company. He instead watched as the trucks lined up on the plateau road to meet Gus at the warehouse loading dock. Gus stood there with a clipboard and pen in hand. In his calm, quiet manner, with his pronounced nose, he pointed the laborers in various directions as they hauled cargo past him. When a truck was emptied, the vehicle moved ahead to the cul-de-sac where it turned around and motored off onto the mountain road. Moving past Gus was lumber and hardware, spools of cable, steel rails, dollies, a crane, a multitudinous variety of furniture and lintels, windowpanes, mirrors, signs, lamps and lanterns, ceramics and statuary, all forms of lighting equipment, framed artwork, pianos small and large, orchestral instruments, music stands, garment racks and more garment racks, sewing machines, bolts of fabric, rolls upon rolls of rugs, pyramids of cases, trunks, and crates, and a great many items to which Bloom couldn't give names. He observed for several hours what equipment and materials entered the warehouse, and as he looked at the procession of trucks, the unloading, the storing, he grew increasingly eager to find out the fate of the man who had been so brutally beaten on the roadside. For the better part of the afternoon, however, the man was nowhere to be seen. Nor, for that matter, was Simon. It wasn't until near the wane of day, when the lead truck of the convoy had returned with its second load, that Simon emerged from the turreted house at the center of the cul-de-sac. He walked to Gus's side, looked over what progress had been made, nodded his approval, then pulled Gus away. They strolled to the house Simon had just exited. Gus now entered and after only a moment hobbled out with the broken man cradled in his arms. Gus, who didn't appear overly taxed by the weight of the beaten man, trudged up the incline to the edge of the estate. When he finished his journey uphill, and he and the man were standing before Bloom on a patch of dappled earth, the young Rosenbloom could clearly see the entire left side of the man's face had been beaten purple. His right eye had ballooned shut, the lid so pregnant with blood Bloom could see capillaries worm over its surface. Near the corner of his mouth swelled a similar, but lesser contusion. Here his lip had been gashed, and the blood spilled from it had dried in streaks down the curly hairs of his beard. On the less injured side of his face, he appeared to be a man of mismatched features. He possessed a prominent nose and a recessed chin, an eye too small for its orbit and a full cheek that would one day soon fall over the line of his jaw. Atop his head was an unkempt mane that flared up about his ears and on either side of a widow's peak.

This is Mr. Dershowitz, said Gus. He keeps our books.

Bloom said with sincere concern, How do you do, Mr. Dershowitz?

As you can see, said Dershowitz out of the less injured side of his mouth, not very well. Not well at all. His good eye moved between Gus and Bloom then turned in the direction of the villa.

He needs a bed, said Gus. The truck with the mattresses hasn't arrived yet.

Bloom said, Why don't you take him to one of the cottages and I'll fetch some ice.

As Gus continued to carry Mr. Dershowitz's weight along the path leading to the courtyard, Bloom ran to the kitchen, where he chipped away shards of ice from the block in the icebox, bundled them into a wet cloth, and carried them outside. In the cottage nearest the studio, he found Gus had removed Mr. Dershowitz's jacket and vest, his shoes and socks, and was now propping up his head on a pillow.

Dershowitz thanked Bloom for the compress and pressed it first to his lip, then arranged it so it rested on his eye. Much better, he said. Much, much better. He now started laughing. I'm accustomed to men finding me a little unpleasant, but never have they exercised their displeasure with me quite like this. I *warned* your brother something of this nature would happen, you know. Only I never expected I would be the victim of his folly. Again he laughed, this time taking hold of his ribs. *Oy!* he groaned. Then: Just my luck I should arrive at the precise moment.

I'm very sorry, said Bloom.

Mr. Dershowitz dismissed Bloom's concern with a *feh* and a wave of the hand. Had it not been me, someone else would have been made to suffer. To ask, *Why me?* It's not worth the breath in my lungs. They were here to menace. To send a message. Here I am: *the message.* Mr. Levy there, he knows the way of the world. He'll tell you the same: the unexpected is always unexpected. And generally unwelcome.

Gus shrugged in agreement.

Dershowitz, whose open eye was beginning to behave strangely, repeated: I *warned* your brother. In a voice now somewhat adrift, he added, There's little profit in animosity, I told him. It didn't take a genius to imagine in what ways the animus would grow. You remember that, he said, jutting a finger at Bloom. The motion was abrupt and caused him to groan. This time with a breathy *ach* rather than an *oy*.

We should send for a doctor, Bloom said to Gus.

Simon already phoned for one. He should be here presently.

Bloom then turned to Mr. Dershowitz, who said with a return of his senses, It'll take more than a mob of *faygala* farm boys to kill off this old Jew. I'll be all right, young Rosenbloom. You wait and see.

I'm going to ask my cook to sit with you until the doctor arrives. She'll have a better idea as to what to do for you.

You're a fine young man.

I'll send her in with some hot water. Should you want her to clean your wounds.

If she isn't too troubled by my appearance, who am I to say no to the soft touch of a *shayner maidel*.

Bloom patted Mr. Dershowitz's hand and went in search of Meralda.

>←

By the time he and Meralda had prepared the hot water and had chipped away a bucketful of ice, the doctor had arrived. He was a portly, red-eyed man wearing a checkered vest and a trilby too small for his wide face. Bloom escorted him and Meralda to the cottage, where Gus continued to sit at Mr. Dershowitz's side. Bloom set the basin of hot water on the bedside table, and to make room in the cramped cottage, he stepped outside. He watched from the window as the doctor and his cook began the work of cleaning the blood from Mr. Dershowitz's wounds. This, however, he decided he needn't see. This whole ordeal had shaken Bloom more than he realized. He took a seat at the edge of the reflecting pool to calm himself. He watched on the surface of its water the sky turn from crimson to violet to black. In it he saw the moon crest over the peak of the villa's roof, and with the moon's arrival the still water of the pool phosphoresced. A silver sheen brightened the air, hung there, as would a vapor. It reflected from the spines of cacti planted on the terraced hill rising to the studio; it mixed with the mist of electric light emanating from the plateau.

He felt at this time Roya's eyes on him. Somewhere. Nearby. He could sense her presence silently maneuvering through the ghostly light. But when he turned to search the courtyard for her, he saw instead Gus's familiar figure, aglow, in motion, moving toward him. When the big man arrived at his side, he rested a heavy hand on Bloom's shoulder and said, He won't be very pretty to look at for a while, but he should be all right. The doctor, Gus told him, recommended he not be moved. Mr. Dershowitz's head had been concussed and he had a broken rib, maybe two, maybe three. Gus and Meralda would sit with him through the night should delirium or a fever take him, in which case they would need to drive Mr. Dershowitz to the hospital in town. Gus asked Bloom if he would please go down onto the lot and tell his brother what he had just told him, and Bloom said he would do it right away. He followed Gus as far as the cottage and continued on through the pergola to the stand of eucalyptus, and there he discovered, on the very boulder where his father had sat the first time he gazed upon Simon as a grown man, his brother. Simon was looking down on what remained of the returned convoy. More props were being hauled into the warehouse, and at the end of the cul-de-sac he could see men carrying furniture and trunks into the strange assortment of dwellings. When Simon saw Bloom standing beside him, the young Rosenbloom delivered Gus's message about Mr. Dershowitz, and Simon, upon hearing it, appeared relieved. That is welcome news, he said. He patted the rock with his hand and Bloom took a seat beside him. He asked if Bloom had been in the tower this afternoon, and Bloom told him he had done as Simon said he should do the last time they were together.

So, said his brother, you saw it all, then.

Yes, said Bloom.

They continued to watch and listen to the activity on the plateau for some time. Breaking the silence, Simon turned to Bloom and said, Gus, I understand, explained the points of contention.

To this, Bloom nodded.

Then you know why those men were here.

Bloom nodded again.

Good, said Simon, nodding along with Bloom. Good. Again he fell quiet for a moment. Had I thought anyone would arrive ahead of us . . . I only learned early this morning there would be trouble, you see, and Hal wasn't meant to be here until later in the week.

If it helps, said Bloom, when we spoke, Mr. Dershowitz sounded accepting, perhaps even a little fatalistic, about what's happened to him.

That's merely the way Hal is disposed. Hal Dershowitz, Simon explained, had been something of an uncle to him; the unwelcome uncle who on festive occasions spoke of nothing but death and disease and suffering. He had looked after Sam's books since before Simon could remember, and now he was looking after his, and, as he had meddled in Sam's affairs—largely to Sam's benefit—he now meddled in Simon's, and almost always landed on the right side of an argument. He warned me of the challenges we would face in the north, said Simon, and he cautioned me against the venture. I would be better served, he advised me, to leave well enough alone. Why, he asked as he extended an arm to the plateau, can't I be satisfied with this? When I made the deal with the water authority, he called it my great folly, my grand misadventure. Perhaps he's right? Simon looked to Bloom for his response, but at that moment a strong gust of wind blew at Bloom's and Simon's backs, rushed through the spindling limbs overhead. Bloom looked away from his brother and turned to the villa to face the onrush. He saw the moon had lifted up in its entirety over the line of the roof, its light bright enough now to cast shadows. On the periphery of his vision, he saw something move within the tower's pavilion, and when he focused on the archway, he saw at its center Roya's silhouette. As if to embrace the oncoming wind, she spread out both her arms, and when she stretched them to their full length, two small birds darted out of her fists into the argent haze. They arced about the moon's circumference and met at its center, where they crossed paths and fluttered out of sight. When Bloom turned back, he found Simon had eased himself off the boulder and was walking downhill in the direction of an approaching truck, his white suit turning black in the night.

PART III

AFFINITY

H al Dershowitz convalesced for the better part of three weeks in a netherworld. Meralda roused him from bed every morning and helped him to a chaise in the courtyard, where she propped his injured head on a pillow and served him a fulvous concoction of iced lemonade and tincture of laudanum. Thereafter, he slipped in and out of consciousness throughout the day, possessing in his delirium little more than the ability to whisper short phrases and mumble gibberish under his breath. Although he wouldn't be able to follow the narrative, Bloom, thinking Mr. Dershowitz might take comfort in hearing a friendly voice, read to him from the back pages of *Little Dorrit*. As a man who had dedicated his life to the manipulation of money, he thought, perhaps he would take some pleasure in hearing under the haze of his laudanum twilight the ways in which hidden and corrupt capital twisted the lives of the Clennams, the Dorrits, the entire city of London. In a few instances while Bloom read of Mr. Merdle's unscrupulous schemes, Mr. Dershowitz briefly emerged from his haze and mistook Jacob Rosenbloom's younger son for the elder. With an arm struggling to lift itself, speaking in a voice that sounded from a nightmare, he said Simon's name, and repeated it over and over until Bloom drew near. The old man crept his fingers up the sleeve of Bloom's shirt to his collar, and using the weight of his arm, dragged the whorl of his ear to his lips, and in a barely audible rasp, he said, *Your appetites will devour us.* On another occasion when Bloom read aloud a section concerning this same character, he said in the same haunting wisp, *Into the abyss you'll plunge us all.* On the final occasion, at the moment of the story when Mr. Merdle was found a suicide in the city baths, he said, *God* will *punish you*. After each of these episodes, Dershowitz quickly slipped back into the dark mists, and remained there. Before sunsets, Meralda escorted him to his bed and fed him some broth, a few morsels of bread and cheese, followed by an evening libation significantly stronger than the one he drank in the morning. In his docile state, the doctor posited, the wounds inflicted upon the bookkeeper healed more rapidly than they would have otherwise—the injuries to his face and his ribs, once plump and plum, deflated, and were reconstituted to the bruised complexion of an overripe peach. Meralda, on the doctor's orders, stopped administering Mr. Dershowitz's morning and evening cocktails, and, after several days of sobriety, he was soon able to walk from the cottage to the chaise on his own steam. His posture gradually straightened, and no longer did he hunch and clutch at his side. The pain that had been masked by the morphine he now expressed in the form of light-hearted jeremiads about dull aches and stiffness, in the same manner a browbeaten man might grumble about his dissatisfied wife; and when his head had cleared and he faced Bloom, he was able to recall who he was, and for his kindness and compassion, he expressed his gratitude. When Bloom asked him if he had any recollection of what had transpired over the course of the last several weeks, Mr. Dershowitz remembered nothing other than the soft touch of the *shayner maidel* who fed him his meals and led him to and from the chaise in the courtyard. But he did say he had many strange and disturbing dreams about the numerous ways Simon had brought about the end of days.

⇥⇤

What Hal Dershowitz had seen of Simon's character in his delirium, Bloom, at times, sensed as well, but in those instances when doubts about his brother's character surfaced to consciousness, he turned away from them until they vaporized into afterthoughts. Even when on the rare occasion he saw fissures crack the veneer of Simon's façade, when he recognized the presence of the dybbuk residing within him, Bloom felt intensely devoted to Simon, and Simon, in turn, appeared to be equally devoted to Bloom. He considered himself to be Bloom's guardian, accountable for his well-being, and he did everything in his power to make certain he was properly looked after. Although he didn't have the time in his schedule to play this role himself, he did assign Bloom his proxies, most notably, Gus, who moved onto the estate, into one of the cottages off the courtyard, to tend to the grounds and the gardens, to wire the villa for electricity and telephone service, to keep Bloom company during his meals, to rouse him out of bed in the mornings, to deliver him to work. On the studio lot, Simon surrounded Bloom with his most reliable people and made it clear to them they were being charged with the responsibility of educating his younger brother. He expected them to attend to their innocent protégé with the same compassion and steadfastness a parent would his or her own child, to shield him from petty squabbles and jealousies, gossip and rumors, and fix Bloom's focus on his craft. Of course, this was hardly a necessary precaution, as Bloom had been set apart from the concerns of society for so long his seclusion had immunized him from the influence of trivial discord. He wasn't any less human than the others—he certainly wasn't above curiosity and intrigue—he was simply unaccustomed to small talk, whether it was composed of gibes or taunts, flattery or fawning. You just go better yourself, Gus told him, without self-pity or complaint. Don't show off how clever you are. Do your work, keep to yourself, and you'll earn their respect. This was all Bloom wanted. To prove his efforts were equivalent to that of his brother's goodwill and his mentors' attentions, to do his job well enough so that he might attract the admiration of Elias Gottlieb.

✵

Not long after Hal Dershowitz departed the estate, Gus awakened Bloom early one morning and escorted him to the plateau. They passed a short convoy of trucks motoring out to the mountain pass.

One was filled with a selection of perfectly ironed cowboys and a gloomy band of snaggle-haired banditos, the next harnessed a Jackass Mail stagecoach, a third had, lashed to its bed, cameras and lighting equipment. Simon had purchased a ranch in the valley to film their Westerns, Gus told him. The trucks were bound for a ghost town they had built on the property. When the roar and grind of the engines drifted off, they were met by a ragtime two-step sounding from the horn of a Victrola set atop a table on Simon's porch. Beside the iron bellflower, Bloom's brother stood conducting the morning orchestration of bodies about the lot. In an open field beyond the dwellings, a circus big top was being erected. There Bloom noticed at the field's edge a chained baby elephant sitting on its haunches. Beside it, several cages on wheels, one containing a screeching chimpanzee dressed in a bridal gown, in another an ostrich garbed in a tuxedo and tiny top hat. Carpenters and set dressers were at work transforming the respective outdoor stages into a saloon, a Victorian parlor, a hospital room, a lady's boudoir, an Arabian tent, the deck of a ship, an igloo, a hall of mirrors, a gypsy's lair. A makeshift sign reading CASTING OFFICE had been posted outside one of the cottages, and there stood a long line comprised of sweating swabbies; overalled men with straw hats; men dressed in black suits and stovepipe hats; musclemen; clowns; grand dames in low-cut gowns; nurses; doctors; nuns; ballerinas; jugglers; acrobats; midget sword swallowers; sheiks; Eskimos; women draped in colorful tapestry. Bloom wanted a closer look at the costumed animals, but as he started wandering to the field, Gus grabbed hold of him by the collar and pulled him away in the opposite direction. Bloom asked Gus, as he was redirected toward the warehouse entrance nearest the estate, if he would take him to watch Gottlieb at work sometime.

No.

Why not?

Gottlieb worked only on closed sets. Behind sheets of muslin. To watch him at work required an invitation.

And how do I receive one?

For that, you do this. Bloom's gargantuan guardian walked him up to the second floor, where, under the enormous skylight of Stage 3, he was introduced to the principal set builder, Percy Evans, a thick man with a thin, tight mouth. And as Gus had done the day he delivered him to the studio to meet the girl with the long braid, he pushed him off, and sent him on his way. Together Bloom and Mr. Evans started construction of what would become a laboratory in which the mad scientist, Professor Kronos, would invent a formula for *The Primal Pill*. They cut and finished long planks of wood, painted them black, lacquered them into a glossy sheen, assembled them into countertops. On their surface, he and the property master, Hershel Verbinsky, whose oily head secreted a camphor-like odor, labored into the night, arranging a complex puzzle of connecting test tubes, beakers, and Bunsen burners. Bloom rejoined Mr. Evans the following morning and helped him raise gray walls against which Professor Kronos's lab coat would stand in contrast. On the walls, they hung cabinets, a periodic table, a piece of slate, arranged bookshelves he and the pungent Mr. Verbinsky would fill with dummy tomes—*The Occult*; *Black Magic*; *Witchcraft*; *Curses of the Underworld*. They displayed strange totems and otherworldly wood carvings of mythical therianthropes, a taxidermy lemur's head topped with a pince-nez, staffs and trinkets, an assortment of tribal masks.

He and the rather mannish scenic artist, Hannah Edelstein, mapped onto the piece of slate an elaborate chemical formula for elements unknown to science: permiam, therbium, delirium; under her direction, they went on to paint pastoral backdrops to be inset into the laboratory windows, which would reveal in the distance the God-fearing town of Integrity. When they had finished the lab, Bloom moved on to the plateau, and there joined a loud and gregarious gaggle of carpenters who assembled on either side of the road's paving stones the town façades.

Before the end of the third week, a Main Street on which townspeople would fall victim to Kronos's diabolical plot had risen. A town hall was constructed, a church with a white steeple, a dress shop, a general store, a telegraph office, a schoolhouse, and stretched across the end of the cul-de-sac was a blank matte on which Bloom would assist Miss Edelstein in painting the reverse perspective of the lab windows—the extension of Main Street; beyond it, rolling hills; at the top, a cluster of columned buildings comprising the professor's bucolic campus home.

With all this in place, Simon, who continued to conduct the lot's activity from his porch to the syncopation of Scott Joplin and Eubie Blake, sent Bloom to Leonard Hertz, the lighting technician, a heavy smoker of a sweet-smelling herb Gus called *drago*, about which, he said, Should he offer you any, you politely decline. Bloom would help Mr. Hertz suspend arc lights from battens running under a scrim stretched below the studio's skylight. They angled the parabolas in such a way that the mad professor's figure would cast long shadows in every direction he turned. They likewise wheeled one of the cranes onto the road outside and equipped it with a reflector. Under it, Bloom stood in for the innocent passersby who, when they saw the lunatic Kronos approach, were meant to look up and appeal to God for help, at which point their faces would brighten. They were meant to bask in the glow for a moment, and then Hertz, in his enervated manner, which was often punctuated with a random and involuntary *Heh*, explained he would slowly pull the reflector away, and with it remove whatever hope the subject had for an act of divine intervention.

The director, Murray Abrams, an intelligent-looking figure who wore a pencil mustache and a powder-blue linen suit whose material billowed over his oxfords like a sail taking the wind, described to Bloom during a rehearsal in what manner Kronos would scatter his primal pills at the townspeople's feet, how when the tablets made contact with the ground they—with flashes of gunpowder—would vaporize upon contact, and in an instant, men, women, and children would become possessed with the primal spirit. To capture this transmutation, Claude Strauss, the makeup artist, showed Bloom how he would shed the constraints of Integrity's prim character: the women's hair, once pulled back, would miraculously unravel by way of a slipknot. He would arrange their locks to hang over the shoulder and brush against the breast, darken the orbits of their eyes with pitch. To the men, he would do the same—tease their hair into demonic tufts, and go so far as to strip them down to their bare chests. The choreographer, Levi Sexton, demonstrated for him the frenzied dance he'd scored to a tribal drumbeat: the women would spin cartwheels and snake along the ground. The men would whirl like dervishes, throw one another up into feats of aerial acrobatics, and drag the women across the road by the hair. When their primitive energy was spent, when they regained control of themselves, when their sense of propriety returned, the cameraman, Stephan Harlow, would wheel up on a dolly, to close in on several of the actors' faces, one at a time, so the audience could see in their expressions the shame they felt for what they had done while under the influence of Kronos's drug, and without consulting one another with words, they would reflect on their undoing. At that moment the town's reverend would lift his head and look up at one of his parishioners, Abrams said, and one by one, they would stand as a congregation and turn to the hills, gather into a mob, and march off in the direction of the professor's lab. Once there, they would pull out the professor by his beard, bind him in ropes, and drag him back to town; in the middle of Integrity's Main Street they would push him atop a mountain of wood and bind him to a stake, at which time a woman shaking a Bible in one hand and a torch in the other would set the heaping pyre, and Dr. Kronos, ablaze. The men would then comb back their hair and button up their shirts. The women would twist their manes into tight buns and right their skirts. And off they would walk, turning their backs on the black smoke lifting into Integrity's clear sky.

They took fifteen days to film *The Primal Pill* and a day to break down the sets they had spent five weeks building. Simon sent Bloom next into the lab, where he sat in the dark with the technician, Max Heinrich, and listened to the reels wind through the chemical baths; he watched Max work through the toilsome process of making contact prints—the positives cast from the negatives, which, when complete, they walked to the editor, Constance Grey, and Bloom, along with six young women, catalogued scenes and hung them by their perforations in orderly rows so the senior Miss Grey could glue together the sequence provided to her by Mr. Abrams. When all was done, and after further prints were made, Bloom walked the final cut to his brother's home, where they sat in his offices on the ground floor, in a black velvet room reserved for screenings, and there, in the dark, they watched, and there, as he judged the first professional picture in which he had a hand in making, he reflected on the extraordinary effort, the time and resources put into each and every frame of film. And he had to wonder . . . He had come to occupy his time so completely with the disciplines of the studio's work, he no longer experienced the passing hours of the days and weeks as vacuous and endless in their movement; he no longer dwelled on the sun's position in the sky, on the smallest barometric changes in the weather, in the reflection of Roya's eyes staring back at him from the still water of the courtyard's pool. He exerted himself so thoroughly, he rarely, if ever, had a reserve of energy to utilize his imagination in the manner to which he was once accustomed. This didn't bother him. Not really. He had come to enjoy the novelty of living in service to others. He took satisfaction knowing his hands and his mind had become an extension of the kind and patient men and women undertaking the task of training him. But for what? For *this* picture? If each frame were a painting or a drawing, the content was sound—the images of the town, the actors who inhabited it, the painted backdrops—but there was something about the transitions from scene to scene, from cut to cut, that bothered him. The movements from one location to the next, from one actor to the other, appeared to him clumsily executed, lacking a fundamental logic, as if done with no awareness of how one form followed the next. Too little attention was paid to something as obvious as to how the direction a character's eyes looked at an opposing character with whom he or she was speaking. When one addressed the other, his eyes moved one way, the other's moved in the opposite direction, and it caused nothing short of a sensation of vertigo. He didn't understand why the props and paintings he, Miss Edelstein, and

Mr. Verbinsky created and placed in Kronos's laboratory, with such tedious care, hadn't been adequately observed by the camera. Why had they built an elaborate set and dressed it so fastidiously, if they weren't going to use its full affect to establish the professor's character? The camera's positioning, its location relative to its subjects, made for an inadequate frame through which to observe their movements. Nor was the camerawork nimble enough in its mobility, particularly when the ensemble of actors filled the screen. It would have been beneficial to have a second or third camera rolling at alternate positions to capture the strongest performances, to give Miss Grey the opportunity to cut between the crowd and the individual dancers. In the few instances Mr. Harlow did trail the movements of the actors, the lens was pulled too far back when it should have been close, close and tight when it should have been withdrawn. The quality of the light, the contrasts of dark to light were often inharmonious with respect to the tone of the story; too light when it should have been dark, too dark when it should have been light. It wasn't at all what Bloom had envisioned when he was quietly tending to his tasks. It wasn't at all what Murray Abrams described—nothing of what the gentlemanly figure claimed to live in his mind had been realized. Bloom couldn't help but think it a grave disappointment. Was it possible none of them really knew what they were doing? Were they merely making it up as they went along? While Bloom possessed the language to express to his brother precisely how Murray Abrams and the others had failed *The Primal Pill*, he wasn't yet confident enough to prescribe the techniques he would engineer to remedy it. He had an inkling, however, that he could do better. A great deal better. When he had this very thought, the lights in the viewing room turned on, and he saw that Simon had already turned to face him. Seeing what expression was on Bloom's face, he said with a laugh, I warned you. I did warn you. And now you see for yourself. You and I, dear brother, are young parents to a precocious infant no one quite knows how to handle. Patience, he advised. Have patience. Believe it or not, you have a thing or two more to learn before you embark on your own enterprise. And you certainly have more than a few things to learn before you embark on an adventure with Gottlieb.

→←

Except for the occasional evening meal they ate together and the brief moments they stole from their busy schedules, he and Simon remained in close proximity to each other, but largely lived parallel lives. If he seems distant, Gus told Bloom, don't take it personally. He rarely sleeps, and when he does, it's never restful. As you've seen for yourself, when he's at the studio, he never stops, and when he's finished on the lot, his attention is on the waterway, and when his attention is on the waterway, he never stops. Making it so he never stops.

In many regards Bloom and Simon's relationship began to resemble the one the young Rosenbloom maintained with Jacob, an arrangement, Bloom, at the outset, felt as disappointed in as he felt about the outcome of *The Primal Pill*, but he eventually came to find it strangely comforting, satisfying even; although their time together was limited, Bloom began to observe in their private moments—when Simon appeared to him the truest and most mild version of himself—something most unexpected: the familial qualities he had been searching for in those weeks they spent together before the others arrived. Perhaps because he was exhausted and at ease in Bloom's company, his brother began to unknowingly exhibit their father's manner, embody his idiosyncrasies, approximate the qualities with which Jacob exercised his ruling passions, and there was something about recognizing these traits within Simon that not only created a sense of continuity for Bloom, but also, to some extent, demystified the competing impulses of his brother's persona. Of course, Bloom told Gus, knowing how Simon felt about Jacob, he wouldn't presume Simon would want him to point out their commonalities.

No, said Gus, I wouldn't recommend it.

Bloom secretly took pleasure when these unmistakable similarities revealed themselves, when, for instance, not very long after Mr. Dershowitz departed the courtyard and the state of affairs on Mount Terminus had normalized, they met in Simon's parlor, in his white room where the furniture and the furnishings resembled his brother's attire—white settees and armchairs, white walls trimmed with white wainscoting, adorned with white filigree, white bookshelves, a white Pleyel grand—and Bloom asked Simon if the farmers' revolt had caused him any further problems, and in a demeanor that was nearly exact to Jacob's, in a display of gestures almost homologous to their father's, Simon contained within him whatever burdensome news he didn't wish to reach his brother's ears; in a pantomime Bloom knew well, Simon drew his hands together, stared at the young Rosenbloom as if he were making an apology, and finishing with a half-formed smile said, You needn't concern yourself with such things. That weight is mine to carry, and mine alone. The accuracy with which Simon reflected the departed Rosenbloom's bearing and diction to deflect Bloom's inquiry gave rise to a prickling of gooseflesh, as Bloom was convinced that Jacob Rosenbloom, however fleetingly, had been raised from the dead for the purpose of inhabiting his son's body.

In the months following, after the studio had gone into production, when the white walls of Simon's parlor had grown cluttered with colorful theatrical posters, productions in which Simon had played roles high and low—*Henry IV*; *Henry V*; *Hamlet*; *Trigorin*; *Gregor, the Straight Man*; *Hollis, the Holy Dunce*; *Favish, the Singing Philologist*; *Calamitous, the Acrobat*; *The Wunderkind, Harvey Plum, Whistler Extraordinaire*—Bloom recognized other reflexive behaviors his brother shared with their father—the way the two rested their chin on the heel of their palm when sitting in an armchair; the habit they both had of rubbing their thumb against their fingers when pausing in the middle of a sentence to search for a lost word or thought; forming the same slight pucker of the lips—as if awaiting a kiss—when they drew a glass above their chin, and Bloom, again and again, would be revisited by the uncanny sensation of déjà vu. It seemed at times, he told Gus, as if Simon had somehow studied his father in the way Bloom imagined an actor would mirror a subject he was to portray on stage.

And Gus said to Bloom, That would be impossible. They spent no more than a few minutes in each other's company. And that was that.

The similitude was never more apparent than the times Bloom watched Simon meticulously attend to the shrine he dedicated to the dead mother he had never known. In a room with thick white lintels framing the canyon road, the basin, the haze hanging at the edge of the sea, Leah, the identical image of Bloom's mother, hung on the walls as the ingénue Eloise, as Medea and Lady Macbeth and Scheherazade, as the subject of paintings and drawings and illustrated songs, blue renditions of *The Little Lost Child* and *After the Ball*, as buxom caricatures captured on cocktail napkins, as a distant figure on a stage enveloped in cigar smoke. Beneath the window's ledge, organized by composer, were shelves neatly stacked with sheet music, some of which, Simon told him, were tunes written for his mother by Joey Haden and Theo Metz, "A Hot Time in the Old Town" his favorite. Then there were the sheets from her childhood, her Bach and Brahms, Chopin and Mozart, her numerous versions of Berlioz's *Symphonie Fantastique*, which, Simon had learned, she devotedly read in silence, claiming to hear in the measures the strings of Berlioz's aching heart. In this same room, at its center, stood an enormous table on which rambled the topography of a raised relief map, Mount Terminus and the valley, the lake, the basin, the reservoir, the aqueduct, an expansion of the studio at the bottom of the switchback road. Like the elder Rosenbloom in his gardens, like the elder Rosenbloom with his shears in hand, Simon often lingered over the rise and fall of the mountains, in the depressions of the valley and the basin, circled it when he talked to Bloom, and, as a small child might, toyed with pins in the shapes of houses and trees, railcars and motorcars, and he would articulate what Bloom was thinking; he would joke about the great tyrants and master builders, about whom he said, All children of one sort or another. Children playing childish games with the lives of men. On the rare occasion Simon visited the estate for dinner, Bloom came to further appreciate the intimacy and continuity he experienced in his brother's company. On these nights, he always visited alone. After Bloom, Simon, and Gus completed their meal, they would sit in the parlor until their conversation lulled, when his brother's gaze would retreat inward as if drawn there by the forces of an interior gravity. On these nights, Bloom would observe the patterns of lines prematurely etching themselves onto the edges of Simon's mouth, across his brow, around the corners of his eyes, onto the otherwise smooth surface of his skin. This sight transported Bloom through time, to the past and the future simultaneously, through whose open doors he could see in what way the ridges and grooves on his elder brother's face would come to resemble the configuration forged on their father's. He easily imagined the direction in which the lines would lengthen their reach and grow more compressed. During these instances of attenuated temporalities, he envisioned his brother aged before his time, becoming the man for whom he felt nothing but bitterness and disappointment, the man whom he had been at odds with in his mind his entire life, and when bearing witness to the ways in which time inscribed its marks into his brother's skin and prematurely salted the roots of his hair, Bloom was often tempted, for the sake of his brother's amelioration, to take Simon by the hand and walk him up to the top of the tower, where, in the company of his birds, they could look out onto the simple wonders of the sky and the sea.

He wanted to teach his elder brother the art of slowing time, so he might ease his anxieties, and prolong his life, but, Bloom suspected, the fiery core of Simon's temperament, his dybbuk, would burn through such a whimsical gesture with the heat of a magician's flash paper. At the very least, he thought, he could insist Simon share his burdens with him, but every time Bloom made further inquiries into his affairs, when he expressed a sincere interest in knowing the particulars about the elaborate plans he'd envisioned for the land on either side of Mount Terminus and the barriers he faced trying to realize them, Simon quietly and patiently redirected his attention elsewhere.

✷

The passage of time at this early stage of Bloom's life could be measured as a collection of dots at the end of a pointillist's brush. Bloom, in his gray years, would be able to relive his rite of passage on the studio lot only as a toilsome series of nonsequential events, a nonlinear pastiche of window treatments and cornices, light riggings and costume changes, painted mattes, dark rooms, and strips of film. Had he ever chosen to revisit these days in any detail, to make any sensible order of them, he would have needed to consult a filmography of Mount Terminus Productions. He could, however, always recall this much: in the time it took for one to see from the peak of Mount Terminus the first glimmer of his brother's metal aqueduct reflect off the eastern range of the valley, in the time it took for his brother to fell the citrus groves across the basin and raze their stumps, in the time it took Gus to arrange and present hundreds of floral bouquets and bowls of fruit to his beloved Meralda, in the time it took Meralda to consent to a dinner out with Gus at the Pico House Hotel, Bloom had worked in various capacities on more than two dozen productions with the unremarkable but kindly Murray Abrams, and two other equally unexceptional but endearing directors, Ned Weiman and Bud Manning. He took part in the making of *The Counterfeiters*; *The Count of No Account*; *The Adventures of Mr. Troubles*; *The Amateur Hypnotist*; *The Hebrew Fugitive*; *The Daughter of the Gods*; *The Gambler*; *Colossus and His Dog*; *Neptune's Daughter*; *The Man Without a Name*; *Beyond Eden*; *A Cry in the Night*; *His Wife, the Acrobat*; *The Muse of the Mews*; and *Master and Man* as well as a multitude of other movies whose titles escaped Bloom not long after they were released to the chain of Freed Theaters, as they weren't worth remembering. In fact, not one of the productions on which Bloom spent his considerable efforts did he think as engaging as those pictures his brother had shown him the day he arrived with his projector and lifted Bloom into the sky on their aeronautical voyage. Not one could compare with the sophistication of Gottlieb's *The Magnetic Eye*, or, for that matter, the half dozen three-reel pictures—*Undine*; *Memento Mei*; *The Face in the Window*; *The Astronomer's Dream*; *A Good Little Devil*; *The Overcoat*—Gottlieb had made since Simon introduced Bloom to his work.

For almost three years, Bloom awoke every morning at sunrise and retired in a state of exhaustion long after the sun had set, and he had still caught only the briefest glimpses of Gottlieb from a distance, as Gottlieb generally kept to himself, except for the occasions he was on stage, when he became a shadow puppet behind the white panels of muslin his minions erected for him. For three years, Bloom waited patiently for Simon to determine that he was ready for Gottlieb's guidance. For three years, he didn't broach the subject. For three years, he waited patiently. But the youngster had become a man. He possessed bushels of black hair under his arms, a woolly nest of black pubis in which a finch could luxuriate with its mate, a face of thickening Semitic stubble that required a daily shave, a ripe musty smell he needed to scrub away after a long day's labor. As he neared his seventeenth birthday, Bloom, looking forlorn, sat across from Murray Abrams on the empty set of a romantic melodrama, *A Long Day in the Sun*.

Why so glum, Rosenbloom?

It's nothing.

You look like you've been fed some bad gefilte fish.

It's a case of disappointment, not indigestion.

Disappointment? In what? In whom?

In the fates? In myself? . . . In Elias Gottlieb, if truth be told.

Gottlieb?

Yes, Gottlieb. I thought I would have had the opportunity to work with him by now.

And this is the cause of your dyspepsia?

Yes.

Better you should consider yourself fortunate. Blessed!

Why?

It's *Gottlieb*! Even when he works *with* people, he works with no one other than Gottlieb, as there is no other human being on the face of the planet when Gottlieb is around, as there is no man more in love with Gottlieb than Gottlieb. *Gottlieb.* The man is a creature. A cretin. Too deformed in body and spirit to be loved by anyone *other than himself.* No one has ever told you this?

No.

And now that *I've* told you, you still sit there like a matzo ball?

What can I say, Mr. Abrams, I think he's brilliant.

Gottlieb? Uhch. He's unruly. Unpleasant. A grotesque. An unintended—unacceptable—consequence of your brother's generosity.

How is that?

Like the punch line of a joke that gets no laughs, he wandered out of the desert while the company was between locations, and your brother, he takes him in as one would a stray dog. *Gottlieb!* He claimed to be a painter and a photographer, considered himself some sort of Plato or Aristotle, or some such *mishegas.* All I know is this, Rosenbloom: he never spent a day of his life working in the theater, knows nothing of production decorum, of human decorum, he's unproductive, unprofitable, and your brother treats him like the fucking messiah. Trust me, Rosenbloom, you want nothing to do with this imp. Gottlieb's concern is only for Gottlieb. To Gottlieb, everyone else is a shadow in a cave.

I would settle for being a shadow in Gottlieb's cave, thought Bloom.

He didn't have the heart to say this to Mr. Abrams, who continued to say *Gottlieb* as if the man's name were a sneeze or a cough or a curse. If it's what you want, go on, I won't be offended. Get up off your ass and talk to your brother. Just stop with the moping and the acting like the love of your life was some Ophelia.

Mr. Abrams . . .

Go on! Go. You think I want to look at that long face any longer?

Bloom apologized to Murray Abrams and walked to his brother's house. He paced the planks of his porch for a half hour until Simon peeked his head out the front door. Aren't you going to come in?

No.

Would you like me to come out?

No.

Then what would have me do?

I would have you talk to Gottlieb.

I see.

I'm ready. I have long been ready.

From within the shadows of his foyer, Simon said, I know.

He knows, said Bloom.

Yes, I know. But it's slightly more complicated than that.

What is?

Everything. Gottlieb included. Stay right there. Simon disappeared for a moment, and when he reappeared, he stepped out under the overhang, took Bloom by the arm, and walked him to his roadster. He opened the passenger door and commanded Bloom to get in.

Where are we going?

You'll see when we get there.

That afternoon, they drove off the lot and down Mount Terminus's winding road. At the bottom of the switchback they turned in the direction of town, traversed the hills of the boulevard for a little under an hour, and not long after they passed the heights of the Griffith subdivision, the dusty clay haze of the city's asymmetrical grid came into view, the shallow channel of the river running through it, the lines of swaying palms and slow-moving trolleys drifting between them. A composite of architecture had risen up since Bloom first arrived at La Grande Station those many years ago. More and more buildings now towered over shaggy palm crowns, shouldered together along Broadway, stretched outward in the direction of Mount Terminus, and with them, people, hordes of them, had crowded there in greater numbers. They motored past old Sonora town, skirted around bicyclists, pushed through packs of pedestrians crossing the avenues, turned onto Broadway, and then into an alley behind a Freed Theater whose Moorish marquee read *Master and Man*. Simon parked beside the back door and told Bloom to follow him. From the bright light of the day, Simon delivered Bloom into a cool darkness choked with tobacco smoke, filled with the melodic vibration of organ music descending its scale to the lower octaves. They walked the length of a curtained corridor, at the end of which they arrived at an enormous screen flickering full of the snow-specked beards of Shelby Riordan and Hollis Grant playing the roles of Vasili Andreevich and his servant, Nikita. Master. Man. The picture was reaching its conclusion, when the two men were caught in a blizzard, unable to find the road to take them home. Bloom watched on as Vasili Andreevich, the selfish, self-important man of privilege, experienced an awakening, a revelation; he covered Nikita's body from the cold, sacrificing himself for his humble but loyal peasant; Vasili, in that instant, becoming noble for the first time in the story, not only in name but also in the manner he conducted himself, in the face of death. Bloom and his brother stood at the edge of the curtain, beside the image of snowy tundra Bloom and Hannah Edelstein had painted together, and as the organ music began to swoon in a dramatic thrum, Simon said, Don't look there. Look at the audience. Look at their faces. Bloom saw through the billows of smoke wet eyes glimmering in the flashes of light, women and men alike moved to tears by the unexpected change in Vasili's character.

They haven't just seen them, Simon whispered. They've become them. They don't see what you see. They don't see the flawed technique. They've forgotten where they are, who they are. They've forgotten those are grown men up there, pretending to be something they're not. They only see what *that* man is doing for that *other* man, and it wrenches them in their guts. They don't know it yet, or maybe they'll never know it, but they are the better for it. They'll walk out of the darkness into the light changed people. That, Joseph, is what you do for them. That, right there, is our business, to manufacture emotions, as quickly and as frequently as we can.

I know, said Bloom. It's just . . .

What?

I see a better way. I see Gottlieb's way. I see it, Bloom said, tapping a finger at his temple, up here, all the time.

Simon stepped close to Bloom and looked at him not unlike the way he had looked so intently at him when they first stood face to face on Mount Terminus, and he said, I know, I know you do.

Then why haven't you allowed me to work with Gottlieb?

I haven't disallowed it.

You haven't encouraged it. You haven't arranged it.

No, said Simon, I haven't. But not because I don't think you're ready.

Why, then?

It's simple mathematics, really. For every picture Gottlieb makes, Abrams makes four, Weiman makes six, Manning eight. And, well, you have been important to each of them. You've made them better at what they do, and I was afraid to give that up, because without them, the studio doesn't run, the theaters don't turn over pictures, and if we don't have pictures to attract new audiences, the waterway doesn't get built, the basin doesn't get developed, families don't buy homes, the rails to town don't get laid, the boulevard doesn't get paved, and we all continue living in a desert, possibly without a business, because, Joseph, I'm all in, well over my head, as deep as can be, I'm drowning in it.

I didn't know.

You didn't need to know. And you don't need to worry about it. Listen, if you want to work with Gottlieb, you should work with Gottlieb. I won't stand in your way. But you have to understand, it's a position you'll need to secure on your own. If I approach him and tell him what a gift you would be to him, he wouldn't trust a word of it. I can mention your interest, but I can't persuade him to do anything he doesn't want to do on his own. Nor would I try.

Why not?

Because Gottlieb is Gottlieb. A special case. His value to me is what I expect your value will be to me one day. He's an inventor, an innovator, in an art form that's at its inception. When he innovates, the members of his crew absorb his innovations—they are transformed by them. When he is great, those who work with him become marginally better. The influence spreads, and that influence, however invisible it might seem to those on the lot, will be the very thing that keeps our studio relevant and profitable in the future. Gottlieb knows this. And he knows I know this. He knows how much I need him, how much I admire him and his pictures. He knows I won't send him packing. So he takes great pleasure in refusing me anything and everything. If this is what you want, you'll need to find a way to do it on your own.

><

Once a week, for months, Bloom sent Gottlieb an invitation to join him for dinner on the estate. And for months, Gottlieb sent no response in return. Over dinner one evening, he told Simon about having extended these invitations, and Simon told Bloom he had a thought about how he might just attract the elusive Gottlieb to the estate. What's that? asked Bloom. Simon said he would share his idea in return for a small favor. Bloom asked his brother what he needed from him, and Simon said he had some business to discuss with Gerald Stern. He wondered if Bloom wouldn't mind writing a letter on his behalf, telling Stern he had Bloom's permission to contact him. When Bloom asked what was the matter he wanted to discuss with Stern, so he might mention it in his letter, Simon told him it wasn't his affair to speak of. An old friend was in some trouble. He promised to find her an attorney, someone well liked and respected around town. More than that, he wouldn't say, due to the sensitive nature of the woman's predicament. In exchange for his advice, Bloom told his brother he would write the letter that night and put it in the mailbag in the morning. And with that settled, Simon advised the following. Rather than implore Gottlieb to do what you want him to do, he said, entice him with something he'll find too irresistible to ignore.

Which would be what?

Well, I can tell you this: I've recently learned my friend Gottlieb has a deep fascination with historical artifacts. In particular? The type of objects you have on display in the library. That, my dear brother, is your way in.

>←

That evening, Bloom wrote to Stern on behalf of his brother, and after he had spent a sufficient amount of time deliberating how he would word his missive to Gottlieb, he wrote:

> Dear Mr. Gottlieb,
>   In the middle of the first century, a ship belonging to soda traders spread out along the Phoenician shore of the Belus River to prepare a meal of fish stew. They had no stones to support their cooking pots, so they placed lumps of soda from the ship under them, and when these became hot and fused with the sand on the beach, streams of an unknown, translucent liquid flowed . . . I have treasures to share with you. They are here for you to view at your convenience.
>   Yours truly,
>   Joseph Rosenbloom

As with his invitations, his letter received no written response. Some weeks later, however, at the most unexpected time of the morning, something entirely unexpected happened. While he was eating his breakfast in the tower's pavilion, an old nag carrying a man plodded through the front gates. When Bloom looked through his telescope and saw who it was, he asked Elijah, Is it possible? Is it him?

He looked again. It was him. It was most certainly him. Up the long drive rode the disheveled Elias Gottlieb, who, at that moment, was hunched over his seat in such a way he appeared to have taken ill. It soon became apparent to Bloom he was leaning over the old plug's neck to whisper something in its ear—words of encouragement, perhaps? This, followed by a loving rub of its hoary mane. Having seen the intimate moment shared between man and beast, the worry and anticipation Bloom felt about engaging this artist he so much admired, the man he had so long been waiting to meet, was to some extent eased. Here, he tried to convince himself, was a good man, a man from whom he had nothing to fear. Hardly the *creature* Mr. Abrams insisted he was.

Bloom was moved to call out and greet Mr. Gottlieb, but when he was about to speak, he reconsidered; he thought it more prudent to wait, to watch. Of course! He would allow Meralda the opportunity to greet their guest. She would, after all, enjoy escorting him inside. Take his hat and coat. Offer him some sweet morsel she had baked that morning. I don't want to appear too eager, he said to Elijah. Overly zealous is not attractive. And so Bloom looked on while the great Elias Gottlieb, the unequaled Elias Gottlieb, tied his horse to the hitching post beside the service entrance and made his way inside. Bloom, meanwhile, stood in the sanctuary of his aviary long enough for Meralda to have engaged their visitor with small talk, to offer him her small kindnesses. He then began his descent. He rounded the first turn in the stairwell and then the second, and when he reached the second-story landing, a horrible sound, a most unsettling and unwelcome sound, rose up to meet him. It was a moan, a bellowing, gut-wrenching moan, punctuated by a sharp jag of sobs. No, he said. No no no. Not now. Bloom halted and listened, hoped his loving cook would regain her composure . . . But no. The noise repeated and reverberated upward through the hollow shaft. Only after he came to the conclusion that the noise was not likely to stop did he proceed down, slowly, apprehensively, and when he eventually reached the bottom of the stairs, he peeked through the kitchen door to see Meralda's shaking shoulders. She stood before the butcher block with her back to the window, in front of which two skinned rabbits hung from strings by their necks, and, to Bloom's dismay, he discovered, clenched to her chest, was Mr. Gottlieb's bearded cheek. Bloom had never noticed when he caught distant glimpses of Gottlieb on the studio lot what a diminutive figure he was—he always appeared to him larger than life, but even when wearing a pair of lifts and standing with a straight back, as he did today, Bloom was surprised to see his face reach only as high as Meralda's bosom. Presently, one lens of his spectacles was buried in soft flesh, while the other magnified an amber eye, bemused in its expression, as if it were looking off to some distant horizon in search of a train. When Mr. Gottlieb's eye caught sight of Bloom arrested at the doorway, the tufted brow residing on his forehead lifted into an arch, at which point Mr. Gottlieb motioned with a hand for the young Rosenbloom to come closer, and when Bloom had done so, Gottlieb rolled his visible eye to the countertop, where Bloom saw what it was that had upset Meralda enough to grab hold of this perfect stranger in the same manner she had so often embraced him when he stood at Mr. Gottlieb's height. There before Meralda was a third hare, its belly sliced open, its viscera neatly piled beside its head, and at its feet lay a dozen miniature rabbits, each the size of a small toe.

In a voice muffled by the buffer of Meralda's chest, the little man said with a crushed smile, Come come. Come, do away with them so I might catch my breast—breath! for God's sake—so I might catch my breath. The hand that was consoling Meralda's flank, he now used to thumb Bloom over to the counter. Please, he said, she is mightier than she appears. His hand returned to comforting Meralda, who was lost to the world she joined when she disappeared from this one. Bloom edged closer to the counter, on which he could see more clearly how carefully she had washed the litter clean and how respectfully she had arranged it. Side by side each unfinished body lay next to its sibling, very calm, very serene, as if they had been prepared for burial by the hand of a skilled mortician.

Go on, said Gottlieb. Out of sight.

Bloom gathered the lifeless bodies into his shirtfront and, proceeding as if the small nuggets were still alive and could feel every movement he made, he walked out the service entrance onto the drive with his vision focused on the creases of the unborn eyes, on the folds of tender skin, expecting at any moment for the eyes to awaken, for the limbs to wriggle. His attention was so narrow in this instance, he was unaware of what stood in his path. He was so concentrated, he didn't see, obstructing his route to the front gardens, the ass of the old nag Gottlieb had ridden in on. With his eyes mesmerized by the sunlight illuminating the capillaries under the rabbits' vellum skin, he collided with the horse's backside with enough momentum that he spilled from his shirt the stillborn litter. It scattered onto the gravel, and as soon as it did, the horse rocked forward, and when it stepped back to right itself, it moved side to side as would an old drunk set off balance, and it proceeded to crush onto the stones with each clumsy step of its brittle hooves the entire brood, and at that moment, Bloom, who had been knocked on his back from the concussion against the nag's ass, heard from behind him a basso profundo guffaw, which, like Elias Gottlieb's eyebrows and nose, belonged to a fuller, taller, more prodigious man. The resonance struck Bloom as would a clap of thunder. So foreign and contagious was the sound of Gottlieb's laugh, Bloom felt forming deep inside him, in the deepest region of his innards, a laugh so sustaining when it reached the narrow passage of his throat, it hurt upon eruption from his body, and once it began he couldn't make it stop—it possessed him. For more time than could be considered dignified, he made a spectacle of himself. He rolled around on the gravel, pounding his fist on the small stones until he felt tears running down his cheeks.

><-

Your brother tells me you and I are kindred spirits, said Gottlieb as Bloom upturned some earth under the purple-hued shade of a bloomed jacaranda. He spoke with a pipe lodged in the corner of his mouth. The smoke departing his lips curdled into the kinks of his mustache and hung in the nostrils of a nose whose bulbous tip was shaped like the bent-over buttocks of a well-fed woman. He thinks you're *something*, Gottlieb said of Bloom's brother.

But you don't believe him.

And why should I? He's a typical *macher*. Like all *macher* money-men, if a man can earn him a dollar, this is enough to make him *something.*

He saw something in you once, didn't he?

He saw a helpless, desperate man wandering the desert without shoes and water. He thought I had an *intriguing face.* His words, said Gottlieb, *intriguing face.* He wanted to put it in a picture. As a destitute man dying of thirst in a wasteland, who was I to deny him the pleasure of putting this *intriguing face* of mine anywhere he desired?

Bloom looked up from his hole and at Mr. Gottlieb's features. There was a feral quality to Gottlieb's appearance. He was broad in the forehead, the bones of his cheeks protruded into a narrowing curve, and his chin—Bloom could see under the thick growth of his beard—formed at an acute angle, and he felt himself nodding in agreement with his brother's assessment. It *is* an intriguing face, he said to Gottlieb.

Let's not kid ourselves. It's the face of the primordial wood. Had I been born with haunches and a tail, if I cantered off in search of a glade after my mother deposited me onto the earth, it would have come as a surprise to no one.

Bloom smiled at this. It's a handsome face.

Gottlieb shrugged. It's a face. Gottlieb watched Bloom fill the hole he'd dug for the remains of the litter. The young Rosenbloom placed the crushed bodies inside the opening, and with the trowel he had used to dig the small grave, covered them over with clods of dirt. When he had patted down the mound, Gottlieb pushed his back off the smooth bark of the tree and walked out from under its shadows in the direction of the courtyard. Bloom left his father's old tool on top of the tiny grave and took to Gottlieb's side. Now tell me, said the man, who gave you the brains to write those words in your last note?

My father.

And where is this father of yours?

Bloom pointed a finger to the center of the rose garden. There. In his grave.

And your mother?

In her grave. A great distance away.

Fatherless *and* motherless.

Yes, said Bloom.

I see, said Gottlieb, and not without pity.

Bloom walked Gottlieb through the pergola into the courtyard and led him inside. They walked upstairs and entered the library. Here, Bloom said, looking down on his companion, this is what I wanted to share with you. With his arm outstretched, he led Gottlieb to a table running the full length of the library's windows. On it were arranged in the order his father had left them the optical devices he'd inherited and collected from the time he was a child. Indonesian shadow puppets on one end, the very first Phantoscope equipped with the Rosenbloom Loop on the other. On shelves behind the objects were notebooks and pamphlets, antiquarian publications written in Latin, French, and German, boxes upon boxes of glass slides from phantasmagorias performed by Etienne-Gaspard. And then, on a separate shelf, there rested leather folders stuffed with designs and descriptions of patents for many of these objects, his father's included. Gottlieb walked the length of the table with the fluff of his beard pressed to his chest, his bony little fingers tugging at curls.

That and my mother were Father's great passions, said Bloom in response to Gottlieb's silence.

Too engrossed in what he saw, Gottlieb made a guttural sound from the back of his throat. Bloom placed his hands in his trouser pockets and took a seat on a sofa, and from there he watched Gottlieb run a finger over the items. Before one of the magic lanterns he stopped and lingered for a while, then did the same when he saw a folio whose front cover read, *Ars Magna Lucis et Umbrae*. This, he said as he pointed to the old book, and that, he said of the lantern, what did your father tell you about these?

Nothing.

Nothing about where he acquired them?

No. Nothing at all.

A shame, said Gottlieb. The little man pulled the folio from the shelf and opened it. Slowly and deliberately—with great care—he turned its pages, paused every now and again to take in what he saw. Would you mind very much, he asked, if I write to a friend of mine and invite him here to examine these?

Of course not.

My friend, he's a scientist, of a kind. He'll be intrigued by such a comprehensive collection. More than intrigued, I should think.

He's welcome anytime.

Gottlieb now walked over to Bloom and looked beyond him to the library's shelves. From the beleaguered looks of you, he said, I'm going to conjecture you've read nearly every book in this room.

Bloom nodded.

Gottlieb began walking along the orderly rows of bindings at Bloom's back and began to quiz him. You've seen the world of Homer.

To this Bloom nodded once more.

Gottlieb pointed to a nearby shelf.

You know Scheherazade and her golden tongue?

He did.

Studied the cosmologies of Copernicus, Ptolemy, and Galileo? He had.

Visited with Dante and Milton?

Yes, he said to these, too.

And on Gottlieb walked some more and pointed some more, and Bloom continued to say yes. Yes to Leonardo and Swift, Diderot and Voltaire, Tolstoy, Chekhov, and all the books Gottlieb catalogued. Yes. Yes. Yes. Yes, he said to all of it.

And you can quote Pliny the Elder to me?

Yes, said Bloom.

Do you know what all this tells me, Rosenbloom?

No.

It tells me, Gottlieb said as he took a seat across from Bloom, you have a mind too bright to waste on that halfwit Abrams and the nitwits he keeps company with—those other journeymen incompetents in which your brother sees *something*.

Although Bloom didn't believe Mr. Gottlieb was inaccurate in his estimation of his mentors, he nevertheless came to the defense of the men and women he considered to be his friends and protectors. They're hardly halfwits and nitwits, he argued.

Why? Because they've been kind to you? Stroked you until you purred? Coddled you in their knowing hands to show you something of their world?

They *have* been kind to me, said Bloom. Kind *and* generous.

Of course they have. Your brother owns them, Rosenbloom. It's his money that allows them their livelihood. They *should* lavish you with kindness and attention if they know what's good for them.

Taking offense at this, Bloom said firmly, I expected no special attention.

Gottlieb leaned forward in his seat and with a seriousness of purpose scrutinized Bloom's face. His tawny eyes lingered on him in the same way they lingered over the lantern and the book. No, he said, I don't believe you did. Gottlieb protruded his lower lip. Allowed a moment more to pass. Clever, loyal, *and* good-natured? he said, waggling a finger. A dangerous disposition for a young artist. He shook his head at Bloom with disapproval and started to once again twist the curls of his beard. So, he said, I've seen what I've come to see. Now what?

I'm not sure, said Bloom.

Well, said Gottlieb, you do away with the pretense and you tell me the real reason why I'm here today.

Bloom searched for a way to begin describing how important this moment was for him. He tried to formulate an argument in which he could articulate the effect Gottlieb's pictures had had on the way he perceived his craft, but he failed to speak.

I am at best, what, Rosenbloom? Four feet, eleven inches in height?

I'm sorry?

Do you generally fear men a little more than half your size?

No, Mr. Gottlieb.

You are what? A *regal* six feet in stature?

Bloom shook his head. I don't know.

And you—a *giant* Jew, a colossal Semite whose ancestors likely commingled with villainous Cossacks—sit across from me like a milksop? Have I not praised you enough? What? Do I need to cradle you in my arms?

I beg your pardon.

Or is it because you believe I'm the intolerant dog everyone says I am? Or maybe you've concluded all on your own, I am that intolerant dog?

I don't know.

Well, you *should* know. What is a man—what is an artist—if he doesn't know his own mind? His own heart. What kind of weakling are you? . . . And your brother thought you and I were kindred spirits? Nonsense!

Bloom now wondered if perhaps Mr. Abrams was right, after all. Perhaps Gottlieb was too enthralled with himself, too devoted to his adversarial role to extend a hand and guide him.

Well? said Gottlieb.

All right, then, said Bloom. *Yes*, if you must know the truth. Yes, I fear that you might be the rabid dog everyone makes you out to be. The instant Bloom let these words slip from his lips, he wondered if he should retract them, but his riposte shaped a broad smile on Mr. Gottlieb's goatish face, a smile he let linger for some time.

What? said Bloom. What is it?

What is it? he asks. Still smiling broadly, now to the ceiling, Gottlieb extended his arms as if he were seeking an embrace, then looked back down to Bloom. A sign of life! Of honesty! This is what *it* is.

Again, without intending to, Bloom in response to Mr. Gottlieb's condescension shook his head with a snarl of consternation. An entirely involuntary reflex.

Aha! Gottlieb, delighted at the sound of Bloom's small exhalation, was now pointing with both hands. Listen to that: a set of *balls* has descended! Come now, he cajoled, his arms waving in toward his chest as if motioning a boat into a slip. Sit up in your seat. Pull back your shoulders. And speak!

Bloom was resistant to do anything this vicious little man asked of him, but, as if he were being pulled by invisible strings, he slowly sat up in his seat and drew back his shoulders. And now at a loss, said, What would you have me do now, Mr. Gottlieb?

Say what you want from me, Rosenbloom! Tell me why you've written to me once a week for more than three months. Say it! Once and for all! Commit yourself to your own cause!

It was at that moment Bloom understood precisely what was happening. He was in the midst of his first lesson. Mr. Gottlieb was, in effect, teaching him how to communicate with him in such a way he could tolerate Bloom's company. Now that he understood what game Gottlieb was playing, Bloom, with as much dignity as he could find within himself after recovering from Mr. Gottlieb's humiliations, said without any constraint whatsoever, I want to work as your apprentice, Mr. Gottlieb.

Gottlieb leaned forward in his seat so his face was near Bloom's. In a tone no longer playful, but dead serious, he asked, And I should accept you, this meek wisp of a boy, as *my* protégé, why?

Bloom now leaned forward in his seat, and with his nose only inches from Gottlieb's grotesque protrusion, he said in a gritty voice charged with a conviction he didn't know resided within him until this very moment, For reasons I can list ad nauseam, Mr. Gottlieb, I'm able to speak of what I find brilliant in your pictures. To my great misfortune, it seems, I've been cursed as one of your great admirers, and, however foolhardy it might be, I want to learn from you everything you can teach me. *If* such a thing is possible.

Now there, whispered Gottlieb as he pulled back from Bloom and nodded with approval, is a man to whom I wouldn't mind imparting my wisdom. Gottlieb rose to his full, stunted height, and said, We'll waste no time! He walked to a nearby desk and pulled out from a drawer a piece of paper, on which he scribbled a few lines. Paused for a moment, then scribbled a few more. Here, he said, a dramatic sketch for you to do with as you please. I give you three weeks to draw up a scenario. Plan for two reels. Twenty minutes, no more. Prove to me you have what *I* consider *something*, and then we'll see. In the meanwhile, you stay away from that stronghold of amateurs and poseurs down there. You remain here on the estate.

But I was meant to be on set with Mr. Evans this afternoon.

I'll inform him—and all the others—you belong to me for the time being. You understand? You belong to *me*.

The thought of this troubled Bloom. He had in the time he'd worked on the lot grown accustomed to the company of Mr. Evans and Murray Abrams, of Hannah Edelstein and Constance Grey. He'd grown accustomed to the discipline and rhythms of his routine. He would especially miss meeting Gus for lunch in the canteen and eating the food Meralda prepared for them each morning.

If you're hesitant to make a commitment, said Gottlieb, if you're unwilling to sacrifice what I think necessary . . .

No, said Bloom. I'll do as you ask.

Not even Simon will drag you down there, understood? If he asks what's become of you, what do you tell him?

I belong to you.

Precisely. Then we're agreed?

Yes, said Bloom, we're agreed.

And with that said, Gottlieb made his exit. Three weeks from today, Rosenbloom.

Three weeks from today, Mr. Gottlieb.

Good afternoon, Rosenbloom!

Good afternoon, Mr. Gottlieb.

Once Bloom heard the front door slam shut, he walked over to the desk on which Gottlieb had scribbled his hand. On the blotter, Bloom read the title, *Mephisto's Affinity*. Following this was a short description of a domestic scene in which Mephistopheles's wife grants her husband leave to visit Earth for a day of long-needed holiday. *He rises up from the underworld and enters the world of the living,* wrote Gottlieb. *He witnesses the sins of sinners, sees the avaricious, the gluttonous, the envious, etc., all in need of his services, but because he is on leave, he resists temptation and turns away from their folly. He is resigned to do as his wife said he should. He is resigned to enjoy a devil's Sabbath. Today, he will write no contracts and make no bargains. Today, he will capture no souls. In which case, where, Mr. Rosenbloom, will Mephistopheles find his joy? How will he experience abandon? In whom will he find his affinity?*

><

For hours after Gottlieb had left him alone, Bloom paced the floor of the library, waiting for the first image to come to him. He paced through the remainder of the day and into the night. He lay awake in his bed, hoping something in the shadows of his room might take hold. The following morning, for the first time in a long time, Gus didn't wake him to go to work. Bloom climbed the stairs of the tower and through his telescope searched the basin, thinking perhaps there he would see something, anything that would stir him. But he found only an image of a landscape ravaged by his brother's endeavors; across the vast stretch of the ancient seabed a number of citrus groves had been razed, their fields left barren. The disheartening image advanced an even duller emptiness than he'd felt before he climbed to the tower's pavilion; his mind void, his spirit enervated, he searched for Roya, from whom—without intending to—he'd grown apart in the three years he'd spent on the studio lot.

For some time after he started work on *The Primal Pill*, she continued to search him out in the evenings, to sit with him in the parlor after his meals, to lie with him on the chaise in his mother's gallery, but when he began to return later and later from the studio, she withdrew from him. Only from great distances did he catch glimpses of her—on the trails, in the tower, standing on the promontory, and soon afterward she seemed to disappear from the estate altogether. He would sometimes awaken in the middle of the night and think she was standing in his room, watching him sleep, but when he turned on the electric lights, he would discover he was alone, at which point he would wrap himself in his blanket and walk to the gallery, where he would stare into the pinholes of Aphrodite's eyes, thinking that perhaps she was there, watching him from inside Salazar's chamber.

For three days, Bloom searched for her, and for three days, she managed to elude him. He wrote notes to her and left them about the house, in his room, in the gallery, in the parlor, all of them saying the same thing. *My dear Roya. Please come back to me. I am waiting for you at the pool.* And for three days, he waited at the pool's edge, much of that time spent looking at the still waters in search of a way into Gottlieb's scenario; but still, nothing came. On the third day, he reclined on the pool's ledge and fell asleep, and when he awoke to a tickling sensation on the tip of his nose, he saw falling over his face the canopy of Roya's hair backlit by the noontime sun. She sat beside him, lifted his head onto her lap, and when Bloom asked for her forgiveness, she stroked away the hair hanging in his eyes, bent down, and kissed him on his mouth. And with the sensation of that kiss, he recalled what had been lost to him in the years he'd spent away from the quiet rhythm of the estate. In the toil of work, in the tedium of labor, he had forgotten the profound pleasure he had once taken in Roya's quiet company; he forgot how uninhibited and free his imagination was with her at his side. As he did when he was a child, he spent the afternoon trailing after his silent companion through the rooms of the villa, sat with her over lunch in the parlor, and in the late afternoon, he meandered with her through the mazes of the front gardens, and there he shared with her the scenario Gottlieb had written for him, and there she showed him what he had been waiting to see. She climbed atop an empty pedestal on which a long-lost statue had once resided, and she playfully struck a pose for Bloom. And then another. At which point, Bloom began to envision in the darkness of his mind all the images that had refused to show themselves to him when he was alone in his solitude. He took Roya by the waist and gently lowered her to the ground. Thank you, he said. Thank you. And he took hold of her hand, kissed it several times, and walked with her to the courtyard, to his studio, where, for the next several weeks, she would keep him company in the evenings, late into the night, and there he would remain, shut away. With Roya's help, he conceived Mephisto's underworld as a hell bathed in white, white light, white walls, a world in which the food and décor, the complexions and garments were white on white on white, so absent contrast when the audience looked on, they would find themselves craving—not unlike Mephistopheles—the smallest divergence. He drew Mephisto dressed in Simon's style, white suit and shoes, white vest and tie. He would stare down a never-ending white corridor, declaring, Eternity! How tiresome! How tiresome! he would declare to the unchanging white horizon out a white window frame. How tiresome, he would declare to the face of a white clock whose white hands he would spend his time starting and stopping at will. At which point, his wife would declare: How tiresome *you* can be! Sweeping white dust from a white broom in his direction, she would proclaim him an idle layabout. Go! she would order, sweeping him off. Be gone! I can't stand the sight of you! Take a holiday! Mephisto would brighten momentarily at the very thought. He would pack a small case and kiss his wife goodbye. One rotation of the Earth, she would say, and not one revolution more. Mephisto, in that instant, would raise his arm and rise into a billowing white sheet, out of which he would emerge through a crevice in the Earth shaded in blacks and grays. In the world of the living, his white suit would turn charcoal, as would the lines about his eyes and the hair of his mustache and goatee. He would pass a picnic blanket on which a man as large as a sedan would be parked before a cornucopia of meats and fruits, cakes, pitchers of ale. Bloom drew an image of a man reclining on his enormous side, pointing a thick pickle at a cadaverous manservant. More! the man would order. The gargantua would rip away chicken legs with his

hands, crunch with his teeth into the heads of squabs, take volumi-
nous bites out of legs of lamb, from frosted cakes and crusty pies.
Mephisto, as he witnessed the cheeks swell larger and larger, would
be tempted to approach the glutton, but would restrain himself
and proceed forward to a circle of men throwing dice. There he would
watch as more and more money piled onto the ground, and he
would witness a man shed from his finger his wedding band, and
from his wrist his watch, and he would observe him go so far as to
extract a gleaming crown from a tooth. For a second time Mephisto
would refrain from conducting business, and move on, to find himself in a meadow, where he would be drawn to a fountain at whose
top would stand a statue of a naked nymph. He would walk over the
water collecting in the catch basin and run his hand over the pedestal, and with a wave of his finger he would bring the marble to life,
and with another wave, turn the living stone to flesh. Together, he
and his naked creature would set out arm in arm into a garden maze,
where they would animate a general and his horse, an ancient god
and goddess, a storybook maiden and storybook villain. He and his
companion would shepherd them to a meadow, where, for a full day
and night, they would dance and dine under the sun and the moon.
Bloom conjured a stage on which each figure would perform a short
pantomime, an allegory in which they would enact the plight of the
seven deadly sins. And when the day would begin again and then
wane into a second sunset, Mephisto's wife would appear in an agitated state. She would be so aggravated by her husband's antics she
would freeze the statues in mid-reverie, and Mephisto along with
them. With a flick of her finger, she would open a crevice in the
Earth, take her beloved by his marbled nose, and drag him down
into a pit of white light.

➤〈

For two weeks and four days, Bloom went without sleep. In two
weeks and four days, he drew and redrew more than eighty panels.
And when he had completed the last of his drawings, he reclined

for a moment in his armchair and fell asleep. He was shaken awake shortly after dawn, when he found Gottlieb holding up Bloom's work in his hands, and he said with a note of capitulation that made Bloom wonder if he wasn't dreaming, Perhaps there *is* something to you after all. Recover today. Tomorrow we make our plans. And off Bloom drifted back into slumber. When he awoke again later that afternoon, he was delighted to find Simon walking along the curved wall at the back of the studio, to which Gottlieb—he presumed— had tacked his drawings.

Simon?

Hello there, said his brother. Simon walked the length of the wall, and when he reached its end, he returned to the middle and stood facing an image of Mephisto clawing his way up out of hell, onto the Earth, his white suit turned black. With his back still to Bloom, Simon said, I've just been accosted by Gottlieb, demanding this and that, a budget, a crew, actors, stage time. It seems you've made quite an impression.

What do you think?

What do I think? He reached out and touched an image of Mephisto, ran his finger down the trim of his white suit. I think you've done wonderfully, he said after some time. In Gottlieb's hands, this will be something to admire.

So, then, you'll give him what he wants?

And then some, I'm sure. Simon now turned to face Bloom, and to Bloom, who had come to know the many faces of his brother, Simon appeared transformed, a version of him he didn't recognize. He stood looking at Bloom as if frozen in time, his eyes searching for something intangible. Like an image from one of Bloom's mother's miniature glass plates, Simon gestured to his brother with an extended arm and an open hand, looking as if he were in search of Bloom's understanding. A long and odd silence passed between the brothers as Bloom waited for Simon to utter whatever thought was lodged in his mind.

What is it? the young Rosenbloom eventually asked. Is everything all right?

Yes, yes, I'm sorry, I have a lot on my mind. That's all. Yet he continued to stand there, unmoving, still unaware his hand remained reaching out, its fingers splayed, like they wanted to grab hold of Bloom, but couldn't.

Simon?

Yes. Yes! He became conscious of his pose and lowered his arm to his side, retracted his fingers into a tight fist, and shook it at the wall of Bloom's images. The quiet here, it's filled you with precisely what you needed. You've done well, Joseph. Very well. Simon approached Bloom, put his arm around his shoulder, and when he gave him a tight squeeze, Bloom couldn't help but notice how he smelled sharp from worry. We'll celebrate the moment it wraps. As quietly as you like, he said with a palm to Bloom's cheek. Simon turned to go, but before he did, Bloom said, Are you sure there isn't anything I can do for you?

Do? Simon halted and looked off to the courtyard, over the pool and the lawn, to the tower's pavilion. No, he whispered to himself. No, he said to Bloom. No. You *are* doing it, aren't you? You're doing exactly what you were meant to be doing. Think of nothing else. Think of nothing more. But now Bloom couldn't think of anything other than Simon's bizarre turn.

→←

Early the following morning, he discovered Gottlieb pacing in the parlor around Hershel Verbinsky, Hannah Edelstein, Percy Evans, Leonard Hertz, Claude Strauss, Levi Sexton, and a half dozen others. And where were you? said Gottlieb. It's time! From that moment on, they met early every morning and worked late into the night. In order to capture the domestic bliss of Mr. and Mrs. Mephisto, Mr. Evans erected white walls on one of the lot's open-air stages, on each of which Hannah Edelstein painted the optical illusion Bloom had devised to make it appear as if the room extended into infinity. Mr. Verbinsky dressed the front of the never-ending room with the white furniture and white props Bloom had drawn for their underworld home, and to a second stage, Verbinsky masterfully whorled a white sheet of muslin into which Mephisto, and later, Mrs. Mephisto, would ascend with the aid of wires, painted white, attached to a harness fitted under their garments. The seamstresses in the costume department sewed to Bloom's specifications a fitted white housecoat and apron for the missus, to which they matched a sensible pair of white pumps for the feet and a white-handled feather duster with white plumage for the hand; and for the mister, they pieced together a white suit and added to it all its accoutrements; they then duplicated all the garments in black. Into the grounds of the estate's grove a deep hole was dug and around this opening in the earth where Mephisto would emerge were set an assortment of rocks and boulders of varying size and shape. Adjoining the big hole was dug something akin to a gopher hole, through which steam would be pumped. Mr. Evans manufactured an enormous canvas-lined wooden catch basin for the fountain, built around it plaster walls, and re-created, from a plaster mold, the base of Bernini's Triton Fountain, in the middle of which a platform was secured to prop up the actress playing the marble sea nymph. When the fountain had been filled, Mr. Evans lined the basin with stones painted aqua blue so it would appear as if Mephisto were walking over the water's surface. Per Bloom's instruction, Claude Strauss devised pantomime routines that followed the themes of the seven deadly sins, all neither too farcical nor too serious, neither too lyrical nor too pedantic. Light humor, he said of it, yet cautionary. Pedestals were secured throughout Jacob Rosenbloom's sanctuary, his garden mazes, and a statue of a horse was driven around from one of the warehouses. The last location built was the stage on which Mr. Strauss's routines were to be performed. Opposite the fountain, Mr. Evans constructed a simple but elegant platform on whose corners he erected tall Corinthian columns. The actors were cast in their roles by Mr. Gottlieb, all except one— the rotund giant with elastic cheeks—who was left to Gus to scavenge from town. When they were all assembled, Mr. Gottlieb sent them off to be fitted in their costumes. The following day, when film-

ing began, Bloom took to Mr. Gottlieb's side, thinking he would
function as his silent shadow, but Gottlieb's method of teaching reflected the man himself, talkative, abrasive, and Socratic, and his
method of filmmaking, it turned out, while full of noise and bluster,
ran contrary to his obstinate demeanor. Rather, it allowed for the
possibility of future indecision, for the likelihood of incertitude, after
the fact. Unlike Mr. Abrams, he labored over each frame of film
exposed. Using Bloom's drawings as a starting point, and all the
time questioning him about what he had envisioned preceding and
anteceding the moment at hand, he blocked and reblocked the movement of his actors, sent them through their paces in a cycle of eternal
returns, positioned three cameras about the stage, and while the actors remained in their places, he supervised the setting of the scrims
and, to Mr. Hertz's displeasure, positioned the lights himself, and
only then would he call action and roll the film through the camera,
taking no fewer than a dozen takes. When the formality of the scene
was captured, he continued on to film cutaways and close-ups, what
amounted to inspired, spontaneous acts. With his mind preoccupied with the scene, he walked the stage or the set with camera and
tripod on his shoulder, as if with a divining rod, and when he felt
moved, he planted the tripod's legs down, positioned his lens on a
subject or an object, and rolled for fifteen, twenty seconds, never
longer. And when this material was canned, that was a day, a process for each take he repeated for three more days, during each of
which he set a new pattern of blocking, used different scrims and a
new arrangement of lights and reflectors, repositioned the cameras,
called upon all to action, over and over again, and again filmed more
spontaneous moments, until there seemed nothing spontaneous
about them whatsoever. For every drawing Bloom had presented to
him, Gottlieb ran through the same routine, and for every fourth
day Bloom worked at his side, Gottlieb asked him to block and light
the same course of action in his own individual way. At the end of
every seventh day, well known to all as Gottlieb's Sabbath—which
just so happened to fall on a Thursday—Gottlieb invited Bloom
to sit with him in the parlor to review the work they had done

together, and when they had seen all the film they had run, which every week accumulated that much more, Gottlieb asked Bloom to map out the sequences—based on the blocking, the lighting, the quality of the acting—he thought worked most harmoniously. By abiding by Gottlieb's Talmudic method, a two-reel picture, that would have otherwise taken no more than five days to shoot under the direction of Mr. Abrams, took seven weeks, and because they had filmed the equivalent of four separate pictures, and, what's more, because Mr. Gottlieb's practice was to have multiple copies reproduced in the lab for each take filmed, he and Bloom would spend an additional month reviewing and compiling the already reviewed material, what, in this case, amounted to four final cuts, all of which Bloom thought magnificent and couldn't be more proud of, especially because each of the final cuts included at least half a dozen scenes he had conceived and directed. Bloom could now understand why Gottlieb was considered insufferable by the entire colony, why so many regarded him with disfavor and took no pleasure in working with him. If Bloom were an actor on one of Gottlieb's stages, a lighting technician, a cameraman, made to stand by in the heat of the day for prolonged periods of time, for reasons no one other than Gottlieb could immediately grasp, he could see in what way they would detest him. But Bloom felt nothing but admiration for Gottlieb's method, as he managed to command his people with an iron will, to keep them in place—to control them not unlike Mephisto did his statues—in such a way he was able to exercise the full capacity of his imagination in public, to work to excess in the same manner Bloom did in the privacy of his studio, cloistered and unseen. And for this feat, Bloom—who without Gottlieb at his side didn't think himself capable of taking such extreme measures—envied him; and he now knew why Simon revered Gottlieb, why Murray Abrams felt threatened by him. In the small realm over which he ruled, Gottlieb was nothing short of a Napoleon riding a monumental steed.

➤✦

After many long conversations between Bloom and Gottlieb about which finished version of *Mephisto's Affinity* was superior, Gottlieb never informed Bloom which cut he presented to Simon for distribution. He merely said he had chosen the right one, and then told Bloom to put it behind him. Better, he said, to leave the business to his brother, and move on to the next conceit. There was little enjoyment in dwelling on finished work, Gottlieb believed; because all one could find in the aftermath of creation were its flaws, he abandoned it as he would an unwanted child. He, therefore, never attended premieres at the theater, and he expected Bloom to follow his example. On the very day Gottlieb delivered the final cut of *Mephisto's Affinity* to Simon, he sat Bloom down in the library and said it was now time to consider their next scenario, before they grew too pleased with themselves for having accomplished their first undertaking together. Only this time he expected Bloom to choose the scenario himself. A choice easily made for Bloom, as he had long dreamed of transforming *Death, Forlorn* into a motion picture, and even before he had been properly introduced to Gottlieb, he knew he wanted to collaborate on it with him. That afternoon he walked Gottlieb down to the parlor, sat him in Jacob's chair and proceeded to show him the slides he had labored on in the dim light of Salazar's chamber. And when he had removed the last slide from the slot of the magic lantern, Gottlieb was so impressed by what he saw, he nodded his head, and then nodded it some more.

Are you saying yes? asked Bloom. We can work on this next?

Yes. Most definitely, yes. But first, I must pause and think awhile.

Why? asked Bloom.

Because, said Gottlieb, that is my prerogative. I must think of what to do with you.

With me?

Yes, you. Gottlieb whirled his skinny fingers about Bloom's chest. There's something missing in there. Something needed before we begin.

What?

I will tell you what. After I've paused and thought awhile!

✕

For reasons Bloom assumed were related to business, and because Bloom himself had been busy on the set of *Mephisto's Affinity*, he hadn't spent any significant time with Simon since their peculiar conversation in Bloom's studio. When, by chance, they passed each other on the lot during the production, Simon would do little more than exchange pleasantries with Bloom. He remained guarded and distant and moody. Bloom pressed him on several occasions to visit the set, but Simon insisted Gottlieb wouldn't allow it. When Bloom suggested they instead eat a meal together, Simon prevaricated. Perhaps, he said, perhaps when you're through filming. And when the filming was through, when Bloom pressed his brother again, Simon lost his patience with him. Please, Joseph, not now. Just not right now, I beg you. In the weeks following, the morning music his brother chose was all requiems. Requiem after requiem hung like a pall of despair in the dry desert air. Mozart's *Requiem in D minor*; Berlioz's *Grande Messe des morts*; Verdi's and Dvořák's *Requiem*; Fauré's *Requiem in D minor*. What, Bloom asked Gus one morning, has gotten into him? And Gus said he didn't want to say, not right away. But then several more weeks passed, every morning now beginning with Simon pacing contemplatively on his porch to the heavy choral arrangements of Verdi's opera *Nabucco*. He played it all the way through and then started it again, at which time Gus approached Bloom and said, I need you to do something for me.

What?

I need you to walk back up to the estate and go out the gate. A car's waiting for you there. Get in it, he said, and do what the driver tells you to do.

What's this all about?

Divided loyalties. A clouded conscience.

I don't understand.

You want to know what's eating your brother, do what old Gus is telling you to do. I've made all the arrangements.

Where, Bloom asked, would he be going?

And Gus told him it would all become clear before the day was out.

Bloom did as Gus said. He walked up the hill and through the grove, down the drive and through the gate, where he found a black sedan idling. The driver was a man he had never seen before, a Negro with a handlebar mustache, young and lithe, dressed in a checked suit, his face narrow and serious. You Joseph? the man asked. Bloom nodded his head. Then get in. He pointed a thumb to the back. Bloom opened the door and took a seat, and off they drove. The driver looked up in his rearview mirror from time to time, but didn't say anything until they were parked in town, on Broadway, in front of the pavilioned sidewalk covering the entrance of the Hotel de Ville, a tall French Baroque pile whose tower rose up from the corner and appeared to be cinched at its neck, just below its onion dome, by a belt. Room five thirty-three, said the driver. That's where you go. He handed Bloom a key and an envelope. Gus says you should go straight on up and keep yourself there until it's time to leave.

When will that be?

Gus says you'll know. I'll be waiting outside when that time come.

All right, said Bloom. Thanks.

The driver tipped his hat.

Bloom exited the car and strode between two lines of potted palms into the hotel lobby. A tidy man with slick hair directed him to the elevator. Bloom told the operator the room number, and they rode up to the fifth floor, where Bloom stepped into a foyer papered in Art Nouveau birds of paradise. When the operator had pushed the gate shut and Bloom could see his head descend below the line of the floor, he turned around to find Room 533 directly behind him, and went inside.

It was a sizable sitting room with a view of the street, a desk, a sofa, several comfortable armchairs, a coffee table set with a plateful of finger sandwiches, a pitcher of lemonade, and a tall glass. Through open windows the noise of the street rumbled in. Bloom took a seat on the sofa and opened the envelope the driver had handed him. Inside was a note from Gus, a list of directions he should follow, the first of which was for Bloom to shut the windows. Bloom got up and swung them closed, and when he did, the room quieted for a moment, and then voices, playful and unencumbered, one a man's, the other a woman's, murmuring through a door adjoining the room next door. The second directive in Gus's note was for Bloom to eat his lunch, which Bloom did—he was rather hungry after his drive; he finished off the entire plate of sandwiches and drank through the pitcher of lemonade. And now, according to Gus's note, he was to wait until two o'clock, half an hour from the present. At that time he was to gather his courage and open the door to the adjoining room, just a crack, absolutely no more than that. If he stood still and quiet, Gus assured him, he would not be seen. Having read this third item on the list, Bloom, now feeling quite nervous about what he would discover next door, paced about the room, keeping an eye on the desk clock, occasionally stopping to look down onto the procession of traffic and hats moving through the thoroughfare below. At two o'clock, he heard the heavy gate of the elevator crash open, and he listened at the door leading to the hallway. There were footsteps and then voices directly on the other side, and Bloom could make them out quite clearly. It was Simon and Gus.

For Christ's sake, Gus, stop looking at me like that.

I know you got misgivings about this.

Of course I do.

Then why go through with it?

Because I can't see a way around it.

The kid'd give you the eyes in his head—he'd give you his heart— if you asked him.

You know it's not that simple.

What I know is you. You love that kid, and what you're about to do is gonna fill you with bile and regret. This is the way Sam would've handled it. You're better than that. Smarter than that.

Is that so?

Yeah, that's so.

Well, apparently, I'm not.

You don't know what you are yet. But, you do this, it's gonna become real clear, real fast. There's no coming back from something like this. I've seen men more golden than you changed inside by less devious acts.

There was a long silence after this. And then: I can't see the alternative, said Simon. I really can't.

Yeah, well, don't say I didn't warn you. I've grown real fond of the kid. Real fond.

I know, said Simon. So have I.

He doesn't deserve this from you. Not from his own brother.

But it's not just his welfare I have to take into account, is it?

Well, then. You know where I stand.

Another long silence passed, and then: Yeah, I know. I'm sorry, Gus. I really am.

Bloom could now hear Simon and Gus walk on, down the corridor, and Bloom followed the direction of their footsteps to the door Gus instructed him to open. He rested the weight of his hand on the knob and slowly turned, pulled it open a crack, and set his eye in the opening to discover Simon walking up to the foot of a bed, on which a thick, curvy woman with a mane of ginger hair straddled the hips of Gerald Stern, whose wrists and ankles were securely tied to the bedposts with neckerchiefs. Mr. Stern was so stunned to see Simon and Gus, he reacted in a manner Bloom couldn't imagine was typical, but what did he know? Stern neither called out in protest nor struggled to release himself. He merely lay there prostrate, half his face pressed into the down of his pillow, repeating to himself with his eyes squeezed shut, I should have known, I should have known, I should have known it was too good to be true . . . The young woman, whose back and hair appeared familiar to Bloom, shrugged her shoulders at the pitiful sight of him, and when Stern had finished berating himself, when there was nothing left in him but a few whimpers, she bent over and gave him a peck on the cheek. She whispered something in his ear and pecked him again, this time on his lips, as she removed what remained of his flaccid member from inside her. As she covered Stern with a blanket, Bloom recalled where he had become intimate with her form—she was one of the women Gus had delivered to his studio; she tucked his attorney in a bit, and walked to a screen standing in the corner of the room on which her clothes were draped.

Thank you, Miss Merriweather, said Simon.

No bigs, said the young woman, then with a twist of her wrist, added, A part's a part. When she'd finished dressing, she presented Gus with the open mouth of her handbag, into which Bloom saw Gus deposit a fat roll of cash. Don't be too hard on the old boy, Simon. He's a soft touch. She blew a kiss in Stern's direction, and off she went.

Mr. Stern? said Simon as the door shut behind Miss Merriweather. Please, Mr. Stern. This'll go much faster if you'll just open your eyes and look at me.

Stern lifted one lid and proceeded to focus his attention on the ceiling.

Over here, Mr. Stern.

Stern now turned his head, and with as much dignity as a man could rally in his position, sniffed a few times and said, What can I do for you, Mr. Reuben?

I don't want to be here, said Simon. In fact, it's the last place I want to be.

Then why *are* you here?

Well, said Simon with a sympathetic grin, it appears that, not unlike you at the moment, I'm caught in a bind. Before I get to that, however—he said with less levity—let me tell you what it is I have on you. Simon, who was carrying a briefcase, opened its clasps and pulled from it two large envelopes. From the first, he removed a collection of photographs. As you can see, said Simon as he sorted through the images—slowly, so that Stern could fully appreciate to what extent his assignations had been documented—some friends of mine have been keeping an eye on you and the lovely Miss Merriweather.

So I see.

It's my understanding you've been married for nearly twenty-five years, Mr. Stern.

Yes.

I also happen to know you have two daughters about the age of Miss Merriweather: Mildred and Hannah, is it?

That's right.

They've recently married well, I hear. A double wedding it was. To two young men whose parents are longtime clients?

The top of Stern's head turned a bright shade of crimson. Yes, he said.

You are a member of the Jonathan Club. You attend shul regularly at the B'nai Brith Synagogue on Ninth and Spring. I know you to be a philanthropist with your various Hebrew charities. All in all, a well-respected man about town.

I like to think so, said Stern with his mouth turned down and his eyes returned to the fine woodwork of the ceiling.

I presume you'd like to keep it that way.

Yes, said Stern, I would.

In which case, you wouldn't want it getting out you've been caught up in a tryst with a young woman who allows herself to be filmed doing the sort of unspeakable acts the two of you have gotten up to, said Simon as he sorted through the photos once again and presented one of particular interest. A woman, Simon added, who, I should probably mention, has been up before the court on charges of indecency and promoting the sale of pornographic material.

Stern's lower lip began to quiver and Bloom could see a tear now run out the corner of his eye.

Right, said Simon. Now, I'm going to be straight with you, Mr. Stern. I'm going to tell you something I trust we can keep between us?

Yes, said Stern, gathering himself. Yes, of course.

What's happening today between the two of us? It's the act of a desperate man. At the moment, you might think yourself the desperate man, but I can assure you I am that man. As I know you're well aware, I've been helping the water authority finance the construction of the Concord Reservoir and the Pacheta Lake Aqueduct.

Yes, I'm aware.

Well, said Simon. And on he went to reveal to Stern the complications he had been concealing from Bloom these past several years. Simon explained to Stern that had everything gone according to plan, all of his investments would have been safe and secure. He fully expected there to be a struggle, but he never expected the farmers and the ranchers to turn into such a steely resistance. They had been dynamiting key junctures of the waterway and taking hostages. Making a real mess of things, said Simon. Just the other day, he told Stern, they destroyed hundreds of yards of piping in three separate locations and kidnapped a member of the water authority out of his bed. They drove him to a remote part of the Mojave and abandoned him there with a small jug of water and a pencil and paper to write a farewell note to his family. For three days the poor man walked westward, only just barely returning with his life. Simon thought, however foolishly, the waterworks would be finished by now, that he'd be well into the construction of his real estate development. The farmers and the ranchers had managed to set his plans back a year, a year at the very least, perhaps longer, and, to the chagrin of the fastidious and dogged Hal Dershowitz, Simon was reminded daily to what extent he had overextended himself. More was going out than coming in, Dershowitz was telling him more often than he'd like to hear. Which had left Simon in quite a predicament. Simon was sure Stern would appreciate that he couldn't readily go to the bank and open a line of credit, as his interests were tied to the public interest, and, like Stern, Simon had an appearance to uphold. If he announced to the world that he was on the verge of ruin without first parting with assets he held dear, How, he asked Stern, would that look? How could he rationalize not selling off his theaters, his studio, the very property he hoped to develop and keep the public's trust? How would that look? he asked Stern.

Stern agreed it wouldn't look good.

No, said Simon. Not good at all. But Simon wasn't prepared to give anything up just yet. He still believed his plans were sound. Which was why he was here today: to speak with Stern in his capacity as the trustee to his brother's fortune. He assured Stern he had no intention of stealing a penny from Joseph. He simply wanted Stern to arrange for him to become a silent partner in this endeavor. He needed Stern to sell off whatever holdings or assets he needed to raise the money Simon required to continue operating the studio and the theaters, to ensure the funds he'd committed to the county were available. He needed Stern to arrange for Bloom to become an investor in all his business ventures. When the reservoir and the aqueduct were complete, when the land was developed and sold, he would return all he borrowed from his brother, with interest, and provide him a small percentage of each enterprise. But—and this was rather important to Simon—Bloom should be none the wiser. That, Mr. Stern, is my aim here today, said Simon. To coerce your cooperation. Simon, at this point, removed a stack of papers and put them on the table beside the bed. Here is everything you need: the contracts, the banking information, the amounts I'll need, and what Joseph can expect to receive in return. I expect you to sign the agreement before the week is out, and I expect to see the funds deposited into my accounts at the same time . . . Do you think you can manage this? asked Simon, who was once again holding up one of the lewd images of Stern.

Mr. Stern studied the photograph and said after a short moment of reflection, Let me consider your proposal?

Of course, said Simon. You have the week.

Thank you.

All right, then. Gus? Simon stood up and Gus joined him at Mr. Stern's bedside. Together they untied the bound man from the bedposts. End of the week, said Simon. Not a minute longer. He offered Stern his hand, and Stern, looking to Gus first, took hold of it and reluctantly shook. Bloom watched as his brother and Gus left Stern's side and exited the room. He now closed the door, but continued listening. He heard Stern begin to moan and cry and curse himself for having been such a reckless fool. Bloom was beside himself. He didn't know what to do. Stern still hadn't let up on himself. After listening a moment longer, he couldn't bear it any longer. He opened the door through which he had witnessed his brother embody a character with whom he would have preferred not to have become familiar, and walked into the room to find Stern pacing about the bed in the buff. Oh, come now! Stern declared. Not you, too! Where in the world did *you* come from? Bloom told Stern to calm himself. He told him to get dressed and sit down, and as Stern went in search of his clothes, Bloom explained to Stern how it was he had come to be in the room next door and assured him everything would be all right. He had nothing to worry about. He swore to him his reputation would remain intact, his secret wouldn't be revealed—he could rely on his discretion, and he and Bloom would continue on as they had, as if nothing had happened today. Here, said Bloom as he took the stack of papers from Stern's bedside. Take them. Sign them. He walked over to the desk and returned with a pen. Go on, he said. Stern looked at Bloom and looked at the pen, and said, You're willing to do this for me?

To which Bloom said, Yes.

Stern deliberated a moment longer and then, without looking at Bloom, signed the documents in all the places that required his signature.

All done. Bloom advised Stern to follow Simon's instructions, to do everything he asked of him today and whatever he might ask of him in the future. It is only money, said Bloom. Had he thought to ask me for it, I would have insisted you give him whatever he needed.

Yes, but he was well aware I would have never permitted it. He knew I would never have allowed you to take such a risk. He was well aware I would have felt obligated to protect you from his folly. He's a shrewd man, your brother. I'll give him that. After a long silence, Stern said, You were good to come in, Joseph. I don't know if I could have gone through with it had you not shown yourself.

For Stern's sake, for the sake of his family, Bloom said he would keep today their secret. And for this, Stern said he was in Bloom's debt, and the poor man started to weep all over again. I should have known when Simon sent her to me. I surely should have known when she took an interest in *me*. In *me*, Joseph? I know what I am. But she was just so, so . . . young and glamorous and . . . liberated. Stern opened his mouth and bit down on the palm of his hand and cried some more, this time, thought Bloom, not from humiliation but because he would miss Miss Merriweather.

><

How does one reconcile something like this? Bloom wondered all the way home. He tried to rationalize the events he'd just witnessed as a necessary deception rather than an act of betrayal. It was an act of a desperate businessman. It wasn't personal. Simon did love him. He heard him say as much to Gus. He loved Bloom and didn't wish to hurt him. There was simply no other way, not without damaging a project years in the making, a project bound to the fates of count-less lives, Bloom's being only one of them. It was a Machiavellian maneuver, he thought, one that would have likely been considered tepid in the time of the cutthroat Borgias. No one had been mur-dered. No one had been irredeemably harmed. Stern, as a matter of fact, had enjoyed exercising a middle-aged man's passion. He reveled in his indulgence, felt the thrill of his lapse in judgment, which, in the end, if he was being frank with himself, significantly endeared Stern to Bloom, who found Stern only tolerable before. A little money would be shifted from one investment to another, there would likely be a handsome return, so, really, what harm had been done?

Bloom tried to be a man about it. He tried all the way home to be as strong-willed, as thick-skinned, as his brother. But the only problem with that: he wasn't Simon. He wasn't nearly as malleable or pragmatic. He wasn't practiced in the art of playing roles, and he hadn't yet experienced enough of life's compromising positions to hold a relativistic view of the world. Was it really too much to ask, he wondered, to expect his own brother's loyalty?

By the time he entered the estate's gates, he had relived the days after his father had revealed the omitted truths of their family history, and as he reflected on that period of time he couldn't mitigate the dull ache of disappointment he now felt in his brother; it rivaled the disappointment he had held for his father. He had been used by Simon to set up Stern, was made to be his unknowing accomplice. He had written that letter, given him his entrée. For months Simon had been planning this, in a cold and calculated manner. And for a young, sensitive man like Bloom, it was all too much. Too, too much. There had been too much sadness, tragedy, and disenchantment compounded in too short a time. Bloom wanted to overcome it all, but he simply wasn't equipped to sufficiently distance himself. Not with humor. Not with irony. Not with philosophies whose bedrock relied on humanity's innate moral shortcomings. When the driver dropped Bloom at the villa's entrance, he discovered Gus sitting on the stone bench beside the front door. He was dressed in powder-blue slacks and a white shirt unbuttoned at the collar. Bloom sat beside him and asked him why he had chosen to reveal Simon's betrayal, and betray Simon in the act of revealing the betrayal. He's gone too far, said Gus. I thought maybe he'd see sense. I thought maybe his heart would overcome his head, but it didn't, and, well . . . I have something at stake here, don't I? Gus looked off in the direction of the kitchen, from which they could hear the sounds of Meralda preparing dinner.

You love her that much that you would do this?

Gus inhaled a big whiff of air through his cavernous nostrils. What would you say if I asked to continue on here? To keep the grounds, look after your general well-being, and such?

I would say, Yes, of course. This is your home now. But what about Simon? You won't have anything to do with him?

Gus shook his head. To do so would mean I would need to deceive you. To deceive you would be to deceive her. To deceive you would be hard enough. To deceive her? I just couldn't do that. I don't have it in me. Not anymore.

But by making this choice, you've deceived him.

That I have.

Why?

For his own good.

Because he's gone too far?

Because he's gone too far.

And now that I know? What am I supposed to do?

I don't know. You should speak with him. Tell him what you know, what you saw and heard.

I'm not sure that I can.

And why not?

I promised Mr. Stern I would keep his secret. If Simon learns that I know what he's done, he might not believe it was you. He might choose to believe it was Mr. Stern who told me.

It will make no difference. He needs Stern's cooperation. It's not in Simon's interests to make trouble for him. So, you let him know, and then . . .

What?

You can choose to forgive him. Or not. If not, I do wonder who will be left to redeem him.

＞＜

Meralda was delighted to spend more time in Gus's company. She often joined him in the grove and in the rose garden, where they lunched together on a picnic blanket, on which Meralda would linger afterward, to watch the enormous man delicately work his pruning shears around the garden's lattices, along the muscular limbs of the fruit-bearing trees. On the few occasions Bloom noticed Meralda's full figure sneaking across the courtyard in the early morning, he was tickled by the need she felt to protect Bloom from her liaison by upholding the pretense that she had slept in her own bed.

Why, he asked Gus one day, didn't he ask her to marry him?

Gus said he had. She refused him.

Why?

She's waiting for you.

For me to do what?

To marry. To find love and happiness.

But she doesn't need to delay her own happiness on my account.

No, but she is anyway. She feels responsible for you. Loves you like you're her own. *Mi'ijo*, she says when she talks about you. My boy. My son. Bloom wondered if he should have a word with her, and Gus said no, he shouldn't, absolutely not. She doesn't know you know about us. If you let on, she'll call it quits for sure. As it is, she's down on her knees every night with her *Dios mio*, praying to Jesus to forgive her for loving a big-nosed Christ killer. No need to complicate things any more than they are. Our lives are complicated enough, are they not?

They are, indeed.

✣

Simon had been to and from the estate several times since Gus had taken up work on the grounds, and so far as he let on, all was right with the world. Pangloss couldn't have been more convincing, thought Bloom. Simon couldn't be more pleased to see Gus taking a well-deserved break from the business. The rate of production on the lot and the progress they were making up north was moving along at pace. The construction of his housing development in the basin would soon begin. The spirit of Scott Joplin and Eubie Blake had returned to the syncopated palaver of his brother's speech and their music once again amplified across the lot. Simon related the details of his business to Bloom while taking photographs of him building a miniature replica of Death's fortress out of stones he and Gus had collected on the estate's grounds. Gottlieb had shared the director's credit with his young protégé on *Mephisto's Affinity* and there had been some inquiries about him by *The Motion Picture Story Magazine*, by the Answer Man himself (a herself, if you must know,

Simon told him), and knowing Bloom wouldn't enjoy sitting for an interview, and knowing Gottlieb wouldn't permit it, Simon took it upon himself to send them a few publicity photos, along with a page or so of hyperbole about the reclusive teenage genius of Mount Terminus Productions—unequaled scenarist, unrivaled production designer, director extraordinaire.

On each of these short visits, Bloom had every intention of telling Simon that he knew what he had done. There was a part of him that wanted to tell him in order to relieve him of the need to put on a false front. But every time Bloom thought to draw the curtain on his brother's performance, he couldn't bear the thought of the consequences. He wondered if their brotherly bond would survive Simon's feelings of shame and embarrassment. If he wouldn't recoil from having been made the fool by Gus. The irony, of course, was that because Simon had been relieved of the financial burdens that had been weighing him down and occupying so much of his time and energy, his visits to the estate had become more frequent. He began to show up for dinner once, sometimes twice a week, which required Bloom to perform his own false role, to pretend that nothing had happened to alter his perception of his brother. After three or four meals like this, in which Bloom did what he could to hide the displeasure he felt about his brother's deception, without really meaning to, without having planned the moment, Bloom interrupted the silence they shared in the parlor after dinner, and said, I know what you did.

Simon, who was sitting in Jacob's chair, smoking a cigarette and reviewing his handiwork in *The Motion Picture Story Magazine*, turned to Bloom and said, I'm sorry?

I know what you did, said Bloom. To Mr. Stern. To me.

How do you . . .

I was there. In the adjoining room. Watching through a crack in an open door.

Simon set the magazine down in his lap and began to nod slowly as he searched his thoughts as to how Bloom could know. How he would have been there. And then it came to him. Gus? he said.

Bloom now nodded.

Gus, he said again, as if in a state of disbelief. Simon discharged a heavy sigh.

Bloom wasn't certain what to say next. So he said nothing. He waited for Simon, but for the first time since he had known his brother, Simon, it seemed, was at a loss as well. He sat there tapping his finger against the chair's armrest. And then it occurred to Bloom to say, I heard enough to know why you did it. And Mr. Stern explained why you hadn't come to me in the first place.

You weren't the obstacle.

I know, said Bloom. Nevertheless . . .

Yes, said Simon. Nevertheless, I should have spoken with you first. I should have thought more of you.

I would have done everything in my power to help. I would have done what I could to influence Mr. Stern to help you. The money, said Bloom, I don't care about the money. All you needed to do was ask for it, and it would have been yours.

Simon returned to nodding and tapping. He was unable to look at Bloom. I'm sorry, he said as he stood up and walked away. At the threshold of the parlor door, he stopped, and said, I truly am sorry.

Wait, said Bloom.

What is it?

Promise me something before you go?

Yes.

Promise me no harm will come to Mr. Stern.

No, no harm will come to Mr. Stern. He's done what I've asked of him. There's no reason for it. Simon now walked off in the direction of the front door. Bloom considered going after him. He stood up, and when he was about to start out, Gus stepped into the parlor and told Bloom to leave him be. Let him live with his shame for a while. It'll do him some good.

There's no need for him to suffer, said Bloom.

Yeah, said Gus, yeah, there is.

>*<

If living with his shame did Simon any good or harm, Bloom wouldn't know about it for quite a while. Simon ceased his visits to the estate for the time being, and from what he had heard from Gottlieb, he was keeping himself busy making frequent journeys to the offices of the water authority, to his various construction sites. Besides, from Gottlieb's perspective they had more serious concerns than Simon. Not long after Simon made his somber departure from the villa, Gottlieb barged into Bloom's studio carrying an enormous canvas sack on his back, proclaiming, I have paused! I have thought! I have reached my conclusion! He dropped the bag on the studio floor and announced, Love! An intimate knowledge of love! *Death, Forlorn* would be significantly longer than *Mephisto's Affinity*, he said, and Gottlieb insisted *love* was the key to bringing the story to life.

Love? said Bloom.

Love! cried Gottlieb. For this picture, you must begin to understand what it is to be in love. Truly in love. Deeply in love. Blinded by love. If the creator of this sort of picture hasn't been undone by the visceral upheaval only a tormented heart can provide, it will be nothing more than a hollow fantasy. And what do *you* know of such a love? Gottlieb scoffed.

To this, Bloom could only say he had witnessed the aftermath of this kind of love. Lived in its shadows. If he had his way, he told Gottlieb, he would rather not love if what he observed in his father was the result of abiding love and devotion.

Nonsense! Gottlieb shouted. You would feel blessed if you were ever lucky enough to be cursed by such love! . . . No. We must find you a woman you can sink your teeth into. Isn't there anyone on the lot who moves you?

No, said Bloom. The only women he had known well were Hannah Edelstein and Constance Grey, and Hannah, he was certain, had no romantic feelings for men whatsoever, and Constance was twenty years his senior. He had loved Roya for a long, long while, but when he considered the kind of love Gottlieb spoke of, their love wasn't that. Their love was unconditional and unspoken, secret, familial. It was a love he relied on to sustain his spirit and his art. It was the love of a muse, not a love through which his body would be overcome by passion or heartache, jealousy or rapture. It wasn't the type of love that had the potential to tear him asunder. He knew nothing about that kind of love. That category of infectious love he had distrusted and avoided for good reason.

Well, said Gottlieb, the hunt is on! He kicked the bag at his feet. Bloom asked what was inside. Letters, said Gottlieb. From *admirers*. *Your* admirers. Readers of that *yenta* column your pimp brother put you in.

I don't understand. What am I to do with them?

Find a goddamned woman, of course.

Like this?

Why not? Can you think of any better way? You go nowhere. You see no one.

I know. It's just . . . I wouldn't know how to begin.

For *chrissake*! Get up! Pick it up! Give it here! Bloom lifted himself up from his collection of stones, from Death's fortress, lifted the heavy bag from the floor, and handed it back to Gottlieb. Come along! Gottlieb marched down into the courtyard and made his way to the kitchen, where he dropped it between Meralda and Gus, who were sitting at the table, drinking tea and playing cards. Gottlieb said to them, Find this virgin Apollo a woman and turn him into a Dionysus.

Mr. Gottlieb? said Meralda.

It's time he knew the true purpose of his heart. And here, said Gottlieb as he turned to Bloom. He removed an envelope from his jacket pocket and pressed it into Bloom's hand. From your brother.

From Simon?

Who else? Remember this well. *This*, Rosenbloom, *this* is why for men like us we enjoy the work when we make it, and abandon it to the dustbin of history after the fact. The *work*! The *work* is essential! Whatever comes of it is ephemeral, momentary, a flicker on a screen, *no more*! he said as he made his exit.

As Bloom made *his* exit and walked back to the studio, he opened the envelope, thinking perhaps his brother had written some further explanation or apology, but the letter Gottlieb had pressed into Bloom's hand was from Georges Méliès, the magician whose inimitable pictures Bloom so admired that afternoon his brother took him up in the balloon. Méliès had addressed the letter to Simon, thanking his old protégé for having sent the print of *Mephisto's Affinity* to him. He was pleased to see his efforts had not been entirely wasted on Simon, that here, finally, was a picture he had produced worthy of his admiration. Mr. Méliès was pained to report that his production company had failed and that he had been insolvent for some time. Bankrupted beyond bankrupt. To feed and clothe himself, to pay his creditors, he had been forced to cede all the film in his archives to the courts. He believed one day it would be returned to him, but now, with his country preparing for war, someone in some ministry, some pecuniary functionary, had decided the film stock should be scrapped and melted, shaped into heels to be cobbled onto the boots of soldiers. *All has been lost,* he wrote. *Nearly every trace of me, of our work together, will soon be marching into oblivion.* Only children appreciated magic these days, he contended. And so he had taken to making toys for them. Stuffed into the corner of the envelope, Bloom discovered a tiny metallic moon whose face spun about on a spool when its string was pulled.

✣

Bloom was informed by Meralda that he had received many letters from many young women expressing in refined penmanship a keen interest in making his acquaintance. She was in agreement with Gottlieb, as was Gus. It *was* time Bloom began a proper courtship. It is what your father would have wanted, she said to him when serving him one evening. And so she took it upon herself to respond to his letters and make invitations. For a period of a month—while Bloom continued cementing his rocks into the shape of the fortress— the young Rosenbloom dressed for dinner and sat in the dining room across from young women whose appearance and manners were as fine as the lines of their handwriting, and with each passing meal Bloom felt himself growing fat and bored. He thought the dozen women to whom Meralda and Gus had extended invitations priggish and prudish and self-possessed to such an extent they might as well have been dead. Not one appreciated the beauty of his birds or his view of the sea; they didn't enjoy a senseless meandering through the maze of the front gardens; they complained about the steep grade of the trail leading to Mount Terminus's peak; they thought it morbid that he would introduce them to his father's burial site; and they all insisted he walk them down to the lot so they might catch a glimpse of their favorite idols, actors, so many of whom Bloom found dull and uninteresting. And Bloom, who, to one degree or another, had discovered the beauty and life within every life model Gus had delivered to his studio some years earlier, Miss Merriweather included, found it deeply troubling that there existed women into whose eyes he could look and see nothing at all. How, he asked one afternoon while standing at the foot of his father's grave, before the eternal lovers, can I love if I'm not moved to love?

Don't worry, said Gus when Bloom asked him the same question, the quivers hit you when they hit you, and when they do you'll wish you never got struck by the little cherubic bastards.

>‹

The outer walls of Death's fortress had been completed, and Bloom had moved on to building the exterior of the cathedral in which Death captured the souls of the dead, when he heard Gottlieb call out from the courtyard, He has come! Rosenbloom! He is here!

Bloom stuck his head out the studio's doorway. Who's come, Mr. Gottlieb?

Dr. Straight. He's come to document your father's collection. Stop what you're doing and come meet him. Bloom put down his tools and met his miniature master and collaborator in the courtyard, followed him into the house and out onto the drive, where Gottlieb, who was in his usual animated state, made the introductions. Upon shaking Dr. Straight's hand, Bloom couldn't help but notice in what ways the man carried himself with a military bearing. He stood well over six feet tall, considerably taller than the taller-than-average Bloom. He possessed a bold nose and a sturdy jaw, wore an imposing mustache. He even had a brawny head, bald and gleaming, as if he applied a polish to it. His eyes looked at everything they beheld with such youthful intensity, they appeared as if they possessed a supernatural ability to see through solid objects. Bloom would have normally felt intimidated by a man of such overt, masculine stature— as he had felt around Gus when meeting him for the first time—but when Dr. Straight reached into the trunk of his automobile and presented to him a large box adorned with diamond inlay, Bloom saw the doctor's robust countenance transform—as if built into the musculature of his face was a childish wonder and topsy-turvy logic—and he understood Dr. Straight wasn't entirely defined by the body that contained him.

Go ahead, he said. The bristles of his mustache spread like the crest of a porcupine over the bridge of his smile. Open it.

Bloom unhooked a gilded latch and lifted the lid to find reflecting back at him his face turned upside down. He was so delighted by this, he shut the box and opened it again to repeat the experience, and upon opening it a second time he could now see there were two mirrors joined at a right angle. From somewhere behind him, he heard the voice of a woman say, Try turning it sideways. Bloom rotated the box and moved it about until he caught within the mirrors' frame a young woman about his age. She had hair as black as the darkness leading to Salazar's chamber and a complexion the color of cinnamon, a rich reddish brown that reminded him of the earth in Woodhaven after the rain had soaked the ground. As she neared, he could discern she stood almost as tall as he. Her shoulders were slim, neither too fragile nor delicate. She wore her hair with a flip at the nape of her neck, and short bangs that framed a face round and full in the cheeks, long and narrow in the chin. The lower half of her face provided an unusual balance to a most prominent nose that was thick along its ridges. In the shadow of this most sturdy feature, her mouth, whose lips spread tenderly when she smiled, appeared affectionate. But countering this warmth were near-translucent eyes, which, in the brightness of the afternoon, picked up the blue hue of the sky. Combined, the rich color of her skin, the pitch of her hair, the pastels of her eyes, made such an arresting image, Bloom felt something of an electric charge surge through him, and without meaning to, he clapped the box shut.

It takes some getting used to. She laughed. It's your true image. Nonreversed.

Bloom reopened the box for a third time, and there within the mirror's frame, he now saw himself looking at an image of himself he hardly recognized. She explained to him that the two mirrors joined at a right angle created the illusion of a single frame. The light hitting you refracts onto the right mirror, which then refracts again onto the left mirror. If you were looking at the right mirror alone, you would see yourself as you would ordinarily, in reverse, but once the light moves from the right mirror to the left mirror, you become reversed once again. There you have your true self.

It's what you and I will see when we turn to face each other, said Bloom.

Precisely, said the woman.

Bloom thought he looked very strange as his true self. To see his hair fall off to the left instead of the right, to find his symmetry reversed in the eyes and the cheeks, the mouth, to see reversed the slight imperfections in his teeth, was all so very disorientating, he averted his eyes to the woman, who he thought much more pleasant in comparison.

I've grown accustomed to it, she said, but I still prefer to see myself in reverse.

Bloom couldn't imagine in what way her beauty would be diminished from any perspective. He now shut the box again and turned to her, and there she was, exactly as she had appeared in the mirror.

I'm Isabella, she said.

I'm Joseph, said Bloom.

They held each other's gaze without speaking, and although he thought he was most certainly deceiving himself, he believed he saw in her expression the same fascination for him as he felt for her. And the mere possibility unnerved him.

PART IV

LOVE

O ver lunch in the courtyard that afternoon, Bloom learned Dr. Straight was an experimental psychologist whose sense of self-importance was equal to that of Gottlieb's and Simon's, as his humble aim as a practitioner was to find a means to curtail the collective impulse to wage war. He held the belief that civilization's instinct toward violence wasn't teleological in nature. If it were by design, he posited, why then would God provide man a conscience? Why would his creator provide him a moral imperative to nurture and sustain life, then ask him to ignore it? A soldier is trained to kill not by appealing to the best of his humanity, but by systematically stripping his humanity away from him, through a methodical act of reshaping his perception of men outside his tribe as something other than men. He had long ago concluded that if men were given the tools to see from an early age beyond the limits of who and what they were at any given time—if they were given the opportunity to foster within themselves a heightened consciousness, one that raised them closer to the aspirations their creator conceived for them—this broader perception of themselves would prevent such methods from being effective. They would more easily see with what narrow concerns authority was wielded and wars were waged. It is a matter of inhibiting the aggression inherent in men, he said, and replacing it with cold, dispassionate reason. It was his opinion that the most effective means to broaden consciousness and inspire enlightened, rational thought was through the means of visual perception.

He's on a mission, Isabella teased him, to achieve peace through optical illusion, to shine light into the eyes of the person living in darkness.

Dr. Straight looked at Isabella and kindly grinned. She likes to provoke me, he said. But she understands better than most what forces—what organized interests—summon men to war, and how these men, once indoctrinated, are irredeemably transformed on the battlefield. Those who have experienced the savagery I speak of, Joseph, the variety of savagery I participated in in the Philippines when I was a soldier, they normally refuse to revisit the horror because they're too haunted and repulsed by the memory, in some instances too regretful for the atrocious acts they've perpetrated, in other instances so overcome by pride they can't admit to themselves they were ordered to act in unconscionable ways, in ways that defy explanation, and in place of shame they choose bravado. Instead of healing their conscience, they choose to lean on the fictions of past glory and dwell in the darkest of silences, leaving the people who dwell in their ignorance of war to remain ignorant. For reasons I can't adequately explain, said Dr. Straight to Isabella, I have been affected differently than many of my comrades. I've been filled with a righteous indignation and am more than prepared to play the foolhardy proselytizer for peace, however naïve I might appear.

But how, exactly, asked Bloom, does the conceit of visual perception aid your cause?

Dr. Straight used his large hands to pantomime a barrier around him, and he explained to what extent man was a self-oriented, self-contained being, connected to others through spoken language, through the written word, through commerce, familial bonds, communal spaces, so much of which was predicated on what the individual saw of himself in relationship to others. I've been asking myself, said Dr. Straight, what would happen if we began to question not what we see on an ordinary day, but the very way we see it. How do we redefine what we take for granted? If we distance ourselves from our own points of view and question our basic assumptions of the world, what then changes within us? Do we begin to question what exists beyond our ordinary range of vision? Beyond the aggregate's accepted beliefs? Beyond its involuntary assumptions of the world?

And now Bloom asked how one created a distance between the self and what one sees.

That is the pertinent question, isn't it? said the doctor. Wearing a mischievous furrow on his brow, Dr. Straight turned again to Isabella. If you're genuinely interested, he now said, turning back to Bloom, if you're willing to give up a few days of your time to take part in our study, I'm sure Isabella will be very happy to administer the experiment.

For that you'll need to consult Mr. Gottlieb, said Bloom. My time belongs to him.

Please, said Gottlieb, use him in whatever manner you like. For however long you like. He's yours for the taking.

No, said Isabella to Dr. Straight. It's asking too much.

Nonsense, said the doctor. I promise you, Joseph, you'll benefit from the experience in ways you can't imagine.

To Isabella, Bloom said he'd be more than happy to participate.

You shouldn't indulge him, she said. He's indulged enough. Between me and his wife, he's spoiled to the core.

Dr. Straight ignored Isabella and began to speak of the work Bloom and Mr. Gottlieb were engaged in. He believed the art nearest to re-creating life—not as men experienced it, per se, but how they remembered it—was the motion picture. What are they, the pictures you make, if they're not a way to dream collectively? The experience, he argued, goes well beyond the solitary act of, say, reading a novel. It's somehow more real in its aftermath than recalling what happened between characters on a stage. He was fascinated with the way the moving images lived inside those viewing them, as if they were memories generated by the very minds they touched. I don't know about you, Joseph, but I've found myself on more than several occasions dreaming of pictures I've seen, as if the characters in those scenarios were men and women I knew from life. The question becomes, therefore, how can one use such a dream to most effectively evoke an inhibition response in the individual who's confronting the prospect of war? Dr. Straight believed it was imperative to bring to life for this individual, who would otherwise be seduced by glory and honor, the horrors of war in their entirety. He proposed that photographers should be sent out onto battle-fields wherever war was being waged, to film its atrocities and present them to the public unadorned. He thought it imperative that artists like Bloom and Mr. Gottlieb feel an obligation to construct *mimetic events* in which the human spirit was shown—through the most uncompromising images—to be crushed by war's barbarity. Damn society's sense of propriety, he said. Damn its precious composure. Whether it should be incidental footage or artifice made real, Dr. Straight desired to introduce an innate hesitation, an instinctual pause, a deeply felt revulsion, that went beyond the hesitation of primal fear and the impulse to preserve oneself. These very rational fears had proven to be too easily overcome by tribal and national concerns. Beyond natural instinct, he argued, there was the need to root within the culture a third hesitation, a hesitation influenced by the artificial memory of violence and its haunting aftermath. On the eve of war, men should not only be reminded of the noble warriors among them, but also the monsters living in those same warriors. Only then would a new morality, a new consciousness, be born. There is no other way, said Dr. Straight, to demythologize the war hero.

>＜

When they had all explored Dr. Straight's various ideas at length, and found they had exhausted all aspects of the subject, Gottlieb rose to his feet and said to Bloom and Isabella that they should get acquainted. I'll take Dr. Straight to the library.

Dr. Straight said to Isabella, Take your time, my dear.

As the two men walked into the villa through the courtyard door, Isabella said of the doctor, There's nothing he says, he doesn't believe. And there is nothing more he enjoys than to play the gadfly.

Don't you believe in what he advocates?

On the contrary, I believe in it all. Her father, Carlos Reyes, she told Bloom, died fighting alongside Dr. Straight in the Philippines. Her father had been an astronomer, and it was he, she said, and her mother, Anna Sorenson, a cultural anthropologist, who influenced Dr. Straight's thinking. When the doctor returned from the war, he often visited Isabella and her mother, and during those visits, she recalled, the two of them would sit together in the garden, and she would eavesdrop on them talking about how they might promote the practice of a pacifist ideal. So, you see, Joseph, it's deeply ingrained in me. It's as much my mother speaking as it is Dr. Straight. In many ways, it's all I have left of either of my parents.

Why is that?

A few years after the doctor's return from the war, she told him, her mother left her in the care of Dr. Straight and his wife, and went on an expedition in the mountains of Central America, where she contracted malaria and died before she made the return journey home.

I'm so sorry, said Bloom.

Thank you, said Isabella. I know you understand what it is to be alone in the world.

Yes, said Bloom, I do.

➤❤

Over dinner that evening, the passion of their afternoon conversation turned to Jacob Rosenbloom's remarkable collection of optical devices. All three of Bloom's dinner companions were well versed in the medieval world of scryers and the writings of John Dee. Dr. Straight was particularly impressed with the two items Gottlieb had pointed out to Bloom the first day he was introduced to the elder Rosenbloom's collection. Bloom would learn for the first time that evening that the device he had used to project the slides of *Death, Forlorn* for his father was a seventeenth-century thaumaturgic lantern designed and forged by an optician named Walgensten, which was known to the world from an illustration drawn by an optics enthusiast and Jesuit priest, Athanasius Kircher, who, in the year 1646, began publishing the journal *Ars Magna Lucis et Umbrae*, all of whose editions were collected in the other item Gottlieb had pointed out. They really are remarkable companion pieces, said Isabella. What's more, they discovered when examining the journal, Jacob was also in possession of Kircher's *magia catoptrica*, a spin wheel with a peephole for viewing images on interchangeable disks. They discovered several boxes of slides specifically designed for the *catoptrica*—*The Crucifixion of Jesus Christ, Son of God*; *The Ascent of Icarus*; *The Descent of Icarus*; *Orpheus in the Underworld*; and *Original Sin: The Fall of Man*. They were intrigued by the *Visionary Phantasmagorias* of Etienne-Gaspard, and spent time viewing *Apparitions, Spectres, Phantoms, and Shadows*; *The Drum of Eumenides*; *His Satanic Majesty*; *Medusa's Head*; *Doctor Young Interring His Daughter: The Head with the Revolving Glory*; *The Head of the Departed Hero*. They tried to imagine how he conducted his hydraulic experiments: *The Turkish Smoker*; *The Lantern of Diogenes*; *The Pneumatic Pump*; *The Ascending Egg Upon the Point of a Waterspout*; *Illuminated Lustre, Upon the Jet d'Eau*. Isabella, it turned out, had seen many of the modern projection devices—the phenakistoscope disk, the zoetrope, the choreutoscope, but she had never before seen a zoopraxiscope, an electrotachyscope, or a photographic gun.

Dr. Straight explained to Bloom how meaningful it was to him to see Kircher's journals, as it was an article on the Jesuit priest that Isabella's father kept in his files at home that had inspired his conversations with Isabella's mother. He, too, said Straight on the subject of Kircher, was a man who dedicated himself to a life of seeing the world anew after having wandered the battlefields of the Thirty Years' War. Like Bloom's father, Straight drew inspiration from Dee's postulate that light was the exuberance of God's great goodness and truth, that mirrors were the divine means to reflect that truth. He, too, believed in the limitless magic of the mind. You must take some time with the journal, he said to Bloom. If only to see the sketches of his magnetic oracle and botanical clock, his diagrams on magnets and sunspots, the stuffed crocodiles and skeletons, geodes, and ostrich eggs. With your permission, Dr. Straight said to Bloom, Isabella and I would very much like to stay for as long as it takes to document the collection. To which Bloom said with his eyes on Isabella, Yes, please do.

>‹

Maybe one day, Joseph, you'll recall the experience Isabella and I are about to give you and apply it to one of your pictures. Maybe one day in the future, you'll recall what it is I'm about to say to you now. Which is this: out of the depths of the mind, new powers are always emerging. And with that said, Dr. Straight and Isabella strapped onto Bloom a shoulder harness, which was attached to a device Isabella had invented and named the invertiscope, an elegant contraption consisting of a series of angled mirrors that rose up in a shaft whose design resembled a periscope's. At its highest point, its neck bent forward and then down; it could be manipulated with a system of pulleys whose cords dangled from rings just above his ears. If he pulled on the cord above his right ear, he could elevate the scope's angle upward and turn it a full 180 degrees around to his back; if he pulled on the cord above his left ear, he could rotate his perception back around and downward. The scope, therefore, provided Bloom a field of vision extending from the front of his body, to the sky, to his back. When the invertiscope had been fully secured to his head, he could now fully appreciate Dr. Straight's short speech in the courtyard, as he clearly understood, quite literally, the doctor's notion of heightened consciousness. He felt himself made strangely tall and elongated, and detached. It was as if he'd stepped out of his skin altogether, released—as Straight said—from his containment to become an invisible interloper looking down on his own life.

It took the better part of the day to learn how to maneuver with the invertiscope towering over him, but the material Isabella had used to manufacture the device, and the shoulder harness she'd designed, were remarkably well engineered, so well, in fact, that before the morning had finished Bloom had grown accustomed to its weight and was able to adjust his balance and gait. As a precaution, however, Isabella remained at his side, her arm entwined in his, advising him along the way when to make small adjustments to the scope with the pulleys. They spent the day walking the grounds, first through the mazes of the front gardens, next through the open field to the promontory, where Isabella held him with her chest pressed against his back, her hands gripping his shoulders, as Bloom stood at the headland's edge. There, he looked down, and saw himself looking down, and he described to Isabella the state in which he discovered his father at the bottom of the ravine. She guided him through the grove, around low-lying limbs, walked him under the canopy of trees jeweled in ripe summer fruit, and there in the shade he looked down on himself and Isabella as a bird might.

And here, when Bloom had begun to question his ability to love, he found this was the perspective he needed. He reached out with the hand nearest Isabella's shoulder and said to her, This space between us, this narrow space separating our shoulders, reminds me of a passage I read in Leonardo's notebooks. He advised painters who lacked inspiration to contemplate with a reflective eye a crack in an old wall, and there the painter, he advised, would find what was lacking. When Bloom said this, he could see from his vantage point Isabella look at his hand and tenderly take hold of it. She then leaned into him to close the gap between them. They next walked with great care up the stairwell to the tower's pavilion, where Bloom introduced her to his birds and demonstrated the various lines of repartee he had developed with Elijah. Here he could see the muscles in Isabella's face relax in appreciation of his aviary; and, later, when he observed with what ease she adjusted the gauges of the telescope to suit her eye, he couldn't help but think how naturally she fit into his private world above the tree line.

Before they entered the dining room for dinner that evening, Isabella said to Bloom, I should warn you, Dr. Straight will want you to carry on wearing the invertiscope for the remainder of the week. If you'd prefer not to, you should say so. He'll grumble a little, but he won't keep it up.

Why a week?

We've discovered it takes at least that long to fully alter your perception.

Meaning?

In that time you'll have adapted to your new point of view. Your orientation will have changed. You'll have grown accustomed to using your hands, for instance, by observing them from above instead of directly before you. But more important, you'll have observed yourself and the world around you long enough to fully comprehend in what ways you're an active participant in your own life. When I remove the invertiscope at that point of separation, you will, in theory, retain a more vivid memory of the divided self. The longer you experience the invertiscope's perspective, the longer it takes to reorient yourself when you shift back to your normal perspective. The process reinforces Dr. Straight's hypothesis, that perception isn't absolute, that the mind and body are capable of adapting to new associations.

In other words, said Bloom, we are not fixed.

Yes, said Isabella, looking up to the eye of the scope. We are not fixed.

When Bloom saw Isabella look at him directly and he thought of the intimacy they had shared without exchanging glances in the traditional sense, he said he was eager to continue on. I'd like very much to experience what that change feels like.

In that case, I recommend I feed you your dinner.

Why?

Handling small objects, she cautioned, will be the last motor skill you perfect.

Bloom found this arrangement agreeable. In the company of Gottlieb and Dr. Straight, Isabella sat beside him at the table and thoughtfully fed him and then fed herself. He related to the doctor and Gottlieb the strange and remarkable sensations he had felt throughout the day. He described them as one would describe a dream. And when he saw Isabella take the last bite from his plate, he confessed to feeling fatigued, which Dr. Straight said was common on the first day when wearing the invertiscope. Your body and mind haven't been as challenged, he said, since the time you were a small child. Isabella took him by the arm and led him up the stairs to his room, where, once inside, she ordered Bloom to shut his eyes, and when his eyes were shut, she removed the scope from its harness, the harness from his shoulders, then proceeded to place a pad of cotton over each eyelid and blindfold him. In the dark, he changed into his nightshirt and lay down in bed. From what point of view are you seeing in the dark? Isabella asked.

I seem to be switching back and forth.

Before the end of the week, you should see only from the eye of the invertiscope.

Will I dream from the invertiscope's point of view?

It's been known to happen. We'll see, won't we? . . . I have a book in hand, she said. Shall I read to you?

If you don't mind.

Not at all. And on Isabella went to read from the pages of Ovid's *Metamorphoses*.

✳

In the seven days Bloom wore the invertiscope, he adapted to his altered perception. He successfully managed to help Meralda prepare a meal in the kitchen, handled a deck of cards and played out several hands of rummy with Gus, navigated his way through the grove to the stand of eucalyptus trees, where, with his back to the plateau, he watched Simon conduct the morning orchestration of the studio lot. When Isabella blindfolded him on the third night and asked him what he saw in the dark, he saw only from the invertiscope's perspective. And that night, he dreamed he was flying, following Isabella through the labyrinths of his father's gardens. When, at the end of the seventh day, Isabella and Dr. Straight removed the scope and harness from Bloom's body, he expected to feel some

profound change take place within him, but aside from his equi-
librium having been set off balance, and his lines of sight feeling
somehow limited and inadequate, the most powerful sensation he
experienced was a feeling of ennui. He described his melancholy to
Isabella before bed that night. She assured Bloom this had been a
recurring theme among their subjects.

I believe, she said, it has something to do with the loss of the
elevated perspective, with the diminution of feeling one experiences
from loftier heights. You've grown accustomed to seeing yourself play
a role in your own life from a position of remove—it's as if a character
in a story has disappeared.

This made good sense to Bloom, and he was certain all this played
some part in the onset of his malaise; but he knew, too, when he
looked into Isabella's eyes as she searched for further theories to explain his altered mood, his sadness had as much to do with the fact
that she and Dr. Straight would one day depart from Mount Terminus and return to the university. The only comfort Bloom took from
the connection he had formed with Isabella was that she appeared
to have grown equally connected to him, and perhaps, he thought,
she would consider remaining behind.

>←

In the coming days, they separated after breakfast—Bloom went off
to work in his studio, Isabella to the library—and they returned to
each other for a walk up the trails after lunch. When her work was
through for the day, Isabella joined Bloom in his studio and sat
with him as he continued the tedious work of constructing the
cathedral within Death's fortress. They left Dr. Straight to Gottlieb's
company after dinners and lounged together in the gallery, where
they read to each other and shared with each other more details about
their pasts. Bloom told her the story of his father and mother, his aunt
and brother, and when Isabella had heard the entire tale, she expressed an interest in meeting Simon. She wanted to see, she said,
what she could expect Bloom to look like in ten years' time. Bloom

was moved to relate to her what had transpired between him and Simon in the months before her arrival, the dull ache he continued to feel in the aftermath of Simon's deception, but he couldn't see how to do this without betraying Stern's confidence, or casting a pall over Simon's character. He didn't want to elicit pity or suggest in any way that he was a cynic on the subject of love, whether it brotherly or otherwise. And because he couldn't invent a good-enough excuse to keep Isabella from meeting Simon, he walked her down to the plateau one afternoon to make the introduction, when, to his relief and good fortune, he learned from Murray Abrams that his brother had departed for an extended leave, to the north, to the Bay Area, where he was consulting with his architects and engineers. I know he intended to see you before he left, said Abrams.

It must have slipped his mind.

He has been overwhelmed.

Bloom sounded a false note of regret and apologized to Isabella for Simon's absence.

Abrams, who Bloom could see was as entranced as Bloom had been when he first set eyes on Isabella, insisted he be allowed to tour Bloom's new friend around the studio. Bloom rather enjoyed the privilege of watching Abrams lord over the lot as if it belonged to him. He told them old show-business stories from his vaudeville days, and grew nostalgic for a time before he involved himself in the novelty act of making pictures. He missed proper show people. He missed the desperate wretches who couldn't survive without the adulation—the laughs, the groans—of a living, breathing, coughing, talking, abusive, overly enthusiastic audience. The applause, Abrams said to Isabella, it filled us up with what was lacking inside. Here, he said as they walked among the hanging strips of film in the editing suite, we are little more than ghosts of the men and women we used to be.

They parted company with Bloom's old mentor, and the young Rosenbloom took the liberty of taking Isabella into Simon's home. He showed her the white parlor and the memorabilia of Simon's past glory on the stage. He showed off photographs of Simon stand-ing in the company of his stars, and from these images Isabella could see one possible outcome of Bloom's physical future. As she turned her head between Bloom and the photograph, Isabella said—as everyone said—There really is quite an uncanny resemblance. To pro-vide her greater context, he led Isabella to the room in which Simon maintained his shrine to his mother, and there she was impressed by the devotion his brother had shown his mother, and she was equally intrigued with the rather forward images of Leah, the bold-ness of her sexuality, the unapologetic manner in which she pre-sented herself to the world, and what that unfettered spirit inspired in the artists she came in contact with. She marveled for some more time over the raised relief map depicting Simon's vision, and she loved the screening room, where she and Bloom spent the remainder of the afternoon sitting side by side, watching pictures he'd helped make, including *Mephisto's Affinity*.

>←

When Bloom completed the construction of Death's cathedral, he returned to the wall, aged it with sulfuric acid, adhered vines to its crevices, and began painting moss and lichen. Isabella had taken to sitting by him in the evenings, reading while he worked, asking him an occasional question about a poem or a story, a point of philosophy. After one such night some weeks into Isabella and Dr. Straight's stay, Bloom awoke to find a note from Roya pinned to the chest of his nightshirt. It read, *Take her to the chamber. When you have seen all you have seen before, I'll reveal to you two items yet to be discovered.*

Upon reading this, Bloom wanted to rush outside to Isabella's cottage and steal her away, but he knew she was expected in the library at any moment. He chose to wait until lunchtime, when she wouldn't be missed. And all the better, as after he dressed and walked downstairs he found Stern waiting for him in the parlor. His attor-ney's health appeared to be in decline. He had lost a considerable amount of weight; the flesh under his eyes sagged and looked bruised. His body effervesced a sweet odor from too much drink, his suit jacket and pants looked slept in, but most untidy of all, the hair about his horseshoe of baldness had grown out into uneven tufts that made him look like a madman escaped from an asylum. When Bloom asked Mr. Stern if he had been unwell, Stern said in a voice entirely depleted of his former self, I've been drinking.

Perhaps you'd like to lie down for a little while?

No, I wouldn't. The news I have to deliver is unpleasant. I'd prefer to get on with it.

What's happened?

Stern's eyes drifted from Bloom for a moment, then returned. Losses, he said. I'm here to report we've experienced substantial losses. Given Stern's conservative nature with regard to Bloom's financial holdings, perhaps, Bloom thought, his use of the word *substantial* wasn't quite as *substantial* as Stern was making out. Perhaps *substantial* to Stern meant a small shortfall. Bloom knew nothing about the rise and fall of fortunes, but he intuitively understood a fortune as large as his couldn't be easily dissolved.

How substantial?

Quite substantial . . . I'm afraid Simon's demands on us, on you, have grown excessive.

What does that mean, Mr. Stern? Am I ruined?

No. Well . . . not quite. But your holdings outside your brother's concerns have been significantly diminished. The short of it is, Joseph, if Simon fails to deliver the water to the property he's developing in the next year, at the latest, you *will* be ruined. For the better part of the next half hour, Bloom made a concerted effort to listen to his drunk and disheveled advocate erratically advocate a method to hide some of his assets from his brother. He proposed he fictionalize the premature purchase of such and such a property, inventing several risky capitalizations that failed to pay off. He concocted stories about an outbreak of hoof and mouth disease at two of Bloom's ranches, a devastating explosion in the oil fields, something about poor crop yields in the tropics, a host of margin calls by the market.

The poor man, thought Bloom, was losing his mind. Perhaps he already had. Stern could think of no other way to stanch the bleeding and reassert Bloom's position . . .

What was Bloom to say?

Stern had never solicited his opinion before. He had only informed and advised and acted on his behalf, and Bloom literally knew nothing of what was being asked of him. You must do whatever you think best, Mr. Stern, Bloom said in the end. I trust you to do what's best for us both.

Stern, half-composed, said, Yes, all right. All right.

Meanwhile, Bloom proposed again, perhaps you should have a rest before you begin your journey down the mountain?

Stern ignored Bloom's offer and instead took hold of his shoulder and looked him in the eye. You do realize, Joseph, it's in your power to do with me as you see fit. You should consider the possibility you might better benefit by letting Simon act on his threat against me. You would be free of him at that point. You could take legal action against him. I wouldn't blame you. In some ways, it would be a relief.

No, said Bloom. We are in this together, Mr. Stern. We must have faith in Simon and his project if we're to get through this.

But all that money, said Stern with widening eyes. A lifetime of your father's work. Don't be foolish. My cousin, Saul, will happily help you find someone else to conduct your business. Given the way I've failed you, I'd consider it a reasonable course of action if you decided to dispossess me of that privilege.

Bloom was now confused. Do you *want* me to release you from your responsibility, Mr. Stern? Do you *want* me to inform Mr. Geller? Is that what you're saying?

Stern looked down to his feet for a moment. When he looked up, he shook his head and said, No. No. My entire life . . .

I know, said Bloom, I know. Mr. Stern, I do know something of life's disenchantments, and this, said Bloom as he pointed to Stern's overstuffed attaché, doesn't trouble me nearly as much as I think it troubles you. That you're so upset by what's happened only inspires my faith in you. I have every reason to believe you'll do everything you can to see us through this. Please, don't make yourself ill over it. You have loved ones relying on you. Feel blessed you have that, if nothing else.

Stern nodded at this sentiment. I do. Of course I do.

Then all is well so far as I'm concerned. As long as I'm able to continue living here, as long as I can sustain the estate and its staff, continue to work on my pictures, I'm very content.

In which case, you have nothing to worry about.

Then I'm not worried.

Very well, then, said Stern, who appeared relatively calmed. That puts me at ease.

I'm happy for that.

Thank you. You've been very kind, Joseph. Too kind. And with that said, off Stern went with his fat attaché weighing down one side of his skinny frame.

><

Isabella entered the parlor just after Stern departed. Who was that sorry-looking man?

That was Stern.

He looks unwell.

I know. He's deeply troubled.

He doesn't look fit to be on his feet.

I said to him as much. But I couldn't persuade him to lie down.

What's happened to him?

He's had a shock. A personal matter.

Isabella pressed her fingers to her lips as if she were trying to hold something in, and then out of her mouth erupted a small burst of laughter. I'm sorry, she said through her laugh.

What is it?

She apologized again and said, He honked his nose at me when he greeted me hello.

Who did?

Your Mr. Stern.

Did he? Maybe you excited him?

You mean to say I excited him with a simple hello?

I've read of such things. About men whose septums work at cross-purposes with their breathing when aroused.

I've never heard of such a thing.

No, said Bloom with a smile. Neither have I.

Isabella tapped Bloom's arm with her fist, then took hold of it. Together, they walked to the dining room and had made their way through half their lunch when Bloom—who could no longer restrain his excitement—said, I can't wait any longer. I can't pretend today is like any other day. Come with me. Now.

What's gotten into you?

Come. Please.

But I haven't finished my lunch.

You won't need to finish when you see what I have to show you. Bloom took Isabella by the hand and dragged her away from the table. He walked her through the kitchen to the cellar door, where he handed her a flashlight.

What is this for?

Don't ask questions. Just follow me.

Bloom led Isabella down the stairs. He walked her through the butterfly buttresses that formed the underground vaults, and when they reached the entrance to the chamber, Bloom stood before Isabella and said, You must promise me something before you go in.

Isabella shone her flashlight about the darkness, and said, Go in where, Joseph?

Ignoring her, Bloom persisted. You'll want more than *anything* to tell Dr. Straight about what I'm about to show you, but you must promise me you won't. I've never shown anyone this place, not Father, not Simon, not Gottlieb. You'll be the only one, so, please, you must promise me this will remain ours, and ours alone.

Isabella once again shone the flashlight around the darkened vault, and when she stopped, she shone the light onto Bloom's face and examined it.

Trust me, Bloom said into the gleam of the light, and make me your promise.

All right, said Isabella, I give you my promise. Whatever it is you make appear in the darkness will belong to us.

And with that, Bloom took Isabella's hand and walked her to the column of bricks. He set her palm against it and said, Push. Isabella pushed, and in the door swung to reveal the chamber and its ladder. In the darkness, Bloom could see her eyes widen. Do you trust me? Bloom asked.

Yes, said Isabella.

Then start climbing. Climb all the way to the top and come meet me in the gallery when you have seen what's there.

Isabella took hold of a rung and paused, then, taking Bloom by surprise, she turned around and embraced him. She held him for some time, the shapeliness of her form snug against him, and when she eased herself away, she returned and pressed her lips to his mouth, hard at first, but then softer, with affection; and when she removed her lips from his, she continued to hold Bloom for a moment longer, and then, without looking him in the eye, she quickly turned back to the ladder and started up. And as she did so, Bloom ran through the vaults, through the kitchen, up the stairs to his mother's gallery, and there he sat on the chaise staring into the pinholes of Aphrodite's eyes, through the wall, to Isabella.

Bloom reclined on the chaise and waited, and knowing he was present with Isabella in Manuel Salazar's room, he found himself relaxed, and he drifted off to sleep. He slept for some time, and was awakened when Isabella snuggled up against him. It's a camera obscura, she whispered in his ear. It must be hundreds of years old. She sounded giddy.

Yes, I know.

But how? she said, looking to the surface of the wall.

Aphrodite's eyes. See the pinholes?

How incredible.

And Bloom noticed now Isabella was holding Salazar's journal in her hand. From those pages, he explained as he touched the book, I learned how to draw.

Have you never read what's written here?

No. I don't read Spanish.

Isabella opened the journal and said she had read it through to the end while Bloom napped.

Please, tell me, who's the woman he pines for in all the drawings?

Miranda. The wife of Don Fernando Miguel Estrella.

And what did he write about them?

A great deal. Mostly about how they came to live on Mount Terminus and how they established themselves when they arrived. At the beginning, he recounts the time just after Fernando and Miranda were married. While they attended a ball in honor of King Philip of Spain, Fernando had a dispute with a member of the royal court over an insult directed at Miranda. The insult led to a challenge, the challenge led to a duel, the duel resulted in Fernando's favor. Unknown to Fernando, however, the king considered the slain man an ally and a dear friend. And for not having acted with the king's consent, Fernando found himself in his disfavor. As a punishment, he was pressed into service. Philip appointed him viceroy of this territory, a position many would have found desirable, but to Fernando, who was content with his life in Spain, the king's order was tantamount to a prison sentence. He considered this place the end of the world. The end of his world. Which is why he named the estate Mount Terminus.

I see, said Bloom.

Manuel, Isabella said, was Fernando's cousin. Poor. Without family. But a trained architect and builder. When Fernando was sent away, his father, also a Don Fernando, commissioned Manuel to build a proper villa for his son. In return for his work, he would receive the Estrellas' patronage. Fernando and Manuel scouted for the land, and when they saw the mountain with the spring, Fernando sent for the priests at the mission.

The priests, they arrived with every intention of reasoning with the people who lived on the land, but Fernando ordered them and his garrison of soldiers to gain control of the mountain and its spring by force, and clear the land of its people. When the natives had been subdued, Don Fernando ordered all men over the age of twelve massacred. A sight, Manuel wrote, that should have blinded him. An event for which he would never forgive his cousin or God. He thought of returning to Spain in the aftermath of the atrocity, but on their long journey to Mount Terminus, he had grown so enraptured by Miranda's beauty and her way of being, he felt compelled to remain near her. He was convinced the love Fernando felt for his wife couldn't compare with his. And although Miranda hardly recognized Manuel's existence—she considered him little more than a servant—he was intent to prove the extent to which he loved her. He was determined to build, over the graveyard of Fernando's savagery, a cathedral worthy of Miranda's beauty.

Isabella became silent for a moment. She turned to Aphrodite's eyes and said, He must have constructed the camera obscura to be near her, to see her, here, in secret. She now turned back to Joseph and touched the curls of hair that hung over his forehead. The shape of her lips suggested to Bloom she was about to say something more, but she instead drew her mouth to his and kissed him again.

✳

The morning after he and Isabella had visited Manuel Salazar's chamber together, Bloom awoke to find on his nightstand a small skeleton key and a note that read, *The key fits the lock at the base of the clock in your father's room.* The clock Roya referenced Bloom knew to be the one built into the wall, the one that hadn't kept time for as long as he had lived on the estate. With the key in hand, he walked down the landing and entered the room in which his father rarely slept; there he stood at the foot of the bed, searching the exterior of the clock's base for a lock into which he could insert the key, but he found none. He next searched under the pendulum, and here, too, he couldn't see where it belonged. He was about to give up looking when he noticed overlying the wood behind the face a tarnished metal disk held in place by a pin. He bent down and pushed it around its axis, and there, underneath, he discovered the lock. Into it he slipped the key and gave it a turn, and when he had rotated it all the way around, a plank of wood that formed the clock's bottom dislodged, and when it did, Bloom lifted it up to find resting on the floorboards a metal box, which he removed and opened, and there inside saw a notebook identical to the one in the chamber.

Before he turned open the cover, Bloom returned to his room and dressed, and with the notebook in hand walked down and out into the courtyard to Isabella's cottage. He gently tapped on the door, and when he heard her voice ask who was there, he answered her. Come in, she said, and he let himself in to find her reading in bed, wearing little more than a slip. When he saw what state she was in, he turned to face the window.

Joseph?

Yes?

Don't be childish. Come, she insisted, sit by me. When Bloom turned, she said, It's all right. I'm not ashamed.

No?

No. Not with you.

In an attempt to control himself, Bloom shut his eyes and took a deep breath, then took another. I wanted to share this, he said, offering her the book.

What is it?

I think it's the second volume of Manuel's journals. Bloom removed his shoes and reclined his back against the headboard of the bed and stretched out his legs. Isabella turned to him and pressed the back of her head into his lap. She then lifted her knees so the material of the slip fell into the open space between her thighs. I was hoping, Bloom said with a small catch in his throat, you'd read this one as well?

Isabella had already opened the cover to the first page, from which she read the title, *The Bathing Habits of Doña Miranda Celeste Estrella*. She then glanced up at Bloom. There's no author cited, but it's in Manuel's hand. Together they looked for the first time at what was depicted in the journal's pages, and here was revealed the most intimate details of any woman's life. All variations of the same image: Miranda lounging in the bath, her attendant participating in one fashion or another in the cleansing of her body.

It's a little naughty, Isabella said to Bloom.

Do you mind?

She hesitated a moment as she read ahead. No, she said, once again glancing up to Bloom. But, in fact, it's *very* naughty.

But if we're to know?

Then, I suppose, it's necessary. Isabella now returned to the opening and concentrated on the pages. The writing isn't like the last. It's more . . . authorial. Here, you see, she said as she ran her finger over a phrase, he describes *the tropical length of her arms*. Her appendages were so long and flexible, it seems, she said with a laugh, she was able to remove her corset without the aid of her chambermaid, Adora. The household servants, men and women alike, Isabella translated, paraded in steaming buckets of water past Miranda, who stood naked before the tall mirrors inside her boudoir. The servants poured the hot water into a tub Manuel had especially cast for the uncommon length of her body. And there she is before the mirrors, Isabella said as she turned the page, and there are the servants, the men and women alike, carrying their scuttles. And as we see here on the page that follows, Miranda did not stand idly by as they passed, but rather, stretched one of her arms high over her head while she used the other to stroke her forearm and underarm, down and up, up and down, alternating limbs until the tub was filled. Isabella paused for a moment and pressed her head back against Bloom's lap, and said, rather playfully, Would you like me to continue?

Would you like to continue?

She smiled at him and flipped several pages ahead. Ah, she

said, here he lists the perfumes and oils and tonics, the flora and fauna Adora added to the steaming water, and then goes on at great length . . .

Yes?

Isabella took in a breath and let it out through her nose. He goes on at great length about a scrub brush whose handle was made of a finely polished glass. An instrument, he writes, she submerged through the rose petals floating over the water's surface, and with it, she formed small eddies that whirled about between the archways of her knees.

Hmm, said Bloom.

Yes, said Isabella. When she emerged from the tub, he continues, the flowers held to her body *leechfully*. And for some paragraphs here, she said, pointing to those paragraphs, he describes the patterns shaped by the cascades of water running down her back, around her shoulder blades, through the valley of her breasts, all converging, he writes, on the triangle of a sparkling pubis. Here, she said, he describes Adora in her maid's uniform, her hair covered in lace. She would hold hand mirrors up to the naked Miranda for the purpose of *self-examination*. He wrote of the care with which this same attendant applied talc to Miranda's chest, in what manner she cupped the weight of each breast with one hand and with the other padded the underside of its heft with a fine brush made from the tail of a horse. He wrote of how Adora parted Miranda's long legs and dabbed at her inner thighs with this same brush, then turned her over so that she presented her ass, into whose crease she sprinkled the powder, and then ran her fingers into its seam.

He describes here, said Isabella, whose legs had begun to embrace the material between them, the hundred strokes the attendant ran through Miranda's hair with a hard marble comb, and he writes in meticulous detail about the application of her face cream, in particular, the white face paint applied to Miranda's skin with a blunt knife and a dry cloth.

Isabella now became quiet. She was reading ahead, and as she did so, the openness of her face began to close. The entirety of this last section, she said with the concerned expression remaining fixed, charts the effects Manuel observed on Miranda's health over several years. The young woman with the pink pallor, the vital woman he adored, turned lethargic and pallid with hollow cheeks and wobbly legs. She is plumbed around the ankles and wrists, he writes. Suffers from what he calls *Saturnism*? Isabella now looked to Bloom, but Bloom could only shake his head. Miranda, Isabella said as she reached the end, grew so hopelessly ill, Manuel could no longer observe her. The sight of her, he wrote, saddened him too much to set his eyes on her.

And there, said Isabella, this volume ends. Isabella shut the cover and held it to her chest. What, she asked Bloom, would motivate her to do such a thing? She must have known what the application of the paint was doing to her. It appeared as if she were doing it deliberately.

I couldn't say.

If it's true, said Isabella. If what he depicts here has any truth to it, it would seem she intentionally destroyed herself. Destroyed her beauty.

Bloom tried to remove the journal from Isabella's hands, but she refused to let him take it. Please, she said, leave it with me.

Of course, said Bloom.

Is there more?

Bloom knew Roya would reveal the third part soon, so he said, Yes. Later. I'll show it to you later.

Isabella rolled onto her side, and when she did she allowed herself to feel Bloom's erection on her cheek. I think I'm going to draw myself a bath.

I think, perhaps, I'll do the same.

I'll see you at lunch?

Yes, said Bloom. At lunch.

Isabella dragged her cheek away from his lap. She withdrew slowly, watching Bloom's pants rise.

※

When Bloom had stepped outside Isabella's cottage, he looked up to the tower's pavilion, where he saw Roya looking down on him, calling him to her with a wave of her arm. He walked inside and made his way to the tower stairs and there found her standing beside the cellar door. Why, he asked her, are you choosing to show this to me now? Roya placed a finger to his lips, then reached for his hand and led him down into the cellar. She pulled him along through the empty vaults, and when they reached the chamber door, she pushed it open and pointed Bloom to the ladder. Why? he asked. Why now? Roya responded to his question by pressing her weight against his body. She pushed Bloom in, set his hand on one of the ladder's rungs, then pointed up into the darkness. Following Roya's command, he climbed, and when he reached the top, he opened the door to Manuel Salazar's room, where he saw the projection table leaning against the shelves opposite the door. Where the table had rested all these years, Bloom now saw a wooden hatch open in the floor, and at the edge of the hatch, a message from Roya written in charcoal. *Follow the silver thread.* Where these words were punctuated sat a lantern and box of matches. Bloom lit the lantern and held it over the opening where the table had been, and found there a ladder leading down some ten feet or so. With the lantern in hand he climbed to the bottom, and there he discovered a narrow passage and was reminded of the floor plans Roya had shared with him moments before he first entered the chamber those many years ago. On the wall of the passage just a few steps away, he encountered a fresco of a nymph draped in white robes. Cinched around her hips was a purple sash, crowning her head, a purple laurel. She stood in profile with her arm outstretched and she held in her hand the limp end of a silver thread that wilted to her feet and wound into a coil. A single mercuric strand looped into oblong circles, then stretched taut down the corridor. Bloom followed the line into the darkness. He turned left and then right, right and then left, until he reached the thread's end, which was woven into a tunic worn by a young warrior loping forward, taking flight, a dagger clutched in his hand. The silver stitching formed on the tunic's back an image of a grand kingdom at whose center stood the nymph and the warrior in miniature, the two of them locked in embrace. Towers rose above them, up to the warrior's shoulders. Turreted walls secured them, their stones hugging at the young man's waist. Held in the grip of these structures' stitching were the straps of a golden breastplate imprinted with a labyrinth so intricately plotted, its multitude of warrens appeared to Bloom as if they were changing shape before his eyes. At the point of the warrior's dagger was an open doorway, through which Bloom stepped, and there he found a room aglow with an image of the library reflecting off a mirror onto a projection table, the lens in this case shining through the eye of a Minotaur. Here, there was no chair, no shelves, only a motley heap of blankets, next to which he saw a decanter and an empty wineglass whose stem had snapped. Beside these items sat a flat box with an inkwell, a quill, and a candleholder. Bloom placed the lantern next to the decanter and carefully touched each of the items near it. When he arrived at the blankets, he pulled back the corner to see dark strands of human hair mingling with the blankets' worsted threads. Bloom considered if he really wanted to pull the blanket back any farther, to see what horrific sight was there. Knowing this was what Roya intended him to see, he shut his eyes for a moment and took a breath, and once he had gathered his courage, he pulled the woolen cover away altogether.

Revealed to him were the mummified remains of a woman wearing the very uniform he had seen Miranda's attendant, Adora, wearing in Manuel Salazar's journal. He reached for his lantern and hung it over her face to find an image he had seen before only in photographs, of the unwrapped remains found in Egyptian tombs. She looked like a doll whittled from mahogany, brown and varnished, with no nose or lips or eyes to speak of. She appeared to be wearing a fright mask too large for her face. Her mouth was agape, her teeth discolored and bucked, all her soft tissue long ago shriveled or decomposed. Bloom sat beside her for some time, long enough to grow accustomed to the sight, and soon he lost his fear to touch her. He touched first her hair and found upon contact it turned to dust. Her skin was a petrified shell, brittle in texture, and when he jabbed at her fingers, which were clasped together over her chest, the digits clattered. He spoke to her now. Promised her that one day he would return to give her a proper burial in the gardens. But for the time being, he covered her over once again, and turned to the box. In it, he found wrapped in cloth, a stack of parchment, each page filled with writing.

>←

Bloom waited until after dinner to show Isabella these papers. When they had finished eating, he escorted her to the gallery, and as they had done that morning, they reclined together, and Isabella translated the testimony Adora had written after she had been entombed alive.

She writes here at the beginning, said Isabella, she's been made a prisoner to keep her from telling anyone what she's seen. Here, Isabella said, she expresses her love for Miranda, and asks God's forgiveness for having transgressed in ways for which she should feel shame, but can't, because the sins she's committed were bound by the love she felt for her mistress.

What had she done? asked Bloom.

She writes that Fernando was a savage and a monster, who from the moment he married Miranda suffocated her with an affection she couldn't return. She recounts the circumstances of their exile. Explains here that the incident between Fernando and the king's man wasn't the honorable confrontation Fernando claimed it to be, but rather an act of murder, a spontaneous assault committed against the man for doing little more than make a passing gesture to Miranda in a corridor, a simple greeting directed in his and his wife's direction. He saw something that wasn't there, she writes, and he grew so impassioned with rage, he dashed the poor man's head in with the silver handle of his walking stick. It was for this they were sent away from everyone and everything they knew. And for this, for having solicited the man's attention, for creating a circumstance in which he was forced to defend her honor, Fernando punished Miranda. He locked her away. Behind the closed doors of the ship's cabin when they made their passage, behind closed doors here in this house. Her only authority, said Isabella, was over her servants, so she took great liberties with them as a form of rebellion against Fernando.

To spite him, she dispensed with decorum. To humiliate him, she paraded herself around as she pleased within the confines of her chambers. Every day she prayed Fernando would tire of her antics and return her to Spain. When this appeared unlikely, she changed her tactic and began to pursue Manuel, whom she knew loved her. One day, not very long after the villa had been completed, Fernando rode out into the valley to inspect his cattle, when, on Miranda's order, Adora carried a message to Manuel. Miranda invited him into this room, Isabella said, and she and Adora together seduced him and made love to him. They repeated this experience for some months until Manuel had grown accustomed to their affections. The women then began withdrawing their warmth, and soon grew cold. He begged them, she writes, to accept his love and devotion. Miranda offered to be his if he could arrange their escape. She said if he returned with her and Adora to Spain, she would devote herself to him entirely. Manuel agreed, and one morning, not long afterward, he sent word with Adora that he'd organized safe passage to the port; the two women, he said, should be prepared to leave that evening. That night, however, passed into morning, and Manuel never came. Miranda sent Adora to him, and Adora found him sitting in his studio on the hill in an agitated state. His work, he told her, his position, was more important to him than he had realized, more important to him than the love he felt for them. He couldn't bring himself to sacrifice Fernando's patronage. To have done what Miranda had asked of him, he explained, would mean the end of his dreams. I am a coward, he said to Adora. You chose your hero poorly. Miranda, Adora writes, now grew despondent. Nothing she could do for her would lift her from her despair. And here, Isabella said, is the answer I was searching for earlier today. Miranda decided she would no longer allow these men to enjoy her as their object of desire. She would show them how she truly felt by manifesting her sorrow in her appearance. So she began poisoning herself in the manner we saw in the notebook. It took only months, Adora writes, before she became thin and frail, and a few months more before she was gravely ill, so ill and so ugly to behold, both Fernando and Manuel were grief-stricken at the sight of her. They diverted their eyes away from her when she passed, wept at the mere mention of her name. And when Fernando began to see how her condition affected Manuel, he began to suspect his sadness derived not from a cousinly concern, but from a deeper affection. Unknown to him, Fernando ordered his man, Roberto, to keep a watchful eye on Manuel, and it was at this time Roberto discovered Manuel's secret chamber. Roberto told Fernando, and Fernando, one morning while Manuel was away at work, climbed the ladder to see his wife take her morning bath, and saw in what manner Adora attended to her, and he saw the poison she had been applying to her face. At the sight of this, Fernando descended the shaft's ladder and charged upstairs to his wife's room, and in front of Adora, he brutalized Miranda, who, as she was being beaten, courageously expressed her contempt for him, encouraged him to beat her harder. And he did just that. And the harder he beat her, the more she insulted him, swore to him that any love she ever felt for him was false. As she bled from her nose and mouth, she bragged of her affair with Manuel, told him what great comfort she had taken in his body. She needn't have said any more than this, Adora writes. She could have saved herself the beating had she only said this at the start, as Fernando in that instant threw Miranda over his shoulder and carried her to the tub, where he submerged her in the bath. With one hand he held her under the water by the throat, with the other he fended off Adora. Miranda struggled for several minutes, kicked and scratched at her husband, but she eventually grew still. Adora, at this point, ran off to hide, but when she entered the courtyard, she saw Manuel descending the steps from the studio. She ran to him and told him what Fernando had done. She told him Fernando knew of their attachment and begged him to run away and hide with her. Manuel, instead, charged off in a rage. Adora, intent to stop him, followed him to the boudoir, where he discovered Miranda on the bed, her body . . . Isabella lifted her hand to her mouth.

What is it? asked Bloom. On Isabella's face was an expression of profound disgust.

He defiled her, she said. It wasn't enough to brutalize her and drown her. He went so far as to . . .

What?

He lodged a candle inside her, she said, and lit the wick. When Adora and Manuel walked in, it had just begun to singe the bedspread. Adora blew out the flame and covered her over, and Manuel, he was now in an even greater rage. He called out Fernando's name. In response, Fernando called his, from somewhere below. And down Manuel went, Adora writes. From the landing she watched Fernando and Roberto drag him out to the courtyard, where Roberto restrained his arms and Fernando drove over and over again the blade of a knife into his chest. They then let him go, to stumble away and fall face-first into the reflecting pool. It was then Roberto turned away from Manuel's corpse to her. He walked upstairs and grabbed hold of her by the hair, dragged her into the cellar, where he struck her on the head. When she awoke, she found herself entombed, trapped in the void of the villa, where she was left with a pen and some paper, three candles, and one decanter of water. God forgive me, she writes here at the bottom. And then at the end, Miranda, my love, I am coming to you.

><

Neither Bloom nor Isabella could have anticipated that this funereal night in which they lay together quietly contemplating the fates of Miranda, Adora, and Manuel Salazar would be their last for the foreseeable future. The following day, Isabella stood in the doorway of Bloom's studio some hours before they were to meet for lunch to tell him Dr. Straight had received a telegram informing him that his wife, Julia, had fallen gravely ill. Bloom followed her out to her cottage and helped gather her things. When the packing was finished, they paused long enough for Bloom to say, You will come back to me, won't you?

She leaned into Bloom and, without saying a word, kissed him.

Please, said Bloom, tell me you'll come back.

Yes, she said, I will.

As soon as you're able.

Yes, said Isabella. As soon as I'm able.

And that was all. In an hour's time of hearing the news, Bloom stood at the top of the drive with Gottlieb beside him, and they watched them motor away.

Do you feel the despair? Gottlieb asked as the sedan dipped down onto the mountain road.

Yes, said Bloom.

Good! Now go use it! The small man reached up and turned Bloom's shoulders, pulled down his chin so they faced each other. I will not tolerate idleness. Not for a moment. There is much too much to do. If you must be forlorn, be forlorn with Death. He awaits you. Gottlieb now turned Bloom in the direction of the door, walked him through to the courtyard, and pointed him in the direction of the studio.

><

Bloom returned to his work that day, but as much as Gottlieb willed him not to allow his emotions to interfere with his work, but to make it better, Bloom felt such a profound absence of spirit, he wanted nothing more than to take to his bed. He somehow managed to continue his preparations for the production of *Death, Forlorn*, stopping every now and again to draw for Isabella a small sketch. He posted in the mail two, sometimes three drawings a day, each a small detail of the villa. If accumulated and arranged at the point of delivery, they would have been a taxonomy of his small world's margins. For some time, he drew objects that hung on walls and in doorways: Oriental cloths, strings of Turkish beads, a Japanese lantern suspended from a silk cord. At other times, he drew bouquets of chrysanthemums, pink, orange, and white. Cushions of Japanese silk. Chinese vases. Elijah in his cage. The view of the courtyard from the windows of his studio.

He received letters from Isabella not quite as frequently as he sent them, but frequently enough that he didn't feel neglected or forgotten. He learned, through the month of desert gales following their departure, that Dr. Straight had been made bereft by his wife's illness, and when she died some weeks after the autumnal gales had ceased, he grew inconsolable. Since his time on Mount Terminus, Isabella wrote, the congenial man who stood with such granite stature had withdrawn from his colleagues and responsibilities and had taken to drinking himself to sleep at night. Isabella wanted nothing more than to comfort him in some way, but found the only way to care for him was to let him be. Bloom considered abandoning his work and leaving Mount Terminus to be with Isabella and Dr. Straight, to help see them through their difficult time. He did know something about loss and its aftermath, after all. But this notion occurred to him too late. Before he could gather the courage to act on his noble idea, he received a letter from Isabella, telling him she and Dr. Straight would soon be departing on a long journey. They had been invited by the Institut de France to conduct their invertiscope experiments in field hospitals at and around the front beyond Paris. The psychologist and philosopher Pierre Janet, who was well known for his studies on hysteria and his experiments in brainwave entrainment, believed the invertiscope could prove a beneficial tool in treating soldiers suffering the effects of shell shock and could, perhaps, be used as an effective therapy to rehabilitate the wounded. I can't tell you, wrote Isabella, Dr. Straight's transformation since he received the invitation. He has rediscovered his reason for being. Not only would they be able to put their experiments to work in the field, but also they could very well serve a beneficial purpose. And, what's more, they would be in close proximity to the battlefield, where they planned to document the war on film. They would collect footage they could one day apply to Dr. Straight's aversion trials.

Upon reading this, Bloom wrote a response in which he pleaded with her not to put herself in peril. Should something happen to you, look to Dr. Straight to see what you will make of me.

I know you understand, Isabella replied. I know you wouldn't want to dissuade me, or the doctor, from doing our work.

Aren't you afraid? he wrote.

Of course I'm afraid, she replied.

I'm afraid for you.

I want to embrace my fear.

When will you return?

I don't know.

But when we return, she promised, I will return to you.

I'm diminished.

Be proud of me. And wish me all the best. Tell me to be brave.

In his last exchange with Isabella before she departed, he wrote just that. I am proud of you. I wish you all the best and more. Be brave. And he then expressed his love for her not with words, but in a miniature drawing of Cupid and Psyche. Take this with you, he wrote on the back, and think of me always.

She allowed him the final word.

✸✷

Bloom would receive no letters or telegrams after this. He would hear nothing about Isabella or Dr. Straight from Gottlieb. Nothing of her whereabouts or what she was doing. She would, nevertheless, inhabit him completely, not unlike the way a series of images inhabited his thoughts when he began to contemplate a scenario for a picture. The images, when they manifested themselves, grew inside him, larger and larger, and spread out widely and clearly until they were complete and ever present in his mind. From here he could survey the entire picture at one glance. *Wie gleich alles zusammen*, Mozart said of this moment when he was composing symphonies. Right away, all together—*Wie gleich alles zusammen*. In this period of Bloom's manhood, this was precisely how his moods were composed when Isabella's image arrived in his mind. He saw her in all her permutations, inside his deepest thoughts, felt her in the innermost regions of his body. *Wie gleich alles zusammen*. To heighten this experience, he often went to the library, where Isabella and the doctor did their work. In their hasty departure, they had left everything exactly as it was the moment they received the news about Dr. Straight's wife. They left a crate beside a table on top of which was a light cabinet, beside this, Walgensten's thaumaturgic lantern, still assembled, its candleholder submerged in rivulets of cooled wax. And hung from the bookshelves before the lantern was a white sheet on which they revived the phantasmagorias they discovered in the wooden boxes. Bloom told Meralda and Roya to leave all these objects just so. They were not to be moved until Isabella returned. Until then, he said to them, I want to be able to look upon everything as it is, to look upon the white sheet, to see Isabella as she was.

>‹

In the months that followed the last of Isabella's correspondence, Bloom found in his deepest solitude the ache of longing. He no longer took comfort in his most solitary moments. Instead he was agitated by his solitude, and for not having been more forceful with her, he was ripe with regret. Had he only fought for her harder, he wondered. Had he traveled to the university to remove her from Dr. Straight's influence, he thought, perhaps, then, she would be with him now. As he completed his work on *Death, Forlorn* and began to review the work he had done, he better understood the husband's obsession and despair. He now knew what motivated him to walk into the apothecary's shop to drink down the bottle of poison, to take on Death's challenges, to sacrifice his life for the life of his lover. He better understood why, when he was a child, his father made him swear that he should protect his love when he found it. He knew now that the failed promises of love weighed down the human heart more so than any of love's hardships. He better understood the wounds that festered within Samuel Freed. He could empathize with his irrational need to torment the one he believed responsible for the loss of all his future affections. He better understood the lengths to which Manuel went to watch Miranda, the impulse that drove his father to his gardens every day. He knew now why Simon, it seemed, never pursued love, why he was suspicious of it, avoided it altogether. For the first time, Bloom knew the hollow nature of loneliness. Before Isabella, he felt whole in his solitude. After Isabella, he knew that feeling to be an illusion.

As he had done for *Mephisto's Affinity*, Bloom drew the storyboard for *Death, Forlorn*. He redrew the images he had spent almost a year composing for his father, made additions, included even more detail. And when he finished his panels, which amounted to more than two hundred, he proceeded to chart out for Gottlieb every aspect of the production. He mapped out frame by frame, scene by scene, every camera angle, point of view shift, approach and retreat. He inserted cutaways and diagrammed lighting arrangements, what lamps belonged where on the battens, in what order they were to be turned on and off. He choreographed each actor's movement to and from their marks, sketched costume patterns for the seamstresses, made notes for makeup changes that coincided with the lighting changes. He went so far as to design an outdoor set constructed from concrete. It would be fitted with copper tubes through which they could run kerosene to stage a controlled fire for the climax, when the husband entered Death's embrace. When it came time to build the sets, Bloom oversaw the work until he was satisfied with every detail. He checked and rechecked the lights. Set out the actors' marks. Laid the rails himself for the tracking shots. They would film the live action first, and then move on to the filming of the miniatures, for which he devised a special track all its own, one that circled the entire fortress wall, so it would appear as if it were being observed by the young couple from their carriage. And for the moment when the wall dematerialized before the husband, he would achieve this through stop-motion animation, by methodically removing one brick after the next. Death would then walk through the opening of a small portion of an identical fragment of wall he would build on the lot. He would then animate the closing of the wall by reversing the process. One by one, he'd replace the bricks in the order they were removed. And on he would move to filming Death's cathedral in miniature, which Bloom built in such a way he could dismantle it into several pieces. Fit together, he could film its exterior. He would then dismantle it, fill it with lit candles, reassemble it, and hoist it up to the ceiling of his studio, where he would set the camera beneath it and there capture Death's captive souls.

Some days before filming was to begin, he reviewed his notes with Gottlieb, who said to Bloom, You are most impressive, Rosenbloom.

Am I?

Yes, said Gottlieb. Be a man and direct this picture yourself.

No, said Bloom.

But it's all here. The entire vision is already directed. You only need to step behind the camera and describe to the actors what they must do.

But it's there, said Bloom, I'll fail. I'm no good with the actors. I haven't the slightest idea how to talk to them.

There is your problem. You think of them as some form of human being. They're not people. They're dogs. Treat them like dogs and they obey.

I've never owned a dog.

Ach, said Gottlieb, you're impossible. All right, then. We do it together as we did before. Only this time as equals. You be the eyes, the technician. We follow your plans to the image. And I'll make the dogs chase their tails.

To this, Bloom agreed. And together they met on the lot and brought to life *Death, Forlorn*. And when Bloom had fit the last of its many pieces together in the editing room and ran it through the projector, he saw what lived in his mind the day his father handed him the story and asked him to draw it for him. And on this day, he missed Jacob Rosenbloom as much as he had in the days following his death.

✦

For some reason, Bloom began to find in the mail letters from war widows who identified with the husband in the story. All expressed a similar sentiment. If they could do for their men what he did for his wife, they wrote, they would. They expressed the solace they had taken from the story's theme of inescapable destinies, and many of them identified with the moment the husband discovered his love was gone, taken from him without warning. They recalled days of limbo, in which they waited for news, for letters, and they described how they shared the dread expressed on the actor's face the moment he realized his love had been taken from him. Letter after letter Bloom received was a compendium of suffering and heart-ache. He wanted to set them aside, but found he couldn't stop pouring through them, and the more he did so, the more precipitously his mood began to decline.

You must stop this at once, said Gottlieb. You have a successful picture on your hands and what do you do with it? You wallow. It's time to push on. Gus said the same. For the time being, however, Bloom wouldn't push on. He would continue to wallow. The world around him, as it had done on so many occasions in his past, began to fill with darkness. One night after he made certain Meralda was asleep in her room, he went to the stable and retrieved a pick and shovel. He walked into the rose garden, at whose entrance Roya was standing. She accompanied him into the connecting circles, and when he reached Cupid and Psyche, he began swinging the pick into the hard earth. He dug and he dug late into the night, and when he had dug his way down to where the crown of his head poked out of the ground, he climbed out of the hole and walked into the villa through the service entrance. He took from the kitchen a ball of twine, then down he went into the cellar and up he went into Manuel's chamber. He followed the silver thread of Ariadne and

moved past Theseus to the eye of the Minotaur, and there he collected Adora's remains. He wrapped her in her blankets, bound them
together, then bound her to him.

Roya had remained in the rose garden, and when Bloom returned
she sat kneeling beside the hole he had dug. With the twine he had
wound around his waist, he lowered Adora into the grave just as the
thinnest line of magenta began to line the top of Mount Terminus.
When he had finished shoveling the earth over Adora's body, Roya
took him by the hand. Bloom wanted to do nothing more than to
bathe and sleep, but Roya pulled him in the direction of the trailhead. Please, Bloom said, later we can walk, after I've slept. But Roya
wouldn't let go. She dragged him along, up to Mount Terminus's
peak, and there she pointed out into the valley in the direction of
the sunrise.

Yes, said Bloom. It is beautiful and glorious, but I want nothing
more than to sleep. Roya stepped behind Bloom, thrust her arms
out on either side of his head, and focused his attention on the sun
casting its light on the silver line running at a declining grade along
the edge of the northern range. She held him there as the sun continued to rise, and there he began to see the taut thread shimmer.

Yes, I know. Bloom turned back to Roya. She lifted her finger
and waved it across the panorama of the basin. She was trying to tell
him something. She was in a panic to show him. What is it? he
asked. I don't understand. She now took Bloom by the hand again
and dragged him back down the trail, and when they reached its bottom, she guided him to the service entrance, and once there, pulled
him up to the top of the tower. There she set his eye against his
telescope, and there Bloom watched sheets of dust licking across
the land, dust originating from large swaths of earth on which the
orange and lemon trees had been cut away. In their place were parked
trucks and piles of lumber. When her face turned back to his, Bloom
said again, Yes, I know. It's beginning.

Roya shook her head in anger. She pointed an accusatory finger at Bloom. She thrust it at him. Eyes wide and feverish. Lips
tight.

No, said Bloom. Not me. Simon.

She thrust her finger at him again.

No. You're wrong. As he was about to ask what had gotten into her, she turned away from him and ran downstairs.

>‹

From atop his tower Bloom witnessed in the months ahead the basin teem with men in the thousands. They dug and poured foundations into the shape of a grid, and across the grid they dug trenches into which they laid pipe, and alongside the trenches they dug holes in which they erected power and telephone poles, and to complete the reticulation, they began running, parallel to the trenches and the high tension wires, a system of interconnected roadways. Every now and then, Simon met him at the edge of the promontory, where they stood together in an awkward silence, and they looked across the panorama, and his brother appeared to Bloom to be growing brighter with light, stronger and more powerful, larger than life. On these occasions, Bloom wondered if what he witnessed was evidence of Simon's better nature shining forth. Or was it the dybbuk strengthening his pride?

The dust generated from below swelled into the air. It blocked Bloom's view of the sea. Ballooned into a red-and-orange holocaust. For months on end the vista that had brought his mother and father to Mount Terminus, the vista to which his father longed to return, the vista onto which Bloom first looked when he arrived here, was no more, and every day now he felt as if a small part of him was dying, and when the news arrived about Isabella, he couldn't help but perceive the horrible image spread across the landscape of the shore as a harbinger.

>‹

The small packet arrived a little over a year after Isabella had departed. Five weeks before the anniversary of his father's death. Five weeks before the Day of Atonement. Twenty-five days before the start of the Days of Awe. The only letters Bloom had ever received from anyone at his home address were from Isabella, and so, when at lunchtime he saw the packet sitting beside his place setting at the table, his spirit was immeasurably uplifted, but an instant later he saw in what condition the paper was in—it was dirty and frayed at its corners, the area under the postage appeared singed—he sat down and stared at it, looked at it with apprehension. He lifted it and felt its weight. It was thicker and heavier than he thought it would be. Its surface felt gritty. He brought it to his nose, and took in its scent. Gunpowder. It smelled of something incendiary and something else, something noxious, like the smells he associated with the chemical baths of the darkroom. And once again he looked at the singe under the postage, and stood up and walked out to the courtyard, and he walked into the cottage where Isabella had slept, and he smelled the sheets and tried to sense her scent. He lay down on the bed and carefully fitted a finger into the fray of the corner. He knew as he had known with his father. He knew the foreboding he felt was meaningful. He pulled apart the paper's seam and out onto his chest fell the images he had drawn for her during those months they corresponded. The chrysanthemums. Elijah. Cupid and Psyche. He arranged them on the bed and then looked into the packet, where he found a single slip of paper. He pulled it out, his fingers forceps extracting a foreign substance from a body, and he laid out the message next to his drawings.

My dear Joseph,
    I've carried this letter and its contents everywhere as a way to keep you close to me. If you're reading this, my love, the news isn't good. If you're reading this, the sad truth of it is I'm no longer with you.
    Just know this: you are my love.
    I've had no other.
    Here, in this madness, I've thought of our friendship, your tenderness, more than ever. I'm often sitting quietly by

your side in the gardens. I am there now. So, please, don't be afraid for me.

If I have met my end, I have only one wish. I only ask you not to be angry with me for having been reckless. So many of the people you've loved have departed this world, and I know you may not be able to forgive me for doing the same, but I beg you, Joseph, to think of me fondly from time to time, with love and affection always . . .

Yours,
Isabella.

＞＜

It wasn't possible.

Did God find it amusing to take everyone away from him in this manner? What more was there to do than laugh at this cosmic injustice? And so Bloom laughed and laughed. He lay in the cottage and laughed until he could laugh no more, and then he lay there paralyzed until he was discovered by Gus, who pried open his fist and read his letter. The big man gathered all the papers together and carefully fit them back into their package, and he said to Bloom, Let's go.

Gus lifted Bloom in his arms and carried him into the villa, to his bed, and he sent for Meralda, who on this occasion could find no words to comfort Bloom. On this occasion, Roya's touch would not comfort him. Simon's Panglossian positivism, his bromides and platitudes, wouldn't comfort him. Nothing would comfort Bloom. Silence and solitude would not comfort Bloom. He remained in bed. Didn't speak. Didn't think. Didn't see. He disappeared into sleep, into a dark sleep without dreams. For weeks he was like this. For a month he was like this. At which point, Gottlieb said, Enough!

Enough! he cried out. He walked into Bloom's room, climbed on top of him, and smacked him across the face. When he didn't react, Gottlieb slapped him harder. When Bloom didn't react, Gottlieb walked to Bloom's washbasin, placed it beside his bed, and said, Fine! You no longer want to live? Fine! And he took Bloom by the scruff of his neck and submerged his face in the water, and he held him there until Bloom began to struggle. Gottlieb lifted his head. Are you prepared to live? Bloom said nothing, and so Gottlieb submerged his face again. And again Bloom began to struggle, this time with greater spirit. What will it be? Life or death? Gottlieb this time didn't relent. He kept Bloom's face submerged. Well? Bloom began to breathe water, to cough, and finally he threw Gottlieb off him, sending the dwarfish man back against the wall.

Bloom's eyes were now open and, when he turned to see where Gottlieb had gone, he saw the man reaching for his throat. His little hands grabbed hold, and once again Bloom found himself in Gottlieb's clutches. Are you ready to live yet? Gottlieb released one hand from his throat and punched Bloom square in the cheek. We-e-e-e-ll? Bloom threw Gottlieb off a second time and started back to his bed. Gottlieb now jumped on his back and forced Bloom to the floor so he was lying on his chest. He pinned Bloom down at the back of his neck, pulled at the hair on the top of his head, and stuck two of his fingers into Bloom's nose and pulled. The pain Bloom felt was extraordinary. You're going to pull my nose off! Bloom screamed.

Aha! screamed Gottlieb. It speaks! He pulled harder and, with the hand pulling Bloom's hair, he boxed his ear. How do you like that? And he did it again.

Goddammit! Bloom bellowed.

It speaks again! Gottlieb leaped off Bloom's back now. He was on his feet. Get up! he insisted. Fight me!

No!

Get up! I'm only just getting started.

No!

Have it your way. Gottlieb pulled his leg back and kicked Bloom right between the legs. Bloom clutched ahold of himself down there, raising his ass into the air. The breath had been knocked out of him. Get up! screamed Gottlieb. Or so help me God, I'm going to kill you! Bloom rose to his knees, too slowly for Gottlieb's taste, and so Gottlieb once again boxed Bloom on the ears, both of them.

Enough! screamed Bloom, who was now holding his groin and an ear.

No! Gottlieb screamed back. Get up! And fight! You piece of shit *faygala*!

Bloom now rose to his feet and turned around to find Gottlieb approaching again, only this time Bloom cocked back his fist and landed a punch directly on the point of Gottlieb's chin, landing the little man on his back. Twitching. Twitching. Then nothing. Unmoving. He'd knocked him out cold? He tried to rouse him, but couldn't. He slapped his face, but nothing. Meralda! Bloom cried out. Gus! He ran out onto the landing and called for them again. Help! he cried. He walked back into his room, and there was Gottlieb sitting up on Bloom's bed.

So, he said, there is someone you care about other than yourself.

You little bastard! Bloom said with clenched teeth. He approached Gottlieb again and punched him so hard this time, he did, indeed, knock him out. His small body flipped back off the bed, and he was out, facedown, for quite some time.

✦

The bruised and battered men limped along the trails later that afternoon. They walked in silence until they reached Mount Terminus's summit. They continued in silence as they watched the dust rise up from the basin. And then Gottlieb spoke. Work, he said. Let us work.

I don't know if I can, said Bloom.

What's so difficult? Tell me a story, and we go from there.

I'm only able to think of her. I need to know what happened.

It will become clear in time.

In time, yes, I know, in time. I'm cursed by the passage of time.

Pitiful. She believed in something. She followed that belief to a dangerous place. Like her mother and her father, like her adopted father, she lived pursuing her ideals. Do you really think she would want you to give up your reason for being on this Earth? Do you really believe she would want you to sacrifice what life and talent remains within you for the sake of her memory?

No. But I don't understand. Why, Gottlieb, why have I been made to feel this way over and over again? I can't see the point.

I *will* put you out of your misery now, Rosenbloom. I meant it before. I mean it now. If your wish is to be dead, I will kill you.

I don't think I can bear the thought of your face being the last I would see on this Earth.

Then live your life and tell me a good story. Tell me a story you told to Isabella.

Bloom recalled the final day he and Isabella spent together. And without revealing from where the story was derived, he told Gottlieb over the course of the afternoon the story of Miranda and Fernando, of Adora and Manuel Salazar, and the telling of the story gave him pleasure.

It's an epic! said Gottlieb when Bloom reached the conclusion. I can see its enormity.

Bloom turned away from the unpleasant sight of the basin and turned his attention to the farms and ranches that had begun to spread throughout the valley.

What do you say, Rosenbloom? Do we work?

For her. For her, I'll make one final picture.

What is this nonsense? One final picture? You are made for pictures. Your soul was born for pictures.

I'll make one final picture for Isabella.

And then?

And then you can kill me, said Bloom.

It's a deal! said Gottlieb. What's the title?

The Death of Paradise.

Gottlieb thought it over. He threw a rock down the rocky slope toward the valley. He then threw another. But before we make this picture, before I have the pleasure of killing you, you must understand what it is to be set apart from this place.

Why?

Because you're a grown man, Rosenbloom. Because you need to see something of the world. As it was time for you to have your heart ripped out of your chest to make *Death, Forlorn*, it's time for you to take a journey.

I don't want to go anywhere, Gottlieb.

Well, you are going. You'll go and then you'll return. But you must go.

Why must I go?

To understand Fernando's rage, you must go. To understand Miranda's desire to return home, you must go. To know what Manuel Salazar saw on his journey to Mount Terminus, you must go, and discover for yourself what it means to be in motion. I hereby send you into exile.

No.

Yes. If need be, I'll have you forcibly removed.

➤✦

You must go, said Simon after having eaten dinner at his house. They sat on the white settee facing the white window frames and looked out onto the disturbed stretch of land leading to the sea. Gottlieb is right. It's time you saw something of the world. All on your own.

But where shall I go?

Wherever you like.

When?

It will have to be in three days. No sooner.

Why three days?

Because Gus has arranged for us to take a short journey tomorrow.

Gus hadn't mentioned his plans to Bloom. Where? he asked.

I don't know. All I know is that I'm to meet you at the estate first thing in the morning, and that we'll be gone until the following evening. The day after that, you can set out on your own adventure.

It had been some time since Bloom sat down to talk with his

brother, and it had been equally as long since he'd found him to be so charming and congenial in Bloom's company. In no small part because the waterworks had been completed: the dam had been finished, its reservoir filled, its spillways feeding the completed aqueduct. Construction in the basin was proceeding at pace, and according to Simon, every plot of land, every home he would build on it, had been sold. Soon tracks would be laid from here to the city center. They would carry families to and from town.

You'll see, said Simon, it will be as fertile and green as Mount Terminus, as ripe as its groves, as bright as its gardens. It'll be a wonder to behold. Bloom's brother spoke as if he had climbed to the summit of a great monument. Soon, he said, all the money he had taken from Bloom would be repaid, at which time, he promised, he would make amends with Mr. Stern.

Over the course of this lazy evening, an acceptance of his brother grew within Bloom. He couldn't fully comprehend Simon's opportunistic nature, but he recognized that Simon's passion for progress was on a footing with his affection and concern for Bloom. Although Simon wouldn't be ceding the property of the plateau back to his brother, Simon explained his plans to make it his domain, his sanctuary. He would be relocating all of the studio's production to a large plot of land at the foot of Mount Terminus, and leave the current lot in the hands of Bloom and Gottlieb, to cultivate artists like themselves, artists they thought worthy of their attention. They could do as they pleased, with no interference from Simon. Should they ever need it, of course, they would have access to the expanded grounds at the bottom of the mountain. Simon walked Bloom to the room in which Leah's memory was preserved and there, next to the raised map of Simon's waterworks and the grid of development, was a new table on top of which was an architect's rendering of the new, sprawling lot. It will be a small city within the city, he told Bloom, a walled fortress in which permanent façades would reside, entire small towns, Gothic towers, medieval castles, Broadways, Parisian cafés, London squares, row houses, African jungles, anything and everything you can possibly imagine. The entire world, said

Simon, will fit here. Its art and architecture, its greatest monuments, its wildest nature. Imagine, he said, everything you can possibly need at your disposal for an epic picture like *The Death of Paradise*. Simon now turned to the other table and stared at it for a good long while. This, he said, what I've built here, Joseph, I've thought through every need, every desire, every small convenience and inconvenience. The people who arrive here from now on, they'll make a life all their own, on my stage. Every day they'll breathe new life into it for who knows how many generations, for who knows how many centuries. Like your pictures, Joseph, my stage, it will last well beyond either one of us. *This*, he said. *This* is *my* one great work of art, one I will never surpass again in my lifetime.

You're still a young man, said Bloom.

No, said Simon, not any longer. Not after this. There will be small triumphs, perhaps. But nothing quite so great as this. Simon looked at Bloom and Bloom looked into his brother's face, and he could see it now. He could see written into the lines of his brother's face the toll this project had taken on him; the lines around his eyes, on his brow, had deepened and grown longer, in every way Bloom had imagined they would. And Bloom now cast his gaze away from his brother's face, back to the map, and while looking over the rows and rows and rows of red tiled roofs, at the repeating architectural forms, over the roadways and boulevards, tramways and tall office buildings his brother had pinned to its surface, Bloom was coming to realize, it wasn't the beauty of the landscape he would miss when Simon's plans were complete. He realized, at this very moment, what it was that had so upset Roya that night they buried Adora in the rose garden. How could he not have seen it? She feared losing the emptiness. The loneliness derived from it, the serenity one felt in it, the solitude one endured in it. She couldn't bear the thought of the open space closing in around them. Where would their minds wander if they had to peer down onto so many restless souls? The noise, he thought. There would be such overwhelming noise and distraction. And, oh, how the mere thought of it frightened Bloom.

✦

Come, said Simon, interrupting Bloom's thought, I have a gift for you. To get you where you're going. Simon walked Bloom out to the cul-de-sac and there parked at the front of the house was a white roadster similar to the roadster Simon drove. It's yours, said Simon as he handed Bloom the keys. In three days' time, you need only choose a direction.

But I don't know how to drive.

It's easy enough. Here, get in.

I don't know . . .

Just get in. We'll practice all night if need be.

But they didn't need the night. Bloom took to it rather easily. He liked the feel of the gears in his hand, coordinating the clutch with the accelerator and the brake. He drove in circles at first and then motored off the studio and up to the estate, and there, circled about outside the front entrance of the villa. And when he had mastered that much, Simon said to him, I will see you in the morning.

✦

In the morning, Bloom awoke to the sight of Gus standing over his bed. It's time, he said. Let's go.

Where are we going?

Tomorrow is the High Holiday. Tomorrow, you, Simon, and I will be written into the Book of Life.

It's been so long.

I know, said Gus.

Everything was prepared. Gus had spoken with Meralda and she told him what to collect. He uprooted three juniper trees that had been growing since the time Jacob Rosenbloom planted them for his final trip to Pacheta Lake. He gathered lanterns, the yahrzeit candle, the camping gear, a hearty meal they would eat when they arrived, a hearty meal they would eat to break the fast, and trimmings from the estate's gardens and groves. All was loaded into the back of a truck.

When Bloom and Gus stepped out onto the drive, Simon was there waiting, and the three men set off on their long drive down the switchback to the boulevard, up through a canyon pass, to a mountain road, on which they followed the line of the aqueduct, its sluiceways and spillways, past its smaller reserve ponds and catchments. They drove parallel to the stream, against the current of water. Bloom was mesmerized by the way the aqueduct dipped and turned to create the optical illusion of an invisible wavelength. For hours they drove until they arrived at a vista, where Gus parked, and the three of them stepped out of the car and walked up to a rail, and there Bloom saw himself standing over the massive pour of concrete whose arc filled the natural boundaries of the canyon pass he had ridden through with Jacob on their buckboard; now held back by the enormous barrier was a great mass of water. Simon pointed out its outlets to the aqueduct, and Bloom, upon seeing this incredible sight, felt proud of his brother for having performed this godly feat. It's sublime, he told Simon. It was truly sublime and wondrous. The sheer enormity of it.

They continued on the road, and he admitted to Simon when they arrived at the confluence of the river and the lake, and Bloom saw how little seemed to have been altered in the graben of the rift valley, that he had expected to find the land more disturbed, the farms and ranches in the distance laid to waste on the order of the basin. And Simon pointed to the green fields and the irrigation ducts in the distance, and he asked Bloom if he could recall what had changed since he was last here. Perhaps the lake's water table was lower than it had been. The juniper trees Jacob had planted had certainly grown out and produced more berries. Otherwise there was no discernible difference. Except, of course, for the sound of the manned pumping station, its combustion, its gears, turning over at regular intervals, to push water into the channel that led to the reservoir. The sound started and stopped throughout the night. It echoed and reverberated against the cliffs and the escarpment. It was

present at the shore when Gus and then Simon and then Bloom
recited the kaddish. Gus for his mother and his baby sister. Simon
for his mother and for Sam. Bloom for his mother and Jacob. And a
special recitation for Isabella. In the morning, they climbed to the
junipers Jacob had planted, and there they sat staring up and over
the current of the river, to the mountains, and there they sat in the
heat under the heraldic poses of the buzzards, and there Bloom
imagined the ice melt and the ice floe, the cascading waters falling
through the maw of volcanic craters, and he grew weak and weary,
and he slept and he woke and he slept again and awoke again, until
the sun kissed the top of the mountain range, and only then did he
and his brother and Gus stand up and walk to the lakeshore, where
they opened the meal packed by Gus's beloved Meralda, and they
ate and they drank, and Simon placed his hand on Bloom's shoulder, and he placed his hand on Gus's shoulder, and he promised he
would try to be a better man. And you, Joseph, you, go be a man of
the world. The motion will heal you. You'll see.

><

The following morning, Bloom packed a small bag, bid all the
birds in his aviary farewell, and asked Meralda if she would prepare a picnic for him. When she asked what he was doing with
the bag, he said he was going off on his own to become a man of the
world. Hearing this, Meralda disappeared for quite a long time,
and when she returned, she had Gus on one arm and Gottlieb on
the other.

So, said Gottlieb, you are heeding my advice, after all.

I am, said Bloom.

Excellent. Have you decided where to go?

No.

An impromptu journey, then.

Yes.

Ah, I've been on many of those.

For how long will you be away? asked Meralda.

I haven't decided.

You want I should go with you? asked Gus with his eyes on Meralda. There's no reason you need to be a man of the world all on your own.

No, said Bloom. I'm going alone. Somewhere. And I don't know when I'll return.

The right frame of mind when starting out for the first time, said Gottlieb.

Please . . . You must stop speaking, Gottlieb, otherwise I'll turn around and walk back to my room.

I'll say no more, said Gottlieb. He mimed the buttoning of his lips.

It's time I knew what was out there, said Bloom to Meralda, who Bloom could see was in distress over his departure.

As you should, said Gus.

Meralda struck the big man on the arm.

He's a man, said Gus. He should go where he pleases.

I have to do this, Bloom said. You know I must.

And hearing this, Meralda started off to the kitchen in a state.

She notices your moods more than you know, Gus said of her. She's concerned you've grown despondent. She fears you might harm yourself.

Gottlieb unbuttoned his lips at this point and said, He is a malignant despondent.

Thank you, Gottlieb. But I have no plans to do myself in. Not at the moment.

I have first dibs at that, said Gottlieb.

Stop speaking, Gottlieb.

I will say no more.

Here, said Meralda as she returned with a picnic basket. It's enough to get you through the day and the night if need be.

I'm sure it'll suffice, said Bloom. He gave Meralda a kiss and a tight hug, and with that, Bloom set out to the drive. He placed the picnic basket in the roadster's passenger seat and turned over the engine. Gottlieb, Gus, and Meralda lined up before the front entrance of the villa, and as he drove off, he saw Meralda bury her face in Gus's chest.

When Bloom drove through the gates and moved beyond them, he began to enjoy this sensation of being alone and in motion. For the first time since reading Isabella's letter, he felt alive in his solitude. And the more alive he felt, the faster he took the turns on the mountain road. He raced his way into the canyon, and when he reached the bottom, he accelerated into the eyesore of the construction zone, appreciating for the first time in what ways forward motion was a form of escape, and he wondered why it hadn't occurred to him sooner that the landscapes portrayed to him in his reading of other's solitary travels wouldn't echo through his own experience of motion. As he hurtled past one open foundation after the next, he became a simplification of himself, a small quantity of immaterial parts whose image, if he were to paint it, would consist of the impressionistic streaks of his mother's brush. To prolong this ascension of spirit, Bloom considered if, perhaps, he should remain in motion indefinitely, if he shouldn't turn up the coastal road and continue driving north, at the very least until he tired of the thrill. But when he reached the shore and saw across the channel the mountain peaks of Santa Ynez Island, he saw in the island's barely visible contours the mirror image of Mount Terminus, and, without wanting it to happen, the euphoria he felt only a moment earlier reversed to melancholy. And while Bloom urged himself to ignore this reversal, it appeared as if his body and not his mind were in control of his actions, as he slowed to a halt. And sat. And stared. Thinking of Isabella. Of her body warm and alive beside him. Of her dead body mutilated in a trench.

He spent what remained of the morning doing what he might have done had he never left his tower's pavilion. He sat and watched. From the seat of his car, he observed vessels small and large moor at and unmoor from the docks. They arrived and departed at a leisurely pace, a pace that intimately appealed to Bloom's sense of time. The more he saw of their comings and goings, the more he felt compelled to unmoor himself from his seat and take a stroll. He carried

with him a tablet and a fistful of charcoals, and with the same im-
petus he felt to explore the docks, he felt a need to stop and sketch
the watermarks and rust patterns he discovered on the nearby hulls
of ships. Over and over again, he found himself rubbing into the
paper the same shape. The very same blemish, he only realized later,
as the mark on Isabella's letter.

When a group of merchant mariners saw him, they gathered
around to watch, and seeing how skilled Bloom was, they asked if
he would sketch them. Bloom spent the remainder of the afternoon
deciphering the lines and forms of these men's figures, hoping in
the process to divine some inspiration that would set him on his
way in one direction or another. And after some time of standing
face to face with these men, he confided he was aimless and looking
for a destination. They were bound for the vanilla plantations of
Madagascar. That, Bloom said, was perhaps a little too far. The largest, most doltish of the men, screwed up his muscular face and said,
Leave it to me. At the insistence of this man who reminded Bloom
of Gus, he took several puffs from a pipe containing in its bowl a
black, tacky substance, which, when lit, smelled edible. Sweet. And
as soon as Bloom inhaled the rich smoke into his lungs, his head
tingled, then turned pleasantly numb, and soon thereafter his limbs
grew weary and his mind began to pattern the world into sequences
of incongruous images and sounds. The seamen sat before him, their
faces indifferent and still. They each pointed at him, but their eyes
stared into the sun. Although their lips were shut tight, Bloom heard
originating from inside their chests hearty guffaws of laughter. Each
of them, one in succession of the other, then shut his eyes. And as
each set of eyes closed, the sound of the laughter—as thunder from
a lightning storm sounds as it passes into the distance—quieted into
whispers. And then there was silence. Then darkness. Then a dream,
in which Bloom was levitating over the surface of the ocean.

Bloom woke up to the sway of water beneath him and felt running through his body the vibrations of an accelerating motor. He
recognized the sensation of being in motion, and when his vision
cleared he found himself in his car. It was parked on the deck of a

ferry, and gathered around his windows was a menagerie of children costumed as swabbies, the group of them volubly discussing their disappointment with the fact that Bloom wasn't dead. He opened the car door and stepped onto the deck, where he saw the port behind them had flattened into two dimensions. The definition of the coastline grew soft, and with the basin and the distant mountain range spreading out before him as would an eroding sandcastle, he had a difficult time locating Mount Terminus.

Watching the coastline slip farther and farther away, Bloom turned to the nearest ferryman—a man with a topographical map of acne scars—and asked him when the next ferry would run back to the port. But this is the last ferry of the day, he told Bloom. All of us, he said, turning his head to Santa Ynez, we now all go home. The soonest Bloom could return would be first thing in the morning. Upon hearing this news he must have looked like a lost little boy, because at that moment, this unfortunate-looking man, who the others unkindly called Guapo, smiled sympathetically and patted Bloom on the back.

He introduced himself as Eduardo and told Bloom not to worry, that there were very nice accommodations on the island. Because Bloom liked the way Eduardo spoke and thought his eyes understanding, he said to him, Have you ever met a grown man who has never spent a night alone away from home? Eduardo shook his head. I'm not sure why I'm telling you this, said Bloom, but I'll miss waking up to my birds in the morning. When Bloom mentioned his birds, Eduardo's entire presence brightened. And then he asked if, like him, Bloom had a great love of birds. Bloom told him he loved his birds very much. Then come, he said, I show you a trick I no show many people.

Eduardo led Bloom to the ferry's stern, where from a compartment he pulled out a metal tub filled with minnows. He rolled up the sleeve on his right arm and in one deft motion sunk his hand into the water and pulled out a sparkling fish. He held on to it by the tail and asked Bloom, You are no' very delicate, are you? Bloom wasn't certain he understood what Eduardo meant, but he shook his head no. Eduardo, in turn, lifted his other hand to the struggling fish, placed his thumb and forefinger over its bulbous eyes and squeezed until the fish stilled. He wiped the pink ooze that had gushed onto his fingers on the legs of his yellow uniform, and now, with a hearty smile that revealed a mouthful of chipped teeth, he pointed the fish up to a flock of gulls trailing in the sky at the back of the boat.

Pick one, he said to Bloom.

What for?

You pick one, any one, I make it come for a visit. Bloom now must have looked at him with disbelief because Eduardo said, You like birds, yes?

Yes, said Bloom.

You no afraid of birds, no?

No.

Then pick one. I make it come for a visit.

To make it easy for him to know which of the birds, Bloom pointed into the shadowy underbelly of the anarchic flock and said, That one, the one farthest to our right.

No pro'lem. And then Eduardo, most certainly the ugliest man on all the seas, showed Bloom the most beautiful display of man controlling the natural world he had ever seen. With the panache of a magician who worked at sleight of hand, this unassuming ferry-man striped his palm with the silver minnow, and using its glimmering surface reflected the sun into the eye of the very gull Bloom had pointed to. By casting the light just so, he lured the bird away from the flock to the rail of the ship, where, as if it were hung on an invisible string, it gracefully hovered with its wings outstretched on the headwind. Bloom laughed with delight. He could feel his smile fill his face. And Eduardo, seeing him smile for the first time, again shared with Bloom his broken teeth. Now you know why it is we call him Guapo! Bloom heard from over his shoulder. When he turned, he found one of the other ferrymen, a fat pink man with a strawberry nose, who added, The birds! They find Guapo irresistible! Bloom turned back to Eduardo then, when, at just the right angle

for the gull to catch the fish in its crooked beak, he lobbed the minnow into the air. The bird snatched it up and with Eduardo's spell
now broken it lifted away beyond the flock and flew into the blinding glow of the sun.

>‹

They motored into a marina in which small sailboats and yachts
bobbed in their slips. The town on the eastern side of the island was
composed of colorful cottages terraced onto steep hills. A levee of
boulders blasted from the side of the mountain buttressed a winding road from the channel waters. To the south was a small patch of
sandy beach on which Bloom could see orderly lines of lounge
chairs and folded umbrellas. As Eduardo had told him, the town of
Santa Ynez was becoming and clean, very dull, very quiet.

At Eduardo's insistence, Bloom was to go home with him. They
drove on a dirt road to the other side of the island, to the lodging
house owned and run by his sister, Estella Maria Tourneur. Her
husband, Eduardo told him, a famous acrobat, no longer lived. The
Great Guillaume one year earlier fell to his death from the trapeze,
and ever since then, to make her life less lonely, Estella rented her
many rooms to vacationers. She calls the house after her name on
the stage, said Eduardo, La Reina del Fuego, the Queen of Fire. This
was how his sister was known across all the deserts and the prairies
and the greatest of the cities when she traveled with the Grand Ver-
sailles Circus, for whom Estella dressed in a bloodred leotard and
ate and blew fire, and walked over hot coals with bare feet, and fearlessly hung and spun over bright orange flames with only her teeth
biting down on a thin leather strap.

It is empty now, Eduardo said of the house, but because you are
a lover of birds, instead of sleeping in one of the rooms meant for
the strangers, I would be honored if you would stay in my room.

But where will you sleep? Bloom asked him.

I sleep where I prefer to sleep. On the water, in my boat, where
I can better hear and feel the sea. After many thousands of years,

Eduardo explained to Bloom, he and his sister were the only Chumash people left on Santa Ynez. The others, he said, had either died from disease or had been collected like pieces of pottery and gold by the missionaries. It is in my blood, he told Bloom, to want the sea near me when I dream. Tonight, my friend, you keep my birds company and care for them since you no' with your own. All right?

They turned off the seaside road circling the island and drove onto an unpaved incline lined with pairs of braided ficus trees. Their tops formed a clattering canopy through which the late-afternoon sun broke and dappled yellow light onto the hood of Bloom's roadster. When they emerged through this tunnel of foliage, they reached the level ground of a cul-de-sac paved in cobblestone and bordered with a vibrant ring of strawberry lupine and amethyst blazing stars whose soft spikes stood nearly as tall as Bloom. The white-and-crimson façade of La Reina del Fuego sat at the edge of a bluff.

It was Queen Anne in style, three stories tall, with a sheltered porch running the length of the house. A turret rose up on one side, and on the other stood a tall chimney slightly taller than the turret's point. Beyond the plantings around the cul-de-sac was a well-kept lawn at the border of which rose an enormous oak, one of whose limbs nearly spanned the entirety of the yard, and had hanging from it the bar of a trapeze. That, Eduardo said when he saw Bloom mystified by the silver rod swaying in the ocean breeze, is where Guillaume lies dead and buried.

Bloom followed Eduardo into the house, and he could see why a rugged man such as himself wouldn't feel at home here. The furnishings were as ornate as they were delicate, and although the Great Guillaume lay dead and buried under the lawn of the garden, this was still very much his house. His likeness was everywhere, enshrined on the walls of the foyer and sitting rooms, in posters and paintings, the Great Guillaume fearlessly tumbling and spinning through the air. On the mantelpiece and on pedestals were planted heroic busts. And covering a grand piano with elephantine legs were standing photographs of the great trapeze artist shaking hands with European royals and American dignitaries, in palace gardens and ballrooms, on the fields of fairgrounds.

Less prominent, but certainly well represented, was also La Reina del Fuego, depicted in images performing all the stunts Eduardo described on the drive to the house. As startling as it was for Bloom to see such a beautiful woman spit brilliant orange flames ten feet into the air or to see her hanging by her teeth over a crown of fire, it was more shocking to discover two siblings could look any more different than Eduardo and his sister. In these images in which she was costumed as a savage, with her face colorfully painted and her hair decorated with feathers and charms, he could sense that beneath the artifice of exaggerated beauty was the symmetry and form and style only the smallest numbers among us are graced with.

There she is, Eduardo said from the dining room at the back of the house. Bloom walked to Eduardo's side and looked with him out a large window down onto the rocky coastline at the bottom of the cliff, where he found a woman with long black hair dressed in a white gown. She stood with her arms extended, balancing herself on the spine of an oblong rock as she looked off at the descending sun. His finger tapping on the glass, Eduardo said of his sister's outstretched arms, Like the wings of the great heron, no?

Yes, Bloom agreed.

He then pointed down the beach. That way, around the jetty, is Willow Cove. This is where I keep my boat. This is where I will go now.

But what shall I tell Estella? asked Bloom.

I will talk with her on the beach. I will tell her you are here as my guest. She will be happy to know you are in my room tonight. The birds are no' as loud when they see in my bed the shape of a man. Eduardo turned to go, but before he left Bloom in this unfamiliar place, he said, I will return early in the morning to collect you. Eduardo exited a side door and walked down a staircase built onto the side of the bluff. He disappeared for some time and then reappeared on the beach, where he called to Estella. From a distance, they spoke briefly, and then Eduardo turned away from her and continued on, stepping with youthful agility over the shore to-ward the cove as if he knew intimately the surface of each rock on which his feet fell.

Bloom was pleased to find a small library in the sitting room. Most of the books were in French and Spanish, but many were in English. He saw titles he had never seen or heard of before and wanted to browse through them. However, because he didn't feel at home, because the books were so pristine and tidily arranged, he was too timid to remove any of them from their shelves. Instead, he stared at their bindings and he began to imagine Calypso's cave, where Odysseus was held captive, where all the time he was left to his solitude, he wept with thoughts of Penelope. In his mind, Bloom imagined from the images he saw of her in her posters, Estella, as Calypso, who stood with the posture of a powerful being, but who possessed eyes as vulnerable as the love she so deeply felt for the soul of her mortal prisoner. Bloom imagined himself as Odysseus, his will weakened by the nymph's never-ending loneliness and beauty. And thus, he saw himself lying with her on a slab of stone with his arms wrapped around her waist and his cheek pressed against her midriff.

He gathered his sketchbook from his bag and quickly drew in pencil these images he saw in his mind. He added an image of Athena, whose face and body he modeled from memory on the young woman who was first delivered by Gus to his studio. He drew her into a panel with an arm outstretched to the heavens, and in another panel with her arm outstretched to Calypso, threatening her with the power of Zeus if she didn't release him to start his journey home. In the next panel, Calypso's shoulders fell with her head turned in profile, her eyes focused on a broken seashell resting in the sand beside her foot. And, in the last panel, as he was about to venture into the hands of Poseidon, Bloom had fallen on his knees before Calypso, and he saw in his mind Isabella, his Penelope, but he nev-ertheless had reached out to Calypso. She had already turned away from him, dejected, moving toward the dark hollow of her cave.

This activity kept Bloom so preoccupied he hadn't noticed Estella had long since entered from the side door and had been silently standing over his shoulder watching him sketch for some time. He was made aware of her presence only when she said in a voice that wasn't quite sure how it wanted to sound, You must be the lover of birds my brother spoke of. Bloom looked up to find her neck and arms bare. She wore a gown whose diaphanous material revealed the curves of her figure and hinted at the lines of her breasts. He could see from the dispassionate expression on her face—not unlike many of the actresses on the lot—she was accustomed to being stared at in a state of near undress. Given how weathered and old Eduardo looked to Bloom, she was much younger than he expected her to be. She couldn't be older than twenty-five. Otherwise, she was very much the way he had imagined her, and, to Bloom's satisfaction, very much the way he had drawn her.

She sat down beside him and without speaking she took from him his sketchbook. I should explain, Bloom said to her as she sorted through the pages and lingered over the panels in which she and he were naked and entwined inside the cave walls. She was quiet for some time, tracing her finger around the curves of their figures.

She then looked up and smiled. There is nothing to explain.

But, Bloom insisted, these drawings, they aren't what they appear to be.

Obviously amused at Bloom's need to explain himself, she said, I know what these are drawings of. She then pointed to the image Bloom had drawn of himself, and, suppressing a smile, said, Odysseus? Bloom nodded, his cheeks burning with embarrassment. But, she asked, now enjoying this power she held over him, who, I want to know, is your Penelope? When she asked him this question, Bloom saw what couldn't be gleaned from an image drawn by a second-rate artist promoting a circus act. He saw in her face the one characteristic she shared with her brother, the same incisive and compassionate eyes.

Isabella, said Bloom.

She nodded and then asked if Isabella was very far away.

No. She's dead.

When?

Recently.

I'm sorry for you. And then Estella said as she looked one more time at his drawings, You have a vivid style. She shut the sketch-book and placed it back in his lap.

She offered Bloom her hand, which he took hold of, and she said to him as she turned his hand over and studied his fingers, I'll show you to Eduardo's room.

Bloom trailed behind the long gown of Estella Maria Tourneur as they walked up the stairs inside the house's turret. She led him to the door of her brother's room, where, hanging in its many windows, Bloom found cages shaped like lampshades, nearly a dozen of them, holding giant macaws and cockatoos and exotic birds he couldn't have imagined existed until he saw these; they were vibrant and colorful, with tall crests and headdresses, with all varieties of decorative plumage. Bloom surveyed the cages and when he was through he turned back to Estella, who was standing in the door-way, backlit from the sun shining through a window across the hall. They're magnificent, Bloom said. Bloom saw in the shadow the tip of Estella's chin lower, then rise. He continued to move from cage to cage and looked more carefully at Eduardo's treasures, and asked Estella where they all came from. Estella told him over the birds' cacophonous squawks and songs that most of them Eduardo had collected in tropical ports when he worked the cargo ships across the channel. Will you be comfortable here? she asked.

Yes, said Bloom, of course. Eduardo's room may have been spar-tan, as the only furnishings were a twin bed and a rather drab throw rug, but with the birds jumping and shuffling back and forth on their perches, and with views of the shoreline and the garden out the turret's windows, he was reminded of the tower's pavilion. I feel very much at home, he told Estella. More than you can possibly know.

Appearing neither pleased nor displeased that he found the room to his liking, she said he should join her for some dinner as soon as he settled in. She then excused herself and shut the door behind her. The birds quieted and grew still upon her departure.

The sun had set and was warming the sky with a blood-orange glow.

✣

To dinner, Estella wore her hair pinned up and a long strand of pearls wrapped once around her throat, leaving the rest to hang loosely over her naked breastbone. They sat across from each other in an intimate silence, and ate a simple meal of Garibaldi, which smelled of citrus, and thin slices of avocado, and a small mound of rice. And together they looked out to the approaching swells. They didn't speak very much; rather, they listened to the powerful waves crash onto the rocks below, sometimes with so much force the dining room window would quaver inside its frame. When they had finished eating, Estella told Bloom to leave the table as it was and invited him into the sitting room, where, without asking, she poured for him a tall glass of whiskey and asked him to sit on the end of the couch where he could best see her sitting at the piano, and then all the time looking at him and never for a moment at her hands, she played for him a slow, ponderous piece of music he didn't know, and when she was through with this, with only a brief pause, she played another. Bloom felt himself too sensitive to the intensity of her eyes to want to look away from them, so he looked to her as she looked to him. It was only after he took his last sip of whiskey that she stopped, and he realized then she had been play-ing all this time for his pleasure. As soon as he had finished, Estella told him to leave his glass on the table, and then she wished him good night, and walked out the side door she had earlier entered.

When Bloom had returned to Eduardo's room, he saw her through the window, on the lawn kneeling under the bar of Guillaume's trapeze, which was twisting about in the wind. He watched her talk to her dead and buried husband for some time before he felt the whiskey and the smoke and the excitement of the day take its toll. He prepared for bed, and the instant he set his head on Eduardo's pillow, he joined the birds in their slumber.

Bloom wasn't quite sure how long he was asleep when he felt the touch of Estella's hand on his cheek. She placed a finger over his lips when he opened his eyes, tilted her head slightly, observed his face, as if awaiting Bloom's reaction to her uninvited presence at his bedside. Bloom, who was no stranger to a nocturnal intrusion, remained passively reclined. He merely looked at Estella's moonlit face and said nothing when she removed her finger from his mouth and slipped this same hand under his shirt, pressed her palm against his chest. Did you make love to Isabella? she asked.

No, said Bloom.

As if both stating a fact and asking a question at the same time, she said, But you've made love to women before.

No, said Bloom, shaking his head. Not in the biblical sense. No.

And then she said in the same tone, Well, you'll make love to me.

Bloom told her he was still in love with Isabella.

Estella said she was still in love with Guillaume.

But, said Bloom, Guillaume is dead.

As is Isabella. Trust me, she said. You'll see. I know your sadness. I intend to help you. As a mother would assist a child, Estella lifted Bloom's shirt over his head, and as he lay naked before her, she ran her fingers down his throat and along the length of his body. Now, said Estella, don't move. She stood up and pulled the straps of her gown over her shoulders and let it fall to her feet, revealing to Bloom in the moonlight a scar from a burn running under her left arm to the curve of her hip. She now returned to him, straddled his waist, and took hold of his hand, ran it over the scar's marbled surface. Next time you draw me, she told him, you can make me complete. When Bloom felt her scar, whatever resistance remained within him, whatever little tug of conscience he felt, faded. He sat up and kissed the burned flesh, tasted with his tongue its uneven texture.

No, she said, pushing his head back onto the pillow. No, she repeated as she lowered his hands to her hips. Now shut your eyes, she said, and dream of Isabella.

Why?

To keep her memory alive.

Bloom shut his eyes and did as Estella said. He searched for a memory of Isabella. He recalled those many times he held her in the gallery, when he touched the soft flesh of her stomach through the seam of her blouse, lifted the material of her dresses to caress the back of her thighs. The memory was interrupted as Estella began to move. Her movement awakened the birds. They began to sing and squawk and shuffle and jump about in their cages, and Bloom recalled the first time he and Isabella stood in the pavilion, before his aviary with the invertiscope harnessed to his shoulders. Estella shifted her weight, and taking Bloom by surprise, her body swallowed him. Bloom had been touched by Roya's hand, by his own hand, he had been taken into the lush paradise of a woman's mouth, but he had never sensed so complete a pleasure as he felt now. Estella bore down on him, her ass rising and falling athletically, steadily, rhythmically. Her hands pressed against his chest to form a beautiful arch in her back, over which her long mane of black hair fell into the darkness behind her. When she rose to her full height over him, she was a Dionysian mystery, the goddess of everything, so far as Bloom was concerned, Ecstasy herself. Bloom braced his arms and set his hands against the attenuated slope of her small breasts. Now say her name, said Estella, as she rose. Say her name and see her face, she said, as she fell. No, said Bloom.

It's all right, said Estella, say her name. Say it, she said as she clenched her thighs tightly against his hips, tightened her grip on his penis, bore her ass down between his thighs. Isabella, said Bloom quietly and clumsily. Louder, said Estella. Clearer. Isabella, said Bloom, louder this time. Again, Estella exhaled. And again, Bloom said Isabella's name, this time with less pause and inhibition, with more feeling, and he could see her face, as clear in his mind as he could see Estella. Isabella, he said, Isabella. Over and over he said her name, and with each mention of it, Estella said, panting now, Yes, good, good, yes. And after several more mentions of Bloom's lost love, a final Yes! arrived most suddenly, and Bloom felt something indescribable. He felt Estella's body temperature rise, her skin hot to the touch; he felt her entire musculature expand and contract around him. He felt her tremble and tremble and tremble. She dug her fingers into his chest and she trembled some more, and then she said, Ready? and with only the slightest movement of her hips, she pressed her stomach against Bloom's, and the moment she did this Bloom was compelled to lower his hand from her breast and grab hold of her scar, which he squeezed with all his might, and now trembling himself, his eyes feeling as if they were about to combust into flames, he began to fill her, and as he did so, he could feel himself crying, in small jags, like a small child in the aftermath of a tantrum.

There now, said Estella as she lowered her weight onto his chest. There, there, that's good. She didn't move. The birds stilled in their cages. She continued to hold him inside her, squeezing every last drop from him. And with her warm breath on his ear, she lulled him back to sleep, still whispering, There now, there, there, that's what you needed.

And it was true. It *was* what Bloom needed. More than he knew.

In the morning, when the birds first began to stir and make noise, Eduardo gently shook Bloom awake and said it was time to go. When he had dressed, Bloom asked him if he should wake Estella to say goodbye. He said she wasn't in the house. She had left him in the middle of the night and had gone to his boat in the cove. She was now there, asleep. She says, said Eduardo, you may return should you feel the need to see her again.

>+<

And he would. Each time Bloom felt the memory of Isabella begin to fade from his mind, he returned to Estella. Each time he felt himself consumed by bitterness and self-pity, he drove to the port and rode with Eduardo on the last ferry of the day to Santa Ynez, and each time he visited Estella, he was able to bear his fate. They would quietly dine and watch the ocean crash against the rocks. She would play music for him as he drank his whiskey, and she would make her exit to visit Guillaume's grave. As she had done before, she would visit Bloom in the middle of the night, and he would shut his eyes and see Isabella. In time, Bloom found himself wanting to take an earlier and earlier ferry, and wanted to stay on Santa Ynez longer than the one night, for days, sometimes weeks. The island was calm and peaceful, unpopulated, and he discovered how clear his mind became when he was there. It reminded him of Mount Terminus before the arrival of his brother. It reminded him of his childhood in Woodhaven. He and Estella took long, quiet walks together, and as they grew more accustomed to each other, she told him stories of the ceaseless days traveling with the circus, on land, on sea, through the biggest and oldest of cities, into the middle of nowhere, to the smallest of prairie towns and villages, always on the move, wandering farther and farther from home. Eduardo, too, told him stories of his endless sea adventures. He had lost count of the number of times he had circumnavigated the Earth. More times than any one man should, he said. Eduardo taught Bloom how to fish off a boat. He taught him how to spear fish in the shallows. They paddled on swells into sea caves and sat under their natural cupolas at low tide, eating lunches Estella had prepared for them. They fed the seals and watched the dolphins play. They caught pigs escaped from the few ranches on the far side of the island and returned them home to be slaughtered, and they took a share of the meat home to be cured. And one night Estella took Bloom by the hand after dinner and led him to her room, to the large bed she had shared with Guillaume, and they enjoyed each other without men-tioning the dead, and they held each other close through the night and into the morning, and Estella that day emptied a room whose window looked off to the sea, and Bloom looked off to the sea, and he could see in its empty expanse *The Death of Paradise.*

He could see his work taking shape in his mind, and sometimes for weeks at a time, he would spend the better part of his days in this room doing no other work than thinking through the picture in his mind, and Estella never bothered him, and Eduardo never bothered him. They left him to himself. To the quiet. To the pleasures of his prolonged silences. To his most natural state of being. They all shared this in common. He loved it here, and there were times Bloom thought of never leaving. And perhaps he would have had Estella asked him to stay. He might have left Mount Terminus behind had she made the subtlest of gestures, but she didn't, so he didn't. He came and went as he pleased. Each time he returned he was warmly welcomed and embraced. Each time he left, they bid him goodbye with a warm farewell.

PART V

PARADISE

W hen the Mount Terminus subdivision opened, fighter pilots recently returned from the war flew planes in formation across the basin and performed feats of aerial acrobatics. Simon, in the company of councilmen, the governor, and members of the water authority, stood before a fountain at the edge of the bluff, and there Bloom's brother proclaimed this the beginning of a new era, at which point water sprang forth from the fountain's spigots and arced high overhead. That evening, while in the same company, Simon lifted a switch on a transformer box, and with it, all the land for as far as all could see illuminated. Street after street, incandescent light shone atop poles, out windows, onto billboards advertising soap and beauty products and Mount Terminus pictures. Rockets shrieked from the earth and exploded into sparkling bouquets over clay tiles topping the roofs, reflected from the boulevard's office building windows, onto the eyes of pilgrims who had driven in to take in the spectacle. There seemed to be a ceaseless supply of incendiaries. The sky burst open over the development into the early hours of the next morning; over the stages and warehouses of the new studio the pyrotechnics continued to brighten the sky until the sun broke the day. When the light show had ceased, Bloom drove with Simon to the new lot, and there, before he opened it to the employees and the public, Simon walked Bloom through streets and town squares, past far-flung places Bloom would likely never visit, and he was amazed by what he saw, and he was amazed at what his brother had accomplished. It was all too big for words. It was as if Simon truly were some modern pharaoh or emperor, some ancient warlord philosopher king. He had built here a small city within the city, and with the size and scope of his endeavor a testament to his power and vision, he easily attracted talent from the East, new directors, actors, writers, photographers, technicians, so many, in fact, Simon said he would need to appoint an army of stage managers to commandeer the new personnel. No longer would he be seen on his porch conducting the action of the studio. No longer, Bloom presumed, would he be seen at all. It was one thing to know the enormity of a man's ambition, another altogether to witness that ambition realized. Simon's achievement radiated out over the wires, and as news of opportunity at the studio, on the land here and in the valley, spread in the weeks that followed, more and more pilgrims arrived. Cars streamed in from downtown, from the desert, from remote places in the mountains, the outer reaches of the valleys. People en masse massed in the streets. Everywhere. Simply to see. To be part of history. To behold Simon's achievement. Even the malcontents from Pacheta Lake were present, but perhaps because the festivities were so popular and lively, they didn't dare disrupt them. They did, however, make their attendance known. Dozens of them formed a quiet protest on the periphery of the fountain, at the gates of the studio, and with the grimmest of faces, they silently held up signs of protest—*Ignore Us At Your Peril*; *We Will Be Heard*; *Just When You Least Expect It, You'll Know Who We Are*—and were bullied away by the police into paddy wagons. When the energy of all was finally spent and the stretch of land had quieted, moving trucks rolled in, and the men and women who had purchased their new homes from Simon's real estate company settled, and soon Bloom saw take life the map his brother had kept in his mother's shrine. The entire basin, it appeared to Bloom, grew more and more green and colorful by the day, and it continued to phosphoresce at night, a shade of violet, or was it lavender, and the stars, he could have sworn, had begun to dim. On nights that held a chill in the air, a scrim of smoke blanketed the pale blue light, and if the current of wind swept in from the ocean, it could lift the sweet smell of burning wood as high as Mount Terminus's peak. They were there. Always there. Their cars roaming the streets. Their trams crating them back and forth to and from the heart of the city. An occasional siren crying a sorrowful wail.

⊁⊀

As much as Bloom admired his brother's achievement, he took comfort knowing a boundary was drawn around his ambition at the base of Mount Terminus. And while he felt a dull ache when the members of the colony departed the plateau for homes on the grid, he mostly felt relief to see them go, including Simon, who had built a sizable home on a fine piece of property that elevated him just high enough to appreciate the entire stretch of land he had developed. The plateau from hereon would remain largely unused. Except on the rare occasion—when the stages and studios of Mount Terminus Productions were overbooked—it was Bloom's to do with as he pleased. It afforded him the time and silence to continue working at an unhurried pace on *The Death of Paradise*. It provided him the right set of circumstances to meticulously re-create under the warehouse skylights the rooms of the villa as he imagined they had been when Fernando and Miranda, Manuel and Adora occupied them. Every now and again, he called on the aid of Hershel Verbinsky and Hannah Edelstein. He mailed them designs for furniture and art, odds and ends, and, on occasion, asked for a helping hand. Usually, however, he relied on Roya to keep him company, sometimes Gus, who helped with heavy lifting, and every now and again, Gottlieb, when his mood and schedule allowed it. Simon had offered the plateau to Bloom and his mentor, to make it their own personal domain, but Gottlieb was fonder of people than Bloom had realized. He couldn't properly be himself if he wasn't being a nuisance. To feel relevant, he told Bloom, he needed to be in the company of people who properly loathed him. If he wasn't agitating his colleagues, he didn't consider himself fully alive. Bloom, who possessed his own idiosyncratic methods, albeit antithetical to Gottlieb's, understood. He often wished he were equipped to contend with Simon and Gottlieb's boisterous world, but if his time on Santa Ynez had taught him anything, he knew he was better disposed to living his life apart, as his father had done, as his mother had done. Upon his returns from Santa Ynez, he often envisioned raising the walls of the estate higher and higher, so high his view from the top of the tower would become obstructed. He dreamed at times of encircling the gardens and the grove behind such a wall, and cutting himself off completely, forever, with little more than a slot through which he could receive the most essential things. He would have been perfectly fulfilled living such a life with Roya, Meralda, and Gus. And when these figments passed, he thought, perhaps after he had completed *The Death of Paradise*, he would make it so. Cut himself off. For good.

And why not? . . . What, after all, did he have to offer anyone? Like Death, like Jacob, like the earliest inhabitants of Mount Terminus, his fate, it seemed, was sealed. God had sealed him into the Book of Life with the mark of misery and sorrow. What good was it to fight against it any longer?

✶

Bloom spent some months trying to work out the details of the Mount Terminus massacre, and for months he felt his attempts a failure. He wanted more than anything else to portray Don Fernando as the monster he was, but he worried that if he provided him the camera's point of view, he could very easily turn him into a conquering hero. He attempted, therefore, to frame the atrocity from Manuel's innocent and observant point of view, as his perspective seemed more compatible with the truth Bloom wanted to show. But knowing what he knew of Manuel Salazar now, of his craven self-interest, of his cowardly disregard for the woman he claimed to love, he didn't wish for the audience to mistake his sensitivity as an artist as a form of romantic nobility. He began to recall the conversations he had with Dr. Straight on the subject of nationalism and tribalism, of defining the enemy as something other than human, and it eventually occurred to Bloom, this scene's success—if he was to get to its essential truth—was dependent on a shifting perspective. If his intent was to charge Fernando as a monster, Manuel as an unwitting accomplice, he must humanize the people whose lives they and the church destroyed, and so he went back in time to the images he drew for Jacob in their early days on Mount Terminus, the ones in which he included his mother as a participant in the mountain's idyllic past, and he decided to make the conquered, not the conquerors, the centerpiece of this movement. As soon as Fernando disgraced himself in Spain, was ordered into exile by the king, put aboard the ship bound for the New World, he would cut away to the spring on Mount Terminus, and dwell there with the children hanging from the limbs of the oak trees, with the men spearfishing in the sea, with the women tending to the fires and preparing for the feasts and the celebrations. Here he would allow the light to shine, here he would make these people as real as Eduardo and Estella were real, and he would show his audience who the true barbarians were, and what darkness they carried in their hearts.

When this idea took hold, Bloom began drawing throughout the days and late into the nights. He relived his earliest days on Mount Terminus and re-created the world he had imagined as a child, the images he had captured in his waking dreams. And on one such night when he attempted to retrieve from his memory an image of his mother, to see her living within the long-lost Arcadia, he paused for a moment and looked out his studio window, into the courtyard, where he saw a dark figure returning his gaze. It stood still for a moment and then walked off in the direction of the cottages. He thought perhaps it was Roya, but Roya, he recalled, had long since turned in for the night. Perhaps he saw nothing at all? He shut off the light so he could better see into the dim light of the courtyard, and now he observed the same dark figure walk under the toupee of bougainvillea atop the pergola. Bloom hurried out the studio door, down the steps into the courtyard, and he followed the figure into the grove, where he glimpsed a slim wisp of a woman's silhouette enter the rose garden. He called out a hello, but there was no sign of her. He continued on to the garden's center, through the passages cutting across the concentric circles, and when he reached the glowing limbs of the enraptured couple sleeping the Sleep of Death, there, sitting on the bench set opposite Jacob's grave, in the glow of moonlight reflecting off the statuary marble, was Isabella, the sight of whom caused Bloom's body to behave in an involuntary manner, one not conducive to sustaining consciousness. His extremities started to tingle, as did the very follicles attaching his hair to his scalp. The scent of the air sweetened, and then the moon's silvery glow grayed and eventually filled with an inky darkness.

><

When Bloom started to come to, he felt his head resting in the warmth of a lap and a hand stroking his cheek. Again his thoughts turned to Roya, but when he opened his eyes, he found what was unmistakably Isabella's face in the darkness, and he thought of his mother searching the windows for an image of Leah, and he thought of the images he saw of her being chased by the phantasm of her dead sister. He reached for the hand running down his cheek and felt its form, its fingers, its bones, and he said to himself, I've gone mad.

No, Joseph, you haven't gone mad.

But you're dead.

No, I'm here, said Isabella, here with you.

She sounded weak, like an imprint of a life, as if something inside the very core of her had been torn apart. She reached for Bloom's hand and raised it to her mouth, and she blew her breath onto it. She then pulled his palm to her breast so Bloom could feel the faint beat of her heart.

See?

It's not possible, thought Bloom. He lifted himself up and turned to her.

But your letter . . .

What letter?

The one you carried with you. The one sealed with the drawings I sent before you departed.

But that letter was lost.

No, said Bloom. No, it wasn't.

No?

No. For almost two years I've been mourning your death.

Two years?

Yes, said Bloom. Two awful years.

It never occurred to me that letter could have found its way to you. If I had thought it even remotely possible . . .

Her voice dropped off, and Bloom could hear what a struggle it was for Isabella to contend with such a strong emotion. After a long moment of silence, Isabella collected herself, and said, Joseph . . .

Yes?

Will you please do something for me?

What's that?

Pretend with me, for just a little while, that I never left. Please, can we act as we once did? With the same familiarity? With the same tenderness?

Bloom could again hear in the hollowness of Isabella's voice the echo of something horrible, and he knew whatever had happened to her was far graver than the misery he had suffered when he thought she was lost to him. He was compelled to share with her how bereft he had been, to tell her what it was like for him after he read what was contained in her package. He wanted to tell her how changed he was by the news it carried, how changed he was by his visits to Santa Ynez. For a moment he wondered how he could possibly pretend to be the same man Isabella had loved. He was no longer that person. He had been drained of hope. Grieved. Mourned. Fallen to despair. He had come to adore another woman, a woman who helped reconstitute and renew his spirit. Her companionship had fundamentally changed him. He wanted to say it all, but as they stood up and started walking in the direction of the courtyard, he could see in the glow of light emanating from the house how thin and frail Isabella had become, and when he walked her inside and sat her down in the parlor, he saw to what extent her once vibrant eyes had lost their vitality. A thick fog had settled within them. And when he began to comprehend what hopeless state she was in, he said, My dear Isabella, there's no reason to pretend. I'm still the same man. The very same. And then he asked if she would let him call a doctor for her.

She gently took his hand and said, Please, Joseph. As if I never left.

All right, Bloom agreed. As if you'd never left. At which point it occurred to him to take her to the library. He guided her up the stairs by the arm, and when they entered the room she and Dr. Straight inhabited for the months they were on the estate, he said, There, see, as if you were here only yesterday.

The smallest glimmer of life appeared in the corners of Isabella's eyes. She approached the light cabinet and ran her fingers over the rivulets of wax in Walgensten's lantern.

I didn't have the heart to move it.

Isabella returned to Bloom and pressed her gaunt cheek to his chest. May I sit in here alone for a few moments?

Of course. Bloom left her, but before he walked off into the hall, he observed her face and saw how absent of color and expression it was. However upsetting he found her condition, however impossible the actuality of her return seemed to him, however much he continued to question whether or not the experience he was having was, in fact, taking place, or if he had gone truly mad, he did as he promised he'd do. He let her be without questions. He found her belongings in the foyer—her valise and a trunk—and carried them to the cottage in which she resided when she was last on the estate, and he set them before the bed. He was tempted for a moment to search for clues within them, to see if he could puzzle together where she had been and what she had been through, but he restrained himself. Rather, he left her things alone and descended into the cellar, and climbed the rungs of the ladder to Manuel's chamber, and climbed down the rungs of the ladder to Manuel's labyrinthine passages, followed Ariadne's thread to the eye of the Minotaur, to Adora's tomb, and he watched Isabella sit in the library. She hadn't moved. Not a muscle. She sat upright, staring at the white sheet she and Dr. Straight had used to screen Gaspard's slides. For nearly a half hour he observed her sit as stiff as death, at which time Bloom couldn't take it anymore. He returned to her and, without a word, lifted her up in his arms, carried her to the cottage, and settled her into bed. He then sat through the night in the courtyard trying to believe it was true, wondering if he had somehow conjured her spirit to return to him during those nights spent with Estella, those nights he called out Isabella's name into the caws and squawks of Eduardo's shuffling birds. Throughout the night, he periodically stood up to look in, to see if her body was still at rest on the cottage's bed. Throughout the night, he sat and asked himself if this was how his mother had begun to see Leah when she was alert and awake. He felt himself at the precipice of madness all night, until early the following morning Meralda discovered him sitting upright in his chair, staring at the cottage's exterior, and asked him what in the world was he doing out here, and Bloom said, Please go to the window of the cottage and tell me what you see. Meralda asked what had gotten into him, and Bloom asked once again for her to do as he asked. She walked to the cottage window, and when she returned, she said, Is it her? Is it really her?

You see her, then? She *is* there?

Yes. She is there. Asleep in her bed.

You're certain?

Meralda clutched hold of Bloom and said, Yes! She is there. In one piece. Asleep. Dreaming. Waiting to awake to see you. And then Bloom's cook proclaimed it a miracle his angel had returned to her dear boy. Thank you, she said to the heavens, crossing herself. Please, may she bring him peace and joy.

>‹

Bloom and Isabella dined together in the early evenings, and then quietly walked through the hedgerows of the front gardens. For several weeks, they continued on in the same silence to which they had, in gradations, grown accustomed on Isabella's previous visit, but what Bloom once found deeply comforting then, he now considered unnatural. He wanted to talk, to know where she had been and what events had taken shape to so dramatically change her. He didn't want to put on this charade; yet he didn't have the heart to disappoint her. They kept to their regimen, until one night—when, Bloom noticed, Isabella appeared to have regained the smallest fraction of her luster—she finally spoke and asked him to tell her what he had done with himself since their last correspondence. If for no other reason than to hear something occupy their silence, Bloom took his time recounting for her the changes he had witnessed take place on the stretch of land leading to the sea. And because he had few of his own stories he could share that didn't in some way relate to her, he talked of Simon. About the scope of vision, the enormity of his will. She asked about *Death, Forlorn*, and he recounted the details of the production for her. And when she asked what more he had done, he said, without stating why, his rate of production had slowed considerably, but he had been preparing to work with Gottlieb on their largest picture yet.

Will you tell me about it?

Better, said Bloom, I will show you. Tomorrow.

The following day, Isabella insisted she had improved enough to walk the trail to Mount Terminus's peak. She was growing restless and needed a change of scene. Meralda packed a picnic for them, and together Bloom and Isabella walked arm in arm as they made a geriatric ascent to the top of the mountain. Once there, Bloom pointed out the aqueduct carrying water to the basin and told her of the thousands of men and the incalculable amount of material it took to build it. He recalled for her the image of the dam filling the canyon pass and the holocaust of dust generated by the construction in the basin, and he described the nightmarish sunsets cast through its cumulous plumes. He spared her the dismay he felt over the loss of Mount Terminus's former serenity. He left unspoken how disheartened he felt by the changes he saw every morning from the tower, the visions he had of walling himself in.

It was a day of gentle breezes, which brought with them the smell of baked earth and the strong scent of citrus and eucalyptus. When Bloom shut his eyes, he was reminded of his earliest days on Mount Terminus, when he was a child, when the mountain and its vistas were open and clear. On this day, the air was still and the chaparral silent enough they could hear the sounds of quail nervously warbling about unseen. And here they reclined and slept, and when she was awake and alert, Bloom read to Isabella Chekhov's *The Lady with the Dog*, and when they finished this melancholy seaside tale, they watched for some time a condor ride the thermal currents around and about the ranches of the valley.

When they had tired of the sun, Bloom walked Isabella down the trail and then they continued ambling farther down to the plateau.

I have a small surprise for you.

Bloom had earlier tied a long sash of black velvet around his waist, which he now removed, and with Isabella's permission, he covered her eyes. He held her shoulder with one hand and folded his other hand over the curve of her hip. He guided her into the warehouse, where, once inside, he walked her up the stairs, sat her in a chair under a skylight, and told her to be still. When he had climbed to the part of the set he had finished only some weeks before her return, he instructed her to remove the blindfold, and when she did, she found herself looking into a vanity mirror, from where she could see in the mirror's reflection the image of Aphrodite.

Where are you?

Observing you from beyond.

Bloom, who was looking down on her from behind the peepholes of the goddess's eyes, stood up on a scaffold to reveal himself.

I had a tub carried into the villa's gallery some months ago, thinking I'd be able to more easily reflect on Miranda isolated in that room, but I couldn't bring myself to remove Mother's paintings. So I reconstructed her room here.

For what purpose?

It's their story I'm going to make into my next picture.

In the mirror's reflection Bloom could see the smallest of smiles take shape. He once again crouched down and looked at Isabella through the pinholes of Aphrodite's eyes, and from here he recalled how carefree and easy she had once been, and he knew from this vantage point, he was no longer looking at the same woman with whom he'd fallen in love. And while continuing to hide behind the façade, he was moved by a feeling of urgency he knew he would soon be incapable of containing. He understood that whatever ordeal Isabella had been through had been infinitely worse than his, but his experience had in its own way devastated him. And so, speaking from behind the goddess of love's mask, he apologized to Isabella.

I'm sorry, he said. I'm so sorry . . .

What for?

I can't continue on this way. I can't pretend any longer.

Isabella fixed her eyes on his, and said, My dear, sweet Joseph.

I need to know. I need to understand.

>‹

Instead of accompanying him to the gardens that night after dinner, Isabella led Joseph to the parlor, where she had set up the projector and the screen and arranged on a table a stack of film canisters. With her hand on top of the pile, she said, I've been here. What you need to know, you'll find inside these. What you will see, I have lived. And then she left Bloom to watch movies he would learn later that evening she had filmed. They were movies of the dead. The dead and the walking dead, the lamed and dismembered, the infected, the fevered, the deranged, the destroyed. For hours, Bloom sat in the dark, listening to the interminable clicks of his father's drive and loop, experiencing with open eyes one repulsive vision after the next. He watched reel after reel of healthy young men cut down by machine gun volleys, witnessed them mined and thrown into the air in pieces. He saw, through the eye of Isabella's lens, men vaporized by mortar and cannon rounds. Men disappearing into gaseous clouds from which they never emerged. He saw the half-faced, the crushed-faced, the gutted, the pulverized, men burned beyond recognition; the

noseless, the eyeless, the jawless, the impaled, men with freshly blood-
ied stumps; the decomposed, the decomposing, the trench-footed,
dead men hung over barbed wire, their sinew, their bowels eaten by
rats, maggots bred within their open cavities eaten by ravens. He
saw ravens shot down from the skies to be eaten by starving men.
Most dreadful of all, Isabella had captured with her camera moments
of death, bodies shuddering in death rattles, bodies exhaling their
final breaths, the widening of eyes, the fixed glare of the newly dead,
the cessation of the excruciating, the unbearable, the unjust, the in-
conceivable, horrific pain of men.

When Bloom had watched each reel to its completion, he searched
the villa for Isabella and found her lying still on the chaise in his
mother's gallery. The night was half gone, but she was awake, list-
lessly staring up at one of his mother's many paintings. He lay down
next to her and took her in his arms and held her. And soon she
began to talk. She explained to him that while crossing the North
Atlantic, Dr. Straight suffered a heart attack. The grief, she said, I
thought it had passed. I thought he was prepared to travel. When
they reached Paris, the doctor had recovered to some degree but
was too weak to continue on. Isabella hospitalized him for several
weeks and then took him to a rented room. He willed his home and
all his possessions to her. He encouraged her to return to Mount
Terminus to be with Bloom. He regretted having taken her along to
experience this. A few nights later, he had a stroke and died. In his
last conscious moments, he saw in a mirror a reflection of his wife.
I'll only be a moment, Julia, he said at the end, and then he was
gone. Isabella sent his body to be cremated, so she might easily carry
it with her when she returned. She intended to inter his ashes beside
his wife's, but they would be lost in the chaos that followed. For a
time, she said, she sat still and read. In the flat was a French trans-
lation of Ivan Turgenev's *Fathers and Sons*. She drew strength from
Bazarov's cold nihilism, from his calculated, unfeeling sensibility.
For a time, she became numb. Until she wasn't. She packed her
things, took along her camera and film, the invertiscope, and volun-
teered for the ambulance corps in time for the Battle of the Somme.

She carried away men from the trenches and drove them to the field hospitals. One afternoon, when she was en route to the aid station, she crashed her ambulance, and she, herself, became a war casualty. She suffered a concussion and broke a bone in her leg and one in her arm, and in the aftermath of the accident she experienced what they said was a nervous state of exhaustion. Her entire body, as if a switch had been shut off inside it, ceased to function. She convalesced at a quiet sanitarium in the South by the sea, where, fate would have it, she was put in the care of Pierre Janet, the expert on brainwave entrainment who had invited Dr. Straight to join him on the battlefield. Dr. Janet helped Isabella recover to the degree he could help anyone recover from the horrors they had seen, and she, in turn, detailed for the doctor how to administer Dr. Straight's invertiscope experiment. One day, not long after the armistice had been declared, she left her invention in Janet's care, packed up the film she had shot, boarded a ship, and, not knowing where else to go, she returned to Bloom.

Bloom expected Isabella to expel the horror of this nightmare with tears after she had recounted her story, but instead she reported these details as if they were part of someone else's narrative. Perhaps this was necessary, Bloom thought. If she felt it right away, all at once, the burden of it might destroy her. Perhaps it was healthier, he thought, that she saw these experiences from a distant remove, as she would have had she been wearing the invertiscope.

><

That night they remained in the gallery and Bloom held her close to him until he was certain she had fallen asleep. He drew the heavy curtains to darken the brightening room and went out into the morning light to the rose garden with a pair of pruning shears. He clipped red roses whose heads had opened recently enough their petals were still intact, yet opened long enough to the elements that they could easily be shaken free. He filled a bucket of these overripe roses and returned to the house, where he requested from Meralda a few items from her toilette, some perfume and bath oils, some powder, shampoo, a scrub brush, and he took all these things to the gallery and set them about the tub. When he returned to Isabella, he found her asleep with her body curled tightly around a pillow, her fingers clenched in fists as if she were shielding her face, and there was a noise, a loud and disturbing sound of pebbles rubbing against one another, grinding and churning, in a tedious and persistent rhythm. Bloom momentarily wondered what Isabella was squeezing in her fists, but it wasn't until the grinding ceased and was followed by an incomprehensible mumbling, and then a restrained whimper like that of a dog who'd been shamed by its master, that he realized the noise was emanating from Isabella's mouth. It was only when he eased her fists away from her face, he saw—as the grinding recommenced—that the horrible noise was being made by her teeth. Her jaw was clenching and pressing, gnashing in communion with an invisible force inside her. To help her release whatever it was she was reliving in her dreams, Bloom took hold of her face and whispered her name. Isabella, he said, Isabella. Isabella, he repeated, sounding the word out in his mouth, accentuating each syllable, speaking it as he had so many times when summoning her memory on his visits to Santa Ynez. He now reached out to touch her, to smooth over her hair, and just as the tip of his finger brushed her brow, she turned to him violently, thrashing her arms about. She grabbed hold of Bloom's chest and pressed herself into him. Only then did she briefly awaken, enough to recognize it was him beside her. Oh, Joseph, she said wearily. I'm so sorry. And when her jaw relaxed and she grew calm, Bloom said, There, there. There, there. It's all right. With Bloom holding her, the rest of her body, the muscles in her face, her arms and hands and legs, relaxed and stretched, and the lines of her body straightened into the self-possessed woman he once knew. In this peaceful state, he could see the Isabella he saw so clearly in his dreams on those nights he spent with La Reina del Fuego, when he dreamed of the Isabella he had held in his arms in this very room, and he knew in this instant the love and affection he once felt for her still lived inside him.

Isabella slept for many hours. She slept through the entire day, and as if this were the first real sleep she had had since she left Bloom, she slept into the early evening. When she awoke, Meralda brought her some chicken broth and bread, and when Isabella had eaten all of this, she asked for some more, and Meralda brought up a little while later a thick steak and potatoes and a jug of red wine. For dessert she dug heartily into a large block of cheese, then ate small pastries and cookies and a custard. Although he hadn't slept in more than a day, Bloom's attention was acute; this sight of Isabella returning to good health filled him with joy. When she asked him to read to her something frivolous and fun, he picked from a library shelf *Alice's Adventures in Wonderland*, and after a while, he handed her the book to read on her own, and he went to the cellar to retrieve two buckets, both of which he filled with hot water. He carried these buckets into the gallery and emptied them into the tub, then, as Miranda's servants had done for her, he repeated this task over and again until the tub was full. Each time he crossed the room, Isabella poked her eyes up over the top of the book, but Bloom chose to ignore her. He added to the water Meralda's oils and a few drops of perfume, and when the room had filled with a soothing aroma, Bloom shook out the roses he had picked from the garden. All of them he shook out until the water's surface was thoroughly disguised.

Isabella now ignored Bloom as he had ignored her. When the bath was prepared, she continued to read until the very moment Bloom snatched the book from her hands and cast it aside. It was only when Bloom felt himself grow serious, when he felt the urge to explain what it was he was going to do, the Isabella of the past, the strong and curious, the impetuous Isabella, who played at seduction with quiet misdirection, returned, and said, No, let's not speak of it. Let's never speak of it.

Yes, said Bloom, let's not. Bloom helped her up, carried her across the room, and set her down to stand before the full-length mirror, where Bloom—with shaking hands—unzipped the back of her dress. He reached to the cuffs of its sleeves and eased them down until the neck folded over her small breasts; and down farther he pulled until she was able to step out of it. She raised her arms as Bloom set the dress aside and when he returned to his place behind her, he lifted her slip, turning it inside out over her head.

Isabella now stood before him with her chest bare and her bloomers hugging her waist and covering her midriff. As eager as he was to tear them away, Bloom, with great care, set her slip on top of her dress, and this time when he returned to stand behind her, he discovered Isabella stroking her arms as Manuel described Miranda—up and down, caressing one, then the other, her head lolling back with pleasure; and as she continued to do this, he slipped his fingers inside the waistband of her bloomers, feeling with their tips the smoothness of her flesh, and from behind, he pushed down, ran his knuckles over the generous curve of her ass, down the backs of her thighs and calves, until he had pulled them to the floor. She stepped out, and as he had done with her other items of clothing, he set her bloomers aside.

Bloom wanted nothing more than to lay his hands on her hips and feel the weight of her body against his, to kneel before her, as if in prayer, and press his nose into places it didn't belong, but he had cast himself in the role of her servant, and was determined to attend to her, to abide by her desires, and heal her. He stood on the threshold and watched as indifferently as he knew how. He watched her step through the rose petals, watched her ease her body into the water, at which point she shut her eyes and disappeared under cover of bloodred petals.

><-

For a week, Bloom waited. For a month, he waited. For two and then three and then four months, he waited. He waited for Isabella to recover. He moved her belongings from the cottage into the gallery, and for four months she didn't leave this room. For four months, she ate, and read, and slept. For four months, Isabella became Bloom's sole occupation. For four months, there existed nothing else but her. Every morning and every night, he clipped roses from the garden and drew Isabella her baths and undressed her and attended to her.

In small increments of time, he could see changes take place in her spirit and body. In his company she grew more round in her belly and her breasts; her arms thickened and her cheeks grew more full, and soon enough, the fog that had settled into her eyes began to clear and her countenance was reconstituted into the mysterious and arresting object onto which Bloom could once again project his wonder. No longer the deeply wounded creature that had returned to him, she stopped asking for books written for children, but rather requested from the library lengthy tomes by Henry James and George Eliot, Trollope and Thackeray, books full of serious contemplation and social intrigues. And she grew fascinated with Jacob Rosenbloom's back issues of *Modern Astronomer*, in which she followed the Great Debate between Harlow Shapley and Heber Curtis on the subject of island universes. When she saw the first photographs of spiral clusters taken at the Solar Observatory, and saw the magnificence of the billions of stars magnified by the telescope's hundred-inch mirror, she speculated along with Shapley and Curtis whether the spirals were gaseous nebulae or distant galaxies or universes separate from our own. Her newfound strength grew from the attention Bloom lavished upon her. And, no doubt, it grew, as well, because— like Miranda with regard to her most caring servant—she granted Bloom more and more liberty to attend to the pleasures of her body. Sometime into her second month of convalescence, after having soaked herself long enough in the oils and tonics and perfume of her bath to spiral the flesh on the tips of her toes, she one day lifted a leg onto the lip of the tub and asked Bloom to soap and massage her feet. For several weeks this became their customary morning. She would bathe, and Bloom would attend to her wrinkled feet. First to the heel, then to the curve of her arch, and then—as if each was its own separate appendage—to her toes. When this therapy alone no longer satisfied her, she asked him to shampoo her hair. And so, every morning thereafter, Bloom washed and massaged her feet and caressingly dug his soapy fingers into her hair, and when he rinsed it clean, he slicked back behind her ears her dark mane to reveal the fullness of her face. As his father had once attended to the leafy statuaries of his mother in his gardens—with such meticulous and calculated care—Bloom attended to Isabella. To her every whim. And soon during her bathing ritual—sometime at the start of her fourth month in the gallery—Isabella began to resemble more and more Manuel's depiction of Miranda at her most indulgent and vital. One morning after he had shampooed her hair, she rose up from the bath with rose petals clinging to her skin and stood before him with her thickening figure, and asked that he now soap her shoulders and arms and hands. He dutifully stood before her and soaped her shoulders and arms and hands and each of her fingers as he had so attentively cared for each of her toes. When he had finished, and Isabella didn't return to the water, he asked if she desired anything else. My neck, she said as she lifted her chin. And so Bloom moved inward along the line of her collarbone, pressing with his thumbs and forefingers, until his hands met at the base of her throat. He then pushed upward over the ridges of her airway to the bottom of her chin, and traced the line of her jaw. And while his hands gripped the circumference of her throat and neck, and as his eyes focused downward onto the water dripping off her pubis, she said to him very mildly, And the rest, please, Joseph. Bloom now worked his hands down the middle of her wet chest, and with one hand followed by the other he passed through the rise of her breasts, around which he playfully circled suds with his fingers until their tips swelled and hardened. Her breathing, he noticed, began to brush the bubbles across the backs of his hands. All of the rest, she now said. He lathered down to her midriff and spread his hands and fingers over her hips and washed upward to the narrow folds under her arms, and then down again to converge on her pubic bone, which she reflexively pressed against the pressure of his palms. All of me, she repeated. But Bloom didn't allow his hands to descend beyond this point, but rather he fanned his fingers out to the tops of her thighs. He knelt before her to lather first the left leg and then the right, which was when Isabella said to him, You're being cruel now. And without warning, she turned and bent forward and unfairly presented to Bloom her ass. Touch me there, she said. When Bloom hesitated, she now ordered in a commanding voice, Touch me there. So Bloom touched her there. His throat swelled as he touched her there, as he slipped his finger through the line of her ass and ran it along the rim of her anus. Again, she said. But Bloom moved on to soap her inner legs and dimple the springy flesh of her rump. Again, she said, more insistently this time. Bloom slowly dipped his finger into the soapy starburst, as she—with one hand against the lip of the tub and with the other hand between her legs—began to touch herself. Blow on me there, she said. And so holding her open, Bloom blew on her there. Bite me there, she said. When Bloom hesitated, she said it again, Bite me there. Pushing her open wider now, he pressed his face into her and nibbled on her there. He could feel the rhythmic motion of her touch on his lips, and excited by this, he now had no control over his desire. He dug his tongue in there. Forced his nose in there. Nuzzled his chin there. He nibbled and pressed and tickled there with his teeth and his tongue, until he felt her quiver in his mouth, the innermost part of her body convulse and clench and release. And as the convulsions eased, he lifted himself up and cleansed her heaving back. Very gently, he rubbed in synchronicity with her breath, and he waited for her to slip down the wall of the tub and wither into the pool of petals. When she did this, Bloom returned to the threshold, and fully alert, smelling and tasting the perfume and oils on and in his mouth, he kept a watchful eye on Isabella as she briefly nodded off in the warm fragrant water.

The day Bloom walked Isabella out of the gallery for the first time in four months, the first thing she noticed on their stroll around the grounds was the state of the rose garden: all of their bushes had been denuded. She insisted Bloom take her for a closer look, and there she found among all the cross-hatched branches the one remaining rose he had intentionally left untouched to remind her that the concentric rings of the garden would once again brim with color. But seeing the dreary circle of land with all its lattices filled with skeletal remains, seeing what result her pain had wreaked on such a thing of beauty, she looked at the one remaining bloom with some distress, and with fatalistic dread in her voice said, If I ever ravaged you as I've ravaged this garden, Joseph . . .

Bloom's response to these words came readily and sincerely: You can pull up every inch of my roots. It will change nothing.

But, Joseph, she said, pausing to extend her arms to the naked branches all around them, look at what I've done.

Bloom reminded her that it was he who did it.

That, she said, disturbs me most of all. Isabella's eyes began to mist over. She walked away from Bloom now, out of the garden toward the grove.

You're overcome, said Bloom as he trailed after her. Let's walk. Let's take a long walk.

You don't understand, she said. She turned around and, with her fists clenched, started bridging the short distance between them. Something's happened to me! Her voice was angry. She drew her nose to his, and said, I feel! I feel, I need, I deeply need . . . Her eyes picked up the vast blue of the sky as she searched for the right words. I've become insatiable. Ravenous. Like a swarm of locusts.

You're alive, Bloom said gently. He reached out to her and ran a finger under her nostrils where a tear dangled on her nose's bulb. And you're healthy. He touched the back of her neck and then took hold of her under the arms. And you're here, with me, and there's nothing you can do to me to make me feel any worse than I felt when I thought I'd lost you . . . Blind me. Maim me. Kill me, if that's what you want. I don't care.

Oh, Joseph, she laughed softly through her crying, don't say such things.

Honestly, said Bloom. I'm your servant. I'm your slave.

She took hold of his face and held his head steady, and looking into him with a strength and resolve he recognized as the fortified young woman he once knew, she said, Ask me to marry you. Ask me to sit still with you on this mountain to make a quiet and easy life.

The idea of this both confused and delighted Bloom in equal measure.

I'm ready to be at peace, she said. I'm ready to feel at home. All you need is ask.

Even though Bloom could clearly see in the pressed shape of Isabella's mouth that she didn't believe a word of what she was saying, and that her desire to be caged by the limits of such a covenant ran contrary to the words she had spoken not more than a few seconds earlier, Bloom asked Isabella if she would be his wife. And she said, Yes.

⊁⊰

They married some months later at the foot of the reflecting pool. A justice of the peace wearing a dusty suit and smelling of tequila officiated, and Gottlieb, Meralda, Gus, and Simon bore witness. They sat in the courtyard afterward and were served by Meralda. Once drunk, Gottlieb toasted Bloom's father—Wherever he may be!—and the memory of Dr. Straight—Who I had not nearly enough time to know!—and the newlyweds—May you reflect in each other all the beauty there is to discover in this world! And after they had filled themselves with food and wine, the wedding party walked Joseph and Isabella to the master bedroom, and wished them happiness and a fruitful sleep.

For several months, Bloom and Isabella continued to live with the same intensity of spirit they enjoyed during Isabella's convalescence, but in the months after these, when the rose garden had replenished itself with blooms, Bloom began to recognize a Manichaean disquiet in Isabella's presence and he could see quite clearly how the sizable plot of land on which they lived and the union in which they were bound had in her mind become the fortress Bloom feared it might become. Something had awakened in Isabella in the brief time they had been married; some force of will deep within her, the same force that sometimes at night still caused her to gnash her teeth, had emerged into daylight, and although Bloom didn't think she was aware of what was taking hold of her, he knew. He knew it to be the same animalistic force he felt inside her when they made love, the same insatiable hunger she attempted to describe to him on the day they were engaged, and Bloom knew he alone was incapable of putting this force to rest. He knew of nothing he could do to make her feel content within the microcosm he had fashioned for himself since the time he was a child. There wasn't enough sex and kindness and love to snuff it out. He could, therefore, only watch this creeping vine work its way into her, into them, with the frosty indifference with which one greets an unwelcome guest into his home.

Bloom encouraged her to search out a man named George Ritchie, an optician who had designed the enormous parabolic mirror at the Solar Observatory. He lived only a few hours away by car. She drove off one afternoon to meet with Dr. Ritchie, and when she returned, she reported to Bloom what she had found when she arrived, an aged and pathetic creature who complained of headaches and insomnia, of maelstroms in his head that plagued him so often he had named them. Whirligus, he called them. As fascinating as Isabella found the observatory and his diverse collection of mirrors and the designs he had made for an even larger telescope that had the potential to unveil that much more of the sun's surface and the unseen sky, she couldn't bear the disappointment she felt for the man himself, and after only a few visits she decided her fascination for the man's work wasn't great enough to tolerate his company. She soon searched out others whose discipline was closer to the work done by Dr. Straight, but in each instance reported a similar story to the one Bloom had heard when she returned from visiting Dr. Ritchie. Not one of the men whose work she admired, and would have enjoyed furthering, lived up to her expectations, not one equaled her memory of Dr. Straight, and finding all lacking in one way or another, after these few brief meetings, too disillusioned to search anymore, she no longer pursued what had until then been integral to her life.

Perhaps Bloom shouldn't have been surprised to see Isabella appear relieved to be free of the past, free from the tether of memory attaching her to Dr. Straight, from the diligence and discipline she had practiced throughout her youth. Perhaps he should have more readily understood when one afternoon she packed away the part of his father's collection yet to be recorded, and placed it back on the shelf to which it belonged. No more, she said to Bloom, I am done. And as soon as she had put away the elder Rosenbloom's artifacts, she said to Bloom, I want to become part of the world. I'm tired of being separate from it, observing it as if I were somehow less animal than the rest. And with this simple declaration, Isabella was Dr. Straight's protégée no more. Nor, it seems, was she content any longer with their quiet life on the top of Mount Terminus.

She had come to understand what Bloom already knew on that day he asked her to marry him. That the union of their commonality, their shared curiosities, had been undermined by all the bodily humors she had witnessed expelled from men, the horrors she had smelled and wretched on. He could hold her. He could ease her suffering. He could provide her pleasure and escape. Invite her into the world of his imagination. But Bloom didn't have it in him to thrill her, to provoke her, to charge her with the sort of electrical current she required to feel fully alive. When Bloom implied such things in the quiet of Mount Terminus's solitude, Isabella claimed this wasn't the case. Not at all. She had, by now, become better acquainted with Gottlieb and Simon; she had grown accustomed to their company, and they to hers, enough so Bloom's collaborator and his brother began to speak freely in front of her about her husband, about how it had been far too long for Bloom to have let his gifts lie fallow. And Isabella agreed.

So she would not be a hindrance, she began to take short excursions into town in Bloom's car, where, one afternoon while eating lunch at the Pico House Hotel, she recognized at the table beside hers, Nora Duncan, the actress who played the fountain nymph in *Mephisto's Affinity*. The two women had a pleasant chat, Isabella told Bloom in the parlor that same evening, and she made plans to meet with her at the theater the following night. The two regularly met thereafter for lunch, and, in small gradations Bloom hardly noticed at first, Isabella started to transform into a woman he hardly recognized. She opened accounts at the fashion houses downtown and spent a great deal of time shopping with Nora. She took up smoking and afternoon cocktails, and—Bloom would learn only after the fact—found a more than willing companion in her new brother-in-law, whom she would come to see much more frequently than Bloom did. Bloom probably shouldn't have encouraged it, but when he learned she and Simon were now circulating at the same dinner parties and nightclubs, Bloom insisted his brother do what he could to keep her entertained, to escort her to his premieres, to introduce her to his wide circle of friends and associates, to help her mingle with the new crop of motion picture colonists migrating here by the day. Simon didn't think it the best idea. He encouraged Bloom to join them. He would arrange for his tailor to visit the estate, to measure Bloom for a suit. He would send Murray Abrams to the estate to civilize Bloom in the ways of society, to practice him in the art of meaningless conversation. They could attend a few parties together, Simon suggested, and after an outing or two, who knew, perhaps Bloom would come to welcome the occasional night out on the town; perhaps he would even take a liking to someone outside his immediate circle. You should make the effort, said Simon. For her, you should make every effort. You do know, don't you, that she's not a woman you can take for granted?

I would only spoil her fun, said Bloom.

Joseph, she needs looking after.

Won't you look after her for me?

My dear brother, how it is you're able to depict the complicated motives of men in your art without truly understanding them will forever remain a mystery to me.

><

Several times a week, Isabella dressed in gowns that displayed the full extent of her beauty and developing tastes, and she and Simon would drive down Mount Terminus into the basin, where the extension of the city had become complete. Out they drove onto the grid filled with more and more elaborate homes, with green lawns and colorful gardens kept alive by aqueduct water flowing ceaselessly from the northeast. Soon enough, Isabella hired a driver and began accepting invitations on her own. Several evenings a week, she left for these parties unaccompanied to homes and hotel suites, beach cottages and ballrooms, and often didn't return to Mount Terminus until early the next morning, when, so as not to wake Bloom, she would sleep in the gallery with the door locked, and wouldn't emerge until late the following afternoon. Bloom would know where she had been only from the invitations that arrived addressed to them both. Otherwise, they never spoke of the parties or the people she'd met or what exciting distractions and entertainments existed in the widening city below. Rather, when she chose to give Bloom her full attention, she was some paler version of his Isabella, the Isabella who, for the time being, tolerated her reclusive husband, whose lifestyle he stubbornly clung to out of habit and fear of a world he couldn't imagine himself being part of. As he never questioned her or complained, she, for now, didn't question or complain to him. Instead, for the time being, when they were together, they talked of the subtle changes in the weather and the night sky, what news she had heard from Simon about his most recent conquests—his most recent acquisitions, the newest actors, actresses, directors under contract, how Bloom's preproduction of *The Death of Paradise* was coming along. And not frequently, but often enough that he didn't feel entirely deprived, they acted out—with more comfort and familiarity than excitement—the passion they once enjoyed together in the gallery.

→←

The more estranged from Isabella he grew, the clearer Bloom's focus became in the studio. For years now he had been dreaming of *The Death of Paradise*, seeing it piecemeal, in fragments, but he had now begun to see it all at once, and knew if he shut himself away for a period of time, if he allowed the story to fully consume him, he would be able to bind all the disparate parts together once and for all, and finally be done with it. He thought perhaps once he was through, once he had put this final picture behind him, he could become more the man Isabella needed him to be. If she saw to what lengths he had gone in making this picture, he believed, she would appreciate the way her absence had affected him. She might see in the complexity of this work he planned on dedicating to Isabella, the complexity and the depth of the love he felt for her. Except to travel down to the new Mount Terminus Studios lot to oversee the construction of the larger sets—those on which the Spanish locales would be shot, the ship on which the Estrellas and their cohort would make their journey, the Mission Santa Theresa de Avila in which the priests would reside—Bloom remained behind the closed doors of his studio, drawing and thinking through the smallest of details, the lighting, the camera movements and perspectives, the blocking, the narrative and text for the intertitles. He wrote many pages of notes on the way he wanted the actors to perform, notes he would deliver to Gottlieb some weeks before they went into production. He feared that the picture, if not treated with the most subtle movements and gestures, could easily be reduced to overwrought melodrama. As was always the case when Bloom immersed himself in this part of his process, he rarely slept, paced a great deal, held elaborate conversations with himself about the elaborate scope of this picture. Its epic length he found stifling—the walls of his studio could hardly contain the many hundreds of panels he had drawn, and although Bloom had the ability to see and feel everything all at once, the energy it required to maintain this vision depleted him. He had grown so lost to his pursuit, Isabella had begun to notice the toll it had been taking on his health and appearance, and she felt it necessary one night to visit Bloom in his studio to express her concern. Bloom hadn't been aware of it, but Isabella had from time to time been observing him work from outside the studio window. What she had seen, she told Bloom, she found disconcerting. She was particularly upset by the sight of him talking with himself, speaking at times as if there were someone there beside him. She found herself haunted by the images of him listening and responding to that invisible someone. When she saw him like this, she told him, she felt something break inside her. She felt overtaken by feelings of shame, and she wondered if her neglect had contributed to Bloom's state of mind. If I'm hurting you by not being here, she said, I beg you to say so. Bloom rejected this idea. As long as she was content with the life she was leading, he refused to stand in her way. Although he most certainly missed her, and wished she would spend more time in his company, he wouldn't keep her from whatever life she wished to lead, no matter how unrecognizable she became to him. Given what he knew of her, knowing so intimately the insatiable hunger inside her, he wouldn't be the one to restrain her. He wouldn't risk being perceived as a barrier to her happiness. He wouldn't allow her to despise him for keeping her from doing whatever it was she needed to do for herself. To preserve and protect their love was his only purpose, and so he said, as a way to placate her, I promise you, you're mistaking my obsession for distress.

To this she said, I'm afraid for you.

I'm hardly in mortal danger.

Nevertheless, said Isabella.

It's true, I do lose myself to my work, but I'm not in any peril.

Isabella eased her head onto Bloom's chest and again said, Nevertheless.

I'm touched by your concern, but, really, truly, you needn't worry.

She then held Bloom for a while, and he could feel from the tightness with which she held on to him there was something more she wanted to say. I know how it goes against your nature . . .

What?

What would you think if we were to host a party here when you've completed your preparations? What would you think if we were to fill the gardens and the courtyard with music? I want us to dance together. I want to see you mindless and frivolous, if only for one night.

Bloom said, I'll dance you through the gardens right now if you like.

Please, Joseph. I'm being serious.

Bloom was reminded of *Mephisto's Affinity*, of Mrs. Mephisto ordering her husband to the surface for a well-deserved Sabbath.

Really, Joseph. It's a wonderful feeling to dance to music and feel yourself moving about with others moving beside you. Try to imagine it. Try to imagine the fascination you might feel for the strangers surrounding you.

You know I'm not inclined that way.

I know, but I want you to experience it for yourself—they're only people, not unlike you or I.

Bloom tried to imagine it, but he couldn't move in his mind beyond the images of faceless shadows pressing against them in the dark. But when Isabella then said, so disconsolately, I've missed you, Joseph, more than you could possibly know, Bloom was unable to say no to her.

Yes, he said, why not? . . . I'll rise to the occasion.

Do you mean it? Do you really mean it?

I'm a grown man, Bloom reasoned on her behalf. If I'm to be your husband, if I'm to be with you in every way, I can't remain apart from the world forever, now can I?

Isabella stopped clutching his ribs and pulled her face from his chest. I know you don't really mean it, but I do want you to try. I really do want you to give it a try.

Then I'll try. For you, I will try. He stood up and walked Isabella outside and down into the courtyard. They wandered together about the trunks of the grove and Isabella asked, You do still love me, Joseph, don't you?

Of course, I do, said Bloom. I'll always love you. Bloom turned to Isabella and searched the darkness for the contours of her face, but found his eyes unable to make out its lines. In that instant, Isabella had disappeared right before him.

><

In a month's time, Bloom completed his preliminary work on *The Death of Paradise*. Every image of the story had been imagined, every transition, every line of dialogue. He had sketched every costume he wished sewn, every prop he wished to have manufactured or found, wrote directions for how every set was to be dressed. He had mapped every movement to be made by his cameramen and his actors, every lighting configuration, for every track to be laid. He scheduled the dates they would appear on what stage, the order in which every scene would be shot. There were five volumes in all, all of which he neatly lined up on his drafting table and presented to Gottlieb, who, upon seeing to what lengths Bloom had gone, nearly wept with joy. I have produced in you, Gottlieb said with his usual hyperbolic flourish, a burning bush! What lives inside of you, Rosenbloom, is a mystery for the ages! And on this day, Bloom departed his studio with no plans of returning to it anytime soon. He bathed for a considerable number of hours. Afterward, Meralda shaved him and cut his hair, trimmed his nails. He dressed himself in a suit and a pair of shined shoes. And he went to Isabella and told her his news. And Isabella was pleased.

><

The gardeners arrived shortly after daybreak. They set about grooming the grounds under Gus's purview as they had done for some years now. Not long after they appeared and began meandering through the labyrinths to clip away the overgrowth of the hedgerows, the kitchen staff and wait staff Isabella had hired to assist Meralda arrived, and soon they began unloading from trucks enough crates of food and wine, ice and spirits, to fortify the entire city. They unloaded dozens of tables and chairs, sets of crystal and silver, bales of linen. From Mount Terminus Productions arrived the makings for a stage and a dance floor, and they brought along as well many bundles of kerosene torches, some of which went to the courtyard and the grove, but most of which were immediately untied by the gardeners, who then spiked them into the ground one by one along the urn-shaped figure formed by the convergence of the gardens; and down the edges of the straight drive they continued hammering on to the front gate. When the last of the trucks had delivered their freight, and the rhythmic pounding of the stage construction had ceased, several of the men from the wait staff, along with the gardeners, took to raking the gravel before the house's entry, down to the street, where, when they had finished smoothing over the tire tracks and had landscaped the white stones into a uniform surface, they swung the wrought-iron gates closed and opened the pedestrian entry beside it. The front grounds emptied now, and Bloom, who had been watching at various times of the day the comings and goings from his tower's pavilion, waited in anticipation for the encroaching city he had witnessed grow up before his eyes to make its entry into his home.

Knowing he would understand the nature of this question without lengthy explanation, Bloom asked Gottlieb when his small, bearded friend climbed up to greet him, Why, Gottlieb, must I see shadows where there are none?

Gottlieb rested his elbows on the pavilion's ledge and placed his fingers in his beard. Simply put. You are blessed. Touched by God. And those touched by God are always a little mad. You, Rosenbloom, are quite normal in that respect.

I am normal in my madness.

Yes, said Gottlieb. You are.

They all seemed to arrive at once, shortly after the last streaks of twilight evaporated from the horizon. They parked their cars on the road, and as couples and small packs they walked as shadows into the orange glow of the torchlit drive. They strolled along the gardens' borders, many pointing and commenting on the sizable grounds.

It's time, Isabella said as she climbed into the pavilion with Bloom. She looked magnificent, and Bloom told her so. She was wearing a long dress made of crushed silk and around her neck a pearl choker. In her hand she carried a leather-bound tablet, which she handed to him.

What's this?

A gift from me, said Gottlieb. To calm the nerves.

If you find yourself feeling uncomfortable, said Isabella, search out a seat somewhere and draw.

The more cruel you are to your guests, said Gottlieb, the more they'll admire you.

You needn't be cruel, said Isabella, kissing his cheek. They'll admire you as you are. When you're ready to come down, I'll be waiting.

She's nervous for you, said Gottlieb as Isabella descended the staircase.

As she should be. Bloom watched Isabella's dress sweep the stairs as she made her exit, and then he and Gottlieb continued to watch them come. They came and they came, and soon enough Bloom could hear the orchestra strike up, and over the din of the instruments tuning he heard Simon's voice cry up to him. Joseph!

Remember, said Gottlieb. You're meant to be affable.

Bloom leaned over the rail and shrugged his shoulders at his brother.

Don't come down, I'll come up! Simon broke from his entourage and Bloom saw him move in the direction of the service entrance, and a few moments later he came charging up to greet them. He looked out onto the sparkle of lights scattered across the basin, and said, It's been some time since I was last up here. I forgot how far and wide you can see from your perch.

You're always welcome to share it with me.

I was told in advance that if I saw you up here when I arrived, I was to escort you down and keep an eye on you. But before I drag you down there, I was hoping you and I could talk for a minute. Simon turned to Gottlieb.

You needn't say it, said the little man. I know you well enough.

I was thinking, said Simon when Gottlieb had left them. I was hoping you'd consider something . . .

What's that?

A suggestion.

With regard to what?

Isabella.

What about her?

She's lost, Joseph. She's in need of a purpose.

I've tried. But this, said Bloom with a hand out toward the on-coming throng, is what she wants.

Which is why you must show her she's greater than all this nonsense.

Isn't this your sort of nonsense?

I didn't say it wasn't right for me. But I can tell you, it most certainly isn't right for her. She is lost, said Simon. I can promise you that. And if she is lost, you are lost, and if you are lost, I . . .

What?

I have failed you. And myself.

How's that?

I've invested a considerable amount of money into your latest effort and I have no intention of seeing the promise of the return dashed because you're blind to the needs of the living.

Simon delivered this line as if it was intended to be funny, but Bloom couldn't find the humor in it.

Just ask her to assist you on *The Death of Paradise*. She's talked about nothing else since you locked yourself away.

Has she?

She's enthralled with the story.

She and I, we discovered it together.

I know.

Before she left. Before she became . . .

My point exactly.

But she's only expressed her concern about me. She's said nothing to me one way or the other about the picture itself.

That's because she hasn't wanted to get in your way. She has it in her mind that you need to be left on your own to do whatever it is you do when you lose yourself to your work. Simon waved his arm around the aviary. She treats you as if you're some fragile creature who must have his plumage fluffed just so, for fear of risking an Icarus-like plummet.

Bloom thought this over for a moment. Perhaps I do.

You and every other prima donna worth my trouble. But you're missing my point. Your wife, the ever-so-lovely Mrs. Rosenbloom, has lost her way. And you, my oblivious brother, need to show her she has a place by your side.

But of course she does, said Bloom. She *must* know that.

I don't think she does.

Here I was all this time thinking she needed the freedom to explore this other side of herself, and you're telling me I've in actuality been neglecting her?

No, said Simon. Not at all. I'm simply saying you should invite her in to our little world of magic-making and let's see what happens.

She won't think I'm pressuring her to give up her new life? Her new friends?

I have a feeling, a very good feeling, she will be receptive.

Yes?

Yes! Even if she doesn't say as much, she needs you to show her the way. She needs a nudge in the right direction.

What can I say? . . . I'll nudge her.

Good.

And Simon?

Yes, Joseph?

Thank you.

Don't thank me. Just come along, or I won't hear the end of it.

><

A clamor of voices, a voracious sound Bloom had never before heard, filled the tower stairwell as they descended. He followed Simon to the bottom and entered the villa through the front entrance, where he found illuminated by bright incandescent light the hundreds of shadows he had watched walk the drive. They stood about in small groups throughout the entirety of the house. Never before—not even in all his years on the overcrowded lot—had Bloom seen so many people crushed into one place or felt the physical warmth or smelled the commingling of scents generated by bodies standing in such close proximity. The biting scents of perfumes and colognes, the briny wafts of damp body odor, the savory whiffs of cured meats and smoked fish, he took it in all at once as they brushed past people acting out private performances in the corridors. The scents and the cacophony of conversation, the monologues, the piano music from the parlor contaminated by the music from the courtyard, all went to Bloom's head. He was relieved to hear one of the bartenders say, when Simon asked if he happened to know where she was, that he had just seen Isabella step outside. Why don't you go ahead, said Simon. I'll bring out the drinks. All Bloom could manage was a nod, and then he slipped away down the long corridor running to the courtyard doors. He made his way outside, where he discovered Isabella standing at the nearest corner of the reflecting pool surrounded by several young men and a young woman who was swinging the head of a dead fox. He knew it would be proper for him to join them and announce himself, but they all appeared so familiar with one another, he wasn't certain how to interject himself without disturbing the festive mood. He instead headed for one of the café tables set around the edge of the dance floor, and there took a seat, and so not to make it appear as if he were in need of anyone's attention, he opened the tablet Gottlieb had given Isabella to give to him, and he took Gottlieb's suggestion: he started sketching, and as Gottlieb had predicted, the movement of his hands calmed him. Perhaps because of the power of suggestion, or because he had manifested in his mood the great discomfort he had felt throughout the day, he found himself making a grotesque mockery out of the woman swinging the dead animal. He extended her sharp nose into an oversized beak. Her slim figure, he made skeletal. He exaggerated the bones of her shoulders and chest, extended the length of her fingers, elongated her jaw, pointed her chin, hollowed her eyes, diminished her cheeks, yet he left unchanged the elegant gown she wore and posed her body with the same glamorous poise with which she carried herself, and he hung over the joint of her bony elbow the fox, to which he added an overly long tongue that lifelessly lolled from the corner of its dark lip. To the men, Bloom did the same as he did to the woman. He turned them into Punchinellos dressed for Saturnalia, well prepared to feast on Isabella, who he drew as full and round, with a softness. However, he couldn't help but notice, as he fixed the lines forming her image on the page, how, as she talked with these creatures—who, with their enormous gestures, appeared to be acting for an invisible camera—Isabella appeared to be mirroring them, and comfortably so, as if for a long time now she had been studying how oversized and artificial emotion was expressed in the features of the face and the physicality of the body. At the sight of this, Bloom felt a queasiness grow inside him. Had he not been so compliant, he wondered, would she have turned to this? Or had he tried to cage her as Fernando caged Miranda, would she have turned into one of these creatures anyway? He began to see all around him grotesqueries from the hand of Hieronymus Bosch. Feral, thought Bloom, and predatory. Sharp in teeth and claw, in the darting movements of the eyes. He could see clearly for the first time since their day in the naked rose garden how Isabella's hunger, her enormous appetite, had in this company manifested itself into a character with whom Bloom felt at odds. For this role, for these absurd people, she no longer pursued her scientific interests? For these mindless conformists, she was no longer satisfied with the quiet subtleties of Mount Terminus? For her place among these ridiculous men and women, she had abandoned him for Simon's companionship?

From Bloom's position in the courtyard, he saw Simon detained at the door by a small throng of mannequins. He parted their closed shoulders with a small movement of his chin and made his way outside. As Simon walked toward him, Bloom noticed Isabella's confidante point the fox's snout in his brother's direction. She then said something that caused Isabella to lift her hand to her cheek. Her eyes now trailed Simon's movement around the edge of the dance floor, and when they reached Bloom, she must have seen with what disappointment, with what revulsion, he had been watching her, because she removed the mask she had been wearing an instant earlier, or, perhaps, Bloom considered, she put one on for him. Some woman wearing a bird of paradise in her hair now touched Isabella's shoulder, and there it was again, an arched brow, a smile wide and open enough for a snake to slither through, her face in its entirety a figure of cartoon surprise. Isabella soon excused herself from her company and walked over.

How long have you been sitting here? she asked Bloom as she greeted Simon with a brush of her cheek to his.

Just long enough, Bloom heard himself saying. He didn't intend his words to sound accusatory, but they did, and he didn't make an effort to correct his tone. When Isabella heard this, her eyes looked to the table on which sat Bloom's open tablet, and seeing what image was there, she now knew better than to ask how he was getting along. She nodded her head in recognition of his mood, and then, after a brief pause, Simon, who had undoubtedly heard the intolerance in his brother's voice, interrupted the awkwardness by saying to Bloom, I don't think I ever told you, Joseph, there was a brief period of time when I was a student that I worked in a department store to make up for the poor wage Sam paid me in the theater. This store, they made the softest, most supple, most elegant gloves you have ever seen. Leather gloves worn by the most fashionable women. To secure my position, I visited Sam's tailor and conned the poor man to put on Sam's bill two of the tailor's finest shirts and two of his finest suits made from the finest material he had available. I went on to Sam's shoemaker and did the same. Once I was in costume, I took on the role of salesclerk, and the manager, seeing how well I had studied my part, put me on the floor. One of my responsibilities—the very reason I was keen to take the job—was to interview the young women who modeled our merchandise. We would advertise for women with delicate hands. Long fingers. Long and thin and elegant to observe in motion. And from this advertisement, in came dozens of beautiful girls, any one of which you'd think were worthy of the position. Simon, now addressing Isabella, said, But you'd be surprised what it takes to show a fine pair of gloves. It takes a very special pair of hands to make a woman of a certain position, a very elegant sort of woman, fall in love with her handwear. Here, he said, motioning to Isabella. She looked to Bloom, then politely offered Simon her arm, at which point Bloom's brother ran a knuckle over the generous length of Isabella's forefinger and up over the curve of her wrist. Here, you see? You see this uninterrupted line? This almost imperceptible line extending from the very tip of the finger to the height of the forearm? This perfect line, right here, on you, my dear, this incredibly rare line that exists only on the rarest of women, this is the continuous line I spent many weeks searching out on God knows how many women, and because of how rare it is, rarely, very rarely, would I ever find it. You wouldn't think it, he said to Bloom, but a fine pair of hands, Joseph, a really fine pair, is as rare as the rarest of precious gems. Simon now paused and leaned his forehead toward Isabella. Had you walked onto my floor, on you, I could have shown our entire line. With you, I could have made a bundle. He now gave her hand a gentle pat, set it down at her side, and pulled himself away.

It was impossible to see in the dim light, but Bloom was certain from the smile on Isabella's face, a smile he recognized from their postcoital entanglements, she was aglow, and seeing in her expression how taken she was with Simon, he could feel himself growing hot.

Simon now leaned over Bloom and shut his tablet. He slid his hand under Bloom's chin and turned it to Isabella's face. Be a gentleman and take your wife for a little twirl.

Bloom pulled his face away from Simon. No, he said. Maybe later.

Then, said Isabella, perhaps Simon will.

Yes, said Bloom, by all means, Simon.

Don't you mind? said his brother.

No, said Bloom, waving them off.

Well, you should.

No. Go. Dance. Be merry.

With a stern look he had never before received from Isabella, she placed her hand in Simon's, and together they walked onto the dance floor. Upon seeing them, the orchestra leader called up the horn section with his baton and waved the musicians into a lively rhythm. Hearing the music change pace, the men and women milling about inside the house started to pair off and make their way outdoors.

The courtyard, Bloom could see, was soon going to fill, and at the sight of this onrush, his physical discomfort began to intensify. How, he thought, could he have handled himself more poorly? His chest tightened at the sight of Isabella's breast brushing against Simon's lapel. His heart began to beat in a flutter every time she turned up her nose and lifted her eyes to look at him. The mentholated air began to smell sweet and inadequate for breathing. A woman of ghostly pallor whose hair was coiled and encrusted with small jewels now sat down across from him and asked Bloom if he was all right.

Why do you ask?

You look faint, she said.

No, said Bloom, I'm fine.

I know faint, she said, and you look it. Weak in the eyes.

Bloom excused himself, and feeling a heaviness in his legs, he stood up. He managed a smile, and leaving his tablet behind, made his way through the crowd, exited the courtyard through the pergola, and moved on into the grove. When he reached the drive he walked between the hedgerows, passing as he went couples embracing in the shadows. He pressed on past these darkened figures to a turn that led to a dead end, and when he found it unoccupied, he blew out the flame of the nearest torch, and with a sweet waft of kerosene filling his nose, he lay down on a bench to look into a moonless sky. And here he shut his eyes and lay still. When his head had cleared, when he was once again able to hear his own thoughts, he felt a hand brush over his hair, and there he found when he opened his eyes Roya sitting beside him. She lifted his head and placed it in her lap, and there, in the dark corner, she continued to caress him, to pacify him. They sat this way for a long time, and when Roya stopped moving her fingers through his hair, she sat Bloom up and took his hand. Together they walked out of the garden and she led him to the cellar door. They descended into the vaults and went to the opening of the chamber, and there Roya sent Bloom up into the darkness, into the quiet of Manuel's secret room.

><

There Bloom sat and stared at the projection table, on top of which he saw, after some time had passed, Isabella walk into the gallery and shut the door behind her. She lay down on the chaise, where she covered her face with her hands. A few moments later, in walked Simon, who, seeing her distraught, sat at her side.

They didn't speak. They merely observed each other. And Bloom could see what was in Isabella's mind.

Simon soon placed a hand on her cheek to wipe away a tear, and he let his palm rest there. Isabella didn't push it away. Rather, she lifted her hand and placed it over his, and held it there. She now lifted her chin so Simon could better see her eyes, and as she turned her face to his, she smoothed over his knuckles with her fingers. She said something to him and he said something in return. Upon hearing whatever it was she said next, he bent down and kissed her forehead. For quite a while he kissed her there on her brow, then turned his cheek and affectionately pressed it to where his lips had been. Simon said something more to her, then removed himself and walked out of the room. Isabella now sat up, her face no longer forlorn, but repaired. She touched the corners of her eyes, righted her dress, then she, too, exited the room.

>†<

Bloom now sat and thought. Was this what Simon meant when he said Isabella was lost? Did he fail to mention that they were lost together?

For the remainder of the night, he considered what he had seen.

He had seen it, hadn't he?

And if it was what he saw, what was he to do?

Was there, he wondered, anything he could do?

Should he react in the ways he knew men to react when betrayed by those they held dearest?

Or should he pretend not to have seen what he had seen? Perhaps he hadn't seen it at all? Perhaps he could convince himself he had imagined it?

Should he not be able to pretend, however, what then?

His instinct was to forgive.

But when he thought of forgiveness, he wondered, How does one forgive such a thing? He began to live out in his mind a future in which he did forgive, and as he did so, it occurred to him what sacrifices this would entail. He thought: If this was true, as it certainly appeared to be from the expressions he observed on Isabella's and Simon's faces, would he have to watch for the indefinite future his wife look upon his brother in that way?

He allowed this to play out, and found this scenario unbearable.

And here in reaction to these unbearable thoughts arrived an anger he couldn't suppress. Here arrived a primal rage that erupted in a primal roar. He lifted his head to the pitched roof and wailed.

Yet, he thought when he had finished howling into Manuel Salazar's void, if he were to act on this primal scream, what good could come of it?

What would happen if he tried to impede them? If he shouted his protest. Disallowed them. Dictated to them. Condemned them. Punished them. Exercised his vengeance upon them.

And here his better nature reappeared.

This was his brother and his wife, for whom he would want, under any other circumstances, love and happiness. He was entangled in their lives so deeply, to seek revenge against them was to seek revenge against himself. To condemn and punish them was to condemn and punish himself.

Yet he was certainly angry enough to condemn and punish, and now that he recalled the way Simon touched her, the way Isabella shared with him the full openness of her eyes—a look he thought until that moment belonged entirely to him—here wrath revisited him.

And again he screamed into the rafters.

And then screamed some more.

Nothing he could do, he came to realize, would leave him in peace.

He now better understood what drove Hamlet so sideways and

upside down. To forgive his duplicitous brother and his duplicitous wife would be in words only. Words words words, and nothing more. To condone their feelings for each other, to say, Who am I to struggle against your desire, your passion? Who am I to dissuade you from what your love demands? would only result in Bloom going more mad than he already felt.

No, he wouldn't be so beneficent. He wouldn't be so accommodating. Nor would he risk repeating the past. He wouldn't give himself over to superstition and orders of predestination and replay the story of his mother and Leah, of his father and Freed.

The option he preferred, therefore, was to do nothing.

And here he contemplated the paradox of Abraham's faith.

He chose to believe in their conscience. He chose to believe that by doing nothing he would leave them to dwell in their transgression alone. Every time they looked at each other, touched each other, so much as had a wanting thought of the other, he would leave them room to suffer their guilt and shame.

He was assured enough in Isabella, at least, that no matter how her concerns had been altered, she was a woman of conscience. She would never forget how devoted Bloom had been to her. She wouldn't be capable of disregarding his kindness and compassion. His love. Their memories together, no matter how hard she tried to ignore them, he was certain, would eventually devour her.

And so, before he left Manuel's chamber the following morning, he was decided. He would say nothing. He would do nothing. He would pretend he had seen nothing. As if it never happened. But he wouldn't forget, and his eyes would remain open.

⊁⊰

When Bloom climbed out of the cellar, he poured himself a cup of coffee in the kitchen and carried it through to the parlor. Meralda had opened all the windows and doors, but the house still smelled of stale champagne and tobacco smoke, of sweat and tinctures of a variety of perfumes. Bloom reclined in his father's chair with thoughts of drifting off to sleep, but after he'd taken only a sip of his coffee,

Isabella entered and with exasperation and some relief said, There you are!

Here I am!

Where have you been?

I went for a walk.

You just left.

I did. I walked away.

Without a word?

It would seem you and Gottlieb were right to have been worried about me last night. And now it's confirmed. I'm not good in a crowd.

Isabella shook her head. She walked over to the chair and sat on its arm with her back to Bloom. I really thought it would do you some good to mingle with people. She looked over her shoulder to glower at him. I certainly didn't think it would do you any harm. And then, the way you looked at me in the courtyard . . .

How?

As if you despised me. Reviled me.

No, said Bloom. You're mistaken.

No, said Isabella. I'm not.

It was only my confusion you saw. I didn't know what to make of you in that scene.

No, you didn't see your face.

Nor did you see yours.

What was it you saw that caused you to react as you did?

It's what I didn't see, said Bloom. I hardly recognized you. I didn't know you.

But that was *me*.

No, said Bloom, it wasn't.

Is it really so hard to grasp that I sometimes flit around a party to gossip and joke? Is it really so perplexing I take an interest in people?

That, said Bloom, I understand. What I don't understand, what I find baffling, is that you've chosen artifice and pretense over every other part of you. The vital parts of you I just happen to love most of all. You've hidden that Isabella somewhere far away from me.

To this Isabella said nothing.

Is she still here? asked Bloom. Somewhere nearby?

Isabella glanced back at Bloom and said curtly, I don't know.

On the off chance she is, would you convey a message?

What?

I miss her.

Isabella sighed.

Would you tell her I'd like to be reacquainted with her.

She sighed again.

And while you're at it, will you ask her if she'd visit my studio?

This solicited a huff. When?

Later this afternoon?

I'll see what I can do.

If you don't think you can . . .

I said, I'll see what I can do.

Good, said Bloom.

In a tone of surrender, Isabella said, What time shall I tell her?

One o'clock?

One o'clock.

⇥⇤

Bloom spent the remainder of the morning posting on the walls of his studio the collection of panels he'd drawn for *The Death of Paradise*. He set them in a linear progression moving left to right around the room. Scene by scene. Act by act. On his table, he stacked the specifications for each set; the costume patterns; the lighting diagrams; the camera positions; every aspect of the production he had mulled over again and again since he had taken it on: all of this, he organized for Isabella to see, to touch, to dwell on. As one o'clock approached there was a small part of him that wondered if she would make their appointment. She had no idea what he had in mind, yet he thought there might be some reluctance on her part to return to him as she once was, to take a step back in time to revisit an aspect of herself she had gone to such great lengths to bury. But there she was at one o'clock, looking up to him as she walked up the stairs to the studio. He greeted her at the door and took her by the hand, and with their fingers intertwined he walked her to the opening panel. She reached out and touched it, and said to him, It's as if Manuel had drawn it himself.

No, said Bloom.

Yes, said Isabella. It's as if you and he were the same.

He directed her eye around the room with his hand. I can use your help, he said.

In what way?

I can't see it any longer.

See what?

What's missing. What's wrong. What's inadequate.

Isabella began to walk along the progression of events. But it's all here. It's all here, beautifully rendered. Perfectly arresting.

Please, said Bloom, keep looking.

I'm just not sure what I'm supposed to be looking for. What more can I possibly say that you haven't already said in each of these images?

Take it all in and then start again from the beginning. Don't look for what's right. Try to find what's missing. If there are any expectations I'm not living up to in your mind. Try to imagine them for yourself. See into it as if you were the one responsible for drawing them.

And on Isabella walked and completed her first revolution around the room. When she finished, Bloom said, Again. And when she finished for the second time, he said, And again and again, until you can see it right away, altogether, at once.

Right away, altogether, at once? said Isabella.

Yes, said Bloom. Take it all in, so you can see it play out all at once in your mind.

Isabella went around for a third time, and then without Bloom saying a word, she went about again.

Can you see it yet?

Yes, she said. As you said. Right away, altogether, at once.

A tablet, she said.

Excuse me?

A tablet. And something to write with.

Bloom handed her a tablet and a pencil, and on Isabella went, looking and writing down what came to mind.

⁂

Isabella stayed in that night. They sat together in the dining room and talked over *The Death of Paradise* in as many dimensions as they could think of. They began with its broadest elements. Isabella was of the opinion that Bloom had placed too much emphasis on Manuel's point of view in the second act. She argued that equal weight should be distributed among the three principal characters. Otherwise, the final scene, in which Miranda and Manuel were murdered by Fernando, wouldn't resonate with authentic emotion. At the moment, she thought Fernando too much a monster, Miranda too much a pawn in Manuel's fantasies. Instead of Manuel standing on his own, observing, as it is now, she said, all three of them should be present throughout, and given a full voice, as it were.

Fernando, perhaps, takes part at the massacre. Leads the soldiers. Gives the orders. Miranda, she can witness it from a distance, and show little concern for what's taking place. I can see her bothered by the inconvenience of having to wait yet another day to be settled at the end of her long journey. As if the clearing of the land were a pesky nuisance. And then there is Manuel, who you've treated exactly as he should be. The reluctant witness, the voice of reason, of conscience, who later dwells in his fantasies of Miranda in order to escape the haunting images he's seen, then turns the pathetic coward.

As for the soldiers, she continued, you would be amazed how casually men like these take to violence, how so many of them are inured to the savage acts they perpetrate. You've depicted them as wild beasts, but in reality, they would be used to inflicting pain and death. They would be numb to it, as familiar with the sickening stench of blood as any man who labors in an abattoir. They would hardly think anything of it to wear the blood of their victims on their armor for weeks at a time. More likely, they would be cold and methodical on the surface, indifferent to the suffering of the people they've destroyed.

✦

They went on talking at length in the parlor after dinner, and for the first time in quite a long time, they went to bed together and held each other in their sleep. When they awoke the following morning, they took their coffee and their breakfast in the tower, and then went to the studio, where they continued to speculate about the movement of the narrative, and soon Bloom began to draft all the changes Isabella had recommended. He neither agreed nor disagreed with them, but he wanted to make them because he had managed to engage her. He had decided this picture would belong to her as much as it belonged to him.

They would now start the story in the past's present, with its emphasis on Don Fernando. They would begin with him and treat him as they would a saint. A man who had for many years governed his territory justly; a man who had sent his crops to the neediest of the surrounding pueblos. Housed the poor. Built a cathedral in which all were welcome to worship and take refuge.

To complicate matters, his old henchman, Roberto, would then arrive on the estate after a long absence to blackmail Fernando. He would threaten to reveal all the dark secrets of his past if he didn't provide him a portion of his land and some livestock. Fernando would agree to this, but before he delivered on his word, the picture would return to the past. To the time of Fernando, Miranda, and Manuel's youth. When Fernando's money and power gave him an inflated sense of importance; when Miranda saw only the promise of Fernando's position and nothing of his demeanor; when Manuel saw both of them for who and what they were, but forgave them for the promise of a better future.

In a series of short scenes, Fernando would be exposed as the hateful character he once was, the man quick to take a life at the slightest threat to his pride; Miranda an entitled beauty who expected the world to be given to her; Manuel, attached to his work, in desperate search of an opportunity to breathe life into the visions he carried around in his mind and his notebooks. And then would arrive the confluence of events following Fernando's exile. Fernando would turn brutal tyrant, destroyer of men, venal public official, Miranda's jailor. Miranda would turn caged bird looking to gain its freedom. Manuel would attain all he had strived for, then betray those who had provided him his chance. All of which would lead to the murders of Miranda, Manuel, and Adora, to Fernando's crisis of conscience. The haunting of Don Fernando by Miranda's ghost. She would show him what great suffering he was responsible for, take him on a journey through the evils of his past, an odyssey that would forge a path to his redemption. When Fernando had been convincingly transformed, the picture would return to its present, at which point Fernando would confront Roberto. He would refuse him the land and livestock he sought, and in doing so, Roberto would grow agitated and slay Fernando. And in the end, Fernando would be venerated and condemned equally, as devil and saint, by the very people he had subjected to death and destruction.

❊

They now held up these images and this progression of events above those Bloom had posted to the walls of his studio and they saw two versions of the same story, and they were satisfied with the work they had done together.

❊

They began filming *The Death of Paradise* some weeks later. Isabella accompanied Bloom every morning to the sets, and over Gottlieb's objections, she helped Bloom keep all the details of the production in order. Without asking anyone's permission, she began briefing the crew and the actors every morning about how the day would proceed, and because she played a significant part in creating the vision of the picture, and often knew what Gottlieb would be asking of them, she coached them on what they could expect from their mercurial director. In turn, both the crew and the actors were often able to provide Gottlieb what he asked of them in the first take. Isabella thrived on the work, and she and Bloom found themselves as happy and connected as they had been when Isabella first arrived on Mount Terminus with Dr. Straight. They had reached such a level of contentment, Bloom convinced himself what he'd seen in Manuel's chamber on the night of the party was little more than an innocent moment between brother and sister. If it was anything more than that, if it were a scene from an affair, he preferred not to know, preferred not to ask. Even if he had learned this was the case, he no longer cared, as Isabella, of her own free will, had chosen to return to him, and this was most important of all. She preferred to stay in with him at night, and on those occasions Bloom felt she had become restless and needed to escape Mount Terminus, he found it within himself to overcome his discomfort with the world at large, and accompany her to town after they had completed their work for the day, and there he would walk with her, look into shop windows, take in a picture show, a meal. He even summoned the wherewithal to accept a dinner invitation on Isabella's behalf, and he began to learn through his wife's example—not unlike what Gottlieb's Myron Bishop had learned from the woman of his affection—how to tolerate the company of people with whom he wouldn't otherwise choose to spend time. He discovered how easy it was to remain silent—to play the role of the observer—when in a room full of people who had cast themselves at the center of their own little dramas and comedies. Bloom would never become entirely comfortable in the society where Isabella circulated, but he would learn to accept it, well enough, so on his own volition, he asked Isabella to teach him how to dance.

They set up the Victrola in the courtyard, and for some weeks after a late dinner Isabella taught him how to fox-trot, and when

Bloom believed he was able to dance without needing to apply his mind to the steps, they drove down the mountain and into town to a music hall, where they danced into the night.

When on a short visit to the set one afternoon, Simon, upon seeing what harmony had returned to their marriage, started to drop in for dinner at the villa several times a week, usually on his own, occasionally with a companion. Bloom noticed from time to time Isabella and Simon exchanging glances; every now and again they would linger on each other's eyes for a while, then move on. But Bloom felt affirmed enough in his connection to his wife, he allowed them this small thrill, as each time Simon came and went, Bloom benefited from a change in Isabella's spirit. After Simon departed, she was often enlivened, but not as if she were inspired by his brother's presence, rather as if she were trying to counteract an urge, struggling against an unwelcome impulse. After these dinners with his brother, she grew that much more affectionate and attentive to Bloom, that much more uninhibited in her advances toward him. Perhaps he should have felt disturbed by this, but he had come to understand this inner tension Isabella needed in order to feel fully alive. He would only be able to recognize it for what it was, the hunger she tried to describe to him that day in the rose garden after she had been sequestered in the gallery all those months. He could only guess it was an inner turmoil derived from having witnessed how random and anarchic was the logic of Death, how indiscriminate and blind it was in its selection of the living. After having lived in the face of such a dark force, after experiencing the darkest human behavior, he presumed, she would never be fully satisfied with peace and tranquility alone. She had witnessed in her brief existence too many enlightened people shatter their most sacred values.

>‹

One night after Simon had visited, Bloom found Isabella had lapsed into a mood as serious as the one he found her in when she first returned to Mount Terminus after the war. As they lay together in bed, in the dark, Bloom asked her what was the matter. There's something I need to tell you, she said. When Bloom asked what it was she needed to say, she told him how she feared to begin. To this, Bloom said nothing. He waited. And waited. And eventually Isabella began to speak. She confided in Bloom about the events that had precipitated the nervous exhaustion she experienced when she came to after her accident. She was alone, she told Bloom. She shouldn't have been alone. But she was. She was transporting to the hospital a man she believed to be a wounded French soldier. The man had a head wound, serious, but one from which he would recover. He lay unconscious on a cot in the back of the ambulance as Isabella drove through wheat fields overgrown from neglect. Halfway between the battlefield and the hospital, she heard the soldier rouse to his feet, and she told him he should lie back and rest until they arrived. He wasn't in a state to be sitting up. When she turned to see if he had done as she asked, she found the point of a bayonet at her nose. The man spoke to her in German and calmly gestured to the side of the road. When she had pulled the ambulance over, the soldier pushed her out of her seat onto the muddy shoulder. He marched her out into one of the fields, through tall stalks of grain, and again he pushed her, down onto her back. She could see he wasn't interested in having her, rather, she could see, from the cold, lifeless expression on his face, he simply intended to kill her and take the ambulance. He turned his rifle on her now, and without acknowledging that before him lay prostrate a human being, he pulled the trigger. Until that moment, she told Bloom, she hadn't feared death. She hadn't felt it a threat to her. In fact, given what she had seen, what she had documented, given the death of Dr. Straight and his wife, a small part of her had wished it upon herself. But when the rifle misfired, she felt all the apprehension one would expect to feel when confronted with one's own end, and she wanted more than anything to live. The soldier's face was unchanged, but Isabella's spirit had been altered. She didn't want to die. Not there. Not then. And so when the man raised the bayonet to check his weapon, she took hold of a rock she felt pressing into the small of her back, and charged the soldier. She sprang up so quickly, in his lethargic state he didn't have time to lower his weapon, and Isabella hit him hard where his head had already been concussed. She continued to beat him back with heavier and heavier blows until he dropped his weapon and fell, and when he fell, she picked up the rifle and turned the bayonet on him. It all happened so quickly, she told Bloom. She pointed the bayonet at his chest and instinctively lunged with all her weight bearing down on him. She drove the blackened blade between his ribs and did as she had seen the soldiers do on the battlefield: she twisted it and twisted it, back and forth, removed it, plunged it in again, twisted and twisted. She felt cartilage resist the blade. She felt the blade scrape and crack bone. She then lunged some more. She lunged and lunged until the man became still, and she continued to twist and lunge until she heard his last breath expel from his lungs, saw the skin around his eyes relax, smelled the putrid evacuation of his bowels. Isabella became silent at this point. Bloom had been holding her as she spoke and now held her tighter. What troubled her, she told Bloom next, was what she hadn't felt when she had acknowledged to herself what she had done. It was what she couldn't feel that preoccupied her so much when she walked back to the ambulance and started driving. For having taken this man's life, she felt neither remorse nor regret. She felt absolutely nothing, as lifeless as the expression on the soldier's face when he pulled the rifle's trigger. And it was the thought of the absence of feeling that distracted her from the road, from not seeing the ditch she drove into.

And when she awoke after the accident, it wasn't her injury or the memory of the death she had seen on such a monumental scale that had so deeply affected her. Her affliction was the absence of conscience. The voice. That small, rational voice that resided in her innermost thoughts had disappeared. She had been reshaped, delivered to a void whose weightless vacuum she had no power to maneuver within. She was frequently horrified by the memory of the killing itself, how it felt when she lodged the blade between the man's ribs, the rank smell of him, the sound of him gasping for breath when his lung had been punctured, the image of him choking on his own blood, but she had yet to feel as if she had acted in an unnatural way. She so very much expected her inner voice to intervene, to plague her in some manner, but each time she recalled the killing in her mind, she admitted to reliving not the torment for having acted against God, but the triumph of having done away with her attacker before he could do away with her. She could still recall the great relief she enjoyed when she had overcome him and was given the chance to live. Never again, she told Bloom, would she hold herself above human fallibility and weakness. And while she abided by the laws of men, she could never again live in harmony with the mores of a civilized society. I often feel lost, she told Bloom. As if I'm balancing between two opposing worlds.

You're not lost to me, said Bloom.

But I am, she said. I am.

No.

I'm afraid I am.

I would have been much more disturbed if you hadn't fought to save yourself.

But I'm no longer the girl you fell in love with. I'm certain you know that to be true.

It doesn't matter.

A Pandora's box has opened inside me and I don't know how to close it.

Bloom reminded her what resided at the bottom of that box, and Isabella said, No, you don't understand. She took hold of Bloom's hand and lowered it to just above her waist. Feel, she said. She pressed his hand harder against her midriff and then moved it about its circumference. Bloom could feel how its shape had changed. How hadn't he noticed? She was swelling. Stretching. The body whose every feature he had committed to memory was transforming into an unfamiliar shape. Before he could become excited about what he was feeling in his palm, on his fingertips, Isabella said, It's been some time now. Understand?

Bloom felt the sensation of ice melting on the back of his neck.

I've been this way for quite some time, she said. Longer than the time we've recently spent together.

I see.

Do you?

Yes. I do. Bloom now understood. He now comprehended in all its complexities what Isabella had just confessed to him. She had known that night of the party. Had Simon known as well? Of course he did. Of course . . .

Bloom instinctively started to remove himself from Isabella's arms, but she refused to let him go. With a strength he didn't know she had, she grabbed hold of him and held tight. She interlocked her fingers with his, and she said, Whatever you decide tomorrow, I'll do. But tonight, please, just tonight . . .

><

Neither of them slept. Neither of them said another word until dawn. All night Isabella clutched hold of Bloom's hand, and Bloom didn't struggle to release it. He felt the warmth of her body against his, the weight of her breasts pressed against his back, but her presence was ghostly. Many times that night he recalled the first moment he saw Isabella in the mirror given to him as a gift by Dr. Straight. And he wondered which Isabella belonged to him. The image of her true self or the image of herself in reverse. He searched his mind for the smallest of alterations of her appearance. And he wondered which of her belonged to Simon. And he wondered which of her belonged to him. And he wondered what he should do. He had so many questions, but when he thought of posing these questions to Isabella, he refrained, because, even if he didn't know the answers, he knew the outcome; he knew in what direction this sort of conversation would take them. And he refused to take that well-worn path. He refused to make his fate the fate of his mother and his aunt. He refused to repeat the all-too-obvious patterns of the past. He chose instead to honor the promise he had made to his father when he was a child. *Blessed art thou, O Lord Our God, Ruler of the Universe, may I protect my love better than he protected his.* He chose to let his love for Isabella prevail over all else. He wouldn't bend to his primal nature. He wouldn't bend to tragedy's architecture. He would allow Isabella her flaws. He would tolerate the duality of her character. He would learn to forget her deception. He would love the child growing inside her as if it were his own. He would forgive his brother for his weakness. He would embrace him as the child's true father. I am a student of the invertiscope, he tried to convince himself. I am its subject. I am its embodiment. He would simply be better, better than all the protagonists in all the world's tragedies who had given themselves over to their basest passions. In all the ways his father was unable to protect his mother, he *would* protect Isabella, first and foremost, from himself. When the sun broke through the bedroom windows and shone its light onto Isabella's face, she asked Bloom if she should pack her things and leave.

To this, Bloom said, No.

What then?

Nothing. We'll do nothing. I can forgive you, he said in a voice as convincing as the voice Isabella had used when she asked Bloom to ask her to marry him. And he told her he could forgive Simon. And he told her he could love the child as if it were his own. And then he asked if Simon knew.

And she said that he did. He knew she was pregnant. But he didn't know that there was no question about who the father was. He thought there was a chance that it was Bloom's.

Then he must be told, said Bloom.

Must he?

Bloom didn't have the answer to this question. He only had another question. There's only one thing I need to know, he said.

What's that?

I don't want to know why, but I must know: are you certain it's me you want to be with and not him?

Yes. With you. Without reservation.

Why? he was tempted to ask, but instead said, Then that's the way it will be.

⁂

That morning they returned to the studio lot down the hill and continued their work. They were exhausted and at times distracted by what had passed in the night. They had thus far introduced all their principal characters and completed the scenes set within the Spanish court of King Philip. The events preceding Fernando and Miranda's expulsion had been completed, as had the scenes depicting Manuel's work as an apprentice to a master builder. On this day, Bloom sat perched on a crane with Gottlieb and his new cameraman, Roland Briggs. Together they overlooked the deck of a balsa wood replica of the *Estrella del Mar* mounted to a fulcrum, at either end of which members of the crew took turns squatting and lifting to approximate the ship falling and rising over the ocean current. An industrial-sized fan blew the sails full of wind, and when the jib boom dipped into the sea, a fire line of men with buckets heaved water up onto the starboard and port. It was a tedious morning followed by a tedious afternoon, one during which Bloom withdrew into the scrolling backdrop of the sea. He could feel himself roiling with the slow movement of the passing waves. Unwanted images of Simon and Isabella appeared. He couldn't help but imagine his brother's seed taking root inside his wife, forming in the well of her a growing replica of his brother, of Bloom. The more he dwelled on these thoughts, the better he comprehended the nexus of his mother's madness. He understood what drove her to Sam Freed's house that day to claim Simon as her own. How, he wondered, would he manage this without losing his mind? I am a student of the invertiscope, he reminded himself. Its subject. Its embodiment. But would he be able to inhibit his basest nature before cold, rational reason took hold and made him a better man? The actions of Isabella and Simon, he could forgive, but these images he had invited would not cease. They only grew more vibrant and real. No matter how concerted his effort to act in a loving and sympathetic manner toward Isabella in the days that followed, when night fell and they turned in to bed, he saw Simon mounting her, entering her, taking from her the most intimate and animalistic part of herself, taking from Bloom what was his. He grew so disturbed and outraged by these thoughts, he needed to remove himself from their room, and on many occasions, he was tempted to get into his car, to drive down the mountain, to confront

Simon, to ask him why he had undermined the love he felt for the two people he cherished most in the world. Was he still motivated, Bloom wondered, by his residual anger toward Jacob? Or did Bloom in some way unknowingly earn Simon's scorn, as Rachel had earned Leah's? Or was it simpler than that? Was it possible his changed wife had fallen in love with Simon, with the complexity of his fractured self, and had Simon fallen in love with Isabella for that very same reason? Was it only their concern for him that was keeping them apart?

Night after night, Bloom walked to Mount Terminus's peak and sat there until his temper quieted, and he then returned to his bed before daybreak so Isabella wouldn't have cause to feel concerned. He did this for weeks, exhausted his body to such an extent he exhausted his anger. And with his anger exhausted, he was able to imagine himself as Simon. He was able to empathize with him. Unconditionally. He was able to rationalize a world in which he had given over his responsibility for his troubled wife to his brother. And he recalled what he saw in Manuel's secret room. In what way the connection between Isabella and Simon was authentic. And he recalled what Simon had sacrificed the night of the party, when, in effect, he returned her to Bloom. And when he was able to perceive their family drama from this point of view, he was grateful to Simon. The images of his brother lying with his wife began to recede, their focus softened, but, night after night when Bloom rejoined Isabella in their bed, he was now awakened in the dark by the same dream he had when Simon returned to Mount Terminus after Jacob and Sam had passed away. Night after night, he dreamed of the mirrored villa filled with his distorted image, of the tower crumbling and rushing asunder, and each time he awoke with a start, an image of Isabella and Simon's child, born and alive, and aging into a man, into a woman, appeared in Bloom's mind. And night after night, he was struck by the same thought. Simon had willingly sacrificed the love of a woman who didn't rightly belong to him, but what of the love of a child who did? If there was no doubt about who the baby's father was, would he remain amicable? Or would he become the

man whose omniscient gaze peered out from the heights of billboards overlooking the basin and the sea?

><

On a morning Bloom was meant to be driving out to meet his crew
in the far reaches of the valley—where Gottlieb had found a location
that resembled the drawings Bloom had made for the Mount Terminus massacre—he discovered his father's old business associate
Saul Geller waiting for him in the parlor. The man looked in good
health, but his demeanor at the moment was sickly. He appeared as
Bloom did, as if he hadn't slept in weeks. He nevertheless possessed
the same warmth Bloom remembered from the time they sat in the
courtyard for the reading of Jacob's will. Bloom told Mr. Geller what
a pleasure it was to see him again, and he explained he was in a rush.
He was expected within the hour, and, as it was, he was already going
to be late. He wondered if Mr. Geller could wait to meet with him
later in the day. Geller took hold of Bloom's arm and apologized to
him. He said it was imperative that they speak now. Please, the older
man asked, when is the last time you saw our Mr. Stern?

Bloom told him it had been some time. Stern, he explained, had,
in the past few years, taken to sending couriers with written reports,
which Bloom admitted to never having read.

Geller stood up and walked to the sideboard on which Meralda
had left Jacob's crystal glasses and a decanter filled with schnapps,
and he poured himself a drink, and then poured one for Bloom.
When he handed Bloom the tumbler, Bloom reminded Geller he
had just started his day. Trust me, Joseph, you'll want the drink
before I deliver the news I have.

What is it? Has something bad happened to Mr. Stern?

If *only* that were the case. I would consider it a blessing. Geller
shook his head and drank. A few weeks ago, I received a distressing
letter from Stern. I want you to understand, I have no way of verify-
ing if what he says about certain parties mentioned is accurate. I'm
only relating to you what he wrote to me . . . Please, Joseph . . .
Geller pushed the bottom of Bloom's glass to his lips. Drink.

Bloom, now sensing the news Mr. Geller had come all this way to deliver was as bad as he claimed, and because he thought it would be impolite not to, drank.

The short of it, said Geller, is that Stern has cleaned you out. This much of what he has written to me I *can* verify. The man has taken you for everything. Your entire inheritance, it's all gone.

Bloom felt the uncanny sensation of blood rushing out of his head. His thoughts departed from the room for a moment, and when they returned, he said, Mr. Stern? We *are* talking about Mr. Stern?

Yes. There is no mistake about it. Mr. Stern, our stern Mr. Stern, has liquidated all your assets. He has raided all your accounts and emptied all your deposit boxes. He has even gone so far as to sell off all the land surrounding the estate. Every square inch of it. He's left you with this property, your home in Woodhaven, and only because he would have required my approval, he left you the controlling interest in our company. Little, very little meat remains on the bone.

Our Mr. Stern?

Yes, said Geller, our Mr. Stern.

Bloom took a seat on the sofa and looked into his now empty tumbler. To the many images of his face reflected in the crystalline diamonds that formed the glass's smooth surface, he said, I'm shocked.

Of course you are. We all are.

I protected him when he needed a confidant. He looked up to Geller as he might have to a rabbi. What have I done to him that he would feel the need to do this to me?

So far as I know? Nothing. Absolutely nothing. He's simply lost his head . . . over a woman.

A woman, said Bloom. Of course, he thought, the woman. The woman Stern never believed would give him the time of day. That same woman who appeared to think nothing of him whatsoever, a caterpillar crushed on the sole of her shoe.

He mentioned in his letter that you know of the woman.

Yes, I know of the woman. But, as far as I knew, he was finished with her, and she was finished with him. So far as I understood it, there was nothing between them to begin with. The woman, he explained, was a prop, an actor, Simon's leverage to blackmail Stern. Simon, he explained, needed Bloom's money to keep his enterprise afloat, and his brother rightly perceived Stern as an impediment to getting what he needed.

Well, on that score, said Geller, you came out well. Stern made a point of saying this. He was considerate to spare your feelings where your brother was concerned.

It turns out he needn't have, said Bloom.

As Geller spoke of short-term losses and long-term gains, of rates of return, Bloom once again fixed his attention to the images of his face at the bottom of his glass. For his deceitful behavior, you can fault Simon, said Geller, and, I imagine, if you want to hold him responsible for the unintended consequences. Had it not been for the ways in which your brother inspired Stern, Simon's manipulation would have done you no harm at all. His example, on the other hand, for that you can hold him accountable. Our Mr. Stern, it seems, had fallen in love with the conniving seductress. And he pursued her after the fact. The problem was he couldn't afford her. So he took it where he could get it. When he saw how easy it was to manipulate your money without you having taken notice—not that I'm casting blame, mind you—he started scavenging your fortune. After Simon had paid back the money he had taken, Stern gradually moved it into one of his own accounts. In small amounts at first, then larger and larger amounts. The next thing he knew, he was liquidating the remainder of your investments and assets, buying property abroad under false names, moving your funds to accounts under the same false identities, and now he's disappeared to God-knows-where with that woman.

Our Mr. Stern?

Yes, said Geller, our Mr. Stern.

Bloom could only shake his head at the thought of it.

I've informed the authorities and I've retained a team of investigators, but, if I'm to be honest, Joseph, I wouldn't hold my breath. Stern is a clever man and it would seem he's highly motivated not to be found. Geller lifted the glass out of Bloom's hand and he returned to the schnapps for a second go. I'm so sorry, said Geller as he handed Bloom the drink. I swore to your father I would look after you, and this, this is what happens.

Bloom was dumbfounded. He wasn't certain what to think about the loss of the money. What did he know of money? He was hardly an extravagant spender. Whatever income was left from the company, he speculated, would suffice. And he told Geller as much. You shouldn't blame yourself, he said to his father's old friend.

But I do blame myself. Who else, if not me, is there to blame?

Mr. Stern.

Yes, but it was I who insisted Stern handle your affairs to begin with. It was I who built this house of cards.

There's no way you could have known it would come to this.

No. But I am responsible. It *was* my doing. And I've decided. I want you to have the shares in the company your father gave to me after he died. I think it's the least I can do to compensate you for such a great loss.

No, I won't hear of it.

You must think of your future, Joseph. You have a wife now. Soon you'll have a family of your own.

Bloom's eyes returned to the empty bottom of the glass, to the multitude of eyes staring back at him.

The income from the foundry? It's nothing to sneeze at, said Geller. But it's not the legacy your father left you. He would have never said it out loud, but he was proud of the fact that you and the children who follow you would want for nothing. And now . . .

I will still want for nothing. There is nothing more I want.

That is the shock speaking, said Geller. When your head has cleared, we'll revisit this conversation. For now, let's leave it.

⁂

After expressing further distress and dismay, after making one too many apologies, Saul Geller departed that morning. He was off to meet the investigators to search through Stern's office and home in hope of finding some clue as to where he'd absconded with Bloom's inheritance and the man-eating Marianne Merriweather. And Bloom went off in search of Isabella. He felt compelled to share Geller's news with her. For the briefest of moments he forgot all the ways in which their life together had been upended, and he wanted her to comfort him, to tell him they would see their way through. But as he ascended the stairs to the landing, Bloom grew increasingly agitated. His only thought was what would become of Mount Terminus. The parcels of land Stern had sold would be developed. It was inevitable. A fait accompli. He easily imagined the city overrunning the mountain. He saw in his mind the physical structures taking shape. He imagined the noise of people overwhelming his peace of mind. And he was reminded of his father's last months, his last days, during which he packed his ears with cotton and sought refuge in the gallery. Bloom better understood now. He better comprehended what was lost to Jacob, what it was that had driven him so deep into the interior of his home. He wasn't merely mourning the loss of his wife; he wasn't merely dwelling in the darkness of regret; he was grieving the end of silence. The silence that had renewed Rachel during their happiest days on Mount Terminus. The silence he dreamed of as a boy in the orphanage. The silence that lasted days on end. And, oh, how Bloom wished he could return the silence to the open vistas, to the open land that ran to the sea and out into the valley, as far out as the dam that now held back the waters of Pacheta Lake. How he wished his brother were a simple man, a man of smaller ambitions, of smaller stature, a man of little means and little experience, a man who held Bloom in esteem, who considered his marriage sacred, who would have shrunk at the thought of touching his wife. Oh, how Bloom wished his father had never gone in search of his aunt after he and his mother had been reunited. How he wished his brother never existed. How he wished he could make him disappear, reduce him to a puff of smoke, a mere shadow in Gottlieb's cave. When Bloom saw Isabella sitting in the gallery, in his mother's chair, her shoulders wrapped in his mother's paisley shawl, her eyes gazing on the outline of Rachel's form in the window overlooking Woodhaven's lake, Bloom couldn't bring himself to subject her to the dybbuk taking hold of him. He would not allow any malcontent spirit to disturb the glow of her motherhood, of her future with her child. He stood and stared at her from the threshold, and then quietly backed away. As noiselessly as Roya, he withdrew, past the library in which he had spent so much time, he withdrew down the stairs to the kitchen and took in the sight of Gus and Meralda looking lovingly at each other from across the table. He would not disturb them either. He walked out the front door, turned over the engine of his car, and sat behind the wheel. As he was about to drive off, he looked up to see Roya looking down on him from the tower's pavilion. What happened next, Bloom wouldn't fully comprehend for as long as he lived. At the moment he was about to wave farewell to her, he noticed Roya had, cupped in her hands, Elijah, who, upon seeing Bloom, tried to break the hold she had on him. Roya gave Bloom's clever bird a kiss on his crest to quiet him, and when she lifted her head, something came over Elijah. He began to peck at Roya's hands. He managed to free one wing, and then the other, and with a final peck directed at Roya's nose, he was free. Bloom's silent companion ran to the rail and let out a silent scream as Elijah tumbled forward. He fell over once and then twice, and then Bloom witnessed Elijah's wings spread. His crest retracted to face the offshore breeze, and for the first time since Mr. Geller delivered his aviary to the tower's pavilion, Bloom watched the beauty of this bird take flight. Elijah circled about the gardens for a few moments, turned back, swooped over Bloom's head, and then flapped on toward Mount Terminus's open gates, and out and up along the mountain road that led to the summit. Bloom threw the roadster into gear, and, with little else on his mind other than the thought of retrieving his beloved friend, sped after him. Elijah flew up and around and kept pace with the car, doubled back every now and again, as if he were intentionally leading Bloom up and over the peak to the valley. Bloom waved his free hand and screamed out Elijah's name over the engine's whine and grind. Elijah, he called. Elijah, I need you here with me. Elijah, who appeared to look down at Bloom from time to time, arced over the mountain and down the canyon switchback, leading Bloom on his descent into the valley. Elijah, Bloom called. Please. Please, come back to me! He lost sight of him as the cockatiel dipped down into the canyon, and he would then suddenly reappear in a long sweep up over the road, and dive down again. Please, Bloom called out, this world isn't for you! And on Elijah flew, paying Bloom no mind at all. For a while the bird flew so high, he blended in with the wisps of haze brushing the washed-out blue of the desert sky. But Bloom felt him up there, felt his presence, and he trusted Elijah would return to him, so he drove. He drove the turns, back and forth, skirting the dry bed of the rusted canyon, passing the folded mantle of chaparral that met the morning sun. He drove to the head of the steep grade of the straightaway that led to the long, long valley road, at which point Elijah sailed down out of the haze, swept over Bloom's roadster, and landed on the remains of a fir tree long ago burned in an autumn blaze. He perched himself right at the end of a blackened limb that hung out over the road. Bloom pulled over onto the road's shoulder and turned off the motor. He held out his arm and called out to his bird, his old friend. Please, he said, I need you here with me. But Elijah wouldn't come. He stared down at him with the same patient gaze as the buzzards of Pacheta Lake who covered his father in the shadow of their heraldic poses and guarded his juniper trees. And Bloom sat looking over the valley with Elijah, and waited and watched, as he did on those days he spent with his father during the Days of Awe, on Yom Kippur. And he was reminded of the mountain's melt cascading down volcanic craters, pressing its way through canyon and gorge, feeding the river that flowed into the graben of the rift valley, and he recalled how the waters had been diverted into the irrigation canals at the desert's edge, and the ways in which his brother had diverted the water through the aqueduct to the immense face of the dam, and he saw his brother's shadow over the world he had delivered to Mount Terminus, with its myriad intended and unintended consequences, and was convinced now, more than ever before, the choice he and Isabella had made together, to remain united as one, was an illusion. For Simon was no simple man. He was no humble man. He had grown so enormous in size he could hardly be considered a man at all. His image had come to hold as many meanings as there were people beholding it; he had become an idol of old, a golden calf worshipped and adored, the producer of dreams at the desolate end of the world, the shaper of implausible destinies, the man who moved living waters to make paradise on Earth, the emperor, the pharaoh, the deity, Simon Reuben. And Bloom had come to know what lived behind his brother's many masks. He knew what formed the core of his humanity, he knew what motivated him, and he knew Simon would never allow Bloom to raise his child. This shaper of the impossible would sooner sacrifice Bloom as a brother before he turned into Jacob Rosenbloom, the abandoner, the missing part, the mysterious ghost. He would not be subject to twists of dramatic irony. He would fight for the child. And, no matter how much he claimed to love Bloom, he would fight for Isabella. Here, thought Bloom, were the unintended consequences of this thread of the tale. Here was the truth of the matter. Here was why stories such as these were told. Here was why men fought bloody battles. Here was why Troy fell. Here was why students of the invertiscope were little more than innocent boys hanging precariously from limbs of trees, filling baskets with acorns in an Eden that had long ago closed up shop.

And then it happened. The unexplainable moment whose timing Bloom would marvel at for as long as he lived. Why, he would ask himself, was he not down there, but up here on the heights of the straightaway? Had Stern not stolen his money, had Elijah not felt an instinctual need to rest his heretofore unused wings, would he have been dead with the rest of them? Would he, too, have been claimed by his brother's hubris? For this is what next came to pass.

Some invisible, exterior force startled Elijah. He jumped from his perch and flew off down the long narrow road in the direction of the valley. The moment after he lifted away, Bloom heard what Elijah had sensed. A percussive boom, like timpani rumbling at the edge of a passing storm, echoed and reverberated against the mountain's face, its canyons. As Elijah's small body began to disappear from sight, Bloom felt the ground shift under him, a tremor, the mildest of earthquakes, strong enough to wobble the roadster on its metal springs. And then he heard the onrush, whose sound was equivalent to nothing Bloom knew of in nature; it was a sound that made his ears ache; as it intensified, it transformed into a vibratory hum that bathed his skin, shook the cuffs of his pants, the sleeves of his shirt, clattered his teeth. He tried to speak, but he couldn't hear his words. Words erupted from his mouth, but the oscillation of the pitch neutralized them. There was no rush of wind, no rustle of leaves or brush, no chips or chirps of insects or birds. Before he ever saw what was producing it, there was only the blanketing sound, an ocean of it, an entire planet's atmosphere of it. From his vista, he could see miniature figures, ranch hands, horses, cattle, all turning northeast, looking off in the same direction. None ran. None moved at all. They just stood paralyzed. And before Bloom had a chance to think a rational thought, the sound's source arrived, and when he saw what it was that was generating what he imagined the voice of God to sound like, Bloom said, and did not hear himself saying, Oh God. Oh God. Oh Gottlieb. Poor Gottlieb. A wall of water, fifty, seventy-five, one hundred feet high, an enormous wave of tumbling brown water, lifted, splintered, devoured all of what stood fixed on the landscape. All that the water had made possible to arise was now being reclaimed. Houses and barns lifted off foundations, tractors and trucks were tossed into the air, bodies of men and women and livestock snuffed out. Like every sentient being who had beheld the maelstrom before it arrived, Bloom, too, did not move. He thought to turn over the car's engine. He thought to turn and run, to climb the dead tree. He could see the trajectory of the water channeling through the valley in his direction. He could see its behemoth force pressing its behemoth mass up the canyon's straight road. He could easily imagine an arm forming from its amorphous heap, and it reach up and out to him, pull him back into the vortex of its maw. Yet he still did not move. Instead, Bloom watched the muddy head of the beast, the golem, crash against the rise of sediment and rock. He watched it funnel its force up the narrow canyon road. He watched its reach extend up at an unimaginable speed, and as it ascended to him, he knew, if he survived this moment in time, what it was he wanted. If he survived the leviathan born of his brother's ambition, from his most feverish dreams, he knew where he would go. If he survived the End of Days foreseen by his brother's accountant, Mr. Dershowitz, if Bloom didn't become flotsam, or some buried archaeological curiosity for some future digger, he knew where he belonged. In this arrested moment of time, he saw it in his mind. It was clear. It was true. He knew now where it was he had experienced his truest happiness. And he knew now the rarity of true happiness. And he knew now for whom his father had decided to live apart, to abandon all. In the face of the oncoming fist, Bloom could see the desk set before the window. He could see the ocean's vast expanse, its uninterrupted view. He could see Estella looking off to the swells rolling endlessly from the horizon. And, he thought, how blissful and at peace he had been there, how easy it would be to lead a quiet life of dreaming there. A quiet life interrupted only by the sound of the sea, the sight of Estella walking the rocks, the pleasant piano music in the evenings, fishing off the coast with Eduardo. Isabella would be free to go to Simon, and Simon would need her now. He would need someone to help see him through this atrocity. He would need her to help him understand the unmerciful ways in which Death visited the world. He would need the child to distract him and comfort him. Bloom was not so cruel as to deprive his brother of these things. Yes, thought Bloom. Yes! he screamed at Death as it rushed to him. Yes! he screamed at what he believed was his inevitable slaughter. Yes! he screamed loud enough to hear his own voice over Death's approach. And he screamed again, Yes! when the muddy fingers were only yards away. He gripped hold of the steering wheel and shut his eyes, and he waited, and he waited, to be swept away, to be pulled in, to be overtaken, consumed, and then . . .

Nothing, nothing except for a misting of water kissing his face. The kiss of Death? Or was it the kiss of life? He opened his eyes to find the muddy water receding, falling back into the valley, into a roiling whirlpool of debris churning at the base of the mountain. The road below was slicked with mud, and the twisted earthly remains of cattle and horses, of men?—perhaps they were men?— began to crust over in the sun almost immediately after the retreat. Bloom thought to look, to see, if anything at all was alive, but nothing stirred, nothing groaned. He stepped out of the car to observe the scene, but he could not bear the sight. Before any more of the grotesquerie was revealed across the valley, he turned away from it. He cranked the roadster's engine, and without another thought, Bloom circled about and drove away from this horrible world of his brother's making. He drove up and over his beloved mountain. He slowed for only a brief moment when he approached the estate, and when he thought of looking through its gate to bid Mount Terminus one final farewell, he stopped himself and drove on, past the road leading to the plateau, and he continued down the switchback, taking turns at precarious speeds. When he reached the bottom, he drove past the gates of Mount Terminus Studios without even taking them in, and he continued on down the long stretch of road leading to the edge of the basin. He continued on through the square blocks lined with stucco homes that once stood pinned to his brother's map. He continued on over paved roads lined with pristine curbs and perfectly appointed streetlamps, with high-tension wires cutting across shining billboards holding his brother's image. He continued on past people who had only just become aware of what had happened on the opposite side of the mountain. They emptied out onto the streets, looked out in the direction of the valley. More and more of them congregated on their lawns, in the street, some weeping, more speechless. They sat framed in open windows, unmoving, and on he continued through the throngs, onward to the port, where he parked his car on Eduardo's ferry, and he stood with his friend, his true brother, his fellow lover of birds, and he told this dear man he had missed him, and Eduardo embraced Bloom, and, in an effort to lighten the mood, he said to him, I have made friends with a pelican who perches on my boat in Willow Cove, and upon hearing this, Bloom was overjoyed, and with Eduardo at his side, he continued on to Santa Ynez, and he continued on around the island road in his car, and he drove under the braided ficus trees up the lane, and he parked near the strawberry lupine and amethyst blazing stars, and he greeted Guillaume hello at the foot of his trapeze, and he walked inside the home of La Reina del Fuego, and he was greeted by her, by the beautiful, melancholy Estella, who, as he was about to tell her about what horrors he had seen only hours earlier, took hold of Bloom's hand and walked him upstairs to a room painted with pink and yellow toucans, and there she lifted up from a small bed a little girl with dark skin and dark curls hanging in ringlets over her eyes, and she placed the child in Bloom's arms, and said, She has been waiting for you to return.

AFTERWORD

B loom would never again set foot on Mount Terminus. For that matter, he would never again leave the island of Santa Ynez. He would remain with Estella and Eduardo and his daughter, Gisele, who he came to realize the moment he held her in his arms was the one true love he was meant to protect over all others.

He wrote to Isabella some days after he arrived on the island, and in this letter he explained to her the reasons why he couldn't return, and he explained to her why he thought it best she go to Simon with the news of their child. Bloom would always love her, he wrote, but it turned out he wasn't the man he thought he was. He was merely a man. An ordinary man capable of feeling the same ordinary jealousies and anger as any other ordinary man.

After some weeks had passed, Bloom asked Eduardo if he wouldn't mind collecting his belongings. Everything in his studio, his clothes, his father's devices, the books in the library, and his birds. He wished also to have Manuel's journals. Meralda, who chose to remain on the estate with Gus, to see Isabella through her pregnancy, had packed the former, and Roya, who chose to leave her sister for the first time in her life, would travel with Eduardo to carry the latter. Bloom added his books and his father's devices to Estella's library and his birds to Eduardo's aviary. The room whose windows overlooked the oncoming waves of the sea, Estella had kept for Bloom's return, and there he looked out onto the open expanse with no threat of it ever changing. In its mists, in its abstractions, in the infinite wonders of the sea, he would dream up island worlds for Gisele as real as any other.

In this room, Roya would sit by his side, and together they would reflect on the ocean in the same manner they reflected on the reflecting pool, and here in this room he would watch her grow old, and together they would draw panels for hundreds of pictures that would never be produced. In this room, among the growing collection of unmade movies, Gisele would visit him, and together they would draw and paint, and like Bloom, like her grandmother, she had a unique eye and a fine hand, but like her mother, she possessed a stately calm that allowed her to control her internal flame. Estella no longer mourned the death of Guillaume. She no longer dwelled in the darkness of her past. The moment she felt her child growing inside her, she knew there was no longer room for her grief. She removed all the artifacts of her former life from the walls, closed the house to visitors, and said her final goodbyes to her long-dead husband, to her nightly rituals.

As for Simon, like ancient rulers of old, like pharaohs and emperors, his legend would grow, for both his remarkable achievements and his monumental miscalculation. Not unlike Don Fernando Miguel Estrella's, his city and his fortunes would continue to rise, despite Bloom's brother being nearly destroyed by this moment of infamy. Bloom wouldn't hear of its aftermath until Gus and Meralda, newly wed, delivered the story. No structure throughout the valley remained standing. Not one. Everything had been swept away or buried. Thousands of head of cattle, all varieties of livestock, mingled with human bodies and fence posts and shards of buildings and heavy equipment. Human limbs, feet, arms, and heads were buried in mud, not among them, to Bloom's great relief, Gottlieb's, nor Hannah Edelstein's, nor Hershel Verbinsky's, nor anyone else who nurtured Bloom for those years he spent on the plateau, as Gottlieb, God bless him, on the day Bloom was to meet them, forced his colleagues to hike up the side of the mountain and join him in the canopy of an ancient oak whose elevation was just high enough on the mountainside to miss the oncoming rush of water when it was released from the dam. And this is how they were spared. Gottlieb, who would complete Bloom's final picture without him, the man who

would be remembered best for this picture, *The Death of Paradise*—
because the timing of its release and because its true creator had
disappeared and was rumored to have been lost to the onrush of the
great flood—would die much later, in a comfortable bed, in his sleep,
on a Mount Terminus estate whose doorways, ceilings, windows,
and furniture were built to accommodate Gottlieb's small stature,
so that when men and women of normal height visited him, they
were made to stoop and crouch and look most awkward and uncomfortable in his presence, which, of course, Gottlieb took great
pleasure in.

Five hundred thirty-five souls passed that day. The anarchists of
the Mojave were hunted down and held in custody for months while
the county conducted an investigation. Several of the men died
mysterious deaths while awaiting the outcome of the report, which
showed, in the end, no one had tampered with the dam. A geologist
determined the structural integrity of the great project had failed,
as it had been built on unstable ground. It didn't matter that Simon
had nothing to do with the actual construction of the reservoir. He
and several members of the water authority were the faces of the
project, but, as the once-heroic bust of progress and renewal, Simon
took the brunt of the public's outrage, and he had no other choice
but to accept the blame. Gus told Bloom he returned to Simon's
side. He couldn't bear to watch him suffer the consequences of this
moment alone. The big man encouraged Bloom's brother to set up a
charity for the surviving family members and influenced him to
make a pledge to rebuild the destroyed property. In time, Gus hoped,
Simon would redeem himself in the eyes of those who had placed
their trust in him.

Not long after the inquiries had concluded, not long after Gus
and Meralda's visit, Simon traveled to Santa Ynez on Eduardo's
ferry, and Bloom saw in his brother's face the toll these events had
taken on him, and he saw to what extent he had been humbled. He
had been stripped of his pride and his arrogance, and perhaps for the
first time, Bloom believed, his brother truly needed him, as a brother,
and nothing more, his unconditional love, his time, his ear. They

walked down the stairs of the bluff together and sat on the rocks and looked off to the sea's horizon, and Simon said how sorry he was for having betrayed Bloom's trust. He had fallen in love with Isabella. There was no other motivation. He loved her, simple as that, and as hard as he tried, he couldn't resist what he felt for her. For what he did to Stern, and for the unintended consequences, he promised to help find Bloom's former trustee, and if he couldn't be found, he would contact Mr. Geller and make a financial arrangement. Bloom learned from Simon that Isabella was now living in Simon's house, and that the estate on Mount Terminus had been shut. Gus and Meralda were now living with them, helping with the baby.

Bloom asked Simon if he and Isabella were happy together, and Simon said they were. But, he said, she still loves you. You must know that. Is it so wrong, he asked, that she loves us both in different ways?

No, said Bloom, I suppose not.

You're happy here, said Simon.

Very. And it would make me even happier if you and Isabella would visit from time to time, so our children can grow up together. After all, we're all that's left, you and I, and them.

They parted company that day on good terms, and they would, indeed, see each other every now and then, and Bloom would find it in himself to forgive Simon, and he would grow accustomed to seeing him and Isabella as a couple, happy in their own way, with their daughter, Anna, who Bloom, too, would come to love. Anna and Gisele would meet on Santa Ynez and swing on Guillaume's trapeze, and lie on their backs for hours in the aviary, thinking up pictures in their minds, and when the desert gales blew across the channel, sweeping away all the mist and dust, they and Bloom would climb to the top of the turret and look through his telescope to Mount Terminus, and Gisele would say, Please, Father, and Anna would say, Please, Uncle Joseph, tell us a fairy tale. And Bloom would tell them stories about the time he spent on Mount Terminus as a child. He hid nothing from them. He told them the sad tale of their grandfather and how he had spent the better part of his life mourning the loss of their grandmothers. And he told them how it was he and his brother were reunited and driven apart, and reunited again. He told them about how he and Eduardo discovered their mutual love of birds. He told them about how he fell in love with Anna's mother, and how his love had been poisoned and transformed. He told Gisele about how he and her mother had come to be joined in love by a grief that in time turned to joy. And he told them stories of imagined worlds he dreamed about in the silence of his days and dreamed about in the darkness of the night.

ACKNOWLEDGMENTS

When I started work on *Mount Terminus*, I had every intention of completing it in three, perhaps four years. For reasons I'm not entirely sure I can adequately explain, the writing came, but it came slowly. My process, it seemed, was more in sync with geologic time than with publishing time. And while I'm sure he was none too pleased when we entered the fifth year of this endeavor, and then the seventh, and then the ninth, my longtime editor, Sean McDonald, never cast doubt into my mind that I would one day finish, that one day there would be a book we could both feel proud of. For Sean's patience, devotion, loyalty, friendship, and sage direction, for his illuminating notes and great instincts, I am deeply grateful. Without him, I could have very easily wandered off into the wilderness and never returned.

I extend similar gratitude and thanks to Jin Auh at the Wylie Agency, who never ceases to go above and beyond. She read multiple drafts, provided valuable insights along the way, and accomplished the impossible task of rescuing my spirits when they needed rescuing. Thank you to Zoe Pagnamenta, formerly of the Wylie Agency, for selling the book to Sean when my children were just out of diapers (they're now in high school), for being a dear friend in the intervening years, and for providing good company and a country retreat, where many of these pages were written. Thank you also to Tracy Bohan at Wylie, who has seen to it that *Mount Terminus* will have a life abroad.

In addition to these very fine people, thank you to Wesley Stace for his unmatched friendship and careful reading, and for sharing his encyclopedic knowledge on all the subjects I most value; to the talented writers and dear friends that comprise the Masonville Collective—Rene Steinke and Beka Chace, who read closely, edited meticulously, and fed me and sang to me; to Errollyn Wallen, for fortifying me with beautiful music; to Minna Proctor, for editorial notes, copyedits, and all-around brilliance; to Gary Shteyngart, for a place to write in Rome and Germantown, New York; to Emily Chamberlain and Ryan Elwood, my research assistants, who hunted everywhere for obscure books and added depth where depth was needed; and to Joel Stutz, for his lifelong support.

Thanks also to the Academy of Motion Picture Arts and Sciences for opening their archives to me.

Christine, my wife, who is the embodiment of the world's most moving lyrical poetry, and my sons, Sasha and Nathanael, the most excellent young men I know—you are the reason I do everything I do.

This book is for my mother, Margaret Stutz, who has given all and asked for so little in return. And for her mother, Bessie Buschel, who, had she lived a few more months, would have turned one hundred upon *Mount Terminus*'s publication. She shared with me her great love of movies and books, and much, much more, and for that I am profoundly in her debt. For a tough old broad, my bubbie had a soft touch.